THE
MORBIDS

Ewa Ramsey is an emerging writer and arts administrator based in Newcastle, New South Wales. She has presented short fiction at the National Young Writers' Festival, won a commendation in the Newcastle Short Story Award and been a finalist in the *Newcastle Herald* Short Story Competition. Ewa has also written for *PC&Tech Authority* and worked as an editorial assistant and pop-culture writer and reviewer for *Atomic* magazine. She is currently Operations Manager for the Newcastle Writers Festival and on the board of the National Young Writers' Festival.

THE

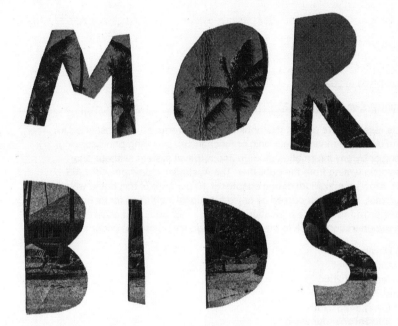

MOR
BIDS

A NOVEL

EWA RAMSEY

ALLEN&UNWIN
SYDNEY · MELBOURNE · AUCKLAND · LONDON

Allen & Unwin
83 Alexander Street
Crows Nest NSW 2065
Australia
Phone: (61 2) 8425 0100
Email: info@allenandunwin.com
Web: www.allenandunwin.com

A catalogue record for this book is available from the National Library of Australia

ISBN 978 1 76087 753 8

Set in 12.2/17.3 pt Aldus LT Std by Bookhouse, Sydney
Printed and bound in Australia by Griffin Press, part of Ovato

10 9 8 7 6 5 4 3 2 1

The paper in this book is FSC® certified. FSC® promotes environmentally responsible, socially beneficial and economically viable management of the world's forests.

For all the real-life Morbids, everywhere

August, Once

There was glitter in my hair. When I moved it sparkled, fell, onto my hands, my lap. Stung.

There was glitter and silence—so loud it hurt my ears. And a smell I knew but couldn't place. Hot. Rusty. Sour.

'Hey,' I said. 'Are you okay?'

Nobody answered.

I looked down. My neck hurt and at the corner of my eye, I saw my hair. Pink, like fairy floss, full of glitter.

'Hey,' I said again, louder. Still, nobody answered.

There was just silence. And glitter.

So much glitter.

So bloody quiet.

Tuesday, April

'It's been three years,' Donna finished in a shaky voice. 'And I still wake up every morning wondering if today's the day.'

Donna was new. Under the fluorescent lights of a nondescript community room in Surry Hills, above a health food co-op and across the corridor from a tax accountant, she looked beige. Her beige-blonde hair hung over her chest, ends crunchy with frizz and bleach, and she wore a beige-blue cardigan, skinny beige hands poking out the ends, fingers curled around each other in her lap, fading into her beige-brown pants.

Like all of us, Donna thought she was going to die. She had woken up one day, three years ago, convinced that the train she caught to work every day was going to derail and she'd be decapitated by a dislodged green leather seat. She was so convinced, she stayed home from work. The next day her fear of trains had passed, somewhat, but there was a strange pain in her calf that Google told her might be deep vein thrombosis. It wasn't, of course, but it could have been. The day after that, she had a headache that could have been a brain tumour, and that fear of train derailment was back, even stronger.

And so here she was.

Geoff sat opposite me. He'd been coming for longer than I had—as long as the group had been going. When Donna said the thing about the train seat, his eyes had widened, and he'd turned to Frannie next to him and said, 'God, I never thought of that. What a way to go.' His voice was full of fear, but also wonder at this new toy to store in his brain box, ready to pull out when his favourite—domestic accident, the more unlikely the better—got boring.

We all had our favourites.

Frannie's was cancer, Carlos's vehicular. Louise had only been coming for a couple of months but it was obvious she was expecting something violent yet premeditated—a stalker or an ex-partner or her childhood enemy.

Mine was mugging gone wrong. Wrong place, wrong time type stuff, killed in a moment of panic or by accident—sexual violence of varying degrees optional, currently waning in frequency.

Some of us had more than one, a primary and a secondary. Louise's secondary was cancer; Geoff's was bad flu. He got his flu shot every year but that only protected you from last year's strains, he told us, over and over.

My secondary was freak accident, not domestic: a shop awning collapsing, unsecured load flying off a truck, lighting rig coming loose from a nightclub ceiling. The kind of thing that would make the news not because it was tragic, but because it was so unexpected, the kind of thing the rest of us would watch on TV and think, *Ooooh . . . good one.*

The primary was the one you thought about all the time, that you'd almost accepted as inevitable. The secondary was more an uncomfortable niggle, a reason to cross the road but not to stay home.

'My shoulder's been sore for a couple of days,' Frannie was saying. 'I did help Owen move the fridge on Saturday, but I don't think it's that. I think it's my lymph nodes.'

'Ohhhh, that's pretty advanced then. Sorry, hon.' Donna's eyes were damp, though it was hard to tell if she was worried for Frannie or herself.

Sometimes people came and they thought we were freaks, that we delighted and revelled in this. Some days I wondered if they were right. I looked at the beige faces, beige hands around their lukewarm cups, and I thought terrible uncharitable thoughts. But then I remembered the first time I'd felt it, walking through the park to my old house in Glebe, glitter in my hair and a horrible sound ringing in my ears. The way my heart had shifted in my chest and I'd felt it so strongly, like a friend walking next to me, arm around my shoulders—heavy and hot and smelling of rot, impossible to ignore. Not a friend at all.

I didn't want to die. I hadn't wanted it then and I didn't want it now—none of us did. I just knew I would. I wasn't as sure of anything as I was of the fact that I was going to die, that it should have happened already and it was only a matter of time.

We were all so sure.

Except we were so rarely right.

Frannie didn't have cancer. She might develop it from the sheer number of scans she got, but so far she was clear. Carlos didn't even have a driver's licence. When Paulie died of a massive heart attack just before Christmas we were all shocked, much more shocked than we probably should have been. He was overweight, smoked a pack a day and his cholesterol was through the roof, but he'd been waiting for an industrial accident (he worked for a printer—in sales, but still).

And yet, we watched and we waited and we ran over our lives with a fine-tooth comb, confused and frustrated and anxious. Trying to outwit it, whatever it was, before it could kill us.

Pretend I didn't say this, Paulie said once, only weeks before his myocardial infarction, *but I reckon I'm safer for having spent all this time thinking about it. I've imagined sticking my hand in a trimmer so many times that when I'm near one I'm the most careful bloke in the room. The guys who are going to do it are the guys who don't think about it, don't see it coming.*

And we all nodded and promptly pretended he hadn't said it, because then it wouldn't work.

◆

We finished up a little earlier than usual, and I was grateful to escape. I had a headache—the same one I'd had for months, probably a tumour—and I couldn't seem to catch my breath.

'You're quiet today, Caitlin,' Geoff said, when my eyes hadn't lit up at Louise's story about being followed out of a bottle shop the weekend before.

Geoff was our unofficial leader. Officially, we were part of a 'unique first-step program for treatment of anxiety, specifically as related to death and dying, led by a team of qualified mental health professionals', but over the years, long before my time, those mental health professionals had been downgraded from psychiatrists to psychologists to counsellors, and then we'd been palmed off onto a series of nurses, most of whom started off with dreams of fixing us but left within months, defeated and disappointed.

According to Patrick, our last nurse who'd only made it to the six-week mark and left just after New Year, we were exhausting and ghoulish. Fiona had been with us ever since, but she spent more and more time doodling at the corners of her notepad, letting us talk among ourselves and nodding at appropriate intervals. I liked Fiona—not that it mattered; I'd liked Bernie, the first one I'd had, too, and Kim and Chris—all of them. They showed up and we let them think they were in charge, but really it was Geoff who led the sessions and asked the questions.

All of this mattered more to Geoff than it did to any of the rest of us. I wasn't sure why.

And, truthfully, I thought Louise was probably reaching. I knew the bottle shop she was talking about. It was long and narrow and only had one door, so there was no way to leave except to follow someone else. And it was cheap, for Pyrmont, so there was always a steady stream of wine snobs and drunks coming in and out, even on a weekday morning.

Not that I ever bought wine on a weekday morning.

Not often, anyway.

I was standing on the street about to roll a cigarette when Donna came out. In the acid-washed streetlights she looked less beige. Her cardigan was teal and her trousers grey, hair blonde, still crunchy. Inside, I'd thought she was about twenty years older than me, but on the street it was more like ten. She looked like the older sisters of the girls I went to school with—cheap bottle blondes with too-long fingernails painted too-bright colours, breasts tucked into too-small bras and then too-small tops, gold bangles on their wrists and gold hoops in their ears. Multiple. Donna looked like one of them, but camouflaged and corporatised. I could see pinpricks along the curves of her ears where she'd taken out a row of earrings.

'Want a tailor?' she asked, holding out her pack.

'I'm good,' I said, finding a filter and touching it to my lip twice before letting it rest there as I filled a paper with tobacco. 'I don't really like the taste.'

I slipped the filter into the end of the paper, licked the edge and rolled it closed, tapping the end with my index finger, quietly proud of how perfectly cylindrical it was.

She lit her cigarette. I could tell she wanted to say something else but she wasn't sure where to start, and when Geoff and Carlos pushed through the door she sighed, a mixture of disappointment and relief.

'Want a lift, Cait?' Geoff asked, like he did every week.

'I'm fine,' I said, like I did every week, putting the rollie between my lips and lighting it. A single strand of tobacco poked out past the filter, and I pinched it out with my fingernails.

'Worth a shot,' Geoff said, patting my arm as he and Carlos walked past. 'See you ladies next week, yeah?'

'Yeah,' I said, smiling, forgetting they were there before they'd even turned away.

'Do you live far?' Donna asked. 'I'm driving.'

'Not far.' I took a proper drag, looking down at my boots, scuffed at the toe. 'Thanks, but I'm okay.'

Her lips came apart like she was going to say whatever it was she'd wanted to say before, but she thought better of it and put her cigarette in her mouth instead.

'How long have you been coming here?'

'About a year,' I said, shrugging, trying not to think about it.

'Does it help?'

I nodded, but didn't answer, wasn't sure how. 'Are you coming back?' I asked.

She paused for a second. 'Yeah. I think so.'

'Good.'

I wasn't sure it was good that she hadn't found us ghoulish or exhausting and run off into the night, never to be seen again. I didn't know what it said about her, or me, but I was glad for it anyway. I put the rollie back in my mouth and hitched my bag further onto my shoulder. 'See you next week,' I said.

She nodded, and as I turned I forgot she was there too.

◆

Carlos didn't have his licence. Frannie didn't smoke, didn't drink, didn't eat bacon or ham or salami and wore sunscreen religiously. Glenn, who wasn't there tonight but who was waiting for a tsunami, hadn't been east of Paddington in seven years. I didn't know, but I was willing to bet Donna didn't get on a train unless she absolutely had to.

I walked home by myself, every night.

Late at night, early in the morning, I walked everywhere. Over the past year or so—maybe longer—I'd mapped out the entire city, walked down every darkened lane and crossed every dodgy park and taken every dodgier shortcut, my skin crawling with goosebumps so permanent they may as well have been tattoos. I walked quickly, always vigilant, hyper-aware, scanning for threats and listening for footsteps or car engines, keys jammed between my fingers the whole way, like I'd been taught in one of the dozens of self-defence talks we were given at school. As though they'd help, as though I'd know exactly where to aim my key-fist when somebody grabbed me from behind and pulled me into a waiting car.

As though I could be bothered.

Tonight, I was skittish and restless and still cold, despite wrapping my hoodie tight around myself. It was cheap and thin, the fabric no match for the wind, which seemed to have picked up since I started walking. I took a right off Crown Street and headed past the towers on Belvoir, smoking my rollie and letting gravity pull me down the hill to Central Station. I crossed Prince Alfred Park and Cleveland Street as it arched over the railway lines, and turned into the back streets of Darlington, cutting through the uni and out onto King Street.

It was early enough that I still had to dodge the odd pedestrian as I walked, hope nobody pushed me out in front of a car or grabbed me and pulled me into an alley, but nobody did, and nobody would have noticed if they had. Shadows danced around street corners and doorways and telegraph poles, reminding me that this was a stupid, silly, terrible idea; a stupid, silly, terrible thing to do. But I did it anyway, waiting for my luck to run out. Ready.

I walked faster and faster until I was at my front door; navy blue and opening right on to King Street, almost invisible between a second-hand bookshop and a convenience store, with a small chrome plate displaying a street number, and an ancient intercom that was more for show than anything. The lock was sticky and only opened if you turned the key in the exact right way, and sometimes it took a few tries and that was when I felt it the most: the presence, eyes on me, creeping up behind me, waiting until that last moment, that last second before safety.

This time it gave first go, and I let myself in, falling back against the door as it shut, as I did every night, my heart pounding so hard I thought my ribs might break.

Alive, still.

Somehow.

◆

It was called the cat-piss house because it smelled like cat piss. According to Marnie, my flatmate, it had been called that for years and years, the name passed down through its tenants along with a threadbare couch and a rusty breadmaker nobody was brave enough to use. Still, not long after I moved in, I hired a machine from the supermarket and cleaned and cleaned, and for weeks after all I could smell was perc and I was sure I was going to end up with brain tumours, but I hadn't—so far—and when the headaches went away the cat piss came back. Marnie just shrugged and told me I'd get used to it.

The cat-piss house wasn't a house. It was a flat over the second-hand bookshop, which, as far as shops to live above went, was relatively pleasant, except some nights when I'd lie in bed, too awake, and I'd swear I could smell smoke and I'd think of the back wall of the shop, lined with layers and layers of browning paperbacks, and I'd wonder how long it would take to go up if someone tossed a cigarette butt into the bin out the back or left one smouldering in an ashtray, and I'd have to get up and make sure nobody had—three, sometimes four times.

Still, it was cheap and close to the city and it overlooked King Street, and when I'd answered the ad Marnie hadn't asked any questions or pretended we'd become best friends, which made it easier to ignore the masking tape holding the windows together and the peeling paint, hanging from the ceiling in sheets.

And I did get used to the smell. Sometimes I barely noticed it.

I walked up the narrow flight of stairs, my pulse slowing, unlit cigarette still between my lips, the end gone damp and cold, cat piss and stale smoke mixing with a new perfume of pad Thai and red wine as I dropped my bag on the kitchen bench. I could see a stack of greasy takeaway containers and two burgundy-stained glasses by the sink, a pile of mail by the toaster, a bright pink catalogue and an envelope from the gas company, and a postcard on top at an angle, tossed there as an afterthought.

Welcome to Bali! it sang in yellow, over a blue sky, bluer water, pale-gold sand, a pink and green beach umbrella over two empty pink and green sun loungers.

Nothing remarkable.

Nothing exciting.

But I stopped anyway, cold, my heart speeding up, strange and uneven and hard against my ribs.

I blinked, looking through the kitchen into the silent, empty lounge room. The glare of a streetlight right outside the window cast a phosphorescent glow over the few bits of mismatched furniture we had, and a flashing mobile phone sat plugged into a charger by the television, which meant Marnie had been here and wasn't far away—probably at the Townie or the Courty, huddled at a table with ten of her closest friends, sharing bottles of pink wine and telling the kind of jokes that weren't really jokes so much as secret handshakes.

We weren't those kind of flatmates—sometimes we didn't see each other for weeks—but we could have been, if I made an effort, if I played along. I could have ignored the postcard, wandered down to the pub and found her, sipped pink wine, laughed at her jokes, been that kind of flatmate. I almost wanted to, but something stopped me.

I glanced at it again.

It could be from anyone, I told myself, pulling a beer out of the fridge and making toast for dinner. It could be *to* anyone. Marnie. A past tenant. The postal equivalent of a wrong number.

The smell of Thai food lingered and made my stomach rumble, but the toast was hard to chew so I threw most of it out and finished my beer, waiting for my bones to soften and my brain to slow down. I thought about Donna and that steady, rhythmic chugging of the train, so familiar and yet so strange. I thought about my best friend Lina and me, years ago, slumped low in those hard, uncomfortable fake-leather seats, not talking, just staring out the window at the blur of graffiti-covered fences that lined the tracks. We'd wasted hours that way, probably whole days, pretending we were going somewhere but not going anywhere.

We were teenagers then. Lina was still my best friend, maybe, but I never caught the train anymore, and I hadn't spoken to her in weeks—longer. Months. Too long. She'd been calling me. Texting. A lot. Wanting to talk, to catch up. Leaving voicemails she had to know I wouldn't listen to. I'd been meaning to get back to her, to find time, to do the things I knew I had to do, but I hadn't.

I didn't know how long it had been, and now there was a blue and gold postcard on my kitchen bench, watching me, waiting.

When I finally picked it up, after finishing another beer, going downstairs to check the locks on the door, checking the ashtrays and the stove and sniffing for smoke, I expected it to burn, to shock, to be heavy and hard and big and breathe fire, but it was just a rectangle of cardboard, slightly bent and too easy to tuck into my pocket, light enough that I could almost forget it was there, could still walk across the flat and into my room without collapsing under its weight.

I opened my window and looked down at the rusty awning beneath, full of so much bird poo and diesel dust and cigarette ash I didn't know how it was still hanging. I wasn't sure it would hold me if I fell onto it, but I leaned out anyway, feeling the cold air on my face.

I smoked a cigarette. Two. Listened.

I heard people on the street, eruptions of laughter and someone who sounded like Marnie asking someone I couldn't see whose house they were going to and demanding a stop for snacks, and then a motorbike drowning them out before I found out if she got her way. And then someone else, something else. A car. A deep booming laugh. Sometimes I hated it—on Friday and Saturday nights when it was all drunken hipsters and engineering students yelling ugly slurs at cab drivers who wouldn't take them home and women who wouldn't go with them—but tonight it was comforting, distracting.

Lina didn't know how I slept with all the noise. When I'd first moved in, she'd startled at every passing truck, at every drunken holler, every siren, and at some point I'd stopped inviting her round, let her off the hook.

She didn't know how I slept with all the noise. I didn't know how she slept without it.

I dropped my last cigarette butt into the old wine bottle I kept wedged in the top of the awning, listening for the hiss as it hit the dregs and went out.

Once I'd closed the window, checked the ashtrays and the locks and the stove again, I sat down on my bed and reached for the shoebox nestled against the wall, opening it and pushing aside a pile of superficially important papers—uni transcripts, tax papers, a copy of my birth certificate—to uncover a stack of postcards.

The top one was from Canberra, a twilight panorama with the tower it was taken from pasted over the top. We'd gone there on a school trip in year six, and I'd taken a photo of the exact same view, but this wasn't from there; it was from an op shop somewhere, years ago. I had a vague memory of choosing it over a purple carpet of jacaranda flowers from Grafton.

I picked up the pile and flicked through it until I found the one I was looking for. Central Park. New York. I had no idea how it had ended up in a Lifeline shop in Hornsby eleven years ago, unmarked and with a hole punched through one corner, but it had, and for twenty cents it was mine. The lines were too crisp, the greens were too green and the blues too blue, as though someone had just figured out how to adjust the saturation and contrast. Still, it made my ribs tighten.

I turned it over. Blank. All the ones at the top were blank. I'd been saving them, until I wasn't saving them anymore. I was just burying them.

Under New York, Amsterdam. When I turned that one over words swam across the cardboard, almost diagonal, handwriting I knew better than my own.

Dear Caitlin,
Okay, I'll bite. Just this once. Weirdo.
  I don't think I want to go to South America. It looks like fun but it's pretty hardcore. And you need to learn Spanish. We should go somewhere easy first. New Zealand has mountains too and they speak English and have cute accents and the chocolate is better than Australian chocolate because the weather is colder so they don't need to put anti-melting stuff in it.
  Did you get invited to Bec's party? I don't really want to go but I will if you do.
  Love you loads, L xx

*PS You know you can just ask me how I am. You don't need
to send me postcards. (I'm fine. I promise. Mum wants me to
see a counsellor but I am okay, thank you for asking. You don't
need to worry. Promise.)*

*PPS Did you know Amsterdam has eight wooden drawbridges?
And like a thousand 'coffee' shops, if you get my drift.
xxx*

That was the first one. She'd run out of room and the postscripts
ran under the address and then curled up the side and around the
stamp. I could only look at it for so long before it hurt my eyes.

From the bottom of the pile I pulled out a panorama of orange
dirt and turquoise ocean.

Caitie,
*Where are you? You're not answering your phone and you
missed coffee. Gus asked about you. He likes you—poor fool.
I rang your work and they said you were off sick. Hope it's not
this flu that's going round. It's brutal.*

*Thanks for coming on Saturday. I know it wasn't really
your scene—I hope no-one bored you with too much
accountant talk.*

*I hope you feel better soon. Let's have dinner this week. Call
me. L xx*

*PS Did you know the world's largest oyster pearl ever was
found in Broome? In 1861.
xxx*

A breeze brushed the back of my neck and I shivered, suddenly
freezing. I put Broome back in the pile, then Amsterdam. I pulled
Bali from my pocket and looked at it for a long time before turning it

over. I knew it would be the same sprawling, swimming handwriting, tilting up as it went, but the sight of it still made my breath hitch.

> *Dear Caitlin,*
> *I know we don't really do this anymore, but I've been trying to call you and you're not answering. I guess you're busy with work and everything, but I have news, and I want you to know first. We're getting married!!! About time, right? I'm so excited and happy and I hope you are too!!*
> *I miss you. Call me. Please.*
> *Lina xx*
>
> *PS Did you know Bali is 'Australia's most popular choice for a destination wedding'? Well, now you do. November 18. Save the date. Book your flights.*

I read it again, and again, and every time it said the same thing and every time the same feeling crept up my spine and seized me around the throat. Guilt, fear, something else. Something worse.

I should have been excited, but it was too cold; the window wasn't sealed properly and the wind sliced through the room like a knife. Underneath me, the sheets were ice. When I moved, a long time later, my joints cracked, ached.

I should have been happy, but there was no air, no space, no light.

Somewhere, a door slammed, a siren sounded, a motorbike roared down the street, so loud it shook the windowpanes and I felt it in my bones and I couldn't move. I read the postcard again and again until my eyes felt hot and the words started swimming and swimming but not getting anywhere.

2

WEDNESDAY, APRIL

'This Saturday?' I asked, wedging the phone against my shoulder as I took stock of the contents of my work locker—three candy-coloured cans of spray deodorant, a rumple of black shirts, a pale pink bra that didn't look like mine.

'Yes. That *is* Jack's birthday, Caitlin,' my mum's voice cracked into my ear, short and already disappointed by a response I hadn't yet given her. A few folded-up pieces of newspaper—crosswords I'd collected to do on my break and then forgotten about. A tangle of sacked-out hair elastics.

'I'm working Saturday,' I said, pulling out an elastic and putting it on my wrist. Probably. Maybe not. Maybe dying. Maybe already dead. Half-a-dozen chocolate bar wrappers from all the times I forgot to eat breakfast before work. Rollie papers. Rollie papers. Rollie papers. I made a mental note that they were there for next time I ran out.

'It's your brother's birthday. Can't you take a day off?'

She was always doing that, like it was so simple. 'It's the busiest day of the week, Mum.'

'What about brunch?' she asked. 'You don't usually work mornings, do you?'

I picked up a shirt, sniffed. 'No, but—' Another. Shook out the least offensive one, inspecting it for stains. Some stale milk on the shoulder, but otherwise acceptable, I thought, pulling the phone away from my ear and lifting my t-shirt over my head.

Sawyer's didn't open until noon, but I didn't want to go to brunch. I didn't want the questions and the furrowed brows and awkward silences, and I really didn't want to talk about Lina and the wedding and how exciting it was. Mum hadn't mentioned it and I wondered suddenly if she knew, and if she knew I knew.

I should've been happy for Lina.

I *was* happy for Lina. She had been my best friend for over half my life and she'd always, *always* wanted to get married. Despite everything, she'd always believed in getting married as some sort of fairytale ending, everyone riding off into the sunset and living happily ever after, like in the movies.

When I put the phone back to my ear Mum was saying something about family. About making an effort.

I exhaled softly, closing my eyes. 'Yeah, brunch is fine,' I said, wanting her to stop. I pulled on the shirt and buttoned it over my dark purple bra. 'I'm closing Friday, though, so not too early.'

She suggested nine as I doused myself in deodorant; Flirt—a baby-pink can of musk and drunk fourteen-year-olds. I coughed, countering with ten, in the city somewhere so I could get to work for eleven, and we agreed on nine thirty. In Petersham. 'That's fair, don't you think? Parking is impossible closer in,' she said.

I wedged the phone back between my neck and shoulder and pulled out my ponytail.

'Fine,' I said. My head hurt. It had been hurting all morning but suddenly it was throbbing. I gathered my hair with my fingers, and twisted it tightly around itself, until I could feel it sting at my scalp. 'Anyway, I've got work. I'll talk to you later?'

Mum sighed. It was like that was all she ever did. I could see her, closing her eyes and pinching the top of her nose with her fingers, a tiny shake of the head. 'Take care of yourself, okay?' Despairing. What had she done to end up with a daughter like me?

I twisted again, tucked the ends under and wrapped an elastic band around the resulting bundle of hair until it stayed put. 'Always. Bye, Mum.'

I didn't wait for her to answer, throwing the phone into my locker as I hung up. It landed on a pile of clothes and slid down onto the floor. 'Shit,' I said, bending to pick it up.

A short raspy laugh from the doorway made me freeze halfway back to standing. I hadn't heard that laugh in months, but I recognised it straight away. The throbbing intensified, a blood vessel fit to burst.

'What are you doing here?' I asked, standing up and putting my phone back into my locker.

More laughter. 'I don't know, Winona. I thought I'd drop by, do some reading, maybe get a bite to eat. You?'

I turned around. Dex—our former head chef and my ex, if I had to find a word for it—was leaning on a locker near the door in his chef's jacket and pants. He looked like he was posing for a photo.

'It's nice to see you too,' he added.

'How long have you been there?'

He smirked. 'Long enough.'

I rolled my eyes and turned back to my locker. 'Hope you enjoyed the show,' I said, looking for my lighter, wishing my bag wasn't so full of . . . everything.

Tampons. An unopened electricity bill. A balled-up t-shirt. A single green sock, not my size. I stared at it for a minute, trying to figure out how I'd ended up with a single man-sized green sock, printed to look like a lumpy, muscular foot. It was dusty grey on the sole, like it'd had a twin and an owner and life experiences before it had ended up in my handbag.

A pull on my shoulder dragged me back in to the present, followed by a snap and a sting. I jumped, and Dex laughed. He'd flicked my bra strap.

'The purple one's my favourite,' he said, walking away.

'Piss off.' I turned around and threw the sock at the back of his head. 'And don't call me Winona.'

He snickered, halfway out of the room. 'You used to love it.'

I shook my head in disgust and turned back to my locker, unable to believe I'd ever found him charming.

The first time he'd called me Winona was about fifteen minutes into my first shift. My hair was short then, and it had taken me a moment to figure out who he was talking to. When I'd corrected him, he'd grinned, like it was a joke, and the next time I walked by the kitchen he called me Winona again.

He does it to everyone, Nic, my boss, said when I asked him about it later. *It's part of his whole . . . thing.*

What thing?

You know—he sighed—*bad boy rock star chef. He gave the contestants on* MasterChef *stupid nicknames too.*

He was on MasterChef?

Guest judge.

I raised an eyebrow, and Nic laughed.

Just play along, he said. *He gets bored eventually.*

I had, and so had he, but not until it was too late.

◆

I found my lighter and my tobacco, and went out to the makeshift staff smoking area in the back laneway. It was filthy and loud, with a few upturned milk crates and a half-dead pot plant, surrounded

by bins and air-conditioning units and piles of flattened cardboard
boxes, crawling with cockroaches. The bins were full, more than full,
black garbage bags pushing over the tops and a couple just thrown
onto the lid in defeat. The sun had been baking them all morning,
and the stench made my eyes hurt and my throat tighten, my cheeks
pulling into my teeth involuntarily. The pizza place across the lane
had left one of their bags on the ground overnight and it had been
torn open by a cat or a rat or a vagrant, the contents spilling out onto
the concrete, blackening lettuce and burst tomatoes and something
that used to be ham.

I sat down on one of the milk crates, rolling myself one last
pre-shift cigarette and tapping the end with my index finger before
I put it in my mouth. The door kicked open and Dex came out, his
cigarette already rolled and perched between his lips. He pushed
his dirty blond hair out of his face and lit it.

'Sorry, Nona,' he said, sounding almost genuine.

I shrugged, lighting my rollie and inhaling hard. 'For what?'
I watched the smoke trail out of my mouth as I spoke. 'Nothing
you haven't seen before, right?'

He laughed.

'So you're back?' I asked, taking another drag.

'I'm back. Started yesterday. I missed you.'

'Sure you did.'

'Nobody made me a coffee.'

I rolled my eyes. 'Diddums.'

I'd been at Sawyer's a few months when it happened. Nic had told
me to play along but he'd also told me to be careful and I'd shaken
my head and told him I could handle myself.

I thought I could. I'd been careful my whole life.

Dex wasn't my type. He was obnoxious and condescending and
sometimes he quoted obscure Radiohead lyrics in the middle of
conversations, as though that made him an intellectual, and he had a

steady stream of fangirls who'd sit at the end of the bar and wait for him to finish his shift. They were all wide-eyed and fine-featured, and looked much too young for him.

Or maybe he was more my type than I wanted to admit, over-confident and cocksure and spoiled, and when he pulled me into a doorway after a long night of drinking and kissed me against a stranger's letterbox, I let him, and I let him take me home.

It was the night after Valentine's Day and it felt like there were couples everywhere, pretending to be happy. I'd been on edge for weeks, dreading it. He was a distraction, a Sawyer's rite of passage, and I was a notch on a bedpost, a tick on a scorecard. We'd used each other, and I'd thought that was it, done and dusted. But he'd walked me home the next night and it had happened again, and again, and then I didn't know what to think. Didn't want to think at all.

I blamed vodka. I blamed insomnia. It was bad then, the insomnia, tempered only by the aforementioned vodka and the exhaustion I felt after a long shift on the floor, and it made me do stupid things. I'd been warned, but I'd let him in anyway. Every cell of my body screamed at me to stop, walk away, be careful, but I didn't, I wasn't. He was like a drug—one I didn't really like but couldn't say no to.

I didn't do relationships, didn't get attached, didn't believe in fairytales or happily-ever-afters. I never had, but when Lina asked how long I was going to let him hang around, rolled her eyes like she knew this routine off by heart, I'd felt sick and scared and angry, clung on tighter.

I was dying, I wanted to say. I was dying and it didn't matter. None of it mattered.

You're too much, he said when he ended it, and I knew what he meant and I hated that he knew it too, but for a brief, shining moment, I'd been relieved.

And then I was just devastated—strangely, awfully devastated, by this thing I'd never wanted anyway. My insomnia got worse.

The Thoughts got worse. Everything got worse. I burst into tears in the middle of service three nights in a row, before finally taking one of the valium pills I'd been carrying around in my wallet and dropping an entire carton of wine behind the bar. It confirmed all my suspicions, the ones I'd had for years. No fairytales. No happily-ever-afters. Just pain. Just death.

Nic had dragged me into the staffroom and handed me a glass half full of vodka, his expression set in a perfect mix of concern and impatience as he watched me drink it. *He's an arse, Caitie*, he said. *But he's Dex. Sorry, sweets.*

He was right. Sawyer's had just been written up in *Gourmet* and everyone knew it was because of Dex, and I was just a waitress, so I sucked it up, got on with it, got over it. Dug up the pamphlet I'd been given after the accident and went along to that support group in that beige community room, just to see. Just in case. Careful again, same as I'd always been.

A couple of weeks later Dex was offered a job opening a new gastropub in Bondi and then he was gone. Lenny, the owner of Sawyer's, stopped saying hello to me when he came in, and every time I went into the prep kitchen conversations would trail off and I only stayed because Nic begged me to. I was dying anyway. It didn't matter.

♦

'So, what happened?' I asked, watching him smoke his cigarette. He had a new row of Japanese characters tattooed on the inside of his wrist and I wondered if he knew what they meant.

'Usual story.' He shrugged and looked past my shoulder. 'It's not the best time in the restaurant business. Bondi isn't what it used to be. Joel has a coke problem. Pick one.'

'I heard the food was pretty average, too.'

'Funny.'

I smiled. 'It is, kind of.'

He shook his head. 'And how are you? Still Nic's princess?'

'Of course.' I looked at him. He looked different. I remembered how he'd looked before, how I'd never thought he was cute but I used to spend hours just gazing at him. 'You know me.'

I used to think he had the most amazing eyebrows. Now they just looked like eyebrows, one cocked up in a way that I used to think was sexy but now just looked over-rehearsed. 'Yeah, right,' he said.

My cigarette had gone out but there wasn't enough of it left to bother relighting it, so I tossed my butt at the sand bucket by the door and stood up. 'See you in there.'

He exhaled, the smoke smudging his face like a thumbprint on a photograph. 'Okay, Nona.'

◆

I'd never even been to Sawyer's before I came in for my interview, never really been in this part of Pyrmont, quietly tucked away between the eighties gaudiness of Darling Harbour and the sprawl of the fish markets. I'd expected something showier and I'd walked past the converted terrace twice before noticing the gold lettering on the front window, the dark, heavy door. The dining room was long and narrow and intimate, like someone's front parlour, if that someone was filthy rich and wanted you to know it, with a long, mahogany bar along one side and a row of antique industrial cage lanterns down the middle. It was designed to impress, to intimidate, and it did. Most newbs would start their first shift whispering out of respect. I'd never been one of them; it was a restaurant, nothing more. Still, sometimes when I touched the bar I was almost overwhelmed by how solid it was.

When I got to the floor the fluoros were on and there was a waitress I half recognised laying out cutlery and Nic was training a newb on the computer. He glanced up and gestured at the bar with his chin.

'Thanks,' I mouthed.

Nic was my boss. Lenny had hired me but Nic had trained me and somewhere amid the dozens of questions I'd asked him and the hundreds of nights when we'd thought we were going to get eaten alive by Eastern Suburbs power couples and the many, many after-work drinks we'd shared, rolling from pub to pub before ending up dancing in some weird club or a stranger's lounge room, we'd become friends. If anyone knew where the sock in my bag had come from, it would be Nic.

I grabbed an apron from under the register and tied it around my waist, positioning myself in front of the coffee machine and wrenching a filter handle free. Nobody had put the music on yet so I could hear Nic explaining subs to the newb in his thick Kiwi accent, her low 'uh-huh's doing nothing to convince either of us that she was listening. I gave her three shifts tops, and clicked a perfect mountain of coffee into the basket.

Sometimes in group, when we ran out of horrific stories we'd seen on the news and near misses that weren't really near at all, we'd talk about coping strategies. Theories and tricks and ways to keep ourselves sane. Sometimes Carlos went on and on about 'mindfulness', which was the technical term for 'distraction'. His psych encouraged him to practise mindfulness, gave him piles of readings on how to do it, which he shared with us, and some of us nodded and went off and tried it—and sometimes it almost worked. None of it ever made much sense to me, but sometimes when I was at Sawyer's I felt like I got close. On a busy night I could go hours without a single Thought, without a single terrible scenario playing out behind my eyes. I was right there, in the present, twisting and timing and steaming and mixing and shaking, and my mind was actually, properly still.

After the accident, Sawyer's was the first place I could breathe.

I'd just finished pouring two perfect macchiatos when Nic said my name. He was standing in front of me with the new girl, her face a picture of confusion and disinterest, eyes glazed like doughnuts, and I slid one of the coffees over to him as I necked the other one.

'This is Emma,' he said. 'Emma, Caitlin. If you have any questions, ask her.'

I made a face. 'I'm here to help.' My voice was slick with sarcasm.

'Aren't you just?' He sipped his coffee, then looked back at the new girl, who was studying us both with the same confused expression.

'Ignore her,' he said. 'I'd say she's having a bad day but she's always like this.'

I arched an eyebrow, and he laughed.

'Seriously, though, Caitlin knows everything there is to know about everything to do with the floor. And she's super-anal about everything being done right. Listen to her, and you'll be right.'

The new girl nodded, and I frowned. She was too quiet. You had to watch the quiet ones—they were either taking everything in and would end up running the place in three months or they were completely and utterly lost and would be fucking up your entire night. I put this one in column B.

I'd already forgotten her name. Tara? She looked like a Tara.

I started setting up my stations, hearing the boredom in Nic's voice as he took the newb through the process of clocking on and off and ordering a staff meal.

'Rachel's the supervisor on today,' he said. 'She's running late— puppy emergency, apparently.'

I sighed. Rachel was my least favourite staff member—or at least she had been, until ten minutes ago.

'She'll be here soon.' Nic glanced at me. 'I'm in the office all afternoon, come see me when you finish.'

'Okay,' Tara said. I could feel her watching me clean out my milk jugs. 'And until then?' She cleared her throat. 'Until my food is ready?'

He shrugged. 'Just, like . . . tidy stuff up.' Nic hated training people, which was why he always rostered newbs on for shifts he wasn't working, and why he always told them to ask me questions.

If you're going to be a supervisor, he told me once, during what I thought were after-work drinks and he thought was a job interview, *you've got to deal with the newbs.*

I hate the newbs, I'd said, shaking my head. *And I don't want to be a supervisor.*

Yeah, you do. Everybody does eventually.

No they don't. They just tell you that so you'll think they have initiative and aren't planning on quitting the second they find something better.

He'd laughed. *You do, though. You're always bossing everyone around as it is.*

We'd had this conversation a lot, over and over since not long after I'd started; me telling Nic this was just an in-between job, just a break from my real career, and Nic telling me I should think about making it more, and me rolling my eyes because waitressing was not something you did for the rest of your life—no matter how short that life was going to be—and that was the whole point.

You're good at this, Cait. You actually care, he said. He always said. *Nobody else in this place does.*

I'd given him a look, hopefully scathing.

You do. You just have to be nicer to the newbs. Maybe start by remembering their names.

Yeah, right.

You'll change your mind, he'd said confidently, and I'd finished my beer and changed the subject, knowing he was wrong, and that even if he wasn't, it didn't matter. This was all temporary.

'You okay?' he asked, when the newb had wandered off. He sighed, pressed a button under the register. From behind me, I heard a soft, brushy drumbeat, a piano.

I looked up from the frothing wand I'd been scrubbing. Whoever had been making coffee for the prep cooks had left it covered with a fine web of hardened milk froth. I thought about pointing it out, but it was probably him.

'Of course,' I said, smiling. 'Always.'

'I was going to message you yesterday,' he said, flicking a switch. The fluorescent lights went dark and the lanterns crackled to life. Everything changed, softened. The bar turned rich and dark and the velvet curtains glistened. Tara was on the other side of the room, straightening an already perfectly set table, and the light from the filaments bounced off her shiny blonde hair like a rose-gold tiara.

'It's fine,' I said. 'Honestly.'

He put his empty coffee cup down on the counter and I picked it up and put it in the washing-up bucket behind me without thinking. When I turned back he was leaning forward on his elbows. Up close he was overdue for a shave, uneven tufts of stubble poking through the skin on his cheeks. 'Are you sure? You look tired.'

'Yeah.' I gave him a smile. 'I just didn't sleep well last night.'

He raised an eyebrow. 'Big night?'

I laughed. 'Maybe.' When I'd first told Nic I wanted Tuesdays off he'd spent weeks pestering me for a reason—his guesses ranging from a second job to a tempestuous fling with a married man on a very tight schedule to Alcoholics Anonymous, which had felt uncomfortably close to the truth—and he still occasionally tried to trick me into telling him.

'You know it wasn't up to me,' he said, as I did a quick check of the spirits. 'Lenny's been desperate to get him back for ages. I swear he sabotaged that whole Bondi thing.'

I rolled my eyes.

'*Good Food* are writing it up as a homecoming. It's a big deal. Expensive, too.'

'No raises for the floor staff this year then?'

He shook his head. 'No raises for any of us. Not when you've got talent to pay.'

I scoffed. 'What talent?'

'Besides, word's out. He only started yesterday and he's only sous until he settles back in, but we're half booked today, only two open tables tonight. On a Wednesday.'

'Great.' I turned around. 'Are they all going to want autographs too? Should I put a reserved sign at the end of the bar for his groupies? Take a tour through so they can see the great man at work?'

Nic ignored me.

I tipped my head towards Tara, walking out of the kitchen carrying a plate of food. 'Have you warned her yet?'

'Very funny.' He smiled. 'I wasn't just blowing smoke up your arse, you know? You really are the only person here who knows what they're doing.'

I laughed. 'Thanks.'

He watched her push the staff door open, the plate too precarious in her hand. 'What do you think?'

I shrugged. 'Not much. You?'

'She's sweet. Young.'

'How young?'

'Nineteen.'

'Jesus.' That explained it. 'One of Lenny's hires then?'

'Shhh,' he chided, glancing around as though to check we weren't overheard. 'Look after her, okay?'

I bit my lip, knowing what he meant. Wishing I didn't.

3

SATURDAY, APRIL

'Seventeen dollars for cereal? But you can't afford a pair of jeans without holes in them?'

I hadn't slept more than a few hours since Lina's postcard arrived. The night before I hadn't slept at all. I hadn't called her despite her plea, and I knew she would be angry. I felt awful, sick with shame and confusion, annoyed that I couldn't just pick up my phone, tap out a generic congratulatory text and hit send. It had been days and I'd tried so many times but I couldn't do it.

I felt scared. I didn't know of what, but at three in the morning that was what I felt the most.

Everything was soft around the edges but deceptively, painfully noisy, every sound bouncing off the polished concrete floor and high, blindingly white ceiling. Someone put a fork down on a table across from ours and I jumped, looking around in alarm.

'I didn't buy them with holes in them, Mum. The ones with holes in them are expensive. These're just old. And it's activated granola.'

'Well, if you didn't spend all your money on granola and cigarettes, you'd be able to afford new ones.'

I heard Jack scoff and caught his eye for a second.

'Activated granola.' Mum shook her head in wonder, as Jack's phone vibrated on the table. He picked it up and started tapping furiously, ignoring us. 'Only in Newtown. And it took twenty minutes to find a park.'

I sighed. I needed to sleep. I hadn't even ordered the granola—she had—but somehow I was responsible for it, because I'd been running late, because I'd misread the time, and I'd called her at the last minute and asked if we could move brunch closer to the city. I picked up my coffee and finished it in one gulp.

'Big night last night, Caitie?' Dad asked.

I didn't answer, just gave him my best half-hearted smile as I dropped the cup onto the saucer off-centre. I felt sick, couldn't concentrate. Mum and Dad kept talking and I tried to listen but everything hurt and their voices were so far away.

'. . . like a brewery, honey. Seriously.'

'How's that job of yours? Have you given any more thought to . . . ?'

'Honestly, Caitlin. What should we . . . ?'

'. . . coming down? Is that it?'

I caught the waiter's eye and flicked my fingers at my empty cup. She didn't stop, but gave me an understanding nod.

'More coffee? Really?'

'. . . ice? I saw something on *A Current Affair*.'

It always went like this, ever since the accident—not that they knew about the accident. They knew something, maybe. They knew that I didn't come home anymore, that I dodged their calls, but they didn't know why. Dad thought I was on drugs. Ice and heroin and benzos, with a side of ecstasy and bulbs. Maybe ketamine. Whatever was in the news that week. I wanted to tell him I wasn't, but it was easier not to.

'. . . just don't want to get stuck there like we did last year. That hotel the insurance company put us up in was disgusting. Didn't even have a pool and the bar didn't sell spirits, remember?'

I didn't know how long I'd been staring at the pepper shaker in the middle of the table, but it was shiny and my eyes clung to it, stuck fast. I blinked, trying to catch the conversation.

'Are you going somewhere?' I asked.

Mum looked at me, exhaled in a heave that made her entire chest fall. 'Yes, Caitlin.'

I stared at her. When I was little, people used to say we looked alike but now you'd be hard-pressed to see the resemblance. She was bigger in every way, years of boxed white wine and desk jobs filling out her torso and plumping her cheeks. Her hair was cut into the customary style of the mid-fifties set, dyed into something that was supposed to look natural but was too blocky, too many shades of copper and gold and ash. Her eyes were frowning at me but her forehead hadn't moved, and I wondered if she'd had her botox topped up recently.

'Oh,' I said, ignoring her tone, forcing myself to sound pleasant and interested, pulling out my ponytail and putting the elastic band between my teeth as I re-did it. 'Where?'

Mum frowned at my mouth, at me. 'Bali, Cait. For the wedding.'

I went cold, twisting my hair tightly and biting on the band so I wouldn't have to say anything.

'I can't believe you didn't tell us Lina was engaged. We had to find out on Facebook.'

I took the elastic out of my mouth and put it back in my hair, waiting.

A plate of food was dropped in front of me, too loudly, the smell of bacon too overwhelming. Another waitress put my coffee down and I picked it up, drinking half of it in one go.

'I thought Jenny would tell you,' I said. Jenny was Lina's mum. She didn't live next door anymore but she still spoke to Mum all the time, at least as far as I knew.

'It's so exciting, isn't it?' Mum cooed over her annoyance. 'And the resort's meant to be amazing. Lina's got such good taste, and it's lucky Matt has that nice job, isn't it?'

I looked at my food, trying to find a place to start. My stomach was churning but my throat was tight, my mouth full of acid.

'Everything okay, Caitie?' Dad asked.

When I glanced at him his expression was odd, and I nodded. 'Of course.' I picked up my fork and stabbed a mushroom, forced my spine to straighten. 'It's really exciting. I can't wait.'

'So has she asked you yet?' Mum asked, pouring milk into her granola.

I paused, the mushroom dangling in mid-air. 'Asked me what?'

'You know! Maid of honour.'

I frowned. 'I don't think—'

'Don't be silly,' Mum said. Her face was all lit up, her eyes too wide open, hard to look at. 'Of course she's going to ask you. You've been best friends for years.'

I put the mushroom in my mouth and chewed it forcefully, understanding for the first time why some people hated them so much. It felt like eating my own toes, still attached.

'Maybe,' I said, shrugging.

'Caitlin.' Mum's voice sounded like a warning.

'What?' Another mushroom. This one oozed dirty water onto my tongue and I nearly gagged, wondering what kinds of bacteria it was harbouring.

'I don't know what happened between you two, but after everything you've been through together, you could at least—'

'Nothing happened.' I didn't want to think about everything we'd been through together. All that ancient history. 'It's fine. We're fine. We've just both been busy, that's all.'

When I looked up Dad was still watching me and it made me uncomfortable, awkward. Over the noise of the cafe I heard a siren, and I wondered where it was coming from, where it was going.

'It's so exciting,' Mum said again. 'Jenny is thrilled.'

I forced a smile at the mention of Lina's mum. 'How is she?'

'Good,' Mum said. 'We're having dinner there tomorrow. They're buying a property in the Southern Highlands, now that Colin's retiring.'

'Oh?'

Mum nodded. 'She's so lucky to have him, isn't she? Especially after everything. She's not big on marriage, as you can probably imagine, but she's thrilled for Lina.'

I liked Jenny. I always had. When Lina had first moved in next door, I'd been around there all the time—with Lina, of course, but also because I liked Jenny. She was so different from my mum, not interested in the kinds of things my mum cared about: whether the P&C should hold a trivia night and whether the cutlery all matched at dinner. Jenny had no patience for any of that—their cutlery never matched—and I'd liked that.

'Matt's a sweetheart, isn't he?'

'Yeah,' I said absently, feeling hot and uncomfortable. Matt was a rugby-playing country boy who worked for an accounting firm. Lina had been crazy about him since the moment they met but I'd never understood why.

'You know, when you two were younger, I used to wonder which of you would get married first.' Mum sounded vaguely annoyed.

I rolled my eyes, didn't even bother hiding it. 'Well, now you know.' As though there had ever been any doubt.

'Caitlin.'

'Sorry.' I sliced into a poached egg with my fork and watched it bleed out all over the plate. 'I'm sorry. I worked late last night and I'm really tired.'

Mum sighed. I glanced up and saw her exchange a look with Dad.

'Leave it, Sue,' he said softly.

'Have you given any more thought to getting a job?' she asked, ignoring him.

I looked down at my plate. Everything was drowning in egg, covered in salmonella, and suddenly I had an overwhelming urge to throw up. At least we were done talking about Lina, I thought. Small comfort. 'I have a job, Mum.'

'A proper one. Doing . . . whatever people with honours degrees in sociology do.'

My eyes met hers, and I knew she was being sarcastic, so decided to play along.

'What? Waitressing?'

'Very funny.' She leaned forward, elbows on the table, studying me. 'You're twenty-eight now. Not getting any younger.'

Not getting any older, either, I thought.

'Maybe I'll go back and get my Master's,' I said, wondering if I could smell gas. 'Then I can become a shift supervisor.'

She frowned. 'You had a job before. I don't know what was wrong with it.'

I shrugged. Bile. That was what the egg looked like. 'Nothing.'

There had been nothing wrong with it. Being a demographic coordinator for a social research company wasn't going to change the world and didn't really use my degree in any meaningful way, but it was corporate enough to keep Mum off my back—just—and edgy enough to impress my school friends at parties. I worked out of a former jam factory in Redfern with bright purple feature walls and jellybean-shaped desks and an office dachshund, and we had cake every Friday afternoon. I wore proper outfits and high heels and my boss talked to me about career paths and progression, and I wasn't going to be there forever but I was going to be there for a while, a few years at least, and then I was going to go somewhere bigger, better.

I had a future, a plan. Climb the ladder. Wear higher heels and fancier dresses and redder lipstick. Date a banker, a doctor, a lawyer. Get invited to industry parties with C-list celebrities we pretended weren't being paid to be there. Save some money. Put down a deposit on a flat. Eventually, I'd have to find my own rugby-playing accountant with a good head on his shoulders, someone normal, someone boring but nice, who ticked all the boxes, and we'd settle down, sell the flat and buy a fixer-upper a few suburbs further out. Keep climbing the ladder, keep buying prettier outfits and higher heels, fix up the fixer-upper, buy another one. Get a gym membership, a dog, a cherry-red hatchback. I'd always known the way it should go. Safe. Comfortable. Careful. No fairytales, but no pain either, just ticking the boxes and climbing the ladder.

And then I had another plan. Lina and I had another plan. Years and years of planning and it had all disappeared in a second, like the back seat of a car, T-boned at speed. Disintegrated.

I swallowed, trying to get rid of the awful taste in my mouth, the sourness in my throat.

Mum made a face. Exasperated. She was always so exasperated. 'Well, could you go back?'

I picked up a piece of bacon and put it in my mouth, licked the salt and fat off my fingers. It was cold. 'I don't think so.'

'Why not? They liked you there, didn't they?'

'I guess.'

They did. They were patient, after the accident. They let me have one week off, then two. Sent flowers. They called a few times during the third week, asking where I was. They didn't fire me until halfway through the fourth, and even then they sounded remorseful about it, my boss calling me personally, leaving a message telling me if I could get a medical certificate I could stay, but I didn't want to stay. I couldn't. I was going to die. It was only a matter of time and it seemed like fraud to keep letting them think otherwise.

It seemed like fraud doing anything.

'Are you really just going to be a waitress for the rest of your life?' She picked up her coffee and took a sip, watching me over the rim of the cup.

Probably, I thought, but at least the rest of my life wasn't going to be very long.

'No,' I lied. 'I'm just . . . taking a break.'

'It's been over a year.'

I shrugged, not sure how to answer.

She stared at me for a while longer then went back to her cereal.

'You right?' Jack asked, finally looking up from his phone.

'Yeah. Tired.' I smiled, wondering if I could get away with ordering another coffee.

'Were you out last night?'

'Just working.'

'Shay and I went to this cool place in Surry Hills.' Shay was his girlfriend. I'd met her once last year. She was a nurse and wore vintage floral dresses and purple Docs. 'All the tables were those old-school arcade machines. You been there?'

I thought for a minute. It sounded familiar, like the kind of sceney bar Nic and I would go to. 'I don't think so. Nice?'

'Yeah, awesome. Shay knows all the best places.'

I picked up my fork. 'You guys are still together then?'

'Yeah, yeah.' Jack grinned. 'We're going to London at the end of the year, did I tell you?'

'No.'

He grinned. 'Just saving up now.'

'That's awesome, I'm jealous.' I meant it, especially about the jealousy, which tasted like tin on my tongue.

'Yeah, it's going to be epic.' But he sounded bored. His phone vibrated again and he picked it up without another word. I stabbed my fork into a piece of haloumi, holding it up and inspecting it for egg yolk.

'What's that?' Dad asked.

'Haloumi. It's Greek.' I held it out to him. 'Want some?'

His upper lip flicked up into a grimace as I put it in my mouth. 'A bit exotic for me, thanks.'

'It's fried cheese, Dad. Not black truffles.'

'Whatever it is, stop playing with it and just eat it,' Mum interrupted, a single comma of a frown appearing between her eyebrows.

I threw Jack a pleading glance as I chewed. He ignored me, kept tapping.

'So, are you flying over with us, or with Lina?'

I stopped, closing my eyes. The cafe was suddenly too small, too crowded and something smelled funny—definitely a gas leak.

'Caitie?' Dad asked.

I glanced at him, at the light fixture over the bar, too heavy. 'Sorry.'

He didn't say anything.

I looked at Mum. 'I haven't decided. It's months away.'

'Only seven,' she said. 'It's not that hard a decision, surely. And you want to book soon to get a good price without having to fly at eleven at night.'

'I can sleep on the plane.'

'That's not the point.' She put her spoon down, too loudly. 'You just don't seem very excited, Caitlin.'

'I am,' I said softly.

'I can tell.' I could hear the frustration in her voice.

'Sorry,' I said again. My voice broke. I wasn't apologising to her, and maybe she knew it. Maybe everybody did. I took a long, hard breath, looked up at the ceiling, at the lights—all that lethal, invisible electricity. The cafe was noisy, impossibly noisy, but I was wrapped in a cocoon of silence, thick and hot.

'I am,' I said, avoiding the eyes I knew were looking at me, forcing out a smile. 'It's going to be great. I think—I just have a headache.' A tumour. Another one; a new one.

'You should drink more water,' Mum said.

I nodded. 'Yeah, will do.' I made a show of emptying my glass then glancing up at the clock above the door. 'Hey, I've got to go. Buses are a nightmare at this time of day, and I can't be late on a Saturday.'

Dad shook his head as I stood up. 'I wish you didn't work in that place. The restaurant business is so seedy.'

I shrugged, putting my phone into my pocket and hoisting my bag onto my shoulder. 'I like it,' I said, turning and walking away.

I heard Mum say something as I left, but I kept going, my eyes on the hard concrete floor, wondered what would happen if I tripped and fell, slammed into it head first.

4

Sunday, April

I did like Sawyer's, honestly. It kept me busy, kept me moving, kept my mind still. It was always the same, even when it wasn't; even after Dex, when Lenny stopped speaking to me and Nic started asking if I was okay, it was the same, and eventually I *was* okay and it all went back to normal. My normal. Work. After-work drinks—maybe too many. Sleep—sometimes. The newbs came and went and the menu changed every three months but the machine churned on, taking me with it.

Still, it was seedy. Dad wasn't wrong about that.

Behind her back, Dex called Emma 'Barbie', and I wondered what he called her to her face. Every time she passed the kitchen his eyes followed her, and when I caught him at it he raised an eyebrow, daring me to say something.

'She's nineteen,' is what I did say, while sorting a crate full of empty bottles for recycling. It was nearly ten and the dinner rush was over and I'd survived, somehow. I'd hardly slept—again—and I'd lost count of how many cups of coffee I'd had. My heartbeat was messy, skittering around my chest like an oversized, overshot pinball, my stomach a tangle of knots wound so tight there wasn't any point even trying to force food into it. Every time I blinked my eyelids threatened to stick shut. I'd had to prise one open with my fingers earlier.

He just shook his head. He was prepping for the week ahead, mindlessly chopping mushrooms and tossing them into a white bucket. Just the sight of them made my tongue curl in disgust.

'You're gross.'

'And you're jealous.'

'Get fucked.'

'Gladly.' He smirked, and then lifted his head. 'Hey, Blondie!'

I turned around, my question answered. She was at the pass, waiting for a plate to complete an order, her blonde hair swinging down her back. Wide-eyed and fine-featured.

'Yeah?' She had studs in her ears, and I was willing to bet they were real diamonds.

'You staying for drinks tonight?'

She giggled. Actually giggled. I rolled my eyes and he caught them, his face loathsome with glee.

'You should,' he said across the kitchen, giving her his most awful Dex smile.

'I've got a history tute at nine tomorrow,' she said. I stifled a laugh.

'That's okay, Blondie,' he drawled. 'I'll make sure you don't stay out too late.'

My stomach lurched as she giggled again. 'Yeah, all right,' she said, as her plate came up. And then she was gone, and Dex was looking at me, his eyes twinkling in victory.

'Wow,' I said, tasting something bitter in the back of my throat. 'I swear you used that same line on me once.'

'Are *you* staying for drinks tonight?' he asked.

'I don't know. Will you make sure *I* don't stay out too late?' I imitated his drawl.

'If you like.' His voice was slimy and slick. 'I can multitask.'

'You're revolting,' I said, shaking my head. 'And I'm tired.'

'Big night last night?'

I frowned, not sure if I should be offended that everyone's assumption was that my current state was self-inflicted. 'Just . . . not sleeping well.' I picked up a bottle and threw it into the bin with more force than it deserved, flinched at the sound of it breaking, the sudden waft of stale beer making me nauseous. Everything was making me nauseous.

'You okay?' His voice changed.

'Yeah,' I said reflexively. When I looked up his face was different too, made me uncomfortable. I looked away. 'I'm fine.'

'You sure? Go have a cigarette. Nic won't care.'

I glanced back at him, standing in front of me with his hands on his hips. For a second, he reminded me of someone else, then it faded.

'I'm fine,' I said, picking up my empty crate and turning away. 'Don't let Emma miss her history tute tomorrow.'

''Kay, Nona.' He shrugged. 'Whatever.'

◆

I went back up to the floor, ignoring the way Nic looked at me, and started making a stock list.

'Hey, can I ask you something?'

It took a second to realise the question was meant for me, and when I looked up Emma was standing at the bar, waiting. Definitely diamonds. 'Yeah, what's up?' I asked, in my best customer-facing voice.

'It's not . . .' She glanced around nervously. 'It's not about work.'

I let my eyes defocus until she was a yellow and black blur in front of me. Even as a fuzzy shape she was perfectly proportioned—

tall, thin, her chest just a little bigger than strictly necessary. 'That's okay.'

'So . . .' My stomach clenched in anticipation. 'That guy in the kitchen . . . Dexter?'

'Dex,' I corrected her without thinking, straightening my cordials. 'Yeah.'

'Yeah?' I noticed Nic busying himself at the coffee machine, too deliberately.

'Is he . . .'

Somehow my face arranged into something neutral. 'What?'

She leaned forward and I couldn't help but notice her cleavage. Definitely Dex's type.

'Does he have a girlfriend?'

I blinked. 'I don't know. I don't think so.'

She grinned, and I felt it in my gut. Nic had told me to look after her, but I couldn't stop this, whatever this was.

'Do you think he—'

'Honestly,' I cut her off. 'I wouldn't go there.'

Her grin faded. 'Why not?'

I went to answer, but suddenly I didn't know how. There were a hundred reasons, but in that moment I couldn't think of a single one. She looked at me, waiting.

'Stock, Cait,' Nic said, a little too loudly, catching my eye and passing me a coffee.

'Sorry,' she whispered, straightening up.

'It's okay.' I gave her a half-smile as she walked away, downed the coffee in one go. It took me a second to feel the vodka burning my throat and I fought back a cough.

'I don't get it.' Nic crouched down in front of the fridge next to me, pulling it open. 'Four milks, three skim, two soy.'

I picked up my pen and started writing, concentrating so hard my eyes hurt. My throat was still on fire. 'What was that? Jesus.'

'Bootleg espresso martini,' he said, without turning around. 'Sunday night special.'

I grimaced. 'Thanks. What don't you get?'

'Three almond. Two rice. Cream . . . two cream. What he does to get all you girls going like that?' He shook his head. 'Make that three cream. And one less almond—there's a stray up the back here.'

'That was Rachel,' I said quickly.

He laughed. 'I know. Seriously, though, what is it? Has he got a really big—' he caught my eye and mouthed the word silently '—or something?'

'Yeah, it's huge,' I deadpanned. 'What about mixers?'

'I'm getting there.'

I saw Emma in the doorway to the kitchen, leaning on the wall, one hand on her perfectly jutting hip, and my smile faltered.

'Ugh,' Nic said, coming upright next to me and following my gaze.

Her ponytail hung straight and neat down her back. I tucked a loose strand of my own hair, neither straight nor neat, behind my ear. 'I know. Less than a week. This might be a new record.'

'You really think he would?' Nic raised an eyebrow. 'She's nineteen.'

'That's legal, right?'

'Ew.' He shook his head. 'I still can't believe you went there.'

'Neither can I.'

'We all make mistakes,' Nic said.

'I don't,' I said, more to myself than to him.

I didn't get attached. I didn't do relationships. I never had.

'Good point,' he said, then crouched down in front of the fridges again. 'Two Coke. One tonic. Two lemonade. Four cranberry. One pomegranate. Two elderberry.'

I frowned, the list blurring in front of me as another wave of exhaustion crashed into me. It was nearly ten and I still had so much to do. I should have had a cigarette earlier, I thought, pressing my fingers into my forehead, trying to make my eyes work again.

'Hello, Caitlin!' Nic was snapping his fingers.

'What?' I glanced at him, trying to remember where I was.

He groaned, turned back to the fridge. 'You're such a brat. Two—'

'Two Coke,' I cut him off, picking up my pen. 'One tonic. Two lemonade. Four cranberry. One pomegranate. Two elderberry.'

'Lucky guess.'

'Every time.'

'Doesn't make you any less of a brat.' He grinned, tipping his chin towards the end of the bar. 'Serve him, will you?'

''Course,' I said, looking up.

A man I couldn't remember seeing before was sitting at the end of the bar, a pale blue shirt rolled up to his elbows, collar undone. Medium-brown hair, not too short, not too long, framing a face punctured by medium-brown eyes and a perfectly straight, medium-sized nose. Medium build, medium height, as near as I could tell, so generic he was practically invisible, but in that Sawyer's way—the shirt was a little too well cut, obviously dry-cleaned, fingernails a little too clean—but still I looked at him for longer than I needed to as I approached.

'Hi,' I said, putting a napkin down on the bar. My voice bounced around my head, too loud. 'What can I get you?'

He looked up and his face cycled through a chart of emotions before settling on the right one. Polite surprise. Not what I was expecting. 'Hey.'

I frowned. Close up, his eyes were darker, hazelnut.

'Glenmorangie, the eighteen.'

'Ice?'

'Water. Just a dash.' He glanced at Nic, smiled. 'Hi.'

Nic smiled back, too knowing. 'Tom,' he said. 'How's things?'

'Good. Busy night?'

'Not too bad, for a Sunday. Lots of couples, though, wouldn't you say, Caitie?'

I tried to say something but I was too tired. The man—Tom—was watching me, a question on his lips. 'I guess.'

'I read your chef was back.'

Nic threw me a look. 'We're so lucky, aren't we?'

I barely suppressed a snort. 'Blessed.'

Tom laughed nervously. 'Well, as long as you don't get so busy I can't come in for a sneaky whisky every now and then . . .'

'Never.' Nic grinned, touching my arm and turning back to the glassware. 'The margins on alcohol are huge.'

'I've noticed,' Tom said, looking back at me as I put a glass on the napkin.

'You've been here before?' I asked.

'Yeah.' He nodded. 'I live down the road. I come in after work sometimes.'

'Oh.' I turned and found the whisky. 'Sorry, I'm terrible with faces,' I said as I poured.

He smiled. 'It's okay. You're usually busy.'

'Still,' I said, as I half-filled a glass with water, 'I'm supposed to notice these things.' I wasn't sure what I was saying. The vodka was making me stupid.

'Have you worked here long?'

I shrugged, focusing on pouring the water over the whisky, trying to get the proportion exactly right. Some people did it themselves but he hadn't stopped me. 'A year or so.' My hand shook and a dribble of water ran down the outside of the glass. 'Damn.'

'It's okay,' he said, reaching for it. 'Thanks.'

'My pleasure.'

'Do you enjoy it?' He looked around. 'Working here, I mean.'

'Sometimes,' I said, not really sure why he was still talking to me. 'It keeps me sane.' I cringed as soon as the words left my mouth but when I looked at him he was still smiling.

'Sanity is good.'

I smiled back, awkwardly, something in my throat—the last of Nic's martini, acidic and hot. 'So I've heard.'

Tom laughed, and our eyes met. I felt drunk, strange.

'You right, Cait?' Nic asked, standing up.

I nodded, blinked, realised I'd been staring.

Tom took a sip of his whisky, put it down and tipped the glass on one edge, studying the liquid inside. 'Sorry,' he said. 'I should let you get back to it.'

Nic grinned, and I didn't know why. I glanced at Tom. Our eyes met again, and for a second he didn't look away. It felt strange, intense but not uncomfortable. 'Okay,' I said, after a pause.

'Nice to meet you, Kate.'

'Caitlin,' I corrected him, not sure why it mattered. 'Caitie—Cait is fine. Whatever.'

'Well, Caitlin. It's nice to put a name to the face.'

I smiled. 'Enjoy your whisky.'

'Thanks.'

I went down the back to get stock, and when I came back Tom was sipping his whisky and reading a book. Nic gave me a look and I ignored him, loading the fridges and making another run down the back. The third time I came up Tom was gone, and I pretended not to notice.

'He's working early tomorrow,' Nic explained, as I put away the wine.

'Who?' I tried to sound bored.

'Funny,' he said. 'You know.'

'I don't.'

Nic sighed. 'He's a good guy, Cait. Excellent taste in whisky, single, a doctor.'

I made a face.

'What?' he asked.

'Have you met many doctors?'

'Have you?'

'One or two,' I said. Probably more, I thought.

It had been a running joke with Lina at one point. *Don't you ever date anyone normal?* she asked once.

They make good money and they're experts in the human form, I'd replied, scrolling through a dating app on my phone. And they thought I was fun and novel and would amuse their friends, but they'd never ask me to meet their parents. *What's not to love?*

Plenty, usually. They talked about themselves endlessly, about how important their work was. Most of them had gone to private schools and had only ever heard the word no when they were the ones saying it. Not that it mattered—I was using them the same way they used me, to fill in time, to keep Lina off my back.

'I mean, he's on the wrong team,' Nic went on. 'But nobody's perfect.'

'How do you know?'

'Ha!' Nic laughed. 'Trust me, if he was on my team, I'd know.'

'No, I mean the other stuff.'

He shrugged, picked up another glass and inspected it. 'He's been coming in for months. He's usually got a book but he's chatty. Like I said—'

'Really?'

'Yes, Cait.' Nic looked at me, bemused. 'You've seriously never noticed him before? Are you blind?'

'I'm too busy doing my job,' I said, putting the last bottle of wine in the fridge and shutting it. 'Usually yours too.'

He ignored the dig. 'He's here all the time. Not once?'

I hadn't. Or maybe I had. Glenmorangie and water did sound vaguely familiar, when I stopped to think about it. 'He sits at the bar?'

'Sometimes. Sometimes out the back if there's a table free, or he's eating.'

I frowned.

'Look up from your dockets sometime,' he said, a little too gently. 'You never know what you're missing.'

I made a face.

'I thought he was going to ask you out.'

'Right.' I snorted. 'And why would he do that?'

Nic smiled. 'You're cute. For a girl.'

'Gee, thanks.' I shook my head. 'I don't do that, Nic.'

'Why not?'

'Because . . .' I glanced down at the kitchen. Dex was cleaning something near the pass. Nic's eyes followed mine. 'I don't have the time.'

'Right,' he said. 'You've just got to get back on the horse, honey— or under it.'

'Jesus, Nic.'

He leaned in, squeezing my arm as he brushed past me to get to the register. 'Just make sure it's a horse, okay? Preferably a stallion.'

I rolled my eyes and picked up a glass. 'Yeah, thanks,' I said, but when I looked up he was gone.

5

TUESDAY, APRIL

Donna came back, like she said she would. She was already there when I arrived, absently stirring her beige coffee with a pop stick while she listened to Geoff and Carlos talking about the weekend's football results. Her hair was pulled back in a high crooked bun, like an old tennis ball had landed on her head and stuck.

Glenn was back too. He was another one of the old-timers. He'd always had Thoughts, but after the Boxing Day tsunami they'd got so bad he lost his job and his wife left him. He was in his mid-fifties, and a former pro surfer. He missed the water the most, he said. Glenn could go months without thinking about the beautiful semi he'd owned in Bondi, or the woman who still lived in it, but he itched for the water every single day.

Frannie and Louise were sitting with their heads bent together, looking at something on the back of Frannie's hand. A skin cancer, probably. Or her manicure, which was such a bright shade of orange I could see it from across the room. Beryl was sitting next to them. She didn't come very often—at eighty-six, she found it hard to get out of the house at night, especially since she'd broken her hip. Beryl thinking about death as much as she did was probably just being realistic, but she liked us and sometimes she brought biscuits—good ones, not a tray from the supermarket—so no-one was going to ask her to leave.

I made myself a cup of sweet, milky tea and sat down next to Donna. 'Hey,' I said.

She gave me a nervous smile and then looked at her hands.

Fiona was scrolling through something on her phone, looking around every now and then to make sure nobody new had come in. When it hit exactly seven thirty, she tucked the phone under her thigh and picked up her clipboard, coughing once, softly. The room went quiet, the football and the manicure disappeared, cups and hands nestling into laps. I blinked, biting the inside of my cheek. Even the light seemed to change. Dim, like during a séance.

'Hello, everybody. Welcome. It's good to see you all again.' She smiled, but it didn't make her sound any more genuine. 'I think we all know each other, but let's go around the room and introduce ourselves anyway. Just your name and something interesting about yourself.' She motioned to Glenn on her right.

He cleared his throat. 'I'm Glenn. Hi, everyone. I'm writing a novel about a surfer who gets bitten by a shark.'

I glanced over. That was new, although not altogether unexpected. Glenn made himself feel better about not surfing by studying shark attacks, and he'd started several novels in the time I'd known him. I wondered if he'd finish this one.

'I'm Carlos. It's been three weeks since my last confession.'

Carlos said that every week, and every week we all laughed, even though none of us really found it funny.

'G'day, everyone, I'm Geoff,' Geoff said, as though he really was in a room full of people he'd never met. 'I'm thirty-four and I'm a plumber. Nice to see you all here.'

'Hi, I'm Beryl. My fourth great-grandchild was born this week. A little boy called Ajax.' She sounded so pleased, and we all made the requisite noises, assuming we'd heard the name wrong.

'Hi, guys. I'm still Fran. And I'm still a teacher.'

Geoff frowned, concerned she was taking the piss.

'Louise. I'm thirty-seven and I like to bake.' Louise had a different hobby every week. So far there'd been knitting, reading detective novels, macramé and rock climbing.

'Hi, everyone, I'm Donna and I like cats.'

'Caitlin,' I said. A long silence followed, sixteen eyes looking at me, waiting to hear my fun fact. 'I'm a waitress.' I used that one a lot.

'Okay,' Fiona said. 'No new faces tonight, so that makes things easier.'

In the year or so I'd been coming, there had been a lot of new faces. Most only came once. They were sent by doctors or shrinks or their local mental health service, but you didn't need a referral and it was free, right down to the tea and coffee, so occasionally we'd get tourists. Most of them made their way here via Facebook, where a post by a bemused and horrified one-time visitor had gone viral and seen us labelled the Morbids.

Death was huge on Facebook, if you knew where to look.

Geoff was a member of fourteen different Facebook groups about death—local groups, Australian groups, groups specifically for the potential victims of domestic accident, for tracking the spread of flu—and he'd joined and left dozens more. Some treated it too much like a joke, some too seriously (*they're so bloody depressing*, he'd complain), some expected members to contribute too much to every conversation and some were so quiet they felt like everyone in them had already been buried. *You need to find your people*, he said once, after telling us how he'd left a group because they focused too much on funeral planning. Some he encouraged us to join, offering to invite us, but online groups weren't for me. I liked being in a room, seeing faces and knowing that these people didn't exist anywhere outside these four beige walls.

I didn't even know their last names.

♦

Donna's dad had been on a train that derailed at Granville when she was a toddler. It had come off the tracks and hit a concrete post, bringing a chunk of road down onto one of the carriages. He'd been at the other end of the train, survived without a scratch, but she was sure she wouldn't be so lucky. 'I didn't even remember,' she said. 'And then a few months back we were talking about irrational fears and I said I was scared of trains and he thought it was the funniest thing.'

'Wow,' Frannie said. 'That's freaky. Maybe you're psychic or something.'

'Yeah, that's what my mum thinks.' Donna shrugged. 'I dunno. I think it was probably a big deal when I was little and I've just suppressed it.'

Fiona was barely listening, back to doodling on her notepad, but she smiled slightly at Donna's self-evaluation.

'Maybe.' Frannie didn't seem convinced.

'It would be freaky, though, wouldn't it? If it happened to me, after Dad being on that train? Like the plot of a movie or something.'

'Like that Dutch woman who survived the Boxing Day tsunami but then died in the one in Japan a few years ago?' Glenn asked.

'Yeah. Sort of.' Donna's eyes were wide with excitement. 'Some nights I can't sleep and I google all the disasters. None of those people had any idea what was going to happen.'

You never do, I thought, looking down at my half-empty cup.

Like I had last week, I thought of Lina, the two of us catching trains, just for something to do, just for somewhere to go. To get out of the house, away from the smell, from Jenny. Not going anywhere, really, but away, into the city. That was when we started making plans—talking about going overseas, backpacking, travelling, living in different countries. They were just dreams, at first, just a way to escape, like the postcards. And then they'd become real. At least, I thought they'd been real.

Bali sat on my bedside table and glared at me every night but I couldn't put it away. I couldn't reply to it, either, and I couldn't call her. I didn't know what to say, and when I rolled away from it to try to sleep it kept me awake for hours.

'Trains are supposed to be safe, aren't they?' Louise asked uncertainly. 'Nearly as safe as flying.'

'I hate flying,' Glenn muttered. 'I know what the statistics say, but there's no way you can convince me a four-hundred-tonne tin can is supposed to be in the sky.'

I stared at the floor. Flying. Falling. Dying.

Book your flight.

Why did it have to be Bali? Why couldn't she get married in the Botanic Gardens and have a reception at some soulless function centre with harbour views like everyone else seemed to? I could handle that. I would be thrilled for her if she'd done that, I told myself, finishing my tea.

'And these days, with those automated engines . . .' Geoff joined in, and I wondered what would kill you first—the lack of oxygen, the impact, or just the sheer terror of those final moments.

A few days ago I'd slipped the postcard of New York into my bag, meaning to write something, to congratulate Lina and tell her I'd definitely be there, to lie and say I couldn't wait—but I hadn't. I hadn't done anything.

Tomorrow, I told myself, as I tried not to listen to Glenn's theory on the plane that had been missing in the Indian Ocean for years. I'd do it tomorrow.

Maybe it would help, I thought. Maybe then I'd sleep.

6

THURSDAY, APRIL

The finance boys were the worst. Private school prefects turned urban professionals, blessed by their parents with endless confidence and jobs they'd never be fired from, dressed in designer suits and pointy leather shoes, hair perfectly slicked.

Once, I'd found that confidence impressive, intimidating, something to strive for, valuable and precious, but now it was just irritating.

There were four of them in a booth near the front, trying to impress an older American client with their drinking prowess and dirty jokes. I'd been keeping an eye on them since they'd arrived for dinner, ordered a tasting menu and a round of Aberlour, neat, shotting it, with beer chasers, because somebody had taught them how to order whisky but not how to drink it. They hadn't stopped talking all night, but not *about* anything. That type never talked about anything, just filled up the room with their big booming voices, making it feel busier than it really was. One of the newbs— not so new that anybody thought to introduce her to me at the start of my shift, but new enough that I'd never noticed her before—was clearing bottles off their table, her lips pressed together so tight they'd turned white.

I finished some cocktails and looked around. Dinner service was winding up, and Rachel was in the office pretending to do paperwork. The newb came around the side of the bar, two fists full of empties. Her whole body was tense.

'Hey,' I said, as she dropped the bottles into the bin. She ignored me, so I said it again, a little louder. Her shoulders hitched both times, but she kept her head down. My eyes scanned the near-empty dining room. Emma was serving one table—a couple on a very obvious, awkward, first date—and the rest were fine. 'You okay?'

She still didn't say anything. I turned to the register and printed out a bill, tucking it into my apron pocket with the credit card reader.

'Swap?'

That seemed to throw her. 'What?'

'Have you worked the bar before?'

She glanced up, frowning. 'Once, only with Nic.'

'That's enough,' I said. 'You'll be fine.'

'I don't—'

'I'll come back if it gets crazy,' I promised, knowing it wouldn't.

I could see her arguing with herself, trying to figure out if this was a trick.

'You're doing me a favour. Nic's always at me to train people on drinks.'

One last flicker of a frown crossed her face.

'That's the coffee machine,' I said, gesturing. 'Spirits up here. Red wine there. Milks on the left, mixers on the right, wine in the middle.' I pointed to a spot by the register. 'Don't touch that power point, it's zappy. There.' I smiled. 'You're trained.'

She smiled back, tight and still nervous, but it was something. 'Okay,' she said softly.

I nodded. 'Okay, good.' I straightened. 'Wish me luck.'

'Good luck.'

They didn't look up as I approached, ignoring me until I was standing right in front of their table, hands on my hips. Even then it took a minute.

'You guys finished?' I asked, when the smallest of them noticed me and put down his beer.

'Not quite,' the one on the end said. He was the biggest—big enough to pick me up with one hand, if he wanted to, leaving the other free to stifle my screams as he dragged me into his car. He had former King's School captain written all over him.

I pulled my shoulders back, trying to supress a shudder. 'Yeah, I think you are,' I said. Not loudly, but firmly.

'I've got half a beer left.' He lifted the bottle as though to take a drink and looked to the others for confirmation, but nobody said anything.

I shrugged. Acting. If it wasn't real, it couldn't hurt me. 'Well, drink up.' I pulled the bill out of my pocket and put it on the table. 'We've got a private function starting in fifteen minutes. Cast party for *Mamma Mia!* or something. You know how it is.'

One of them—the smallest, probably the youngest—started to say something, but I ignored him.

'If it were up to me,' I said apologetically, 'I'd tell them to go somewhere else and let you guys keep doing shots of fifteen-year-old whisky until your bill hits four figures, but it's not.'

The big one scoffed. Everyone else had gone quiet.

I smiled as sweetly as I could manage. 'So, if you could just sort this out and get going, that would be great.'

The big one opened his mouth to say something and I glanced at the American. He was watching me, his face a mix of surprise and amusement and something else, just under the surface. He was the ticket here, and he knew it. If he tried to argue, they'd all join in, and then Rachel would get involved and word would get back to Lenny, and likely the newb or I would end up in trouble. I gave him a look, a silent plea for help from a damsel in distress. His eyes dropped, and for a moment everything went silent.

'What about—'

'Leave it, Pete,' the American cut him off. 'Didn't you say there was a tequila bar somewhere around here?'

Pete hesitated, then shrugged, pulling a credit card out of his jacket pocket and holding it out to me.

I didn't reach for it. I wasn't in the mood for the inevitable game of keep-away. Instead, I looked to the American again as he finished his beer. One eye flickered closed over the bottle.

Finally, Pete sighed and put the card down on the table. I picked it up and scanned it, wordlessly holding the machine out for his pin number.

When the receipt finished printing I folded it under his card and handed it back, standing aside as the four of them slid out of their booth. Pete was easily a foot taller than me, but his face dropped right down to mine as he passed. 'Whore.' His breath smelled like stale beer and onions, and I sucked the insides of my cheeks. The American was last, inching out behind me, and he said something too but I didn't know what it was, felt something against my palm as he brushed past.

I didn't exhale until the door swung shut, but when I did it was like all the air and sound flew back into the void, the music and the hum of conversation from the other tables and from the kitchen, an impatient bell. Emma was clearing a table, and the newb was just standing at the register, staring out the front windows. I tried to catch her eye but she seemed determined not to let me.

I looked at the door. They were gone, but I didn't know where. For all I knew they were waiting just out of sight. For all I knew they'd still be there when I left in an hour. They were the type.

Entitled. Mean. Maybe more. I closed my eyes, but that just gave the Thoughts more of a hold. 'Fuck,' I swore under my breath.

I turned, heading back to the bar, heart thundering in my chest. As I passed the register I glanced down at the hundred-dollar note and business card in my hand.

'All yours,' I said to the newb, softly, slipping the hundred between her fingers. My voice trembled.

She stopped. 'Hey, I don't—'

I looked straight ahead, pretended I wasn't aware of her out-stretched hand. 'You earned it. Nic will have you behind the bar every night if I'm not careful.' I smiled.

She hesitated. 'We can split it?'

I shook my head. 'It's fine. Just—' I realised I was still holding the card. Chief financial officer. MBA. Some other initials I used to understand but didn't anymore, a hotel name and room number scrawled in black ink across the middle. I threw it into the bin and wiped my hand on my apron. 'Don't tell anyone.'

'Okay,' the newb said, as she tucked the note into her pocket. 'Thanks.'

I nodded, let my eyes close as she walked away. My chest felt impossibly tight, and it was hard to breathe. I could hear Emma talking to someone, laughing, the kitchen bell, the door swinging open and closed, a coffee cup hitting a saucer at slightly the wrong angle, but I wasn't there. I was in the laneway a few doors up, pinned to the wall, surrounded by the stench of stale beer and onions. Thrill kills, they called them, when those nice boys did them. A game gone too far. A tragedy, so many young lives ruined, futures ruined. They'd never get good jobs with something like that on their records.

'You okay?'

I opened my eyes, let them adjust to the light, let them find my place. Medium Tom was sitting at the bar, in a green shirt this time.

My mouth opened to tell him I was fine but nothing came out. He frowned, a question mark forming between his eyebrows.

'I will be,' I said instead. I would, I told myself, straightening, touching the bar. Solid. Always solid.

He nodded. 'Good.'

'Drink?'

'Thanks.'

I turned around, looking for the right bottle. It wasn't where it was meant to be.

'Those guys come out of here?'

I blinked, found it by the gins, pulled it out. My heart was still thumping. 'What?'

'There were some—' I turned, and he stopped talking. He was watching me, his expression strange, thoughtful. 'Never mind.'

I smiled—tried to—put down a napkin, a glass. 'It's fine,' I said, trying to keep the tremor out of my voice. Poured the whisky, probably too much, my eyes focusing on the glass and beyond that his elbow, the green of his shirt perfect against the dark timber of the bar. When I looked up it was like looking at a picture in a magazine, the pendant over the register lighting up his face. 'We get them all the time.'

'Yeah?'

'It's Sawyer's,' I said, rolling my eyes and turning back to get some water. 'What did that *Gourmet* article say? *It's easy to forget you're not in a gentlemen's club in the roaring twenties.*' I gave him a wry smile as I topped up his glass. '*You can almost smell the cigar smoke,*' I went on.

He laughed, picked up the whisky. 'Still, it keeps you sane.'

I touched the bar again. 'What?'

'This place. The other night you . . .'

I remembered, cringed at the memory.

He pretended not to notice. 'Despite the cigar smoke.'

'I like cigars,' I said. 'Entitled, over-cashed private school grads whose parents still pay their rent but never taught them to keep their hands to themselves, less so.'

He raised an eyebrow.

'What?'

He shook his head, obviously amused. 'Nothing.'

'So Nic tells me you're a doctor?' I went on, changing the subject.

'I am.'

'What kind?'

He gave me a quizzical look.

'Come on.' Something flipped in my stomach, exhaustion and terror giving way to delirium. 'Doctors love telling people what they do. It's almost like part of the training.'

'Is it?' His eyebrow came up again.

'Yes.' I grinned. 'You're supposed to have a God complex and want to remind me of how important your job is at least once in every conversation.'

'Am I?' His eyebrow was still up. Still amused.

I raised an eyebrow of my own. 'Are you really a doctor? Or is that just something you told Nic to impress him into giving you free drinks?'

He laughed, properly.

'You can tell me. I won't let on.'

'Caitlin . . .' He leaned in as though to tell me a secret. The way he said my name made me feel warm, the fact that he remembered it at all. 'I am really a doctor.'

I smiled. 'So, what kind?'

He hesitated, picking up his drink.

'You've seen what I do,' I said, raising my hands as though to show off the bar. 'It's only fair.'

'Okay then,' he said. 'I work in emergency medicine.'

'Oh.' A chill rolled up my spine, and the warmth faded. 'Sounds intense.'

'Sometimes.' He took a sip. 'Sometimes it's boring. Boring is probably better.'

I nodded as though I understood, not sure what to say.

I wanted to ask what happened when someone came in after a car accident, their blood so thick on their clothes there couldn't possibly be enough left inside them. I wanted to ask how it felt when he realised there wasn't any point even trying. I wanted to ask if he'd been there that night, or any of the hundred other nights that this happened. But it wasn't the time, the place. I touched the bar again. Still solid.

'Sorry.' He held up his whisky, smiled at me over the glass. 'That killed the mood.'

I shook my head. 'It's my fault.'

He went quiet. I looked around the room for the first time in what felt like hours. Rachel was still upstairs. The newb was putting desserts down at a table near the front windows and Emma was clearing another. There was a docket sitting in my machine that I hadn't noticed come in. 'Sorry,' I said, reaching for it. 'I should get back to work.'

'Yeah, of course.' He smiled.

'Enjoy your drink.'

'Thanks, Caitlin.'

I gave him one last look, then moved over to the coffee machine.

'Everything okay?' Rachel asked, coming up next to me as I finished two cappuccinos.

I nodded. 'All good.'

'Want a cigarette before stock?'

'Always,' I said, not needing to be asked twice. My eyes flickered over to Tom, but he was looking at something on his phone, not paying any attention. I turned and went down the back.

♦

I smoked slowly. The blank postcard of Central Park sat on my lap, a pen in my free hand. I was still trying to find the right words—any words.

Dear Lina, Congratulations! That is amazing and I am so happy for you and I can't wait. I love you.

Leen, I'm sorry I've been MIA. Just working a lot, you don't have to worry. When can we celebrate?

I'm sorry.

Hey.

Hi.

It had been nine days, I realised. I had to call her. Every morning I got up and told myself I would, but I didn't, and all day I felt sick and guilty and ashamed, and angry. I could see her, that cold disappointment turning more furious, more fed up, with every day that passed. Or maybe Mum was wrong—maybe she hardly cared. She had Matt now, her happily-ever-after. She didn't need me anymore. Maybe she never had.

In the end I didn't write anything. My cigarette went out, and I threw it at the sand bucket, put the postcard and pen back in my apron and went inside. When I got back to the bar Tom was gone, and I felt a sting of regret, but I didn't know why.

I worked until close and then I walked home the longest way I knew, until I was so tired I couldn't hear and my legs had turned to lead. I had a beer in the kitchen—Marnie was out, again, always—and another in my room, leaning out the window smoking cigarette after cigarette and reading Lina's old postcards one by one.

Caitie,

I think it's unlikely you'll fail all your exams and have to drop out. Knowing you, you'll end up with a neat column of HDs. Seriously, you worry more than anyone I know. But if you just don't want to come to Bec's 21st, that's fine too. She won't be offended. She probably won't even notice—not because you're not fabulous, but she's ordered so much alcohol it's not even funny.

But we're going out next weekend, yeah? You'll be finished exams and there's this DJ I met at a party last week and he's put me on the door for a club night he does. All fun disco stuff. You'll love it. Promise.

Love you. L xxx

PS Did you know Seoul has the longest bridge fountain in the world and it pumps out 54 tonnes of water a minute? And you worry about wasting water . . . xx

Dear Caitlin,

Greetings from Fiji!

It's so nice here! The weather is a bit crappy but the water is beautiful and we got the unlimited meal package so I've been eating non-stop. Mum's loving it too. She just swims all day. We went snorkelling. There were turtles. You should have come. I know you had work but Mum would have loved to have you here. And me too, I suppose.

I'll probably be home before you get this, but I'll call you. Dinner soon.

Love, L xxx

PS Did you know Fiji has 28 airports? How, Caitlin? HOW?

Hey hey,

Plot twist: you know that guy we were talking to the other night at Freya's—the tall one with the hair? I ran into him again. Literally. I was coming out of Fino's with all the office coffees and he was on his phone and it was not pretty.

(Okay, I guess technically he ran into me. Whatever.)

Anyway, his name is Matt, and he works just down from me. He paid for all the coffees—as he should—and then offered to buy me lunch, and I know I said no guys for a month but oh my God he's cute.

Come over Saturday. I have to make a cake for work—long story.

Love you, L xxx

PS Did you know 'Ulladulla' is an Aboriginal word meaning safe harbour? But really, why is Ulladulla on a postcard at all? So weird.

Some of them I knew by heart, even though I hadn't looked at them in years. Others I could have sworn I'd never seen before.

She'd sent me a postcard from Perth when she went over for Matt's grandmother's funeral, and one from Katoomba when they went there for their anniversary weekend, and lots from the postbox at the end of her street, their pictures a comforting lie. And I'd sent them back; one from the Gold Coast on a family holiday, another from Melbourne when I went down for a work trip, but mostly they came from op shops. I searched everywhere for the best ones, bought five at a time and sent them one by one, filled with meaningless news I'd tell her on the phone before she got the postcard anyway.

I read them and read them, until my eyes hurt and my breathing got heavy, and then I put them away, got into bed, the pillow flat and the sheets scratchy. A bus rumbled past, stopped, door hissing as it opened and then clanging as it closed. I shut my eyes but nothing happened, counted my breaths. One, two.

Thirteen. Sixteen. Forty-two.

Lost count, but nothing happened. Another bus, meaning another hour had passed. This one didn't stop.

A truck. Another.

The trucks always went past between three and four on their way to the airport. I sighed, gave up, opened the window and had a cigarette. Then another. It was cold now, and properly still. I considered making myself a cup of tea (chamomile was best, Mum always said), a shot of rum, whisky. Glenmorangie, the eighteen—as though I had a bottle. I shut the window as another bus rolled past. A hiss. A clang. I considered tea, rum, whisky, beer, a quick orgasm—anything to make me sleep—but I didn't have the energy. I counted my breaths again, gave up at seventy-three. My pulse was racing, oddly, too fast, too hard. I needed to sleep.

But my eyes stayed open.

Somewhere, footsteps. Maybe Marnie going to the toilet, maybe a burglar, an intruder, a deranged ice addict. Or just the creaking of the building as the beams settled, fought, ready to give.

A truck, too close, barely missing the awning. Another, maybe a fuel tanker, one wrong move away from taking out the entire block.

I closed my eyes. Counted. Considered tea, rum, beer, a cigarette, an orgasm, prayer.

Dear God, please let me sleep. I'll be good, I promise. I'll do anything.

Somewhere, a bird chirped.

'Fuck.'

A bird meant it was dawn. My heart hurt as I sat up, giving in. When I pulled the window open this time the light was different. Grey. And there were people, voices, cars.

I picked up my phone. The screen blurred, my eyes so tired I couldn't see straight, but I found Lina's name and I texted her, suggested we have lunch. It was barely dawn, but she replied too quickly, like she'd been waiting, and my stomach churned with guilt, so hot I nearly threw up.

7

Monday, April

I'd known her for so long that I could barely remember not knowing her, but the woman sitting opposite me in one of Sydney's hundred vaguely Irish-themed inner-city pubs, picking at her Caesar salad, was a stranger. She wore a navy shift dress and a baby pink cardigan and her hair was chocolate brown and swishy, blunt at the ends. I wanted to tell her it looked nice but I didn't want to hear the disappointed sigh as she pointed out it had been that way for months. Maybe it had.

I was late—deliberately, because I didn't want to arrive first and have to wait alone among the crowd of cheap suits and sensibly priced shoes and expensive fragrances—and when she hugged me it was too tight, too forceful. She smelled like vanilla and money and I tasted anger, with a guilt chaser.

'So they've spent weeks installing this new system at work,' she was saying, between bites of her salad, holding her water glass like it was wine. 'It went live this morning and all the scheduled reminders have disappeared.'

'Oh no,' I said, more in response to her tone than her words, which flew past me without making contact. She'd been talking since we sat down, filling every awkward silence with an observation, about the pub or the weather or the construction work outside—all the meaningless things. It made the guilt bubble up from my gut into my throat.

'So, guess who gets to go through every single patient file and manually re-enter their next check-up date so we can get the reminders out?'

Lina was a receptionist for a chain of dentists, had been for years. Originally, she'd worked in their Parramatta practice, but a few years ago she'd transferred into the city. *We'll see each other all the time*, she'd said, and at first we had. She came to Redfern for drinks or I met her near Central for breakfast, and we had coffee every Monday near Wynyard, because the barista was cute and she thought he liked me. *Not that you'd ever date a barista*, she'd joked, faintly bitter.

'Crap,' I said, taking a long sip of my beer, putting it down and looking too intently at the label.

She shrugged. 'It happens.' She made a face. 'Oh God, and remember Nicole? The dental assistant I've told you about? With the boobs?'

I didn't remember, but I nodded anyway.

She leaned forward, hair falling dangerously close to her salad. 'Well, she got caught with one of the surgeons, this really old guy who owns part of the business. Turns out she'd been servicing—' she made a gesture with her fingers '—a couple of them. Everybody knew but then one of the wives came in for a surprise lunch date and . . . yeah.'

'Ew,' I said.

'I know.' Lina put a crouton in her mouth. 'What a slut, right?'

I frowned, and she caught it.

'Sorry.'

'No.' I shook my head. 'It's just kind of gross that they were all—'

'I'm not judging, Cait.' She straightened. 'We all do stupid stuff. It doesn't matter.'

I shifted in my seat, feeling unsettled. I wondered if Emma was just doing stupid stuff, if it mattered. I wondered if I should warn her, but about what? Lenny liked to surround himself with pretty young things, but as far as anyone knew he'd never done anything beyond look. And Dex was Dex. A mistake. Hopefully non-fatal. I sighed, suddenly exhausted.

'Seriously, you and Mum . . .' She chewed, swallowed. 'I told her and she was like, *the poor girl.*' Her face hardened as she reached for her water. 'Besides, Nicole's already got another job at a radiology place. Senior practice assistant or something. She'll be fine.'

'Oh, good,' I said, as though I cared.

'Anyway.' She shrugged, taking a sip from her glass. There was a shake to her voice. 'What about you? Anything exciting happening? I haven't seen you in forever.'

I looked down at my nachos. I was starving but they smelled like packet seasoning and fake cheese and it made my mouth pucker and my stomach churn. It struck me that I'd barely eaten in days. Weeks. I picked up a chip and forced myself to chew it.

'I know,' I said, swallowing. 'Work's just been . . .'

'It's okay,' she cut me off. 'Me too. I've been so busy.'

'But,' I went on, carefully. Her face was fixed on mine, waiting. 'I heard a rumour my best friend was getting married . . .'

She broke into a huge grin. 'She is. Oh my God. I'm sorry,' she said, too fast, too relieved. 'I felt so bad, telling you in a post-card. I tried to call you the night it happened. Matt rang his mum and I tried to ring you. I wanted you to know first. You've had to listen to me prattle on about getting married for a million years.' She hesitated. 'I figured you were probably at work, and busy and everything.' She laughed, but it sounded forced. 'And then I didn't know if your phone was still working or you'd changed your number or you were mad or . . .'

'No,' I said, not sure it wasn't a lie. 'Of course not, Leen.'

'I know.' Her voice was pitched high, breathy. 'I *know*. It's just a piece of paper and the patriarchy and everything, but I just wanted to tell you. And the postcard—I was worried it had got lost in the mail, or someone else would tell you first and it wouldn't be the same. I was so glad you messaged. *So* glad, Caitie.'

I picked up my beer, took a sip.

'I miss our postcards,' she said, still breathy. 'I know we're grown-ups now and maybe they're a kid thing or whatever, but I miss them. And I thought it would be cool to, you know . . .'

'It was.' My head was spinning. 'I was going to send one back but—'

'It's okay,' she interrupted. 'It's fine. I know you're busy. Your mum said—'

'You spoke to my mum?'

Lina paused. 'She was over at Mum's last night. She said you were acting weird at brunch last Saturday.'

I rolled my eyes. 'I just had a headache,' I said.

'She thought you might be upset about the maid of honour thing.'

I shook away a rush of annoyance—at Mum, at both of them. 'What? No, it's . . .'

'No, Cait.' She stopped me, sat up straight, nervous. 'Of course I want that. More than anything.'

My heart thundered into my ribcage.

'Please.' She looked at me. 'Will you be my maid of honour?'

I don't know what my face did, but the rest of me went cold, and I saw Lina's eyes flicker.

'You don't have to do anything,' she added. 'I know you're super busy with work and you're not into weddings or marriage or any of this stuff. I promise I am not going to expect you to organise anything. Not even the hens' night. Matt's sister has already said she wants to organise that—she's starting some sort of business, I think. You don't even have to come to the hens' if you don't want to, but I promise it won't be gross. God, not like Madi's one last year. No-one is going to be drinking anything out of anyone's underpants, I swear to God.'

She was talking too fast, and I wanted to stop her, but my throat had tightened up. Anaphylaxis.

'I just want you there, Caitie. Not just there, but next to me. You're my best friend.' She took a breath. 'You're the only one who . . .'

'Leen.' I swallowed. Tried to. I'd never been allergic to anything, but anaphylaxis was the sort of thing that could develop at any time. I remembered Frannie once telling us a story about a woman who died because she developed an allergy to hair dye. *The first time her scalp just itched, the second her throat closed up and she choked to death in her ensuite.*

'And your mum said you didn't know about flights yet, which is great, because I was going to ask you if you wanted to go early, you know? Just us? Chill out. Get massages. It'll only be a few days but it would be nice, if you can get the time off work. For all that planning, we've never gone anywhere together, so I thought . . .' Her voice ran out suddenly, and then she just looked at me and the air grew hard, impossible to breathe. There had been nuts on top of my nachos, which didn't make any culinary sense. It had to be a mistake. A fatal one.

I pushed a smile onto my face and reached for her hand. She gave it to me, too eager.

'Of course, Leen,' I said softly. 'That sounds great. Of course.'

She exhaled, her whole body relaxing.

'And I'm not mad. I wasn't mad. I was going to reply,' I said. 'I had a postcard.' I hesitated. 'I don't think it's kids' stuff.'

She shrugged, and I could tell she didn't believe me. 'It doesn't matter, Cait. It's fine. Whatever. I just want you there.'

'I'll be there. I promise.'

'And you'll be my maid of honour? You can pick your dress.'

I laughed. 'Of course.'

'Good,' she said, her voice thick with relief. She picked up her water and took a long sip, then put it down. 'Thank you.'

'It's okay.'

She shook her head, like it wasn't. 'I feel as though I never see you anymore. And I know I'm busy with Matt and work, but . . .'

I looked down at the table, willing her to stop. Sharp edges; a slip and fall could be lethal.

'It's like since what happened . . . I don't know. We don't really talk much. I miss you.'

'We talk all the time,' I said. But we didn't. We had at first. After the accident, it was like she was always around, more than she had been in years, calling most days just to say hi, asking what I was doing, and then it was less, and less. I swallowed. Guilt. Not anaphylaxis at all.

She paused. 'Not like we did.'

'Leen . . .' I didn't mean it to come out as a warning, but maybe it did, because she stopped, shook her head. 'I'm fine. And we're all good. Really.'

Her eyes flicked up and down my face, made me itchy.

'Anyway,' she said, glancing past me, 'I know I'm getting married and that usually means dropping off the planet, but I really hope . . . I want us to do this together. I need you, Caitie.'

I raised an eyebrow, steadied my breath. 'For what?'

'I need you to keep me from going mad.' She laughed. 'And if I turn into a bridezilla and start demanding ice sculptures, I need you to shoot me, yeah?'

I looked at her. She looked smaller. Younger. I felt a pang of something—regret, sadness, need. I had to try, I reminded myself. I had to.

'Ice sculptures would melt in Bali,' I said finally. 'You want some of those living statues. The ones they have busking at Circular Quay. And a magician.'

'Honestly, Cait, don't even joke.' She smiled. 'So if I go off the deep end, can you kill me, please? Don't just threaten to. Mum will help you. She hates weddings as much as you do. God.' She shook her head then, before I could argue, she went on, 'Last night, your mum was talking about the flowers and mine's just on her feminist thing about the patriarchy and how I'm going to take his name.'

A question formed on my tongue, and I bit my lip.

'And look at you.' She laughed again. 'You're thinking it too. If I didn't know it was impossible, I'd swear we were switched at birth.'

I flinched. 'I thought your mum was excited.'

'She is.' Lina looked away. 'But you know her. Overthinking everything. Besides, it's not even Mum's name, I don't get why she cares; Dad certainly doesn't. I called and told him and he was like, *Oh, it's a busy time in the office, Lee-Lee. I'm not sure I can get the time off.*' She made a face. 'Honestly, I know it's Bali, but you can fly in on Friday and out on Sunday. You don't even get jetlag. Matt's invited a few of the partners at his firm and they can be so weird about time off but none of them are even fazed. He's just being difficult.'

'Arse.'

'I know. Always has been, though, right?'

Lina's parents had divorced right before we met and her dad had drifted in and out of her life ever since. The last time we'd talked about it, they'd been on good terms, but that only meant he was taking her calls. I'd only met him once, and he hadn't said anything to me—to be fair, it hadn't been a good time—and all I remembered about him was his expression, annoyed, irritated that his damn child wouldn't stop crying, that he had to take care of her. And on a workday, no less.

It had been an ugly divorce, an ugly everything, and Lina had taken it hard. Jenny had taken it hard. She'd been crazy about him. For all his flaws, she'd adored him, for years and years, until he'd broken her heart. Broken her.

'I'm sorry, Leen,' I said, meaning it. 'I know I haven't—'

'It's okay.' Lina finished off her water. 'I'm just glad you texted, Cait.'

'Me too.' I was. I was hoping I'd sleep now.

'And I'm so glad you're coming. I couldn't do it without you.'

I laughed. 'Yeah, you could.'

'Okay,' she conceded, grinning. 'I probably could. But I wouldn't want to.'

I wasn't sure what to say, so I just nodded.

'Besides, who would Mum complain to about the misogynistic symbolism of wedding rings if you weren't there?'

This time when I laughed, it nearly felt genuine.

July, Once

'So what happened with the guy?'

'Which guy?' I asked, picking up my glass of wine. I hadn't seen Lina in a couple of weeks and when we'd texted it had mostly been about work and Matt. Dinner had been my idea, but she'd chosen the restaurant. Thai, in Glebe, just around the corner from my place so we could stroll back there afterwards and watch bad TV. She was going through a *Pretty Little Liars* phase.

'You're impossible.'

I sipped my wine. 'This is good,' I said, changing the subject.

'Yeah, it's not bad. Matt joined a wine club.'

I raised an eyebrow.

She grinned. 'You know—you sign up and they send you a dozen bottles every three months?'

'I know what a wine club is, Leen.' I wrinkled my nose. 'But don't they have bottle shops in Westmead?'

'Funny.' She smiled as our eyes met. 'It means we get to try all sorts of different things. You know me, I'd just buy that same King Valley pinot with the grapes on the label every time, if I could.'

I took another sip. She would, too. 'It's a good wine, though.'

'Isn't it? And it has no preservatives, so it doesn't give me hangovers.'

I laughed. 'That just means you're not drinking enough.'

'You'd know,' she teased, giving me a look. 'But we weren't talking about wine.'

'Weren't we?' I asked, pleading ignorance.

'Tell me what happened with the guy.'

'I honestly don't know which guy you mean.'

'Jesus, Cait.'

'What? It's been weeks.'

'You're impossible,' she said again. 'The orthopaedic surgeon? House in Paddington with a plunge pool?'

'Oh yeah. He has a name, Leen.'

'Yeah, well, I can't remember it.'

'Neither can I,' I said, flicking a lock of hair off my shoulder. It was freshly dyed, pinker than usual.

'Cait!' She sat back in her seat.

'I'm kidding!'

The expression on her face suggested she wasn't sure.

I straightened. 'I *am*. It's Justin. I even remember his last name.'

'I'm surprised you even know his last name.'

'We did go on five dates.'

'Oh, five. That's serious.'

'Very.' I touched the stem of my wineglass but didn't pick it up. I wanted a cigarette. Not that that was new. I'd wanted a cigarette every three and a half minutes since I quit a month ago. I wanted a cigarette so much more often now than I ever had when I actually smoked, despite the industrial-strength nicotine patch stuck to my ribcage, giving me bad dreams and leaving me looking like I had some sort of tropical skin infection.

'Yeah.' I shrugged. 'He was nice.'

'Was?'

'Yeah, was. It was just . . . I don't know. He ticked all the boxes, but I just wasn't feeling it, you know?'

Lina looked like she wanted to say something, and I could guess what. I'd heard it all a hundred times. *You need to give it time. You're too picky. It's not like the movies. Give them a chance.*

'Anyway . . .' I touched the stem of my wineglass again, looked at my fingers. I didn't want to give him a chance. A chance to do what? I liked being on my own. I didn't need a man, didn't need anyone to look after me. 'It's not a good time. Work is really busy. We're doing a major presentation next week and I have not stopped, and it's not going to get any better for months. And then we're going in six months.' I took a sip, ignoring the look that flickered across her face. 'Matt's going to have to drink a lot of wine by himself come February. Or he can save it all for when you get back. It's only three months, right?'

Three months. We'd fly into LA, then slowly drive across the country—she'd drive, unless by some miracle I got my licence by then—finishing with a month in New York. We'd been planning it for years, since we finished high school, long before Matt and our jobs and all the orthopaedic surgeons, and it was finally happening. We even had a date. February fifteenth, the day after Valentine's Day, because Lina was a sucker for Hallmark holidays. We just needed to book our flights.

I can't believe how excited you are, Lina had said last time we'd talked about it. *You're never this excited about anything.*

It *was* exciting. It was everything we'd been planning for years. But when she'd said that I'd felt funny. Sometimes I didn't even want to go. New York was dangerous. America was dangerous. Flying was dangerous, and the logistics were almost overwhelming—so many bits to line up. But then I thought of Lina and none of that mattered. This was our dream.

When we'd first started planning three months seemed like a lot—it was all we could afford—but the more I read the more it didn't seem like long enough. Three months, and then we'd come back and I'd settle down at last. That was the plan.

'Honestly,' I said, ignoring the long silence, 'now I think about it, what kind of wine drinker are you if you only drink a bottle a week? We get a case in at work every fortnight and it goes like that.' Something twitched in my chest and I laughed it away. 'There needs to be a wine club for the advertising industry. They could just ship it out by the barrel. Or skip the wine altogether and sell gin in IV bags.'

She tried to smile, but didn't quite make it.

'Are you all right, Leen?' I asked finally.

She took a breath. A waiter walked past and put a bowl of green curry on our table, mentioned something about rice, but I wasn't listening.

'So,' she said. Her voice was hesitant, and the thing in my chest twitched again. My expression must have changed, because she put a hand out, nearly knocking over my wineglass. Her fingers were cool on my forearm. 'It's fine, Cait. Everything is good. Like, really, really good.'

'Okay.' I blinked. Relaxed, but only a little.

'It's just . . .'

A bowl of rice and a stir-fry, steaming hot, appeared as though by magic.

'Enjoy your meal,' the waiter said.

Lina looked up at him and smiled. There was a hesitation in everything she was doing. She'd hate me for pointing it out, but in that moment she looked like her mum.

'God, you're scaring me, Leen. Is everything okay?'

She laughed. Half laughed. It was strange; everything was strange.

'I'm sorry,' she said when the waiter was gone. 'It's fine. It's all good.' But she looked like she was about to cry.

She picked up the rice and scooped some into her bowl, held the rice out for me to take. I did, putting it down without serving myself.

'You'll probably think so too.'

I frowned. 'What?'

She took another breath, sat up. 'So,' she said again. 'You know how the owners have been talking about putting our place on the market?'

I nodded, not sure where this was going. 'Yeah?'

'There's been a shit-ton of construction in the area. Lots of new builds. Lots of investment. But it seems to have slowed, and Matt was talking to his uncle. He's a mortgage broker.'

'Uh-huh.'

'And he was saying that it might be a good time to buy, you know? Get in before things pick up again.'

'Okay,' I said like I agreed, like I knew what she was talking about.

'And then on the weekend we were driving by this little complex of townhouses just down from where we are now. They're not quite finished, but they were open, and Matt suggested we go and check one out.'

She looked at the stir-fry, remembered it was there, picked up the bowl and ladled a pile of chicken and vegetables onto her rice, her lips pressed tight together.

'It was so nice, Cait.' Her voice changed; thoughtful, but something else too. Excited. Cautious. Apologetic. 'They've still got to finish off the landscaping, but the kitchen is beautiful. Six-burner stove, butler's pantry, this gorgeous butcher's block island bench . . . I hate the kitchens in these places usually—they're always white and sterile and cold—but this one is different. There's a little balcony off the master bedroom and a courtyard and walk-in wardrobes.' She smiled. 'It's so cute. You'd love it.'

I nodded, even though I wasn't sure I would. 'So when do you move in?' I joked.

'We settle in eight weeks. We bought it.'

'What?' I exclaimed. 'That's amazing, Leen! Congratulations!'

She smiled, her face alight. She didn't remind me of her mum anymore, just someone who was getting everything she had ever wanted. Happy.

I let out a breath I hadn't realised I was holding. 'I can't believe you didn't tell me you bought a fucking house!' I picked up my wine and sat back in my chair.

'Townhouse,' she corrected.

'Still.' I laughed. 'It's a house. You're a grown-up now. Can I help you paint it?'

She grinned. 'Of course.'

'Bright purple?'

'Funny.' She sat up, took a deep breath. 'See, I knew you'd be happy.'

I rolled my eyes. 'Of course. I mean, it's pretty bougie and you know how I feel about commitment. But why . . .' Even as the question formed on my lips, I knew why.

Lina hesitated. 'Matt's uncle got us a great deal. Like, amazing.' She sighed. I wished—again—for a cigarette. 'And we can afford the repayments—more than afford them, somehow—but to avoid mortgage insurance, we've had to put *all* of our money into the deposit.'

'Oh.' And there it was. 'Right.'

'Matt's looked at it all, and once we're settled and we've thrown all our money at it for a year or two we can probably refinance, but until then . . .'

I felt my chest tighten, my eyes get hot.

'No road trips for me,' she finished. 'I'm so sorry, Cait. I know how long we've been talking about this.'

I inhaled. The air caught in my throat but I forced it down, reminded myself where we'd started, why we'd been doing this in the first place. 'It's okay,' I said.

'Is it?' She looked uncertain. 'Are you sure?'

'Of course it is. I'm so happy for you.' I looked away. The food was getting cold but I wasn't hungry anymore. This wasn't about me. This had never been about me, but the thought of Lina in some cookie-cutter shoebox in the suburbs made me shiver, no matter how cute the island bench was. 'I just thought you wanted to . . .'

'I did. I *do*. I mean who doesn't want to road-trip across the States? It's like something we're all conditioned to want to do by television. It's a fantasy. But this is forever, you know?'

I nodded. I did, and it made me feel sick, for a hundred reasons.

'God, Cait . . .' She smiled, but she looked serious. 'I know how much effort you put into this for me. Honestly, it's meant so much. All that planning. You're fucking amazing. And I know you were excited too, and I'm sorry.'

I bit my lip.

'But you don't have to do it now. You can do whatever you want. You can apply for that job I sent you a couple of weeks ago.'

I frowned, barely remembering. I thought she'd sent it as a joke, hadn't even read the ad.

'Or call that hot surgeon again, or anything you want.'

I must have looked strange—I felt strange; confused, tired—because she stopped. Why was I so tired suddenly?

'Can we still go somewhere?' she asked, after a long pause. 'Maybe in a couple of years? A shorter trip? I won't make you plan it all again, don't worry. I'll do it.'

I hesitated, then reached for the bowl of rice. 'It's okay, Leen.' I forced my hand not to shake as I filled my bowl. 'It was a ridiculous plan anyway.'

A fantasy.

'No it wasn't. It was fun. And I loved planning it with you.'

I nodded. That was the point. That had always been the point.

'Thank you, Caitie.'

I put down the rice and reached for the curry. It wasn't even steaming anymore. 'It's okay.'

She put a forkful of chicken in her mouth and chewed. Swallowed. 'Are you mad?'

'Of course not, Leen,' I said. 'I'm just glad you're happy. I still can't believe you bought a house.'

She tried not to smile, but it broke through anyway, and as I poured green curry over my rice she started talking about twin showers and bamboo flooring and I let her. She sounded so happy, and I wanted to be happy for her, but something in my chest had gone hard, and I couldn't loosen it up.

8

TUESDAY, MAY

'I can't sleep.'

It hadn't helped, seeing Lina. One brand of guilt had been replaced by another, this one a physical presence, a hot ball of acid that had formed in my gut after lunch and stayed there ever since, growing every time I let myself think about it, and I couldn't stop thinking about it.

I *could* sleep, but only in snatches—short, shallow, easily broken—or on the couch in the afternoon, suddenly so exhausted I couldn't fight it. I'd got almost four hours after lunch the day before, waking up nauseous with the stale taste of artificial cheese coating my tongue.

Fiona was sick, or so we were told. Abraham was tall and skinny in that almost alien way, and he clutched his clipboard like a shield and gave us all suspicious looks as we walked in.

'I just keep having these dreams. The other night my best friend Lina and I were on a train, but when we were kids. And she was on her phone, even though she didn't have a phone then. I was looking out the window and I could see the smoke, and I tried to tell her but she wasn't listening, and when I looked around it was just the two of us and then the carriage jumped, and jumped again, and—' I looked at Donna. She looked ill. 'God,' I said, suddenly cold. 'I don't want to be one of those people who talks about their dreams, but it was just so real, you know?'

'I have nightmares sometimes,' Geoff said. He'd been watching me more intently than usual. 'I keep a diary by my bed so I can write them down. I read somewhere that it helps.'

'No,' Carlos shook his head. 'You need to break the pattern before they happen. Guided meditation as you get into bed. You just have to get used to falling asleep with earphones in.'

Geoff scoffed. 'That just sounds like a strangulation hazard.'

'Not if you use wireless.'

'Still,' Geoff said, squinting, 'what if a fire alarm goes off and you don't hear it?'

My eyes flicked between the two of them, grateful for the distraction.

'Not noise-cancelling ones,' Carlos explained. 'Tanya got some for running a couple of years back. She still needed to hear cars and things. They're waterproof, too, so if you drool in your sleep . . .'

'I don't, but thanks, mate.'

'Not what I've heard.'

'Caitlin,' Abraham said, bored. 'You were saying?'

I looked around, caught Geoff trying to suppress an eye roll. Something about his face seemed off.

'I just haven't been sleeping well,' I finished, 'and it's starting to affect everything.'

'Can you think of anything that's happened to stir up your insomnia like this?' Abraham asked.

I paused. I could. But I didn't know how to say I wasn't sleeping because my best friend was getting married in Bali. I was supposed to be happy for her.

Most of the others would understand—flying was dangerous, and once you were there Indonesia was a hotbed of earthquakes and tsunamis and terrorism and black-market alcohol made with lighter fluid—but I didn't know how to say it. I couldn't.

'It happens sometimes,' I said. It had happened before. After the accident. After Dex. 'I'm sure it'll pass.'

It happened, and then it passed. Everything would be fine.

'There was that thing in Centennial Park last week, did you see that?' Louise asked, in a tone that suggested she was trying to help. 'The guy in the Daffy Duck mask flashing joggers? I only caught the end of the news story but it was so creepy.'

I frowned, wondering if that was supposed to make me feel better. 'I think so.' I may have heard something on the radio in the staff-room, but I hadn't paid much attention. Still, now that she said it, I felt it, as viscerally as if I was there, felt the fear of what happened next. 'Maybe it's just that,' I said, letting it wash over me, letting it numb the guilty spot in my gut.

Not long after the accident, I'd told Lina about the Thoughts. I'd told her that I kept feeling like I was going to die, that I was convinced of it, and some days it was like I couldn't breathe because all I could think about was how it would feel. She'd looked at me with the strangest, saddest expression. *God, Cait*, she'd said. *You can't think like that.* As though I could just stop.

Nobody said that here. Nobody told me to get over it or looked at me with that expression. Sometimes the nurses would let the mask fall as they were on their way out, but it was easier here. Safer. I felt nearly normal.

Lina asked about the Thoughts a few months later, and I told her they'd passed. *Good*, she said, then changed the subject. The next time she texted I'd told her I was busy. I was suddenly busy more and more; it felt like was better that way, for both of us. Easier. Safer.

9

Friday, May

I hadn't stopped moving all evening. Faces and voices blurred into each other and I could barely hear over the sound of my heart pounding, pumping too much caffeine through my veins. Sawyer's was full and everyone was drinking and I did what I was best at. Two cappuccinos, latte, skim flat white. Pinot gris, three glasses. Vodka soda, gin and tonic, sparkling mineral water. Sav blanc, two glasses. Long mac, short mac, two flat whites. Two IPAs and three pilsners. Gin and tonic. Gin and tonic. Glass of shiraz, espresso martini, cosmopolitan, mojito. Weak flat white, strong latte, soy cappuccino. Four peach ciders, one apple. Glass of sav blanc. Glass of sav blanc. Glass of sav blanc. Amaretto sour and a long island iced tea. Short black. Beam and Coke. Mindful. Distracted. Sane. My hands were shaking and the glasses kept skittering onto the bar in a way that made Nic glare at me every time he walked past but I didn't spill a drop and I didn't miss an order.

Two long blacks, skim flat white. Glenfiddich, on the rocks. Two ciders, two glasses of semillon. Gin and tonic with lemon. Gin and tonic with lime. Gin and tonic with strawberries. Mindfulness.

It was stupid busy and Nic was doing bar service so I didn't have to talk to anyone for what felt like hours, didn't have to look up.

'What can I get you?'

'Oh, fabulous. That's my favourite.'

'What can I get you?'

'Excellent taste, sir.'

'What can I get you?'

'Yes, we are fully booked but I'll grab our bar menu for you.'

I never wanted it to stop, because every time it slowed my head started pounding and my vision blurred and the Thoughts came back, so many of them, and I had to grab something to keep from falling over. I couldn't stop thinking about it, thinking about what would happen if I didn't sleep properly ever again. About walking in front of a bus or falling off a train platform or leaving the gas on or tripping through a plate-glass window, nicking an artery. About slipping in the shower or drowning in the bath or tumbling down the stairs.

About how long my body could keep going before it just stopped.

And then I thought about Lina, about everything I didn't want to think about—the wedding and Bali and Jenny and my mum, pinching the top of her nose in frustration—and I felt so nauseous I could barely stand.

I needed to try harder.

I put three ciders down on the counter and looked at my docket rack. Empty. I realised I was sweating and puffed, like I'd just been running. I leaned back, trying to catch my breath, gazing out at the dining room for the first time in hours. It was calm, under control, a pristine picture of sophistication. Everyone was eating, drinking, talking, laughing softly. The redheaded waitress from the other night was clearing a table, Emma was running my ciders. Nic was standing at the register, looking as worn out as I was.

'Okay?' he asked. He opened it and pulled out a pile of credit card receipts, fingers flicking through them.

'Always.'

'That was crazy. You did well.'

'Thanks,' I said.

'Quick close tonight. I have plans.'

I glanced at him. 'Oh?'

'Mind out of the gutter, darling.' He bundled up the credit card receipts and put them back in the drawer.

I laughed. 'But then yours would be all by itself.'

He closed the register and came around to me. 'His name is Alex and he's a photographer and he's six foot four. Happy now?'

'Cute?'

He grinned. 'You have no idea.'

'Well—' I smirked '—I guess you'll be helping me stock then?'

'Ha ha.'

But he did. He made my stock list while I took care of the trickle of orders that came through. We didn't talk, didn't really acknowledge each other's presence, but we moved around each other like we were dancing, a perfectly choreographed ballet of service and cleaning and stocking.

The dockets stopped, and Nic was counting bottles of wine, his face fixed in concentration, so I opened the register and started bundling ten-dollar notes.

'And what are you doing later?' he asked, coming up for air.

'Huh?' I wrapped an elastic band around a bundle and dropped it back into the drawer. 'Nothing. Going home.'

'Nothing?' He raised an eyebrow.

'Yeah. Why?'

'Holly wants to go out.'

'Who's Holly?'

He gave me a look, as though to ask if I was serious. I looked back to let him know I was.

'Nobody tells me anything around here,' I complained, half joking. 'You just take it for granted I'll figure it all out.'

'That's because you always do.'

'Whatever.' I shrugged, moving on to the twenties, counting under my breath.

'Holly,' Nic explained, 'is the redhead with the tatts. She's on a break at the moment.'

'Oh.'

'Oh?' He rolled his eyes. 'How do you not notice these things? Entire people. I swear she's run most of your drinks tonight.'

'It's been busy!' I protested. Honestly, I had noticed her when she'd come in, but she'd seemed determined not to make eye contact, so I'd left her to it.

'She's good, too. Almost as good as you. And nicer.'

I frowned, and it made him laugh.

'She's in a band. You'd like her. You should go. Besides, it's not like you to skip drinks.'

'What are you saying?'

'It's not like Dex stays, if you were worried about that.'

I looked at him. 'I wasn't.'

'Good.' He met my eyes. 'But even if you were, you shouldn't be.'

'I'm not,' I said, bundling up the twenties and pulling out a pile of fifties. 'I'm just tired.'

My fingers tripped over the notes, moving too fast, and I tried to slow them down, determined to keep my place. Nic would be furious if the till was out and he had to redo it after close.

'Cait . . .' he said, in a tone that suggested it wasn't the first time he'd said it.

'Yeah?' I lost count. 'Shit.'

'Service.'

'Oh.' I looked at him apologetically, putting the fifties back and closing the till. 'Right.'

I turned, plastering on a smile.

'Hi,' Tom said, putting a book down on the bar.

'Hi.' I blinked, only a little surprised to see him.

He looked around. 'Busy tonight.'

'It was. It's settled a bit now.' I glanced at the book. 'Probably a bit noisy for reading, though.'

He picked it up so I could see the cover. Bold type over a dark picture, something you'd find at a newsagent. 'I'm not exactly reading Proust.'

I put a napkin down in front of him, a glass on top of it, turned to the whiskies.

'So,' I said, pouring a measure and trying to keep my voice casual. 'Is that a thing? Going to posh restaurants and reading trashy paperbacks on a Friday night?'

He laughed. 'Sometimes. It seems less miserable than sitting at home by myself and reading trashy paperbacks on a Friday night.'

I added the water and pushed the drink towards him.

'Thanks.'

'Have you been working?'

He nodded. 'Just finished.'

'Busy?' I asked. 'I mean . . .'

He smiled. 'Not really—for a Friday night, anyway.'

'Okay,' I said, as though that made sense.

'Nobody died,' he added. 'Which is the important bit.'

I hesitated. Nic was at the register, re-counting the cash and pretending to ignore me. 'That's good.'

Tom picked up his whisky, took a sip. 'How are you?'

I looked at him. Still a picture in a magazine. A postcard, waiting for an answer.

For some reason, I wanted to tell him the truth—all of it, about Lina and the wedding, and not sleeping. And more. About the accident and the Morbids and . . . everything. It was confusing and alien. 'It's a long story,' I said instead, touching the bar.

He went to say something, and then stopped as a docket rolled out of my machine. 'And you're working. Maybe later?'

I frowned.

He shrugged, his voice changing. 'Or not. I'm sorry.'

'No, it's fine.' I took a long breath. 'Maybe?' I exhaled, touched the bar again. Solid. When I looked at him he was smiling.

'Okay; maybe is good.'

I laughed. 'Enjoy your book, Tom.'

His eyes met mine. 'Thanks, Caitlin.'

I nodded, not looking away until Nic said my name.

♦

He stayed until close, reading his book and sipping his whisky. I tried to ignore him but I was aware of his presence in the same way he seemed oblivious to mine, and to the noise and the room slowly emptying around him.

'You right, Caitie?' Nic asked, as the last tables cleared.

'Always.'

He came up next to me and dropped his voice. 'He's waiting for you.'

'He's not,' I said, focusing on rinsing the coffee machine. 'He's just reading. Decompressing from his big important job.'

'Okay,' Nic said. 'I'll get him to leave then?'

I shrugged. 'Okay.'

'Go talk to him.'

'No.'

He raised an eyebrow. 'Why not?'

'It's complicated.' I didn't need complicated. I needed to sleep. Wake up. Work. Sleep. Group. Easy. Constant. The opposite of complicated. 'I don't have the time.'

'Why, because you're doing the fridge seals tonight?'

I made a face. The fridge seals needed to be scrubbed with a toothbrush, flecks of stale milk and juice and beer going everywhere. Usually they were done by whichever newb Nic liked least that week.

'I could,' I said, calling his bluff. 'But you can't leave until I do, and you don't want to keep six-foot-four Alex waiting . . .'

'Shhh.'

'And what about Holly?'

I heard Tom move, and when I glanced over he'd stood up.

Nic elbowed me in the ribs. 'She'll keep. Go. I'll do this.'

'No.'

'Go,' he repeated, loud enough for everyone to hear.

I shot him a look and turned to the end of the bar.

Tom had his jacket on, hands in his pockets. 'Sorry,' he said. 'I didn't notice how late it was.'

'It's okay.' I hesitated. 'It must be a good book.'

'Not really.' He shrugged. 'Some terrible crime thing my sister lent me. I just wanted to see how it ended.'

'And?'

He laughed. 'Nobody died.'

I looked back at Nic. He was watching us shamelessly, leaning against the coffee machine with his arms crossed. Tom looked at him too, then back at me.

'So, how long a story?' he asked, smiling.

'Pretty long.'

'How does it end?'

I shook my head, too slowly. A reminder, a warning—to him or to myself, I wasn't sure. 'Everybody dies.'

His eyes flashed and his face hardened, jaw twitching.

'Well then,' he said, his voice tighter than I'd heard it before. 'I guess I'll see you later.'

I watched him turn, my ribs aching. When I glanced over at Nic he looked annoyed, and for some reason it scared me.

'Wait,' I said.

Tom stopped, tilting his face up to the ceiling.

'I'm sorry.'

I expected him to keep walking, but instead he turned around, his expression wary.

'I'm sorry,' I said again. I didn't know what I was doing. Or why. Or if I was doing anything at all.

'I don't even know why I said that.' I exhaled. 'It's long. Mostly boring. Slumps in the middle.'

I caught his eye. He smiled, but only just.

'But I have other ones,' I went on. 'I don't know. Maybe.'

'So, maybe . . .' He looked at me for what felt like an unbearably long time. 'Come for a drink?'

And despite myself, I nodded.

◆

I didn't know what I was doing, I thought, as I changed out of my work clothes. Or why. I didn't like him; not the way Nic's raised eyebrows and oversized grin suggested I should. I didn't really like him at all; he was a doctor, and I'd met enough doctors, self-important and cerebral and ultimately out of my league, even before, when my hair didn't live in a bun and my boots had heels and weren't scuffed. But something about him sparked something in my gut: a memory, or the memory of a memory. A memory of something that had never happened.

The clothes I put on were only marginally cleaner, jeans and a t-shirt so old I couldn't remember where it had come from. I doused myself in more candy-coloured deodorant—Sassy, this time: vanilla and the back seat of a school bus in February, toxic enough to make me cough—and re-did my hair, pulling it back neatly.

As I walked out, Nic grinned at me. 'He's waiting outside,' he said, much too cheerfully. 'Have fun, Caitie.'

'You too, Nic,' I answered. 'Give Alex my best.'

Outside, I planted myself in front of Tom, staring at his shoes. Ancient, faded trainers, but even they were clean, looked after.

'Hey,' I said to his feet, suddenly nervous.

'Hi.'

I glanced up. He was smiling, and I wasn't sure why.

'Ready?' he asked.

I shook my head, wishing we could go back inside, where I knew what I was doing. 'I'm sorry,' I said, when his smile faded. 'I don't— this is a terrible idea.'

'What? The drink?' His voice was light, but I caught a note of resignation.

I shook my head again, forced myself to hold his gaze.

'Do you do this a lot?' I asked after a moment.

'What?'

'This.' I looked at the space between us. There wasn't enough of it. 'Pick up waitresses at fancy restaurants.'

'All the time,' he said, then laughed softly. 'No, I only go to one fancy restaurant. And I'm not picking you up.'

'Oh.' I bit my lip, suddenly desperate for a cigarette.

'One drink,' he said. Gently.

I frowned. 'Why?'

He shrugged. 'I don't feel like going home yet. And I want to hear your story.'

I hesitated, not sure what to do, not sure why I was here at all. 'Okay,' I said finally.

He grinned. There was a dimple in his cheek I hadn't noticed before. 'Come on,' he said, turning his body as though to show me the way.

I took a breath and followed him.

◆

The pub was down near the water, away from the city. It was the polar opposite of Sawyer's, all formica and pine and plastic, brightly lit, loud, even though there was only a small crowd gathered around the pool table and a smattering of people around the edges of the room, couples and trios and one or two bigger groups sitting around buckets of beer and near-empty bowls of cold chips. I found us a spot in the far corner of the courtyard while Tom went to buy drinks, opening my pouch of tobacco to roll myself a cigarette.

'Those'll kill you,' he said, putting a glass on the table and sliding onto the bench next to me.

I touched a filter to my lip twice. 'So I've heard,' I said, letting it rest at the corner of my mouth as I found a paper, filled it with tobacco.

He laughed, and took a sip of his beer.

I finished rolling the cigarette, tapped the end with my index finger, put it in my mouth and lit it. He was watching me. 'What?' I asked, exhaling.

He looked thoughtful, and I wondered again what I was doing here, why I'd agreed to this. Nic would have got over it eventually. Holly probably was cool.

'Nothing,' he said, to my shoulder. 'It's nothing.'

'This certainly isn't a fancy restaurant.'

'No.' He picked up his beer again. 'It's a good local, though. You've never been here?'

I shook my head. 'We go into town, usually. Or to the PBH.'

'We?'

'Sawyer's people.' I smiled. 'You know, your typical hospitality drunks.'

'Ah.' He said, nodding.

I looked at my untouched drink, the outside of the glass wet with condensation, wee-yellow lime cordial floating on top of the vodka and soda, and took a drag of my cigarette. I felt like I was in group but not, so far away. I felt like I could say anything, and it would be okay, and it scared me how much I wanted to. A memory of something that had never happened.

'You live near here?' I asked instead, trying to find a thread to pull me back from telling him all the things I wanted to, trying to be careful.

'Yeah, down near the water.'

'Nice.'

'It is. I'm still getting used to it.'

'Where were you before?' I asked.

He hesitated.

'Sorry, I'm just . . .'

'It's fine.' He shrugged. 'I used to live over the bridge, in Cremorne.'

'That's different,' I said. Crossing the harbour always felt like crossing into another world. One with wider streets and more pearls, with pastel cardigans and sturdy shoes. I hadn't been there in years and I didn't miss it.

'A bit.' He took a sip of his beer. 'I was living with someone, and she liked it.'

'She?' I asked, curious, teasing. 'And where does she live now?'

He laughed, a little nervously. 'Still in Cremorne, last I heard.' He gave me a look. 'Anyway, you had a story.'

'It can wait,' I said. 'How long were you together?'

He paused, still nervous. 'Nine years.'

'Nine years?' I exclaimed. The idea was completely foreign, both impressive and horrific. 'How can you be with someone for nine years?'

Our eyes met, and he laughed at my expression. 'Surprisingly easily. Too easily.'

I frowned, not understanding, not sure I wanted to. 'So, what happened?'

He opened his mouth, hesitated. 'Life, death, the usual.'

I went to ask a question, but he stopped me. 'So, your story . . .'

I shook my head. 'There's no story.'

'There's always a story.'

'There's really not.' Only there was, and again I considered telling it.

'Okay,' he said, not entirely convinced. 'So, why hospitality? Why Sawyer's?'

'It's a job.'

'You seem to like it. You're good at it.'

'Yeah,' I admitted. 'Sometimes. But it's not exactly a career.'

'So what is?' he asked, with a playful smile. 'What do you want to be when you grow up?'

I grinned, playing along. 'I am grown up.'

That made him laugh, kind but sad. 'I know.' He nudged my arm with his. 'But you know what I mean.'

'Yeah . . .' I wished I didn't. I picked up my drink, took a long sip, again fighting off that urge to tell him everything. The way he was looking at me made me feel strange. Safe. Not safe at all. 'My parents think I'm going through a phase.'

'Are you?'

'I don't know. When I was a kid, I guess I wanted to do things. All the normal stuff. I wanted to be a writer, for a while, and a marine biologist, because dolphins are cute, a dancer . . .'

'A dancer?' His eyebrows hitched up.

I looked at him. 'Why not?'

He tried to control his face, but failed. 'You just don't seem the type.'

I smiled. 'I'm not. I did two terms of jazz and it was hideous and the costumes were hideous and I have the rhythm of a donkey, but until about five minutes into my first lesson, I thought maybe I had talent.'

He laughed.

'I was seven.'

'Fair enough then.'

I exhaled, wanting to tell him more stories about Miss Diana and the Rockettes and their big fluffy topknots. 'I got good marks at school, so I went to uni, because everyone told me to, but I didn't know what I wanted to do so I did sociology, because it seemed interesting. And then I got a job at this social research company.'

I caught the question on his lips.

'Advertising,' I explained. 'Sort of. Market research for the social media generation. I worked on demographics and social segmentation.'

His eyes found mine, faintly amused.

'God, I don't even know,' I said with a laugh, stubbing out my cigarette. 'My job description was just a page of random buzzwords. It was one of those companies you see in magazines—everyone under thirty and hot and tattooed. We did Martini Tuesdays and a masseuse would come in every second Friday.'

I touched my glass, my fingers suddenly at sea.

'I don't have any tattoos,' I added, before he could ask. 'I had pink hair instead.'

A real-life Manic Pixie Dream Girl, Lina had called me once, her voice hollow.

'It was a long time ago.' I looked away. 'I was a different person.'

He turned, leaned forward, elbow on the table, head on his hand, watching me. 'What happened to her?'

'Life, death . . .' I caught his eye, smiled. Comfortable.

Too comfortable.

'So why did you become a doctor?' I asked, catching myself.

Tom shrugged.

'Come on, you have to have a reason.'

'Honestly? My mum's a doctor. I went to one of those schools where everyone was going to be a doctor or a lawyer or a banker. It was just what you do.'

'Right,' I said. 'It was an accident.'

'No.' He picked up his beer. 'It was a lot of work. It still is. But it wasn't some grand plan.'

I studied him, not sure what to say.

'Okay, it was probably my parents' grand plan. But it wasn't mine.'

'What did you want to do?'

He frowned, like he hadn't considered it. 'I didn't really know. I wanted to go backpacking for a few years and figure it out. But they weren't so keen on that idea.'

I took another sip of my vodka, steadying myself. 'So?' I replied carefully. 'You could have gone anyway.'

'Maybe, but not without their help. I could have got a bar job or something but . . .' He looked at me, his hand reaching up to the back of his neck. 'It was easier just to go to uni.'

'Really?'

'Yeah. My dad promised that once I finished my degree he'd pay for me to take a year off to travel, but by then it was all about internships and residencies.' His hand pulled at the hair on the back of his head and I heard the hesitation in his voice. 'And Sophie was never interested.'

'Sophie? The ex?'

'Yeah.'

'Is she a doctor too?'

Tom shook his head. 'Lawyer. Well, law student then. Now a solicitor.'

'Jesus.' I rolled my eyes. 'You really did just step out of a Lexus commercial, didn't you?'

He laughed.

I looked down at the table, something cold against the base of my skull. A thought, an itch.

'Where did you want to go?' I picked up my tobacco, opening the pouch. 'Backpacking?'

He shrugged. 'Everywhere. I shouldn't complain; Soph and I, we went places. Fiji. The States for a wedding, Tokyo for a week. Ticking things off lists. She liked those nice pre-packaged tours.' He sighed. 'I wanted to do more. I wanted to actually get to know places. Live in them, you know?'

He was looking at me like he wanted an answer, but I couldn't speak. My chest hurt and my eyes felt hot. I hoped he couldn't tell.

'Did you know,' I began in response, taking a breath, trying to stop it shaking, 'that every train station in Tokyo has its own jingle?'

He smiled. 'I did. It was in the hotel guidebook.' He studied me for a second. 'Have you been there?'

I shook my head. 'I haven't really been anywhere. I just read it somewhere.'

I touched a filter to my lip twice so I wouldn't have to say any more, flicked out a paper and pulled at a tuft of tobacco. Smoking might kill me but this ritual—the filter and the paper and the tobacco, the pulling and nudging and rolling, licking and pressing and the final inspection, tapping my index finger on the end—it had saved me so many times it might be worth it.

'Do you still want to?' I asked, as I reached for my lighter. 'Travel, I mean?'

Tom hesitated then picked up his beer, finished it. Our eyes met. 'I don't know. I put it on the backburner years ago and I haven't really thought about it since.'

'You could.' I didn't know if I was talking to him or to someone else.

'I know,' he said, gesturing to my empty glass without looking away. 'Another?'

I nodded. 'Yeah,' I said, not looking away either. 'Thanks.'

◆

When he came back from the bar he slid into the seat like we were old friends. We talked about terrible TV shows and movies we wanted to see and where we grew up. He had a younger sister who'd just had a baby, and he showed me pictures and it felt nice, warm and normal.

He *was* normal, I realised. Hyper-normal. He had impeccable manners and impeccable teeth and he looked like he belonged on a postcard, sitting outside a cafe in Paris or standing on a bluff in San Francisco or walking down a cobblestone street in Prague. So normal he was hardly real, a hologram from some other world who'd ended up in mine by mistake. He listened to me, properly, eyes on me, or half closed, thoughtful, nodding as I spoke, even if I was just telling him how Lina and I used to get dressed up to watch *The OC* together.

When the pub closed I was disappointed and maybe he was too. 'Where do you live?' he asked, as we stepped out onto the street. 'Newtown.'

He put his hands in his pockets. 'Can I get you a cab?'

I shook my head. 'I like to walk.'

He didn't say anything, and the awkwardness crept back, the silence becoming uncomfortable. 'I haven't been sleeping very well lately,' I said, filling it. 'Walking helps.'

He looked at me thoughtfully, the same way he had been all night. 'Are you sure? It's not very safe.'

'I'm careful,' I said. I was always careful. 'It's fine. I promise.'

He opened his mouth as though to argue, stopped. 'Okay.'

I wrapped my hoodie tighter around myself. It was cold, and the air was pulling my eyes wide open, sobering me up. The streets were too quiet for a Friday night, like the sudden onset of winter had driven everyone inside. I needed to move, to keep warm.

'Where do you live?' I asked. 'I'll walk you home.' I hoped it didn't sound like something it wasn't.

Tom smiled, turning, and we started walking down towards the water. I could smell the harbour—salty and alive.

'You don't sleep?'

'Not a lot. A few hours here and there, I guess.' I exhaled. 'Not enough.'

'Has that been going on for long?'

I glanced over at him. He was looking straight ahead. 'Are you doctoring me?'

'No.' He laughed. 'Well, a bit.'

'It happens sometimes.' Lina's face flickered in front of me. 'It'll pass.' It had to.

'Are you sure?'

I nodded. 'I'm okay. Like I said, walking helps. It wears me out.'

He stopped, throwing me for a second. 'This is me.'

I turned and found myself facing the glass entrance of a very new-looking apartment building. If I hadn't known better, I would have sworn it was a hotel. I could see the water at the end of the street. 'Geez, what a dump,' I joked, trying to lighten the mood.

He grinned, letting me. 'It's not that bad.'

I thought of the cat-piss house, the peeling paint. 'You've got no idea.'

'I have some idea.'

'Is this like a doctor thing?' I asked.

He shrugged. 'Is that more or less objectionable than a family thing?'

'It depends.' I couldn't help smiling. 'Do your parents pay your rent?'

'They paid the deposit,' he said, feigning innocence. 'Is that worse?'

'God.' I shook my head. 'So much worse.'

'They did teach me to keep my hands to myself, though, if that helps.'

I laughed. It felt odd, too breathy.

'Wait,' I said, giving him a look, shifting course. 'Where exactly did you go to school?'

'Caitlin . . .' His smile widened as he leaned in, and I saw the dimple again. 'You don't want to know.'

I cringed. 'Oh, wow. I'm sorry.'

'No, you're not,' he teased, easing back, still watching me. 'But you don't need to be.'

I smiled, maybe too tightly.

He straightened. 'Are you sure you're okay walking home?'

'Of course,' I said. 'I'll be careful.'

'Good.'

'I'm not even that drunk.'

He laughed. 'That's good too, I think. Will you message me when you get home?'

I hesitated. 'I don't have your number.'

'I could give it to you.'

I thought about it, what that would mean. Slowly, I shook my head. Too complicated. 'Let's just . . .' Neither of us moved, and I started to feel an unsteadiness spreading up from my feet. 'Um, thanks, though. For the drink. Drinks. I'll get them next time.'

I hadn't meant to say it, and he raised an eyebrow.

'If there is a next time, that is.' I was cringing before the words even left my mouth.

He nodded. 'For sure, Cait.'

'Yeah, right.' I smiled. 'Anyway, thanks.'

'Night, Caitlin.'

'Goodnight.'

But I didn't move.

10

SATURDAY, MAY

I walked for hours after Tom went home, trying to calm the crackling and the fizzing and the bubbling that had started in my chest, trying to remember the last time I'd talked to anyone as much as I'd talked to him.

Before the accident. A long time before that.

Lina and I used to talk. In between postcards we used to have dinner or lunch or watch bad TV shows at each other's houses and talk for hours and hours. We'd catch trains and slump down in those seats and not stop talking for the entire trip. We made plans, read too many travel blogs and plotted out itineraries and the postcards were just asides, with their own threads and their own rhythms. I didn't know if she still had the ones I'd sent her. I didn't know where they belonged in a brand-new townhouse with a timber island bench and twin shower.

Caitlin,
So do I blame you for the fact that I went all the way to
Liverpool this morning because I was reading somewhere that

they had a really good op shop? Or the fact that the other day I was on eBay and for some reason considered spending twenty dollars on a collection of unmarked postcards from Europe? I would have bought them, too, except it's the end of the month and I'm so poor. (I'll send you the link if you want.)

Speaking of . . . Matt asked me to move in with him. I don't know if I want to, but it makes sense. All my stuff is at his place already. But it seems too soon. Is it too soon? Answers on a postcard lol.

L xxx

PS Did you know when Big Ben bongs it plays the note E? I did not!

Caitie,
I don't know if I've just been watching too much Gossip Girl but I think we should stay in Williamsburg. It's close to Manhattan but not as expensive, and it's got lots of really cute bars and restaurants and things. You're probably all over it.

Work is so boring today. Everyone's at a conference except Dr P, who is here for emergencies. I've reorganised the magazines and sorted all the free toothbrushes by colour and now I'm looking up places to rent in W'burg. It's not cheap. Remind me why NY again?

L xxx

PS Did you know Melbourne used to be the capital of Australia?

If you could go anywhere, I'd asked her once, before I sent the first postcard, where would you go?

I don't know, she'd said. We were on a train and she was curled into the window seat, staring at the fences and the car parks and backyards. Anywhere.

I'd go to New York, I said, full of certainty. I'd only ever seen it on TV, but it shone like a beacon. A place where anything could happen, busy and noisy and big and wild. The perfect place to escape to. Never quiet, never still. The exact opposite of the suburbs we'd grown up in with their big too-empty houses and the miles of lawn—and the quiet.

She'd blinked, like she was waking up. *Yeah, let's do it.* And she'd laughed, genuinely happy, for the first time in weeks. I'd never forgotten that laugh, the way it burst out of her without any effort at all, when everything else seemed to be an effort.

That was when it started, with that laugh.

We'd finished school. I'd gone to uni and she'd got a job and we'd talked about it all the time, planning—dreaming, maybe, but it felt like planning. I never forgot that laugh, and New York settled into my heart, exciting and amazing and oddly uncomfortable, like it was too big to fit in there.

And I *was* all over it. I had websites bookmarked, pages and pages of must-sees and must-dos. Places to eat and drink and see and just be. Places I thought Lina would love, but some I'd never even told her about. Some that were just mine, I realised, with a shock of guilt. That always had been.

I put the postcards away, suddenly exhausted, my throat sore from all the talking. For the first time in weeks, when I got into bed and closed my eyes, they stayed that way for hours.

◆

Sawyer's was quiet, and when Nic let Emma go early she sat at the end of the bar and scrolled through her phone, waiting, while the rest of us cleaned and packed down. Dex came up, still in his chef's pants and the same jacket he'd been wearing since I'd known him, and as they left together he gave me a look—victorious—and it made my stomach churn.

I stayed, working slowly and methodically, mopping the bar floor before I clocked off. Everybody was sitting around a table in the courtyard and I slid in next to Nic.

'How are you, Caitie?' he asked, handing me a beer.

I eyed him suspiciously as I took it and put it down on the table so I could get out my tobacco.

'Fine, Nic,' I said. 'Why?'

'You tell me,' he drawled, elbowing me lightly as I rolled a cigarette.

I elbowed him back, a little less lightly. 'Nothing to tell.'

'So you struck out?'

I rolled my eyes. 'It's not like that.'

'Right,' he said. 'So you say.'

He'd hugged me. Quick and awkward and it was over before I figured out what to do with my arms, and then he'd told me to be careful and turned and walked into his building, waving at me from behind the glass.

It was strange, and I'd been thinking about it more than maybe I should have been, about the whole night and everything he'd said, and combined with nearly five hours of sleep and as many cups of coffee it had left me wired, delirious. I could see why Nic was thinking what he was. I touched the end of the cigarette with my index finger and put it in my mouth.

'It's not,' I said, sparking my lighter and taking a drag.

'Why not?' He was pouting like a petulant schoolboy.

I laughed, short and sharp. 'Why do you think? He's a doctor.'

'So? You're cute.'

'For a girl,' I finished, picking up my beer. 'No, he's nice. But he's not my type.'

'What is? Celebrity chefs? Arseholes?'

I shook my head. 'Not doctors from the North Shore, that's for sure.' They never had been. 'How was your date?'

'Don't change the subject.'

'I'm not.' I smiled. 'This is how conversations go. You asked me a question and I answered it—'

'Hardly.'

'I answered it, and now I'm asking you a question. We're *talking*.'

Nic looked at me like he was trying to solve an equation. 'Right.'

'So . . .' I took a drag on my cigarette. 'How was Alex?'

'Alex was lovely. And even taller than advertised.'

I raised an eyebrow. 'Go on.'

'No.' He shook his head. 'I'm not telling if you're not.'

I shrugged, taking another drag. 'Fine. You'll tell me eventually.'

'So will you.'

'Maybe later.' My voice sounded funny. Far away. A wave of exhaustion came over me so forcefully I thought it was going to knock me over. I eased back against the bench, sipping my beer and smoking my cigarette, studying the awning hanging over the door to the courtyard, the bolts attaching it to the bricks, wondering if they'd rusted through yet.

'Caitlin?'

I turned my head. Holly—the redhead with the tatts, almost as good as me, but nicer—was holding a second beer out to me. It was the first time she'd spoken to me since the night with the finance boys, and I caught a tiny tremor in her voice.

I looked at the beer I was holding, surprised to find it empty. 'Thanks.'

'We're going up to the casino after this. Wanna come?'

I snorted. 'The casino? Jesus.'

'I know,' she said, 'but it's open all night and Nic wants to play the pokies. He's convinced he's going to win this time.'

'You know they have pokies in regular pubs too. You don't have to go into that hellhole.'

Holly laughed. 'Come on . . .'

'I hate the casino,' I said. 'It's so garish and full of tourists and every time we go there someone gets lost and everyone else gets lost looking for them.' I turned to Nic. 'And you never win. You have literally never won any money on the pokies.'

'I won ten bucks the other week.'

'How much did you put in?'

Holly laughed again and Nic just glared at me, trying not to smile.

'Why the casino?' I asked again. 'Really?'

Nic gave in. 'She likes someone.'

Holly finished off her beer. 'Shut up,' she said to him. To me, she said, 'Maybe.'

'And he works at the casino?'

'She,' Nic interrupted. 'Tegan. She works in one of the cocktail bars. She's cute too. For a girl.'

'Right.' I looked at him. 'You're a regular cupid at the moment, aren't you?'

'I try.'

'You should never tell him anything,' I said to Holly. 'He's terrible.'

'I've noticed.' But she was smiling. 'So come? I need backup.'

'She needs someone to pretend to be her girlfriend,' Nic said.

'I do not!' Holly squealed. 'I just hate going in there when it's just me and Nic. He's so obvious.'

'Does he do that googly-eyed thing at her for you?'

'Yes! He's so gross. Please?'

I closed my eyes and took a long, deep breath. 'Okay.'

She squealed again. When I looked up, Nic was sitting back in his seat, satisfied, like this had been his plan all along.

◆

And that was how I ended up at the casino, sitting in one of the hundred near-identical cocktail bars under a gold and crystal chandelier the size of my bedroom, so big it could have crushed us all into the ridiculously patterned carpet, drinking Black Russians until four in the morning, arguing with Holly about whether *Clueless* was better than *Mean Girls* and listening as she told me about her band—'we're like punk you can dance to', she said, with a growl and a flurry of drunken air guitar—and how they were putting together songs for their first EP but their drummer was in their final year of law so they never got any time to play. Her enthusiasm lit up the vodka in my belly, making me warm all over, making me laugh.

We watched Tegan make cocktails and plotted and told silly stories with no endings that got sillier and more endless the more we drank, the tinny melodies and shrill songs of the pokies such a constant soundtrack that eventually I stopped hearing them.

I got too drunk too fast and I should have gone home but I didn't want to. I didn't want to be cold and I didn't want to be alone and I didn't want to stare at that water-stained ceiling for one more second, and it didn't matter that it was the cocktails talking but I felt almost human, almost normal, almost like someone else. A normal girl who could do anything—laugh and drink and talk and not be constantly thinking about what would happen to all of us if there was an earthquake, a tsunami, a catastrophic structural failure. Someone different.

◆

And that was how I ended up outside Tom's building, silence ringing in my ears, staring through the glass at the rows upon rows of letterboxes and wishing I knew which one was his, wishing I had his number. Not for any reason—just because Holly and Nic had gone home and I was wide awake and my bones were cold but my skin was hot and I wasn't ready to stop talking, and I had liked talking to him, more than I wanted to admit.

It was how I ended up down by the water, looking back at the rows and rows of apartment buildings and wishing I lived in one of them, that I could sit in bed and look out at the harbour instead of at a brothel. I imagined all the people in those apartments, sleeping soundly.

Tom, sleeping.

My phone vibrated in my pocket—Nic asking if I'd got home all right, and I lied and told him I had. I found a bench and rolled a cigarette and smoked it, staring at the sky for so long it started to change colour, pulling my knees up to my chest, letting my eyes close and my head fall onto my knees. I was shivering, and I brought my knees in closer, tucked my hands into my hoodie and tried to make myself smaller, warmer, safer. I thought about falling asleep, about being found, blue and frozen, by an early-morning jogger, after half-a-dozen early-morning joggers had already gone by, politely ignoring me. About being snatched, dragged into a nearby laneway, too tired to fight. About having a heart attack, my body giving out.

So quiet, so still, so cold. Minutes, seconds, hours passed. I had no idea.

King Street was never this quiet, never this still.

Lina didn't know how I slept with all the noise. She didn't know that sometimes I didn't, that I needed it to mark time, to keep me sane as I lay there staring at the ceiling for hours and hours.

So bloody quiet. It drives me crazy.

I pushed the thought away, buried it.

Jenny didn't sleep much either. When I'd stayed at Lina's, I'd always wake up in the middle of the night, hear the television still going or the clattering of her making a cup of tea.

You and Mum, honestly.

Lina said it all the time, rolled her eyes and told me we were alike. I always wanted to argue, to point out the differences, but I never knew how. Maybe she was right.

I took a breath and the ground seemed to tremble under me, and as I looked out at the water I wondered why it hadn't leaped up and pulled me into its blackness, wondered how long it would be until it did.

11

TUESDAY, MAY

'I was so lucky.'

Geoff had tripped over his front step and cracked a bone in his hand. He had a cast on his wrist and his eyes were wide with adrenaline as he recounted his brush with death.

'If I hadn't put my hand out, that would have been my head, right into the corner of the bricks. Right in the temple. I was so lucky I wasn't holding anything or playing on my phone or looking the other way.'

I frowned. I felt like I'd heard this before. More than once.

'How terrifying,' Frannie said, staring at her hands. 'I'm so glad you're okay.'

'Thanks, Fran.' Geoff smiled. 'It was just such a wake-up call.'

'I can imagine.'

'I'm thinking of moving, to be honest. That place is a death trap.'

Geoff had moved three times in the past year, but every apartment tried to kill him—gas stove, wall-mounted dryer, loose balcony railing.

'You know they reckon single steps are the worst? I did a safety course once—for work, not just for myself, but it was so educational—and they said single steps are deadly. Your brain doesn't see them properly. And if you trip carrying a pair of scissors or a knife or even a glass and it breaks . . .'

Carlos winced at the thought.

'I'm going to get some hazard tape, just for now. But I really think I need to move. It's a shame, though; there aren't many places in that price range with a garage.'

I sank back into my seat, hands deep in the pockets of my hoodie, feeling my eyes drift closed. Geoff talked for a little longer, and then he stopped and Louise started, but I could barely hear her.

I hadn't slept, again. I'd been dying all day, all the day before. Without Sawyer's I couldn't seem to find a reason to get out of bed. I tried. Told myself I would do it on the hour, at eight, get up and shower and get dressed. Think about it until two minutes past, aim for eight fifteen, then miss that too. Stare at the ceiling until eight thirty-four. All morning, and most of the afternoon.

And I thought about dying, all the time. Mugged. Murdered. Car accident. Plane crash. Train derailment. Loose railing. Dodgy stove. All the time, all the things trying to kill me. I couldn't stop thinking about them.

I was so tired. I'd had a couple of good nights, but I could feel it getting worse, and I didn't even know what 'it' was.

Lina had called earlier to tell me about the dessert buffet she wanted and just before she hung up she asked what I was doing and I'd lied and said I was getting ready to meet friends. It had come out so easily I wondered if there was something wrong with me, something awful. A brain tumour, or maybe mad cow disease.

I balled my hands into fists and felt the air moving in and out of my lungs and listened.

Beryl had come down with a cold and she was worried it was pneumonia. Fiona, who was back but didn't seem thrilled about it, asked her a series of questions, and I could tell from the sparkle in Beryl's eyes that this was the highlight of her week.

'How are you doing, Cait?' Geoff asked, when Beryl was satisfied she was going to live at least another four days.

I opened my eyes. He was staring at me intently. I wondered how long he'd been doing that. 'What?'

'You look like you might be struggling.'

I shrugged, annoyed. Usually you didn't have to talk in group unless you wanted to. Carlos went for weeks without saying anything about himself, and Glenn often just sat quietly and listened. He wasn't a big talker, he'd explained, in one of my early sessions, but it helped him enough to be there.

'I'm okay.' I looked at Fiona. She was reading something on her clipboard, frowning.

'Are you sleeping better?' Geoff persisted.

'A little.'

'I read about a guy who died from not sleeping,' Frannie said.

'Yeah, me too.' Carlos was frowning and smiling at the same time. 'Multiple organ failure. Everything just got so tired it stopped working, you know?'

I sighed. 'That's not going to happen to me.' I shook my head, tried for a laugh. 'I'm fine, just tired.'

But as Louise started to share her theory about an old unsolved kidnapping case, I felt something cold stir at the back of my neck.

I closed my eyes again. Multiple organ failure.

12

THURSDAY, MAY

'Hey, are you at work?'

I hadn't recognised Lina's work number, or I wouldn't have answered. The thought made me feel terrible.

'I'm starting in a few minutes,' I said, taking a seat at the table in the staffroom. My bones were cold, stiff, like my body didn't have the energy to warm them anymore. Everything was an effort. 'What's up?'

'Have you booked your flights yet?' she asked.

I hesitated. I didn't know the right answer, if the truth was acceptable.

'Because I was just online,' she went on, 'it's so dead today, don't ask me why—and flights to Bali are so cheap right now. I'll book for us, if you want. When can you go?'

The door opened and Nic walked in, still in his street clothes, carrying a plate of toast. I tried to give him a smile but it must have come out wrong, because he frowned in response.

'You still there, Cait?'

Nic put the toast down, walked over to his locker. 'Yeah.'

'Good. Do you still want to go early? I have the whole week before off work so I could go on Saturday.'

'I don't know.' The smell of warm jam and butter was making me dizzy. I hadn't eaten breakfast and suddenly I was starving. 'I think I can only take one weekend off.'

Nic turned around, shirt off, eyebrows raised in shock. I hadn't taken a single day off since I started. Not even after Dex.

'Of course,' Lina said. 'I forgot.'

'Monday?' I said, feeling sick and hot. Nic was still watching me, and I pulled my spine back, deliberately. I shouldn't have answered the phone, not here. I should have called her back later. 'I have Mondays and Tuesdays off, so I could go then, until the next Monday.'

I'd have to miss group, too, I thought suddenly.

'Okay,' she said distantly, like she was reading something. 'Monday to Monday. That works with the resort anyway. Means we don't have to move if there's a wedding the weekend before. I'll tell Amanda.'

Nic turned, dressed. He picked up a piece of toast and gestured to me. I smiled and took a slice, holding it in front of my face for too long, no longer hungry. 'Who's Amanda?'

'Oh.' Lina laughed. I took a bite. It was rubbery and hard to chew. 'She's our wedding coordinator. At the resort.'

I tried to swallow. 'You have a wedding coordinator?'

'Of course!' She sounded amused. 'It's so much easier than doing everything ourselves from over here. She's great, and she's organising everything—all the accommodation and the food and flowers and the legal stuff over there. All we have to do is tell her what we want and who is arriving when.'

I took another bite of toast so I wouldn't have to speak, the first piece still lodged in my throat.

'I swear, Caitie, organising a wedding in Bali is so easy. You can book out a whole resort and nobody has to bus it in or anything.'

'You've booked out a whole resort?' My mouth was still full, dry, dryer now.

She paused. 'A little one. For the weekend.'

'Oh.'

Nic looked in my direction again, a question on his lips, and I shook my head. Nothing. It was fine.

'It's so pretty, Cait.' Her voice rose, sped up just a fraction. 'All the villas have freestanding baths right there in the rooms, and they all open on to this pool and lounge area with a cute little bar, and the beach is just there. They have this little coconut grove down the side with a stream and a path and timber pavilion over a waterfall. That's where we're having the ceremony.'

I went to say something, to make a noise like I was listening, but she went on before I could.

'We only have the whole place from the Friday to the Monday, but we can book rooms during the week, we just have to tell Amanda. I'm emailing her now.'

'Okay.'

I could hear her typing. 'I'll book the flights as soon as I get off the phone. You have your passport, yeah?' But before I could answer she said, 'Of course you do. Who am I asking?'

'I'm not sure when it expires though,' I lied.

'That's okay.' There was something in her voice. 'I don't need it to book the flights. I know your name. You can pay me back later. Or . . . whatever. I can take care of it. I'm planning this one, remember.'

I felt a crackle of anger along my spine. A resort. A wedding coordinator. It was all too much, too expensive. And she talked about it like it was nothing.

'Just make sure you get the time off work, okay?'

'Sure,' I said, looking at my hands, imagining them transparent, rotting away. Leprosy. 'I will.'

She made a muffled sound. 'Hey, my other line is ringing, I have to go. I've got to organise an appointment with the dress place for us, so I'll call you soon, all right?'

'Sure,' I said.

'Okay, good. Bye.'

'Bye.' But she was gone. I looked at my phone for a minute, then put it down on the table, taking a long, deep breath and trying to settle my stomach.

'You all right, Cait?' Nic asked.

''Course,' I said, standing up and heading over to my locker. 'Just family stuff.'

'Going somewhere?'

'What?' I started looking for a clean shirt. 'No, not really.'

The words startled me even as they came out of my mouth.

Nic coughed and stood up. 'Okay, then,' he said. 'I'll see you up there.'

I nodded, and before I turned around again he was gone.

◆

'Jesus, Caitie. What is up with you?' Nic asked, after the dinner rush. I couldn't tell from his tone how he meant it, and I didn't want to think about it. I didn't want to think about anything.

Talking to Lina had rattled me. I couldn't stop thinking about that resort, all that money.

'What?' I kept my eyes on the coffee machine, bouncing up and down on my toes, trying to keep warm as I twisted a portafilter into the group head. My jaw was locked tight along with it. 'Have I fucked something?'

He laughed. 'You tell me.'

'I already have, Nicholas.'

'That's not my name, Caitlin.' He paused. 'Tom came in last night. After you'd left.'

I frowned. It had been quiet and Nic wanted Holly to learn to stock, so he'd sent me home early. 'So? I'm busy, Nic.'

'You're fine.'

'I'm not. I'm behind.' I wasn't, but looking at the bar, it was impossible to tell.

'I'll help you then.'

It sounded more like a threat than a favour. I shook my head, but when he came around the bar and started opening beers, I let him.

'He asked about you.'

'Okay.' I poured skim milk into a jug.

'So?' He raised an eyebrow.

I started warming the milk, waiting for the metal under my fingers to heat up. 'We're friends. If that. We had a drink. Once.'

'And nothing happened?'

I tapped the jug. Tapped and then pressed. I could tell from the steam that it was hot but I could barely feel anything. 'Nothing. And nothing will. He's not my type.'

'So you say.'

'It's true.'

'Hmmm.' He walked back around the bar and picked up the beers. 'Who was on the phone before?'

I feigned ignorance. 'When?' The steamer made a hissing sound and I knew I'd burned the milk but I didn't care. I poured it into the waiting coffee cups and pushed them away.

He laughed. 'You're such a shitty liar.'

'Order up.' I gave him a look.

'I'll figure it out, Cait,' he said.

I rolled my eyes as he walked off with the coffees, then I set out two wineglasses and turned to find the right bottle of white in the fridge. Another docket came through the printer and I pulled it free. The words blurred but somehow I made them out, like I always did. Beers. Then more wine, two more coffees.

'Emma's disappeared again,' Nic muttered the next time there was a lull.

'What?'

'She said table three needed bread but she's been down the back for ten minutes.'

I shrugged. 'It's her funeral.'

'Nice, Cait.'

I picked up a notebook and dropped it on the bar, a little too hard. 'She's young. She'll get over it.'

Nic sighed.

'I know, Nic. We all know. Maybe she knows too. Maybe she thinks she'll be the one to tame him.' The crackle of anger I'd been fighting since the start of my shift turned into something else, something bigger. 'Why is it on me to look after her? Why do I have to look after everyone?'

I wasn't talking about Emma. Damn Lina. Damn her and her stupid, expensive wedding that was going to end up being like every other stupid, expensive wedding. Boring and pointless when they got divorced in five years, when he left her for someone skinnier and cooler and her whole world fell apart and I had to look after her. Again.

And then she'd get better and move on and I'd still be here, doing this.

Or maybe I'd be dead by then. Maybe that would be better. Probably.

A docket came through and I picked it up a little too forcefully, tearing the paper. I pulled two beers out of the fridge and opened them.

'Fuck,' I said, as one erupted over my hand.

Nic was still watching me, confused, concerned.

I shook the froth off my fingers. 'I'm sorry,' I said. 'It's just . . .'

'It's okay.'

I sighed. 'He's a sleaze. He'll fuck her and then he'll get bored and fuck someone else and she'll get hurt and he won't care, and Lenny won't care.'

'Cait.' He looked around as though to see if anyone could hear me.

'I'm sorry,' I said again. 'I'm just tired. Over it.'

He stared at me for a long time, like he had no idea what he was looking at, and then he smiled, out of nowhere. 'That's lucky, isn't it?' He tipped his chin, and when I turned I wasn't even surprised to see Tom sitting at the end of the bar and lifting a hand to wave.

◆

He waited for me to finish and didn't even ask if I wanted to go for a drink—although to be fair I didn't even think of saying no. As I left, Nic told me to have fun and I smiled tightly, still feeling bad for getting angry at him.

'So what was that I walked in on?' Tom asked as we headed to the pub.

I shrugged, hands deep in my pockets. 'Family disagreement. We love each other really. I'm just tired.'

'Still not sleeping?'

'I sleep,' I said, as we reached the pub. Tom held the door open for me and I walked inside. It was warm, too bright. 'Just not enough. And sometimes Nic is a lot.'

'He seems nice.' He let the door close and came up beside me, heading for the bar.

'He is, I just had an off night.'

The bartender came over and Tom ordered our drinks, remembering mine from last time. I offered to pay, but he brushed me off.

'Thanks,' I said, picking up my drink.

'You're welcome.' He smiled, genuine. I couldn't help but return it. 'So, what happened?' he asked, as we claimed a table in the courtyard.

I shook my head, getting my tobacco out and finding a filter. 'He just expects a lot from me sometimes.' I touched the filter to my lips twice, then let it rest, pulled out a paper. 'And I can't fix everything, you know?'

I didn't know what I was talking about, or why. Tom nodded, watched me finish rolling my cigarette. My anger had faded—at Nic, at Lina—and I just felt guilty. I put the cigarette in my mouth, picked up my phone and texted Nic a quick apology.

'Sorry,' I said, putting my phone away without waiting for a response. 'I told you—boring and sags in the middle.'

Tom laughed. 'It's fine.'

'So . . .' I lit my cigarette, desperate to change the subject. 'Tell me about this ex.'

He raised an eyebrow, suspicious. 'Why?'

I shrugged. 'You were with her for nine years. Obviously there's a story there.'

'Yeah, but . . .'

'Come on, humour me. I've had a crappy night.'

'It's not very funny.' He looked serious, somewhere else.

'What happened?' I asked, softening.

He took a breath. 'Everything was fine. She was—is, probably— great.' He sighed, wistful. 'Soph is the whole package. Smart. Funny. Gorgeous.'

I felt a pang. An ache.

He studied his beer, thinking. 'And then my dad died.'

'Fuck,' I whispered, stunned, wishing desperately I could start the conversation again, steer it somewhere else, anywhere else. Off a cliff, into an iceberg. 'I'm so sorry.'

'Last year,' he went on, like he hadn't heard me. 'Heart attack. No warning. No signs. No risk factors. He was sixty-six, had been swimming his whole life. Did triathlons sometimes, when he had the time to train.'

He touched his beer, but didn't pick it up.

'It was so weird. One day he was alive and the next he wasn't and there were all these flowers everywhere.' He shook his head.

'I'm sorry,' I said again. 'I didn't mean to . . .'

'It's okay. I don't talk about it much. Maybe I should.'

I sat back next to him, both of us staring straight ahead. There was an old, bent mushroom heater in the middle of the courtyard and it made me feel cold. I took a drag of my cigarette, then put it down in the ashtray.

'It's just weird.' He shrugged, his shoulder brushing mine. 'Do you ever think about it? Death?'

I tilted my head like I didn't know what he was asking.

'Because I didn't. I mean, I'm around dying people all the time. Most days, in fact.'

I felt my cheeks get hot.

'But not anyone I know.' He lifted his hand, tugged at the back of his neck and looked up at the sky. 'Well, my piano teacher died a few years back; I read about it in the paper. And a guy a few years above me at school—but not anyone . . . I guess I've been lucky.'

'I guess,' I said. 'Were you close?'

'Yes and no,' he sighed. 'The yes part makes it hard; the no part makes it harder. Regrets, you know?'

I nodded, not sure I did. He was quiet for a minute, thinking.

'Anyway—' he shrugged again '—it spun me out. Made me think about things. Soph and I—we'd been together forever. Mum had us married off. *Soph* had us married off. House in the suburbs, three kids, some big ugly stupid dog.'

I smiled.

'It made me take stock.' He rolled his eyes. 'As they say. Soph thought it was grief, and that I'd get over it. She kept trying to fix things, and I probably didn't handle it well. It was . . . messy. I'm pretty sure she hates me now.'

'I'm sorry,' I said, wishing I could say something else but not knowing what.

I picked up my cigarette. It had gone out so I relit it.

'I'm getting over it,' he said, as I took a drag. 'As much as you do, I guess.'

I nodded, trying not to think all the things I was thinking.

'So,' he said, when I didn't say anything. He picked up his beer and finished it. Reset. 'That killed the mood.'

'It's okay.' I gave him another smile. 'I asked.'

He looked at me. 'I'm not sure why I told you all that.'

I blinked, trying to bring myself back, bring everything back. 'It's because I serve you drinks,' I said eventually.

He raised an eyebrow. 'What?'

'It is.' I took another drag. 'I read this study once. People are more likely to form attachments with service staff who serve them drinks than with anyone else. They find us trustworthy and nurturing.'

He laughed.

'It's true. Bartenders mostly, but baristas too. And I'm both, so . . .'

'Someone did a study on this?'

'Yeah. I read it . . .' I hesitated. At work. Before. 'Ages ago.'

He looked quizzical, and I went on.

'Take my best friend. She's been with the same guy for, not nine years, but at least five.' I felt a stab of guilt. 'But still, whenever we find a new coffee place she always gets a crush on the barista and tries to set me up with him.' Or she used to, I thought.

'And does it work?' His eyebrow came up again. 'Or are you immune?'

'Oh,' I shook my head. 'I'm not really into . . .' I trailed off, suddenly awkward.

'What? Baristas?'

'No.' I took a drag, stubbed out the last of the cigarette. 'Well, them too.'

He smiled, waiting.

'Relationships. All that stuff. I don't know.' I looked past him. 'I've never really been in one,' I said, before I could catch the words, repress them.

His eyes widened, his expression landing somewhere between confusion and shock. 'Really?'

I nodded.

'Never?'

'I've dated, obviously.' I laughed. 'I used to date a lot. Too much. I've had flings and things.'

Things. Drunken hook-ups and friends-with-benefits situations that petered off into weird awkward miscommunications; endless message chains with men who were so far out of my league that nobody could be surprised when it didn't work out; hours spent trawling dating apps with Lina looking over my shoulder telling me I was being too picky, too careful, asking what was wrong with this one and that one and me feeling like she was really asking what was wrong with me.

'But no grand romances. No *honey, I'm home* or roses for Valentine's Day. It's just not my thing.'

There was nothing wrong with me, nothing wrong with not believing in fairytales or happily-ever-afters; nothing wrong with not needing anyone else to make you happy. I was just being careful.

The thought startled me, unsettled me. I sat forward, reached for my hair and pulled out the elastic, sliding it onto my wrist and gathering all the hair back again, twisting and rolling and finally knotting it. His eyes followed my hands, his expression unreadable.

'Anyway,' I said, as I finished redoing my bun. I wasn't sure if my voice was shaking or if it was just my hands. 'I can't even keep a houseplant alive, so I probably fail on the nurturing, but I'm pretty trustworthy, so you're safe with me.'

Our eyes met, held for a long time.

'That's good to know,' he said, finally.

I smiled, feeling both much too awkward and much too comfortable.

13

TUESDAY, MAY

'Sometimes I don't want to know,' Frannie said. 'Sometimes I think it would be easier not to. Just let it grow and grow until it's so big there's no point doing anything.'

She looked different, but I couldn't figure out what it was. Her eyes were wider and her mouth looked smaller, lips dry and cracked. 'I don't want my kids to remember me being sick for years and having chemo and losing my hair. I don't want that to be the thing they talk about when they talk about their childhoods. I want them to remember us being happy and having fun.'

My mum's sick.

We'd been neighbours for a while then but were only starting to become friends. It was the school holidays and she'd wanted to come to my house for a change. She didn't want to be at home, and when I asked why that was what she said.

What's wrong with her?

Don't know.

She was lying on my bed and looking out the window. It was

before the postcards. Before the train. Before everything. I didn't know what I wanted to be then either. Not a dancer.

She just gets weird sometimes. It's why my dad left.

Is she going to die?

I'd said it mostly as a joke, but Lina took a long time to answer. *No*, she said at last, sitting up, flicking her fingers through her hair. *Not sick like that, don't worry.* She'd looked at me, annoyed, frustrated, like there was something I wasn't getting.

'I was eleven weeks pregnant with Ollie and I found a lump,' Frannie said finally. 'You know, in my breast.'

I sat forward. I'd heard this before too, but her voice was tighter, more urgent.

'I went and got it tested. Not at first—at first I thought I was imagining it, that it was just one of those pregnancy things, like your feet getting bigger. But then I couldn't stop thinking about it, so I went and got it checked out.'

She looked at her hands. Her fingernails were a perfect shade of Cadbury purple, just starting to chip.

'They couldn't find it. They did everything. An ultrasound. A mammogram. All clear.'

Abraham looked up from his notepad, knotting his eyebrows together. He was back. *I'll be looking after you from now on*, he'd said when we started. He'd given Geoff a look, as though to check if that was okay with him, and I'd nearly laughed.

'I couldn't find it either. They said—they said it happened some-times. Hormones. But I knew it was there. I knew. I thought I was going to die before Ollie was even born, just keel over, and they'd cut me open and I'd be riddled with tumours.' She straightened her fingers, still studying them. 'And then I didn't. But the feeling never went away. After he was born, they diagnosed me with post-natal depression. Put me on drugs. It didn't help.' She shrugged. 'Nothing ever really has.'

Louise reached over and put her hand on Frannie's shoulder.

'It will be fine, Frannie,' Donna said. She looked tired. They all looked so tired.

Frannie sat up, shaking her head. 'I know. We're going camping this weekend. The kids are so excited. Then I've got another appointment next week.' She smiled, but she didn't look happy.

'You'll be okay,' Geoff said. He didn't look happy either. I looked around the room. None of them did. Everybody looked . . . beige.

Frannie nodded. 'I hope so. I'm just so tired.'

I closed my eyes. All these stories, over and over, and every time they ended the same way.

◆

I hadn't slept properly for weeks. I didn't know how many. Some nights were better than others; if I worked hard enough, walked far enough, stayed out drinking for long enough, sleep slammed into me like a Mack truck on the freeway, dragged me along and left me groggy and sore and feeling hungover—or more hungover. Other nights it was nowhere to be seen, and it didn't seem to matter what I did. I tried everything, but nothing worked.

It had never been this long before.

Tom came into work every few nights and we'd drink, talk. Mostly talk. About safe things, like politics and childhood holidays to the beach—his somehow exactly like mine, only in a holiday house instead of a caravan park—and meaningless chatter about the books he read while I worked. He liked crime novels, pulpy and gritty, liked how they pulled him out of a long shift at work, despite their darkness.

Sometimes I wanted to tell him. I looked at him and I almost believed I could, that it wouldn't matter, but I couldn't figure out how to start. Once he asked why I never worked Tuesdays and I told him some meaningless lie about a standing dinner engagement with Lina, changed the subject, told him about the novel Nic had been writing for fifteen years.

When his work schedule shifted for a fortnight he warned me he wouldn't be around and put his number in my phone. *I know you don't want it*, he said, *but just in case*, and I wanted to ask just in case what, but I didn't. I went out with Nic or Holly, or both, and whoever else was around. Drank. Teased Nic about Alex. Talked about nothing. Sawyer's was safe. Nic was safe again, too, the awkwardness drowned at the bottom of too many glasses of cheap wine.

Mum called and all she ever wanted to talk about was Lina and the wedding and I nodded along, counting the seconds until I could get off the phone. Sometimes I didn't answer it at all.

Lina had booked plane tickets but all I could think about was how the plane would skid off the runway, or disappear in the middle of the Timor Sea or a hundred other things that could go wrong.

The days kept disappearing, the end getting closer and closer.

I went to group every Tuesday. Geoff moved. Frannie got more tests done. Louise deactivated Facebook, reactivated it to keep in touch with her grandparents, deactivated it. Glenn started writing a new book—I didn't even listen when he told us what it was about. I was too tired, barely there.

I was still carrying around the postcard of Central Park, still meaning to send it, once I figured out what I wanted to say. Late at night, early in the morning, I lay in bed re-reading postcards from years ago. Finding out all over again that Lina's mum had a new boyfriend: *He seems really cool. He's a builder, and just very chilled out. So different to that other arsehole.* And that Matt was allergic to shellfish: *Honestly, Cait. Only I would try to surprise the cutest guy I've ever met with a special birthday dinner and have him end up in Emergency!* And that Seattle was home to the world's first petrol station and about traditional penis sheaths from Vanuatu and that the Big Banana was built in 1964 and that the train stations in

Tokyo all had their own jingles. Facts and stories and Lina telling me she loved me, over and over again, while I felt less and less like I had ever deserved it.

Tom's schedule shifted back and I was surprised at how happy I was to see him, how easily we fell back into the same routine. Sometimes, after a few drinks, I caught him watching me, half a question on his lips. And I'd smile awkwardly, start talking before he could ask it, tell him a story about something that happened at work until the question faded. He was so normal, and around him I felt normal too. I wanted to tell him but more than that I wanted not to have to. I wanted there to be nothing to tell.

But some nights, I didn't sleep at all.

My hands always shook and I jumped at the sound of people's voices and I had a permanent headache from squinting against the daylight, and I felt it. Just over the horizon. Murder. Multiple organ failure.

All the days, disappearing.

August, Once

One of the airlines was having a sale.

Every single ad on every single website I visited flashed red and white and told me to book now. A few weeks earlier, I would have sent the link to Lina and she would have called me and we would have talked about it, whether they'd get cheaper, whether we should book finally, or hold off, just in case.

It occurred to me suddenly that we'd been holding off, just in case, for months.

'Cute nails.'

I hadn't heard Annaliese come in. She was standing by my desk, a plastic cup of something iced and milky in one hand. I smiled, looked down at my hand. Bright yellow. I'd started painting them to stop myself from chewing on them. All the brochures about quitting smoking went on about how it would improve my skin and make it easier to swim laps and make food smell better but not a single one mentioned the constant desire to gnaw my own fingers off. 'Thanks.'

She put down her drink. 'It's lunchtime, you know?'

'I know,' I said. 'I'm just finishing some things off. Rob and Carly wanted that report ready to go out by five, so . . .'

Annaliese looked around the empty office. She was wearing gold eyeliner, so well it almost looked natural. 'You don't see them here, though, do you?'

I laughed. It was Friday, so like everybody else, they'd gone to the pub for lunch. 'It's fine, I'm avoiding temptation.'

'Still not smoking?'

I nodded. 'Six weeks tomorrow.' The first four had been rough yet manageable, but ever since dinner with Lina the cravings had turned into something more, something almost primal. My entire body itched for nicotine. I'd seen someone smoking on my walk to work that morning and the phrase 'I'd kill for a cigarette' had felt so true I'd clamped my lips between my teeth and bitten down until my eyes watered.

'Good for you! It's a filthy habit.'

'Yeah, I know.' Filthy. Expensive. Deadly. But the spare pack in Rob's top drawer had been calling to me ever since he left for lunch.

'Doesn't make me miss it any less,' she added.

'Does it get easier?' I asked, hopeful.

She rolled her eyes. 'God, I wish. Hugh turned into a complete evangelist after he quit. I think that's the only way.' Hugh was her husband. 'But let's be real,' she said, 'it's all denial in one form or another, isn't it? How's the report looking?'

I pushed on the corner of my screen, angling it towards her. She came around beside me as I clicked off the web browser and back into Word. The flashing rectangle screamed at me from the side of the screen. 'Good, I think.'

She leaned in over my shoulder, her blonde hair brushing my arm. 'This looks great. When did we get the data in?'

'Yesterday.'

'Jesus,' she sighed. 'You make us all look bad. This is excellent work.'

I shrugged. 'It's really not that much.'

'Stop, Caitlin.' She straightened, studied me. 'How many times do we have to have this conversation?'

'Fine.' I smiled. 'Thank you, Annaliese.'

'Better.'

She looked around, checking that the office was still empty—as though anyone was going to be back from lunch before three. 'Have you given any more thought to what we were talking about last week?'

I bit my lip.

'Carly's got six weeks left. I don't want to advertise. And Liv keeps asking me what I'm planning.'

I took a breath. Carly was our head of campaign strategy, several pay grades above me, and seven months' pregnant. Liv was her assistant, which meant that in theory she was first in line to take over while Carly was on leave. *But she just doesn't have that spark,* Annaliese had said to me a couple of months ago. Last week we'd been having lunch and she'd asked me if I'd consider stepping up.

'Not really,' I replied.

It was a lie. When she'd first mentioned it, it had seemed like perfect timing, too good to be true, but the more I thought about it, the more wrong it felt.

Once, I would have called Lina and talked it over with her, but I knew what she'd say—that I should do it, think of the money, that it would look amazing on my résumé, that I was worrying too much and I should just do it.

She'd say it was a sign. She'd probably say that first, before all the other things. I wasn't sure I could handle it if she said it was a sign. I'd been telling myself the same thing; first Lina had bought a house, and now this—it was all part of the plan—but I didn't want to hear it.

I was free. I could do whatever I wanted. For the first time in years, since we were teenagers, I didn't have to think about her, worry about her.

I could do anything, and it made me feel sick. There was something in the hollow of my chest, almost too big. I took a breath. When I glanced back at the screen, the red and white rectangle screamed BOOK NOW. My eyes got hot, my throat tightened.

'You should. I need to make a decision.'

I had a lot of leave banked. In four years I'd only taken a single holiday—a Friday and a Monday, for Lina's birthday one year, because she'd wanted to go up the coast and drink wine in a holiday house. When I'd floated the idea of three months off with Annaliese at the start of the year, she'd been fine with it, so long as I gave her plenty of notice—*we'll need time to hire three people to do your job*—but that was before Carly got pregnant. I hadn't given her any dates, so she'd probably pushed it to the back of her mind as a thing that would likely never happen. And now maybe it never would.

I'd been so careful. My whole life. I'd been so careful and suddenly it felt like a prison. I felt trapped, sick. Angry.

I felt so angry.

BOOK NOW.

I inhaled. The room spun, shrank. The converted warehouse suddenly felt too small, too empty of air, boring and insignificant.

'I don't think I can.'

She shifted, surprised.

'I'm going to do this trip I was telling you about. Three months from February.'

The words felt strange coming out of my mouth, reverberated around my head, bounced off the walls. I couldn't quite believe I was saying them.

A frown flickered across Annaliese's face, disappeared. 'Oh, that's right,' she said. 'I'd forgotten about that. New York, yeah?'

I nodded slowly.

'I fucking love New York. Hugh and I used to go every year before the kids.'

I smiled, felt sick.

She picked up her cup. It left a ring of condensation on my desk and I traced it with my eyes, shifting focus. Around and around and around. So sick. Dizzy.

'I'm sorry,' I said, not sure who I was saying it to.

'It's fine. Liv will be thrilled, anyway. I'll make sure she buys you a really nice going-away present.'

I laughed. 'It's only three months.'

'So you say. It could be longer.'

I went cold. Colder. She didn't say anything else, just gave me a knowing look and walked into her office.

As she closed the door, all the air went out of the room. I looked at my fingers, bright yellow nail polish, at the ring of condensation, at my computer screen, all the work I'd done that didn't mean anything. I could keep doing it. For years. Until my hands knotted up with arthritis and I got a hump in my back from too much time in front of a screen and my eyes went. I could keep doing it and that would be fine. More than fine. Safe. I could change my mind. Be careful. I was always careful. Even this trip, it was me being careful, it was for Lina, making Lina happy, looking after her when nobody else could.

I didn't even want it, I thought, as I closed the document without saving it and stared at the screen, the flashing red and white box. I never had. It was about Lina. It was for her, for that laugh. But my eyes were hot, watering, and my throat was tight and suddenly I wanted it more than anything.

I wanted this. I wanted go somewhere shiny and big and noisy and completely different. Somewhere I didn't know anybody, where I could do anything I wanted.

Somewhere it was impossible to be careful.

For three months. Maybe longer. Maybe forever. I didn't want to be careful anymore. I wanted to be different.

Be careless, for once.

I took a breath and clicked on the red and white box.

14

MONDAY, JUNE

♦

I knew it was coming. Lina had told me. *Keep an eye on the post,* she'd texted. *I know it's just a formality but I'm stupid excited anyway!*

It was so pretty—from the large, square envelope that felt like silk between my fingers, to the wishing well card tucked into the back. It was lilac and silver, and Lina's and Matt's names sparkled against the background. There were little silver stars in the corners and they got shinier and shinier as my eyes filled with tears. It arrived on a Friday but it took me until after work on Sunday to open it, and I wanted to call her straight away to tell her it had arrived, tell her how beautiful it was and how much I wanted to go, but instead I went to the casino with Holly and drank cocktails until my fingers went numb and I couldn't feel anything, inside or out.

♦

'This damn city,' I sighed, staring at the skyscrapers across the water, black and tall, studded with lights, perfectly in focus. It was too clear for how cold it was, or maybe that was why it was so cold.

'It's nice,' Tom said, next to me, handing me a bottle of vodka. 'I like this view.'

I shrugged. 'It's okay.'

He looked at me. 'Just okay?'

I laughed, lifted the vodka to my lips. It burned all the way down. I died.

I'd been dying all day.

The seat in front of me pinned me down, crushing my chest. There was no blood. No head injury. I was awake until the end, delirious when I was no longer able to get enough air into my chest, but awake. Breathing got harder and harder and then everything went grey.

The jolt of the train jumping the tracks threw me into the window and my neck snapped and it was over in seconds.

I saw it coming, as though in slow motion. A van. White, ladders on the roof racks. It didn't stop and the driver's eyes caught mine and I knew he was going to die too but I couldn't do anything.

The pilot said it was turbulence. It would be fine, but we should all fasten our seatbelts anyway, just in case. I stared straight ahead and I tried to count but my stomach was dropping. The cabin was getting colder and I couldn't think. The pilot started yelling something but I couldn't make it out. It was so cold. So so so cold.

It happened over and over again. Every time I closed my eyes, and when the sun came up I tried to move but I couldn't. Couldn't do anything.

It was getting worse, and I still didn't know what it was.

I'd stayed in bed all day, only getting up to go to the toilet and smoke cigarettes out of my window, and it was getting dark and I was scared, I didn't know of what, and I'd sent him a message, just saying hi, asking what he was doing. Nothing important.

He'd responded within minutes, and the rush of relief had almost knocked me out the window.

We met outside our usual pub, but I couldn't go in. I tried, but my feet wouldn't work—it was too bright, hurt my eyes. *Let's do something else*, I suggested, before it got awkward. The vodka had been my idea but Tom had picked the location. He told me nobody ever came down here and I didn't want to tell him how many hours I'd spent sitting on the bench nearby after he went home. He asked if I was all right and I told him I was. *Always. But you know what they say about change and holidays.*

I took another sip of vodka. 'I think I'm just bored of it.'

'What?'

I hesitated. 'The city. The view.' I shook my head. 'I've been looking at it for years, you know?'

I passed the bottle back to him and wrapped myself in my hoodie. It was finally winter and being outside was probably stupid, but the air kept my eyes open.

'I know.' He swayed, bumped his shoulder into mine. 'You cold?'

'A little.'

'We could—'

'No,' I said, not sure what he was going to suggest. 'I'm fine. This is nice.'

'Okay.' He shrugged. I felt his shoulder again.

'If you could pick one . . .' I started, reaching for the bottle of vodka. I didn't need any more to drink, but I was thirsty. My throat felt raw, my voice sounded strange. 'What would it be?'

'One what?'

I took a sip, felt the heat. Somewhere, just behind my ears, something was biting at me, telling me to stop, but I didn't.

'One view.' I didn't want to. 'One place.'

'One view?'

'Yeah.' My chest hurt. I had another sip but it still hurt.

He frowned, catching my eye and then looking away. 'It depends.'

I didn't say anything, waited.

'I like mountains. Nepal. The Himalayas. Not that I'd ever climb one—I'm not insane or rich enough.' He laughed. 'But they're impressive to look at.'

'Did you know,' I went on, passing him the bottle, 'that Nepal's main export is carpets?'

'I did not.' His eye caught mine again and this time he held my gaze for a second. I felt a shiver down my spine, a sudden breeze.

'Well now you do.' I looked away, finding my tobacco and searching for a filter. Something was off. Something was different. Him. Me. Definitely me. I was different—drunker than I'd realised. Giddy. 'Is that your one place?'

'What?'

I found a filter, touched it to my lip—eventually, my hand shaking so much I missed the first time—twice, let it rest. 'Your one place that you'd go. If you had to pick one.'

Tom laughed. 'Probably not. I just think the views would be amazing.'

Paper. Tobacco. Rolled. Touched the end. Perfectly cylindrical. But I didn't feel like lighting it. I looked down at my feet, dangling over the water. His feet, next to mine. His were perfectly still while my heel kept bouncing off the stone, keeping time.

'So where?' I asked. It seemed important suddenly.

'Just one?'

'Yeah.'

'I've never really thought about it.'

I shook my head. 'Come on. Everyone has *one*. Even people like me who've never been anywhere.'

My voice felt funny forming the words, and I regretted them right away, even more so when his eyebrow came up. 'Really?' he replied. 'And what's yours?'

I pulled back. 'I asked you first.'

'So are we talking country? City? Experience? Landmark? What?'

'Anything. Just the one place.' I reached for the vodka and took a sip—more than a sip. 'If you found out tomorrow that you were going to die, where would you go?'

He looked at me again. Neither of us had moved but suddenly it felt like he was sitting too close. 'How long have I got?'

'Funny.' Too close, and yet I tipped my shoulder to the side, nudging his, closer. He was warmer than me. I was drunker. 'Say a month. What's the first thing you'd do? The one thing?'

He took a breath, turned to face me. I felt like I'd miscalculated at some point, but I didn't know how to get back. And I wasn't entirely sure I wanted to.

'Wait,' he asked, one eyebrow edging up again. 'One place, or one thing?'

I frowned, not sure of the difference. His eyes were locked on mine. I tried to shrug. 'Either. Both.'

His jaw twitched. 'Honestly?'

I nodded, tried to blink, but I couldn't.

He took another breath and moved, almost too quickly, blurred, until I felt his lips against mine. Hesitant, gentle, but definitely there, definitely coming apart, hands definitely coming up to my face and pulling me closer. Warmer. So much warmer. Something caught in my throat, broke, and I kissed him back. I didn't even mean to but I'd miscalculated and I didn't know how to get back and as his chest pressed against mine I didn't want to at all. I didn't know what I wanted. To touch his hand, his arm. To—

You're too much.

I kissed him harder, tried to ignore it. I felt him smile, felt him pull me even closer, one hand at the back of my head, tugging, the snap of an elastic and my hair falling over my shoulders. For a second I felt everything, so many feelings, tumbling on top of each other, so much.

Too much.

His fingers curled into my hair, brushed along my scalp. I saw my hair in waves around my face, felt his hands, felt—

'Wait.' Glitter. My voice pushed out of my throat, pushed him back. 'Wait.'

So much glitter.

He stopped, eyes locked on me as we both caught our breath.

'Tom . . .' I didn't know what I was going to say, but my voice was sharp, hard.

He frowned, pulled his hand away, shifted his body along the wall until we weren't touching at all.

My heart was still thundering in my chest, my mind trying to make sense of what had happened. I could still feel him, taste him.

He took a breath, then exhaled. 'Sorry. I thought you . . .'

I opened my mouth to answer but I couldn't.

'It's not . . .' I said at last. I tried for a laugh. 'It's just a terrible idea, remember?'

His frown deepened. 'Why?'

For a million reasons, but at that moment I couldn't remember any. 'You're a doctor. I'm a waitress, and I'm—' I stopped, closed my eyes, took a breath.

'What?'

When I opened my eyes he was looking at me, genuinely curious.

'I'm sorry,' I said.

'No, it's not—'

'It's—'

I laughed. Or maybe he did. That awkward laughter which wasn't even laughter; the kind that nearly breaks the tension but doesn't.

'I'm sorry,' I said, looking down at my hands. My fingertips felt funny, like they'd just touched something hot. 'It's not . . .'

'Cait,' he sighed, tired. 'Are you about to tell me it's not me, it's you?'

'Maybe.' I made two fists and then released them, stretching my fingers all the way out. 'But it is me.' My voice was shaky. 'It's clearly not you.' I smiled, just. 'Have you met you? You're a doctor and you're smart and nice and normal and you live in a nice apartment and I . . .'

I looked at him. He was waiting, eyebrow raised in question.

'I'm a waitress.'

'You're a good waitress.'

'That's true.' I shrugged, and he laughed softly. My hands still felt funny. *I* felt funny. 'I just don't do this. I can't. I'm sorry.'

He didn't say anything for a second, just watched me. 'It's okay. I'm sorry.'

'No.' I swallowed. 'It's fine.'

'Are you sure?'

I nodded, bit my lip. I could still taste him. The vodka bottle was on the wall behind him and I wanted a drink but it would mean reaching past him and I wasn't sure that was safe. He noticed, picked it up and passed it to me, careful to hold it away from himself, like I was careful not to let my fingers touch his as I took for it. At some point, I'd dropped my cigarette. 'Thanks.'

'This is a bit like being sixteen again, isn't it?'

I laughed, giving him the bottle back and picking up my tobacco, opening the pouch. 'Which part?'

He didn't answer. A strand of hair fell off my shoulder as I touched a filter to my lip, twice. I brushed it back, half expecting to feel the sting of broken glass.

'You all right?' he asked instead.

'Always,' I said, rolling myself a cigarette. I waited for him to ask again but he didn't. He didn't say anything. I glanced at him as I put the rollie in my mouth, and he was staring straight ahead, completely still except for his fingers, twisting together in his lap.

'Good,' he said, with the slightest hint of a nod. 'That's good.'

15

Tuesday, June

Donna's Thoughts were getting worse. She was having nightmares about her car breaking down and having to catch a train, just once. But once was enough. 'There's always someone on those trains who's not meant to be there,' she said. 'You know: the person who usually catches the one before or whose mother has a doctor's appointment.'

Everyone was getting worse.

Louise's ex-crush had messaged her. He hoped she was well. She'd deactivated Facebook again, had her locks changed and quit her pottery lessons. He was married with three kids but she just got a vibe.

There had been an earthquake off Sumatra—nothing major, it had barely made the news—and Glenn was on edge. 'It's not the earthquakes we have to worry about, though,' he said. 'It's the underwater volcanoes.'

Abraham just watched us, didn't say anything. Sometimes it felt like he was about to, but then Geoff or Carlos or Louise cut him off and he stopped, sat back.

I was getting worse.

I was trying not to think about Tom. It had been a week, and I'd spent most of it trying not to think about him. Working and drinking and not sleeping, and trying not to think about him.

Every night as I lay in bed, I felt his fingers in my hair, pulling, heard him sigh as he leaned in to me. Tasted him. It had been a week, and I'd smoked a hundred cigarettes and stayed after work for drinks every night and brushed my teeth twice a day but when I bit my lip I could still taste him.

I'd been right to stop it. Careful. But the memory made me feel awkward, sticky.

He hadn't been into Sawyer's. Every night from about nine I started looking up whenever the door opened, but it was never him. Every night as I slid into the bench next to Nic or Holly for beers, I checked my phone, thought about messaging him to ask where he was, to say hi, to apologise.

I was trying so hard not to think about him. Failing.

'You okay, Caitlin?' Geoff asked, his eyebrows up.

I avoided his gaze; he looked too eager for a story. 'Yeah,' I said, looking at the lino on the floor. 'Just a bit tired.'

At least that part was true.

◆

Afterwards, I walked home, more slowly than usual. It was early but it was cold and everyone was hibernating.

At Cleveland Street, I stopped on the railway bridge, leaned over the railing to watch the trains, to roll myself another cigarette. I wasn't ready to go home, but I was too tired to walk. It was quiet enough that I could hear the leaves rustling in the shrunken street trees, the faint sound of eighties pop music from an apartment somewhere nearby, a motorbike on a side street. And then footsteps. Slow, deliberate footsteps. And whistling.

Sometimes, when I slept, I woke up from the boot of someone's car, still feeling the sensation of an arm coming around my chest and a gloved hand pushing itself over my mouth. It pinned me to the bed, as brutal as it had been that first time. Sometimes it followed me around while I was walking, my skin prickling and my eyes darting around, assessing every movement and shadow.

It was always there, and I thought I was used to it, ready for it. I had my keys in my fist and I knew exactly what I was going to do—scream *Stop! Leave me alone!* at the top of my lungs, as close to his eardrum as possible, while kicking him in the shins and then kneeing him in the groin—but I knew it was all useless, and I was ready for what happened next.

I'd thought about it so much, talked about it at group, accepted it. I was ready. I knew that it was inevitable, that no matter what you did, death would get you in the end. The rest of them—Geoff and Carlos and Frannie and Louise, the ones who'd come and gone—they thought they could prevent it, that they could outrun it, but I knew better, and I was ready.

Still, when I saw the shadow out of the corner of my eye, I had no idea what to think. And then I wasn't ready at all.

My chest tightened and my spine went rigid. I felt my blood heating up, a roar starting in my ears, something cold running down my back. I kept my head down, only my eyes moving, watching the shadow and then the figure form on the footpath. Whistling. He was whistling, and I could barely breathe.

I listened to the careful, even footsteps, wondering if he'd seen me, if he'd sneak around and try to grab me from behind, or if he'd ask me for a light or a cigarette first. If we were going to a second location—never go to a second location—or if he was strong enough to just pick me up and throw me onto the tracks below. If that would kill me or I'd have to lie there, my legs broken, and wait for a train to finish the job. I thought of the houses and apartments, of the cars passing by, wondered whether anyone was watching, whether anyone would have details for the police later. I wondered if there were cameras. If the security footage of the moment before he dragged me into the shadows would make it onto the news and be discussed on Facebook, whether people would argue over if I'd fought hard enough, or if we knew each other, or if it looked like I went willingly.

I thought about Lina. She'd be devastated. Dad, Mum. Mum would blame me, shake her head and ask what I'd been doing there. Nic and Holly—they'd be sad. Nic would be annoyed he had no-one to run the bar. And Tom.

Would he be sad? How would he even find out? Would he read about it on the internet but not put two and two together until he caught a photo of me on the morning news? Would they use one of me with pink hair? Or one from when I was at uni, during my brief goth phase? Would they paint me as a good-time girl, drunk and stupid? Or go back earlier and choose something innocent, from high school?

Would he recognise me? Would he care, if he did? I bit my lip and I could still taste him and for a second I wanted more than anything for him to care.

And then I wanted to scream. I wanted to scream and beg and run.

I wasn't ready.

The thought overwhelmed me, pushed through my chest.

I wasn't ready.

The footsteps stopped, and I tried not to look but I looked, saw the figure still at the end of the overpass, broad shoulders and a dark head of hair, maybe a beanie. He fumbled for something, arms coming forward and up, and I heard the spark of a lighter. I tried to breathe deeply, as deeply as I could. Smell the exhaust fumes and the Chinese food and stale piss. The last things I would ever smell, unless—

The footsteps started again as he resumed walking towards me. I looked down, eyes on the tracks below, made two fists, nails digging into my palms, toes curled up in my shoes, stomach in knots. My keys were in my bag. I considered reaching for them but I didn't want to move, didn't want to let him know I knew. I hadn't learned well enough—all those self-defence tips and I'd left my keys in my bag. So stupid. Everyone would think I was so stupid.

I took another breath, trying to make myself as small and invisible as possible, to disappear, so he couldn't see me. I wished away the smell of my shampoo, my sweat, which suddenly seemed so strong.

I closed my eyes, waiting. Counting. Listening to the footsteps, the rhythm, steady, a barely perceptible skip as he passed behind me. A mumbled greeting.

I inhaled sharply, not sure how to respond.

I could smell it. Hot and rusty and sour.

Are you okay? Are you hurt? Can you count to ten?

Yes. No. One two three four five six . . .

Okay, that's okay.

Glitter. Not glitter.

This was the way it was going to end. This was always the way it was going to end, the way it was supposed to be. Still, my chest was so tight and there was a coldness creeping up my neck, over my face, an invisible hand cutting off the blood flow.

I wasn't ready.

I tried to take a breath but my throat was closed, a roaring in my ears.

Can you tell me what happened?

I couldn't. I hadn't been paying attention. I'd been looking out the window, at the houses, rows of houses, imagining the same rows of houses in a city on the other side of the world.

I hadn't been ready and it had happened anyway, nearly happened. *That was close.*

I was paying attention now. Always. Vigilant. Paying attention to everything, to all the things that could go wrong, waiting for it. But I wasn't ready anymore.

If I were you, I'd be buying a lottery ticket tomorrow, that's for sure.

The footsteps faded, moved further and further away.

I blinked, looked around.

Whoever had been there was gone. I was alone.

I turned, saw the back of a figure heading towards Chippendale, barely a shadow in a faint cloud of cigarette smoke.

The roaring stopped, and all I could hear was my own pulse, heart thumping against my ribs.

I wondered when he'd changed his mind.

I wondered if he'd been there at all.

The silence pressed into me, suffocating and hot, and the pounding in my chest continued for so long I thought I was going to die.

I wasn't ready. All this time I'd thought I was ready but I wasn't ready at all.

16

WEDNESDAY, JUNE

'Wait,' Holly said, leaning in and picking up a piece of cold garlic bread. We'd just finished and she'd been trying to convince me to go to the casino, and for some reason I'd said no, and when she'd asked why, for some reason I'd told her what had happened. And then regretted it instantly. Her eyes were too wide, her expression too gleeful. 'He kissed you?'

'Shh,' I whispered, glancing at the door. 'I don't even know why I told you.'

So wide. So gleeful. While I just felt awful.

He hadn't come in since. He hadn't called or messaged, and nobody else seemed to have noticed. It was as though I'd made him up in my head and he'd never really existed at all, and now he'd disappeared into a cloud of smoke, like the figure last night.

It had been nothing. Just someone heading home from work, from the pub, from dinner out. But it had felt so real and for some reason it made it so much harder not to think about Tom. I'd walked straight home afterwards, too fast, too terrified. It had been nothing but it had shifted something inside me and I couldn't shift it back.

'When did this happen?' she asked. 'Is that—'

The door pushed open and Nic came in. 'Well, that was a shitshow.'

I gave Holly a warning look, and she pressed her lips together with a smile.

'I know,' I said, opening my tobacco and touching a filter to my lip. 'Sorry about the wine.'

'What wine?'

'The riesling?' I touched the filter again. It had been early in the night, before it got busy, and I'd misread a docket, sent a bottle of our most expensive riesling out to a table instead of a glass of the cheaper one.

'Oh.' Nic shrugged. 'It's fine.'

He'd said that when it happened, too, but it hadn't felt fine. I pulled out a paper and filled it with tobacco. It had put a knot in my stomach that stayed there the rest of the night, slowed me down as I read every docket twice, made it hard to find a rhythm.

'It was a hundred-and-fifty-dollar bottle, Nic,' I said, taking the filter off my lip and sliding it into the end of the rollie.

'Ha!' He got a cigarette out of his locker. 'Not to us.'

'Still.' It had been a stupid mistake, and I didn't make stupid mistakes. But this past week, I'd made a few. Most of them so small Nic didn't even notice, but I did. The dockets were harder to read. I put the rollie between my lips, wondered absently if I needed glasses.

Holly nudged my calf with her foot. 'What do you think, Cait. Casino?'

I looked at my phone. Nothing. No messages. No calls. I didn't expect any, but it still bothered me, bothered me more, had been bothering me all night and all day.

One thing.

'Cait?'

I took a breath. Not ready.

'She's coming,' Nic said, pulling his shirt up over his head. 'She always comes.'

Holly snickered.

I frowned, ignoring them. It didn't take much effort. My mind was somewhere else, the same place it had been for the past week.

One thing.

'I don't think so,' I said, unlocking my phone and opening the message screen. My fingers shook as I tapped on the screen, jumbles of letters my phone had to sort into words, and even then I wasn't sure they made sense. 'Maybe later. There's something I need to do first.' I hoped my voice didn't sound as strange as I felt.

I hit send before I could stop myself, before I could re-read what I'd written and worry about whether it sounded too needy or too blunt or too . . . everything. When I looked up Holly was grinning like she knew exactly what I was doing. I was glad somebody did, because I had no idea. I exhaled.

'Okay then,' she said, before Nic could ask. 'Have fun, Caitie.'

I didn't answer, just gave her a small smile and stood up, putting the cigarette back between my lips.

One thing.

◆

I stepped out of Sawyer's and into the cold, looking at my phone, willing it to vibrate, to light up. The sudden burst of bravado faded as the door swung shut and I stopped for a second, trying to decide where to go. I knew I should just go home but I knew I absolutely wasn't going to.

I tried to think about anything but the phone in my hand, stubbornly silent. Work. Holly. Nic.

Lina.

The cracks in the footpath. Broken backs.

One thing.

I put the cigarette back in my mouth, lit it, took a long drag, so hard it came out in a cough. Cancer. Heart disease. Stroke.

If you found out tomorrow that you were going to die, where would you go?

What's the first thing you'd do? The one thing?

I'd been dying for months. Longer. Nearly two years. Known it like I knew my own name. I was going to die and I hadn't done anything. Not one thing.

I looked at my phone. It vibrated in my hand.

◆

Tom was standing outside when I got to his building, leaning on the glass next to the door, hands in his pockets. He wore a hoodie older than mine, but thicker, warmer, over a t-shirt, and his hair was messy.

'Hi,' he said when he saw me, straightening, but still keeping his distance.

My breath caught at the sound of his voice. 'Hey.' I took a final drag on my cigarette, dropped it at my feet.

He didn't say anything else, just watched me, waited.

'You weren't working tonight?'

'I was.' He shrugged. 'Earlier.'

'Busy?'

'Cait.' He sounded impatient, tired. Our eyes met for a second and then he looked down, jaw tightening.

'Did I wake you?'

He shrugged again. Guarded. 'It's okay.'

I exhaled, tried for a laugh. 'So where have you been? I haven't seen you all week. Have you found another waitress at another fancy restaurant to go drinking with?'

He didn't answer, kept looking at the ground. Something moved in my chest. I didn't know why I was here. I'd miscalculated but I didn't want to fix it. I didn't know what I wanted. Or I did.

One thing.

'So, anyway,' I said, maybe too loudly; it felt loud, in the silence. 'I was thinking. Lina, my best friend . . .'

He glanced up, frowned.

'I've told you about her.'

He nodded.

'She's getting married. In Bali. In November.' I took a breath. 'She's booked out this really nice resort. It's on the beach but it's near a rainforest and there's a pool and a bar and the villas have freestanding baths, right in—'

'Cait.'

I hesitated. He was looking at me now, properly, making me giddy. I had no idea what I was doing. 'I know Bali is probably a little touristy and basic and you've probably been a dozen times, but I thought, if you're free, you might want to come with me?'

His face did something. The twitching of his jaw intensified and I saw his hands move.

'It's not a big deal,' I lied. 'I just have a plus one.'

He nodded, thinking.

'You don't have to answer right now.' That was a lie too. My whole body was aching, waiting for him to react, my voice shaking. 'But think about it.'

'I will.' He hesitated. 'But why?'

I shrugged. 'Why not?'

'Because—'

'Why haven't you been in to Sawyer's?' I asked, cutting him off. 'You usually come in all the time. Nobody's drinking the Glenmorangie. It's going to go off.'

He looked at me. 'Whisky doesn't go off, Cait.'

'Still.'

I took a step towards him. He didn't move but I saw him inhale.

'Have you been working different shifts?'

I could see him consider it, deciding whether to lie or not. 'No.'

His voice was pained, and it made my chest tighten even more. I stepped forward again, looked at the ground between us, trying to figure out how much more there was to cover. Too much. Too little.

'So?'

He exhaled. 'I thought you might want space.'

I paused, thinking about it, thinking about how I'd felt all week. Terrified of what was going to happen when I saw him again. But not just terrified. Not the way I'd been on that overpass. Something else.

I took another step, looked back up at him, shook my head.

One thing.

'I don't want space.'

'Okay.' But he didn't sound convinced.

'I don't want space,' I repeated. When I stepped forward again he was right in front of me, hands still in his pockets.

'So do you want to go for a drink, or . . .' His voice was unsteady.

'No.'

I blinked, and then he was closer, and I didn't know if I'd moved this time or he had. He was so close I could see the curve of his neck, the twitch of his jaw, the pulse in the hollow of his collarbone. Fast. Mine was fast too. And loud. All I could hear. I forgot what I wanted to say. I forgot—everything.

How to breathe.

'What *do* you want, Cait?'

My eyes met his, hot, stinging. It hurt, everywhere.

All over. Ached.

One thing.

'I want—' My throat tightened, and then I couldn't talk anymore.

'Cait.' His voice broke. Broke me. Broke down every wall I'd ever built. Every single excuse I'd made. And then there was no space between us at all.

I kissed him. Softly at first, my lips barely grazing his, giving him a chance to pull away, to stop me, and then, when he didn't, harder, hungrier, my hands coming around to the back of his head, his around my waist. He moved into me, pulled me against him. I couldn't breathe and I didn't want to, just wanted to kiss him, deeper and faster and harder. My toes were curling in my shoes and my fingers were grabbing at him, at his hair, his neck, inside the collar of his hoodie, finding his skin, his pulse. Alive.

I crashed into him, terrified it was a dream and the alarm was about to scream, that at any moment he was going to come to his senses and stop it all. That I was going to die, and I didn't know when, soon, any minute, and I wasn't ready at all. This had to happen first, this one thing.

His hand moved and he gripped my hip, pulling me closer, impossibly closer. I felt my teeth scrape his and I thought I should care but I didn't.

'Cait . . .' He tipped his head back, pulled away. His eyes were huge, pupils black all the way to the edges. 'Are you sure?'

I was. I was so sure it burned. I nodded, heard a whimper break out of my throat, a strangled yes. He hesitated, then kissed me again, harder this time. I moaned and felt him react, one hand pulling up my t-shirt, the other in my hair. I couldn't remember ever being so sure of anything, wanting anything, needing anything as much as I needed to be feeling his skin, his hands, his mouth, just once, just this time.

His fingers tightened as his mouth slid off mine, along my chin and onto my neck. 'Come upstairs?' he breathed into my throat.

'Yes,' I managed, kissing his ear and his jaw and tugging at his hoodie. 'Please.'

I don't know how he got the door open, how we made it to the lift, but he pushed me into it and lifted me up. I wrapped my legs around his waist, fell back against the wall as he kissed my throat and bit my ear and kissed my mouth again, bit at my neck until it stung. My hair had come loose and it was everywhere and he kept touching it and I didn't want him to stop, ever. My whole body and my whole mind were screaming for him, wanting him. I don't know how we got out of the lift and down the hall to his apartment, how he got the door open with me pressing him against it, my hand already undoing his pants, but we only barely made the bed.

It was frantic, furious, ferocious. He scraped his chin against my skin, and I dug my fingernails into his scalp and his back and his legs. Desperate. Hungry. I needed him, wanted him, wanted this—I'd known that, somehow, for weeks, maybe from the very beginning, but the force of how much slammed into me so hard it hurt, tearing me in two. Weeks of delirium and madness and needing. He clutched at me like I was drowning, holding on, so tight, and when I came my whole body shuddered over and over, almost violently; painful and intense and insane. Utterly insane, utterly perfect, alive. So alive.

And then everything slowing, hearts and breath still racing but our bodies too heavy to move; the smallest, most gentle kisses, warm and tiny and beautiful, fingertips wiping away tears I hadn't realised I'd cried, tears I didn't understand, and his arms around me, holding me. His fingers in my hair, lips on my forehead, saying my name, over and over again, and my face buried in his shoulder and my mouth on his throat, kissing him and kissing him, my eyes closing and my breath softening and everything falling away.

17

THURSDAY, JUNE

'Cait . . .'

I didn't know where I was, what was happening. My eyes were stuck shut, lids so heavy.

'Caitlin . . .'

Something touched my shoulder. Something warm. Someone. I rolled over, forcing my eyelids up a fraction. Clean, soft, warm bed. Bright. Everything was bright. Tom was sitting on the side of the bed, freshly shaven, his hair damp, wearing a dark green button-up shirt that brought out the warm, deep, rich brown of his eyes. Chocolate. Caramel.

'Hey . . .' His fingers brushed over my shoulder again, tracing their way down my arm, over my palm, sliding between mine. His touch sent something rumbling through me, warm and familiar and delicious and frightening.

'Hi.' My voice cracked. 'Um . . . hi.'

He smiled. 'You're awake.'

'Barely.' My body felt heavy, bones soft. I could smell coffee.

'You okay?' His voice. That voice.

'I think so.' I found his eyes again. So warm. Okay. 'You?'

'Yeah.' He squeezed my hand. 'I didn't want to wake you, but I don't know what time you start work.'

I frowned, confused. Wake me? 'Wait . . .' I shifted my head, looking around. Everything was bright. The sun was up, properly up, not just licking the horizon. 'What time is it?'

'Nine thirty.'

My eyes grew wide, and he smiled. A big, goofy smile I couldn't help but return. 'What?'

'Honestly, if I'd known that was how to get you a solid eight hours.' He laughed, raising an eyebrow.

I felt too shy to look at him, everything too real. 'I . . . This bed is just really comfortable.'

'Maybe.'

I looked at our fingers, knitting together, then at his face. He caught my eye, smiling, but different; smaller, almost scared. I could see the dimple in his cheek and it made my heart skip a beat. I had to look away.

'Jesus.' I finally noticed the room. Pale grey sheets, white walls, enormous windows, blue-white sky beyond, and I knew we were up high. I propped myself up on my elbows and felt them sink into the thick, pillowy mattress. It wasn't a lie—no wonder I'd slept. Light grey carpet. Those windows. That view. 'This place is crazy. You live here?'

He shrugged. 'Like I said, I have a nice family.'

'Really nice.' I looked around. 'You're never coming to my place.'

He frowned.

'I'm serious. You'd catch something.'

He smiled. That dimple. 'It'd be worth it.' His eyes flicked towards the bedside table. 'I made you a coffee. I don't know how you have it so I made a flat white.'

'Thank you,' I said, squeezing his fingers. He squeezed back. 'That's perfect.'

'I didn't put any sugar in it, but I can.'

I shook my head. When I looked at him his eyes were doing that thing again. Huge. Impossibly big. I wanted to drown in them. 'Thank you.'

He hesitated. 'I didn't expect to see you last night. Sorry if I was—'

'You weren't.' I bit my lip. 'Sorry for the late-night booty call.'

He laughed, but there was something else in it. Faintly sad. 'Was that what it was?'

I squeezed his fingers again, pulled his hand closer, suddenly struggling to find my voice. 'No. It wasn't that.'

'Okay.'

'I wanted to . . .'

His eyebrow arched up and it made me laugh, despite myself. 'God, I'm so bad at this,' I said, cringing.

'At what?'

I looked around, then back at him. 'All of this.'

'Caitlin—' his voice was low, flirty '—that is definitely not true.'

I laughed again.

'Sorry,' he said, clearing his throat. 'You were saying?'

I took a breath. How was he so relaxed? So at ease? How could he form sentences and make jokes and I could barely remember my own name?

I sighed. Caitlin. That was it. 'It wasn't a booty call.'

'So what was it?'

I wasn't sure I could answer. I still couldn't be sure this wasn't all a dream or heaven or a cruel, strange trick of the light, but I could taste him on my lips and I didn't want to stop.

'Are you working today?' I asked.

He nodded. 'At twelve. You?'

'Eleven.'

'Do you need to go home first? I can give you a lift.'

I hesitated. 'No, it's fine. I've got spare work clothes in my locker.'

He opened his mouth as though to say something, ask a question.

'King Street is a nightmare,' I went on, maybe a little too fast. 'It's really not worth the trouble, but thanks.'

He nodded, easing back. I pulled myself up to sit, picked up the coffee. I had to let go of his hand and he put it in his lap, seemed to study it.

I took a sip. 'This is perfect.'

'Probably not as good as you'd make.'

I smiled. 'I didn't just mean the coffee.'

'Oh?' The eyebrow. The dimple. Those eyes, drilling into me. Waiting.

I took a breath. It shook on the way out. I sat forward and put the coffee down. It was going to get cold but I didn't care.

One thing.

I looked down at his hands in his lap. Mine, in front of me, not sure what to do. My eyes got hot, the way they had the night before, and I couldn't speak.

'Cait,' he said, sighing, filling in the silence. 'I know. It's okay. You don't have to—'

I felt a sound escape my throat, a protest.

'I'm not going to lie. I'm glad you came here last night. I'm glad you're still here.' I heard him swallow. 'But I know you're not into all of this. If you don't want—'

I kissed him. Put my hand on his cheek and pressed my mouth onto his and caught his breath. I almost didn't mean to, except that I meant to. I wanted to. He kissed me back, like I'd known he would. After a minute, I pulled back, hand still on his cheek. His were still in his lap and something thrummed inside me at the memory of them on my skin.

'I want this,' I said, before I could think myself out of it. 'You. So much. Probably—' My voice cracked. I wanted him so much. I'd wanted him for weeks, felt like I'd wanted him my whole life. 'Probably more than I should. I don't know what it is and maybe it's a terrible idea but I want it anyway.'

His eyes flashed. His face was perfectly still. Perfect. Eyes locked on mine, big, warm.

He took a breath and his whole chest rose and fell and I felt it, right in my bones, so deep it hurt.

'I want this. I want to try.'

He looked at me, then grinned. 'Are you sure?'

I nodded. 'Yeah. Yes.' So sure.

He kissed me, more than kissed me, over and over, and the coffee went cold like I knew it would, but neither of us noticed for the longest time.

◆

'Can I have another wineglass? This one's dirty.'

We'd kissed at his front door for what seemed like hours, like seconds, said goodbye over and over until we were both late and I had to run up the hill to work. It was hours ago but I could still feel him, his fingers on my waist, in the back of my hair, everywhere.

'Cait! Glass?'

I felt soft, warmer than I'd felt in years, the noise I'd grown so used to muffled, diffused, far away. There were no Thoughts, nobody died, nothing went wrong. Everything I looked at sparkled and when I thought about him I couldn't stop smiling.

Bali, huh? he'd said at one point. Whispered it into my ear and made it sound like poetry. My knees had weakened. *Did you mean it?*

I hadn't answered, but I'd kissed him so hard my mouth hurt, and when he said yes I'd had to grab on to him to keep from falling over.

'Caitlin?'

My face hurt from smiling.

'Jesus, *Caitlin*.'

I jumped at the sound of my name, turned to see Nic staring at me. He looked annoyed, tired. 'What?'

'Finally. Christ. Can I have another wineglass before table three dies of thirst?'

'Huh?' I blinked again, trying to remember where I was, what time it was.

Nic sighed, and I looked at the clock. Nine thirty. Tom finished at ten. He'd messaged me earlier, and then again, cute little messages that maybe didn't mean anything but felt like they meant everything, made me grin like a loon. I passed Nic a wineglass.

'You're in a mood tonight,' I said.

He laughed. 'You're one to talk.'

'Can I have a cigarette?'

He picked up the glass and studied it. 'Stock list first. Then cigarette.'

'But—'

'No.' Short, sharp, exhausted.

I sighed. 'Sorry.'

I made a stock list, somehow, possibly the worst stock list I'd ever made. I couldn't count and I kept forgetting how much of what we were supposed to have. When Nic was satisfied it was finished he glared at me. 'Seven minutes. A second more and you're fired. Bring some of this stuff back up with you, okay?'

I nodded then nearly sprinted to the staffroom. I was in trouble, and I barely cared.

I slipped my phone in my pocket and went out the back, rolling a cigarette and lighting it, inhaling hard. I'd hardly smoked all day and it made my head spin, in a nice way.

'Nice hickey.'

I froze, needing a second to process the words, the voice. When I turned my head, Dex was leaning against the wall, watching me. I frowned, looked away. 'Yeah, right.'

'I'm serious. It's a good one. Did it hurt? It looks like it would have hurt.'

'Get fucked.' I put my free hand up to my neck. I'd only noticed it in the staffroom at the start of my shift, peeking over the top of my collar. It made me feel sordid, like a horny teenager, but something else as well. Touching it had set off a memory that made me whimper.

'Gladly.' He flicked ash onto the ground. 'Seeing as you did, I guess I have permission now?'

I didn't answer.

His face broke into a smile. 'Kidding, Nona. It's about time, frankly. I just didn't expect you to be so obvious about it.'

'Sorry.' I wasn't.

'Don't be.' He smirked. 'I don't care.'

I ignored him, pulled my phone out of my pocket. The light blinked and I unlocked it.

I'm standing in the hospital shop wondering if I should buy you flowers or if you're more of a chocolates girl.

I laughed softly.

Chocolates, definitely.

My phone beeped straight away.

Too late. They're closed now. You'll have to cope with a blue elephant that says 'It's a boy!' when you press its belly. I'll see you soon?

I'm counting down.

'Ohhh,' Dex drawled, pretending to come to a realisation. 'You finally nailed that doctor guy. Nic will be thrilled.'

I rolled my eyes.

'No, really,' he said, pushing off the wall and dropping his butt onto the ground carelessly. 'Well done. I wouldn't have thought he was your type, but what do I know?'

My phone buzzed in my hand.

Leaving work now. Can't wait to see you.

'Not a lot,' I looked at him. He looked so small and pathetic I almost pitied him.

Me too.

Dex just shook his head and went back inside.

I finished my cigarette and followed.

◆

Tom wasn't joking about the elephant.

He slid onto his usual stool and sat it on the bar in front of him and my breath caught in the same way it had that morning, harder maybe, like I'd forgotten how brown his eyes were and how warm his smile was and how—

'Caitlin, fuck,' Nic said from the register, not noticing Tom, just that I'd stopped cleaning the coffee machine. 'I have plans tonight, so . . .' He looked up. 'Oh.'

'Sorry,' I said, turning on the steamer and then straight away turning it off again. I walked to the end of the bar. It took too long. 'Hey.'

Tom smiled. 'You still open?' he asked, like nothing was happening.

'For you?' I tried to keep my voice even. 'Always.'

'Caitlin.' His voice dropped, and the charade fell away. I wanted to jump the bar.

'Drink?'

He nodded, and I nodded back. When I turned to the whiskies Nic was right next to me. 'You sneaky little brat,' he whispered, while turning all the bottles the right way.

I tried to be annoyed but I couldn't suppress a laugh.

'Wow,' he said.

I found the Glenmorangie and lifted it up, checking how much we had left. 'We need more of this.'

'It's about fucking time.'

'Is it?' I asked blankly.

'Ha!' he exclaimed, much too loudly. 'It will be once you've finished cleaning up.'

I grinned.

'Well done,' he said, his voice softer. 'I'm so happy for you.'

'Thanks.'

'I guess you did have time after all.'

I was thrown for a second. 'I guess.'

I turned back to Tom. I assumed at some point the sight of him would stop shocking me right into the base of my spine, but it seemed a long way away.

'How was work?' I asked, setting down a glass and pouring a little bit too much into it.

He shrugged. 'Quiet. Long. Or maybe it just felt that way because I was thinking about other things.'

I poured a finger of water into another glass, balanced it over his. 'Like what?'

'You.'

My hand shook, and the water jumped out, too much of it. 'Shit,' I swore. 'Sorry.'

'Everything okay?' he asked. 'You seem nervous.'

I caught his eye. 'Distracted.'

'By what?'

I didn't answer, pushed the glass towards him, and he reached for it before I let it go, his fingers locking around mine. For a second I forgot where I was.

'Caitlin,' he said, tugging on my fingers again. He was looking at me, so intently I couldn't move. Then he blinked and his whole face broke open into a laugh, and I laughed too, almost relieved. 'Sorry,' he said. 'This is weird. You're working and I just keep thinking about . . .'

I smiled. 'Me too.'

I glanced around. Nic was back at the register. There was only one table left and Emma was clearing their dessert plates. I'd barely noticed her all night.

'Cute elephant.'

'It's a present for this woman I know.' He picked up his whisky. 'But she has to finish work first.'

I looked at him for a minute longer, memorising his face, and then went back to my stock list.

◆

We went to his place after I finished. He jokingly suggested the pub but I shook my head and I could tell from the look in his eyes he was thinking the same thing I was, the thing I hadn't been able to stop thinking all day.

We barely talked. We'd talked so much for weeks and weeks, and now we did all the things we'd wanted to do when we'd been talking. Kissing, touching, laughing, curling into each other and wrapping around each other and finding each other. When we did talk it was in whispers; it was hardly talking at all.

I slept, cocooned into his chest. When I woke up he was still there, the room was bright and white, and again I wondered if I'd died and gone to heaven, and then he was there and it happened all over again.

When he went to work I walked home. The cat-piss house smelled worse than usual, but I needed clean clothes and my own toothbrush. Marnie was asleep in her room and mine was a mess, postcards strewn all over the bed, and it seemed like so long since I'd looked at them. It seemed like another person had been there, lying in that bed and reading postcards and wishing for sleep. I picked them all up, put them back in their box. For the first time since it arrived, I picked up Bali from my bedside table and read it again. Lina sounded so excited. So happy. I could almost hear her. For the first time, it made me smile.

◆

He came in that night, and the next night, and the next. I stopped counting, and the nights blended into one, broken up only by long lunch and dinner services, with Nic pestering me for details and Dex giving me strange, meaningful looks every time I went near the kitchen. I floated through them, making coffee and pouring wine and shaking martinis and waving cloths over benches.

Holly accosted me in the staffroom, asking for details, and my mouth tripped over the words when I tried to talk. 'You're so weird in a relationship, Caitie,' she said. 'All smiley.'

I laughed. 'Sorry. It'll probably wear off soon enough.' But I couldn't imagine it ever wearing off. I didn't want it to.

And Tom was there, all the time. Everywhere, all around me, all the time, all in, and I didn't want it to ever end.

18

TUESDAY, JUNE

'This is perfect,' I said. I'd been saying it a lot and I meant it every time, but I meant it the most lounging on Tom's balcony under a blanket, with his arms around me, my back against his chest, looking at the city. The remains of dinner littered a low table in front of us; cheese, meats, olives, bread, an empty bottle of wine.

We'd been together every night for the past week. The night before he'd been working so I'd gone home and done some laundry, but it had been too cold and too loud and I'd been much too pathetically grateful when he'd messaged as he was finishing his shift, offered to come over or to pick me up, and I'd suggested I meet him at his place.

This was the first night we'd both had off. He'd promised me dinner—*I don't cook, but I can cut things up*—and wine, and I couldn't remember ever being so happy.

It was perfect.

'I've been told the view is boring.' He kissed my ear.

I took a breath, ran a hand along his leg. I couldn't stop touching him. I couldn't remember ever having touched anyone this much, ever having wanted to. My fingers sought him out constantly. So warm. So everything. 'It's not that bad.'

'I don't know. Maybe we could find a better one.'

The words spun me around, until I was facing him. I wasn't sure what they meant, but when he kissed me it was different, deeper. I felt it everywhere. Felt so much.

'Was Lina okay?' he asked, pulling away, as I tried to catch my breath.

It took me a second. 'Yeah.'

'Did you tell her I was sorry for mucking up her dinner plans?'

I looked down at our legs, wound together.

'She's fine.'

'How's the wedding planning?' He brushed a curl of hair behind my ear, so gently.

'Good. She's taking me to see her final two dresses on Thursday.'

'She's down to two?'

'Yeah, she's going to race them.'

He laughed. I didn't want to think about Lina, about the wedding, about how he'd asked if I had to cancel dinner with her and instead of telling him the truth I'd lied and said I did. It made me feel sick, but it was done. Group was done. I hadn't thought about dying once since that night and I didn't need it anymore.

His words hung in the air. I couldn't stop hearing them. Everything felt so big, so real.

A thought slid into my head, an idea. I felt giddy, much too drunk given I'd only had two glasses of wine. 'You are right, though. About the view.' I took a breath, hesitated. 'Maybe after Bali, we could go find another one.'

He looked surprised. 'Really?'

I shrugged, tried to. My face felt warm. 'I don't know. Maybe.' I shifted until I was almost on top of him, tilting my face up at his, felt that familiar ache as I looked at him, never wanted to stop looking at him. 'I know you want to travel. Maybe we can go together.'

I tried to keep my voice calm, but I could feel it shake. I hoped he hadn't noticed how much. I felt his hands tighten on my back, run down my spine to my waist. The blanket had fallen and he pulled it back up over my shoulders, tugged me closer. I felt so warm, so safe, like I could do anything. Say anything. Giddy, drunk, floating. Flying. I closed my eyes, giving into it.

'We could just get round-the-world tickets. Jump on a plane whenever we feel like it.'

'I don't think that's how round-the-world tickets work, Caitie.' His voice was low, thick.

I opened my eyes, tried for a laugh. 'Humour me.'

'Do you really want to?'

I nodded. 'If you do.'

He exhaled, pulling me closer. 'I do.'

Giddy.

Flying.

'So where should we start?'

'How about . . .' He tipped his head back, thinking. 'Norway.'

I laughed. 'Birthplace of both the paperclip and the cheese slicer.'

'Really?'

'So the rumours suggest.'

'Those clever Norwegians,' he whispered.

I pulled myself up over him. Kissed him gently. His eyes caught mine and for a moment I couldn't breathe. 'Where next?'

'Denmark? It's almost next door.'

'Did you know . . .' I swallowed. 'There are more than four hundred islands in Denmark?'

Something flickered across his face, his hands tightening around my waist. 'I didn't.' That same voice, barely there, lighting something inside me.

I kissed him again. I wanted to kiss him forever. Over and over. The kiss deepened, turned into something more, and I lost my breath. When I raised my head, he looked like he had too.

'Where then?' I asked. My voice was barely my voice. Cracking.

'Amsterdam?'

I nodded. 'Of course.' I dropped my head again, my mouth an inch from his. 'We have to see all eight drawbridges.' He grinned, so wide I felt it all the way through to my bones, and when I kissed him this time I didn't stop.

19

Thursday, June

Lina was wearing eggshell, the attendant—Marla, maybe?—told me. I'd mistakenly called it cream and she'd corrected me without taking her eyes off Lina's chest and the half-a-dozen pins she'd inserted into the bodice.

I didn't know what I'd expected. Lina had been eyeing off wedding dresses since we were kids but nothing this lacy, this covered in beading, this . . . much. She looked beautiful in it, even with her hair up in a ponytail and another elastic band on her wrist. It felt like the first time I'd been able to look right at her in years.

'So,' she said, when Marla went to get more tape, 'tell me about this guy.'

I sat back on the oversized velvet ottoman I'd claimed as we'd come in, the smaller sibling of the one Lina was standing on. *So you can see how it finishes*, Marla had said, but I didn't understand how standing on an ottoman was different from standing on the floor, except that it made Lina look like she was hovering, a ghost of weddings future.

'Well, his name is Tom.'

She rolled her eyes. 'You told me that already. This morning. I can't believe you've been seeing this guy for over a week and you only told me about him this morning.' But her voice skittered, like she could more than believe it, like she was surprised I'd told her at all.

She looked in the mirror. 'Do my boobs look funny?'

I shook my head. 'They look good.'

'The other one made them look bigger.'

'They look better in this one,' I reassured her. 'The other one looked too small.'

'Tom,' she said, testing it out.

I nodded.

'It's very plain.' She moved around to another part of the ottoman, looking in another mirror. 'But I am marrying a Matt, I suppose . . .'

'He's a doctor. He's thirty, lives in Pyrmont.'

She raised an eyebrow, hitched her shoulders up and tried to look over them at her back. 'Really?'

'Really,' I said, glancing at my phone. Ten thirty. I had to be at work at twelve.

'And how did you meet him?'

'He comes into Sawyer's a lot.' I shrugged. 'We got talking.'

'And you like him?' She lifted her arm, put it down, then straightened and squinted at her reflection.

I nodded, not sure how to answer, gestured to her shoulder. 'Pull it up under there.'

'Damn,' she sighed, disappointed. 'It's going to move too much.'

'It'll be fine. That's what the tape is for.'

'Honestly—' she stepped off the ottoman and the dress rumpled at the bottom '—this is supposed to be romantic. At this point Matt's going to need scissors and eucalyptus oil to get me out of it at the end of the night.'

I laughed. 'He could just rip it off.'

She snorted. 'And take my skin with it.'

'That sounds hot.' I leaned back against the wall, watched her rummage in her bag. When she bent over her boobs wobbled and for a second I worried they'd fall out.

'Well, that too. Bali is stinking in November. Maybe a short one would be better.'

'You used to want a short one,' I said.

'Yeah, I remember.'

She pulled out her lipstick, put it on in the mirror.

'That's better.' She grinned, her lips bright red. 'The eggshell was washing me out.'

'It's the light.'

'I can't wear a short dress.' She sighed. 'I can't make everyone come all the way to Bali and then wear a party dress.'

'Of course you can, Leen.'

'You could,' she said, more to her reflection than to me. 'I can't.'

Lina turned, the dress following a fraction too slowly, and stepped back onto the magical ottoman.

'So when do I get to meet this fabulous doctor?'

'Soon,' I said, the thought making me shiver. I wanted her to meet him, but first I had to tell him that there were no Tuesday dinners, or I had to leave it long enough that it wouldn't matter anymore. Maybe until November. 'He's coming to the wedding.'

I didn't mention the rest. Couldn't. Still, something flashed across her face. 'He is?'

I frowned. 'I'm assuming I get a plus one?'

'Of course,' but she sounded wary. 'If you want one.'

'Well, I do.'

She hesitated. 'Cait.'

'Yeah?'

She looked at me for a minute, then shook her head. 'Nothing.'

'No.' I sat forward. 'Tell me.'

'I just—'

The door swung open and Marla came back in with a handful of tape strips. She climbed onto her stool by the ottoman and started working at Lina's chest.

'What?'

'Just . . . ow.'

'Sorry, love.'

'You've only been seeing him a week.'

I blinked. Ten fifty. 'Higher on the right,' I said. Marla glanced at me, pulled at the dress. 'No, *her* right.'

Lina grimaced, lifted her arms.

'I've known him for a lot longer. Months.'

'I know, but . . .' She exhaled, with her whole body, and her boobs sank into the dress.

'I'll get the shoes.' Marla stepped off the stool and walked out of the room again.

'You're just moving really fast,' Lina said, stepping down and sitting on the ottoman. The dress imploded around her.

'Am I?'

I was. Even I knew that. I spent every single night at his apartment and he messaged me on every single break.

She paused. 'Does he know?'

'About what?' I asked.

'Cait.'

'You need jewellery,' I said suddenly, trying to change the subject. 'Something up around—'

'*Caitlin.*'

I straightened. 'Maybe a cuff? They can look sort of weird but if you—'

'Stop.' She closed her eyes, took a breath. 'I'm worried about you.'

'Leen.' I looked away. 'You don't have to worry. I'm fine.'

'I don't want you to get hurt.'

I shook my head. 'Tom's not going to hurt me.'

'Neither was Dex.'

She said it kindly, almost too softly, but it felt like a slap, and I stared at her for a long time, then sat back, checking the time again. Eleven. I had to go soon.

'Tom isn't anything like Dex,' I said, my voice echoing in my head.

'No, Cait.' She stood up. 'You. You're the same. I just want you to be careful, Caitie.'

Careful. The word stung.

'There we go,' Marla said, pushing the door open and holding a pair of four-inch heels. 'Not the real ones, obviously, but they'll give you an idea.'

'I'm always careful, Leen,' I said. 'Too careful, remember?'

Lina lifted up her dress and Marla kneeled in front of her with the shoes.

'I know,' she said softly.

'I am. This isn't like Dex.' I felt bruised. Tired. I wanted to go. 'This is different, Leen. Tom is different.'

Lina frowned, wobbling onto the heels. 'I know. It's just . . . I don't want you to get hurt again.'

I bit my lip, shaking away a flash of uncertainty. *Too much.* Why was she doing this? All our lives she'd told me I was too careful, played it too safe, and now this. 'I won't.' It was hard, and she looked at me for a moment, her face unreadable, before shaking her head.

'I know.' She smiled. 'I'm sorry.'

Marla rocked back onto her toes, fanning out the dress as she did so. 'There we go,' she said, before standing up and moving back to the wall, disappearing into it. I wondered if she'd deliberately dressed in the same colour as the curtains.

Lina looked in the mirror. 'Holy shit.'

'What's wrong?' Marla frowned.

Lina shook her head, looked at me, her eyes pleading. 'What do you think?' It was soft and thick and I could hear the wanting in it. I looked at her, our conversation forgotten, fading into the curtains.

She looked beautiful. The schoolgirl had disappeared and she looked like a bride. Not like Lina at all, but beautiful. My breath caught.

'I love it,' I said, grateful for the diversion, but it wasn't a lie.

'Okay.' She looked at Marla. 'Okay. Can I have a minute?'

Marla smiled, looked at both of us. 'Of course. I'll be back.'

The door closed, and Lina turned again. 'Holy hell, Cait. I'm getting married, aren't I?'

I frowned. 'Well . . . you'd hope so.'

'No, no, I mean—I'm getting fucking married.' She took a deep breath. 'I've been running around like a headless chicken since we got engaged but it's all been about the wedding and this is . . .' She looked at me. 'It's real, isn't it?'

I was still for a long time, not sure how to respond. 'It is, Leen.'

'I'm so glad you're here, Caitie,' she said, her voice almost a whisper. 'I'm so, so glad.'

'Me too.'

I looked up. Her eyes were damp, and I realised that for the first time I meant it.

♦

Lina bought the dress. She told me I could wear anything I wanted as her bridesmaid and before we left I looked at a whole wall of fluffy shiny silky things and none of them looked right. I held a dark green slip dress up against me and Lina sucked in her cheek and frowned.

'What?'

'You're so . . .' She shook her head. 'I always forget how skinny you are.' And the way she said it made me put the dress back, embarrassed.

Later, before work, I looked at myself in the mirror for a long time as I got dressed. I smoothed down my work shirt and tried not to think about the ridges of my ribs. I was sleeping now, eating now. Things had been rough for a little while there but they were better now. There was nothing wrong with me, nothing wrong with my body. I thought of how Tom told me I was beautiful, how he kissed his way down my stomach sometimes, and I shivered. He was a doctor and he didn't think there was anything wrong. I was fine.

August, Once

'Caitie!' Lina flung her arms around me, her smile wide, eyes glassy. 'You made it.'

I hugged her back. She felt unexpectedly fragile. 'Of course,' I said, letting go. 'I said I would.'

'I know, but I haven't seen you in ages!'

'We had coffee last week.'

She laughed. She was drunk, I could tell. 'For all of fifteen minutes. You're so busy and important. How did your presentation go? Did they love you?'

It took me a moment to remember what she was talking about. There hadn't been a presentation, but coffee had been awkward so I'd made something up. 'Obviously,' I said, forcing a smile. 'It went well. Sorry I had to run off. Annaliese is in total boss mode at the moment.'

Annaliese was anything but. She'd just taken a week off to go to a health retreat near Byron and the other day she'd left a New York City guide on my desk, wrapped in a piece of gold ribbon with a bow.

Lina made a face. 'God, I know the feeling.' She curled her hands around my arm, started leading me through the crowded bar to the courtyard. 'I'm glad it went well, though. I knew it would. You're my smartest friend.'

I rolled my eyes. 'Right, Leen.'

We stepped out of the bar and into an equally packed courtyard, loud and smoky. So smoky. Eight weeks. The cravings were supposed to be easing off but they were just getting worse. We passed a guy holding a cigarette and a bottle of beer and my eyes stuck. He wasn't my type at all—longish hair, old band t-shirt, probably a tradie, from the roughness of his hands—but when he lifted the cigarette to his mouth and took a drag it was the sexiest thing I'd ever seen and it was only Lina still holding on to my arm and leading me to the back of the courtyard that stopped me from walking over and grabbing him. I was almost grateful when he disappeared, and I dropped my gaze to the pavers, deciding that was safer. 'I need a drink.'

'They're doing retro cocktails. I have a jug of illusions.'

I grimaced. 'Really?'

'Tastes like being fourteen again.' Lina laughed. 'I can't believe Matt's turning *thirty*. I can't believe I'm dating a thirty-year-old.'

I hadn't seen her so drunk in months.

'I can't believe I bought a fucking house with a fucking thirty-year-old.' She laughed again. 'I own a fucking house, Cait. Can you believe that?'

I laughed too. 'Townhouse, remember?'

'God. That's even worse!'

We reached the back of the courtyard and a long table scattered with drinks and crushed cigarette packets and the remnants of several bowls of chips. Lina let go of my arm and slid into a seat. She pulled an empty glass out of a small stack in the middle of the table, placed it next to another one and filled them both with something green and toxic-looking. 'Here,' she said, handing me the fresh one. 'You've got to catch up.'

I took it, studying the contents.

'How come you're so late anyway?'

I shrugged. 'One of those days, that's all.'

She raised an eyebrow, then her glass. 'Cheers, big ears.' I touched my glass to hers, then took a sip. Toxic was right. 'I was worried you weren't coming.'

'Of course I was coming. It's Matt's birthday.' I nearly hadn't. I'd taken ages to get ready—everything had been weirdly slow. 'Where is he, anyway?'

She glanced around, unconcerned. 'Dancing. I don't know.'

I looked at her. I could tell her now. She was drunk enough that she wouldn't care, might not even remember tomorrow. I'd woken up in the morning and decided I had to tell her tonight. It had been three weeks of coffees cut short and phone calls full of awkward silences as the words caught in my throat. I had to tell her.

I didn't know why I hadn't yet. She probably wouldn't care. She had Matt, a house, a whole world I couldn't keep up with. She wouldn't care.

For some reason, though, the thought made me nauseous. I didn't want to ruin her night, didn't want to upset her. But if she didn't care at all, then . . .

I put the drink to my lips, downed half of it in one go.

'There we go,' Lina said.

I'm going to New York. I bought a ticket.

That simple. She was drunk, it wouldn't matter. She wouldn't care. She'd be excited for me, like I was excited.

I was excited.

When I thought about it my insides got all hot and I wanted to tell everyone, yell it from rooftops and start planning, properly, but I hadn't told anyone yet. Just in case.

I finished my drink, put the glass down with a flourish. Lina grinned, pleased, picked up the jug and refilled it.

'Come on,' she said, raising her glass with one hand and passing me mine with the other. 'Let's go dance.'

I thought about stopping her. But only for a second. Instead, I stood and followed her inside.

◆

I didn't know how long we danced. We had another drink, and another and another. Too many, too fast. Whenever I looked at Lina, she looked like she was winning and she *was* winning. She was happy and laughing and she looked like she'd never had a single bad thing happen to her, like she'd never collapsed onto me in tears, told me she couldn't stand being at home and begged me to get her out, get her away, as far away as possible.

We ended up back at the table, Lina and me and Matt and a few of his friends who looked like accountants, with neat haircuts and rolled-up shirtsleeves and slightly oversized jaws, everyone talking over the top of each other, yelling to be heard. It hurt my ears, gave me a headache.

'And the kitchen!' Lina's voice pulled me back. She was talking about the house. Again. 'The kitchen. I love the kitchen. Dinner at our place every Sunday. I'll roast something. Two things! The oven is huge—I can do a turkey and a chicken at once.'

I looked at my glass. Empty. The jug of toxic green liquid was gone too, probably a long time ago.

'I can't believe you're still not smoking, Cait,' she said, nudging my arm. 'I'm so proud of you.'

I smiled, awkward.

'Those things will kill you,' Matt said, too seriously.

'Well, something has to.' I laughed, feeling something strange at the back of my neck, cold. 'It may as well be something I love.'

'It stinks too.'

'Yeah,' Lina said. 'I've never wanted to say anything, but . . .'

'Okay.' I made a face. 'Point made. I've quit anyway. My lung capacity has increased twelve per cent and I'm already ninety-two per cent less likely to get lung cancer, after only eight weeks!' I was pulling numbers out of the air.

Lina gave me a smile.

'Besides,' I said, 'you're one to talk. You're the one who got me smoking in the first place.'

Matt looked at her. 'Really?'

'I've told you this.' Lina rolled her eyes until they settled on me, irritated. 'I smoked for about ten minutes in high school. It was gross but I knew it would annoy my mum.'

And she smoked every time the two of us got drunk together and he wasn't around, I thought, but I didn't say. I just smiled at her.

'I didn't even smoke, really,' she explained. 'It was disgusting. I just left lighters and empty packets in the pockets of my school bag so she'd find them.'

Matt smiled tightly.

'It's true,' I added. 'She bought them and gave them to me. I'd put her jumper on and smoke them. They made her green out.'

Matt's eyes flickered between the two of us. 'I can't decide if that's cute or fucked up.'

'Both, probably.' I shrugged. Jenny hadn't cared about Lina smoking. She'd pretended to, given her the lecture about lung cancer and some relative of theirs dying of emphysema, but it had sounded rehearsed, like she was reading from a pamphlet. And she had her own secrets. I saw her from my window sometimes, late at night, down the end of their backyard, a tiny orange glow moving up and down, a shadow of smoke. 'It was my idea.'

Lina caught my eye again, grateful this time. Through all the alcohol, I felt a trickle of guilt down my spine, sobering me up.

Matt stood. 'Another?' he asked us.

Lina nodded, but I found myself shaking my head. 'I'm good,' I said. I glanced at her. 'I think I'm going to head off.'

'But you just got here.' She pouted.

'I've been here for hours, Leen.' It felt like days. 'I've just got a headache.'

Matt shrugged, turned his attention to his accountant friends.

'I'll walk you out,' Lina said, sliding out of her seat. I thought of telling her no but I knew she'd do it anyway. I let her curl her arm through mine as we stood up, walk me through the pub as I booked an Uber on my phone. 'Are you sure you're all right?'

I nodded. 'Just a bit tired.'

'Are *we* all right?' she asked out of nowhere as we stepped onto the street. I looked down at my phone. My ride was two minutes away.

I frowned, like I wasn't sure what she was asking. Too sober. 'Of course.'

'We'll do a shorter trip soon,' she said, squeezing my hand. 'I promise.'

'It's fine, Leen. It might not be the best time to go to the States anyway.' I didn't know why I was lying. I needed to tell her. I could just tell her. She wouldn't care. February fifteenth. The day after Valentine's Day. The date we'd talked about.

'Can we still do the postcards? I love the postcards.'

'Leen . . .'

'Yeah?'

My phone vibrated. One minute. But I could tell her. I could cancel the Uber, wear the fee, tell her.

'You okay?'

'I'm good.' I decided. Not now. I would tell her, but not now. 'Of course we'll still do the postcards. I love them too.'

'I can't believe you still haven't had a cigarette.'

'Me either.'

A red SUV pulled up on the other side of the road, and she eyed it off. 'This you?'

I nodded, and she pulled me into a hug.

'Coffee Monday?'

'Always.'

'It's such a pity you don't date baristas. I swear Gus fancies you. He likes the pink hair.'

I laughed as she let me go.

'Bye, Cait.'

'Bye, Leen.'

And I turned and crossed the street.

20

TUESDAY, JULY

We were moving really fast. I kept expecting it to slow down, but it didn't. If anything, it sped up. Questions became assumptions became routine, in the best possible way. We worked, we went home together and slept wrapped up in each other, woke up and did it all again. Over and over.

'Humour me,' I asked, over and over, late at night. And every time he grinned, and I saw that dimple, so perfect it made me whimper, and his eyes twinkled and he did. London, Paris, Santiago, Montenegro. I stopped asking, and he kept doing it, grinning, eyes twinkling, and it felt less and less like humouring me and more and more like something real, something I could almost touch. A plan. Ridiculous, maybe, and much too fast, but real. Guatemala, Sri Lanka, Rome, Athens.

Lina and I had booked our tickets to Bali and Tom was just waiting for his leave to be formally approved before he booked his. Lina had a dress, she had a cake, flowers. She'd even written her vows.

It was the coldest winter in a few years but I barely felt it, lost track of the days. I was warm all the time, safe all the time. I didn't walk anywhere, except to and from the cat-piss house some mornings to switch over my clothes. Every time I did there was a different empty wine bottle on the kitchen bench and it was the only way I knew anybody lived there at all.

The sun came out every day, and it was cold but it was a nice cold, invigorating, refreshing, and then Tom was there and he warmed me up from the inside out, over and over again.

◆

'Caitie.'

I was dreaming and I didn't want to wake up. Cobblestones. We'd been talking about cobblestones, and I'd dreamed about them. Walking along them, down alleyways and around corners, stopping every now and then to kiss.

'Caitlin.'

His voice was soft. His breath on my neck. Barely there. But everywhere.

I rolled towards it.

'I have to go, okay?'

Still dreaming. Sighing. A mouth on mine.

'I'll call you later on.'

I said something. Maybe. Cobblestones. Bright white sheets. Warmth. Little words, murmured. More kissing and more words and then I was asleep again.

When I woke it was midday. I rolled over and pushed my face into Tom's pillow, inhaling deeply. It smelled like him and I could have suffocated on that smell, happily.

I got up, went to the bathroom. The sun was streaming through the windows and I felt warm, even though it was winter, even though

Tom wasn't there and it was too quiet. It was the first time I'd been in the apartment without him, but I could feel him, everywhere.

The kitchen was pristine, all white and light grey and shiny, a small stack of cookbooks on a shelf over the bench. A half-full plunger of black coffee sat on the benchtop, ice-cold but I found a mug and poured it out anyway, adding more sugar than it needed.

I found my bag and my tobacco and went out onto the balcony. The view was so amazing it churned my stomach. The whole city was spread out, a postcard but not a postcard.

Prague. We'd been talking about Prague. That's why I'd dreamed of cobblestones.

Home of the oldest university in Central Europe, I'd said. He'd laughed, like he always did, pulled me closer, and then I'd dreamed of cobblestones.

I perched on the edge of the lounge and rolled a cigarette, smoking it and sipping my cold coffee and feeling the air moving in and out of my lungs. The whole day stretched out in front of me, the evening. Tom would finish at eight, maybe later, and I'd see him then, but that was hours away.

I finished the coffee and went inside, rinsing my cup and setting it by the sink before wandering back into the bedroom, the bathroom, showering. I felt like I was floating, my limbs soft, completely at home.

I found my phone, sent him a message. *You didn't wake me. I'm trapped in your apartment.*

I tried, but you wouldn't move. There's a set of keys on the bench by the door. Use them when you need to go.

Okay. I can leave them in the letterbox.

Keep them. Another message. *They're for you anyway.*

I felt something leap in my chest. Without thinking, I dialled his number. He picked up on the first ring.

'I'm on a break,' he said. 'You've got three minutes.'

'You're giving me your keys?'

I heard him laugh. 'Is that what you're calling to ask?'

'Yes.'

'Caitlin.' His voice was so kind. I smiled, wished he was here.

'So are you?'

'Maybe.'

'Maybe?'

He laughed again. 'Yeah, maybe.' He paused. 'How are you?'

'Good. I miss you,' I said, looking around, at the pictures on the wall. I'd seen them all dozens of times but now I studied them. A wall of photographs, of musicians on a stage under pink lights and pristine beaches and over-saturated sunsets and rainbow-coloured graffiti, of the Paris skyline. Framed postcards from Rio and San Francisco and Iceland that had made my breath catch the first time I saw them and still did. 'I've used up all your hot water and finished off your coffee and now I'm going to eat some of your food and watch your television and then I'll go, okay?'

'You don't have to go.'

I headed across to the bookcase, past two guitars on stands—one acoustic and one electric, black and white and shiny, but obviously well used. I wanted to crawl inside his brain, live in it and see all this through his eyes.

'I don't?'

I loved the bookcase, overstuffed with piles of books in no order; ancient sci-fi paperbacks that I knew he'd started reading as a kid in between more recent bestsellers and serious, heavy classics; Shakespeare and Umberto Eco and Stephen King and Isaac Asimov and Roald Dahl and Kurt Vonnegut and Nick Hornby. A pile of comics and choose-your-own-adventure books and then Jane Austen and Tom Stoppard and a small cluster of poetry anthologies and Bill Bryson and Hunter S. Thompson and books about maths and the universe and television shows, a stack of science magazines.

'Of course you don't. I'll be home after eight. Use up as much hot water as you like. I think you'll find it doesn't run out.'

I smiled.

'Unless you've got things to do. Or you can go and come back. You've got keys.'

Again I wished he was there, so much. 'Are you sure you trust me here, all by myself?'

'I trust you, Cait.' I heard him move, a chair leg scrape on lino. 'I have to get back to it, though. I'll see you later?'

I touched an atlas at the end of one shelf. Thick and well worn, the kind of atlas he would have been given as a child and never looked at anymore but would never throw away. Or maybe I was making that up.

'I'll be here.'

'I'm glad.' He hesitated. 'Bye, Caitlin.'

'Bye, Tom.'

I stepped past the bookshelf to the sideboard, and a row of happy snaps—family shots, mostly, and a couple where I picked a much-younger version of him out of a crowd of schoolkids. Smiling. Relaxed. Alive. So alive, in every shot. Tom in a graduation gown between two people I assumed were his parents, grinning with pride. They looked—perfect. Like he'd picked them from a catalogue, like the family in a car commercial. I'd teased him about it, more than once. One with his dad, right near the front.

At the end, under a small bowl full of change, was a single photo frame, lying face down, that I'd never noticed before. I moved the coins and picked it up. It was a shot of Tom with his arm around the waist of a woman in a green dress, a string of pearls around her neck. Sophie. She was nearly as tall as he was, with long naturally blonde hair curling over her shoulder, every strand in place, everything about her . . . in place. Perfect. Smart, funny, gorgeous. A perfect girlfriend smile, her perfect body arched perfectly into his. He was smiling too, wide and careless.

It was dusk, the light giving everything a golden glow, and they were leaning against a brick wall that came to his elbow. Just over her shoulder I could see the unmistakeable outline of the Empire State Building in the background.

A hard, painful lump formed in my throat and when I tried to swallow it down it doubled in size. I put my fingertip on the glass, touched her face. It felt warm and I was cold and when I pulled back I'd left a smudge.

Fiji. The States for a wedding. Tokyo for a week.

I hadn't asked where in the States.

We never talked about New York. When we talked about places to go, he mentioned South America or Europe or remote parts of Asia. Not the States.

Not New York, because he'd already been there.

I felt the air go out of the room suddenly, and I couldn't breathe. I put the photo back, bowl of coins on top, went back outside and rolled myself another cigarette, touching the filter to my lips twice, tapping on the end when I was finished, smoked it, then another. And another, so fast my head spun. The balcony railing seemed suddenly too low, too flimsy.

He'd told me, he just hadn't told me everything—didn't know there was anything to tell, had no reason to think it mattered— but still, anger and hurt sparked deep in my gut. The sky was blue but the city looked cold and alien and flat.

Dead.

I closed my eyes. *Humour me.* That's all he'd been doing. The grin, the dimple, the twinkle. He'd done it all before with someone else—someone smart, funny, gorgeous. I'd thought it was more, but for him it was nothing. He was just humouring me, like I'd asked him to.

A fist. A blade. A blood vessel, rupturing. I tried to shake it, but it wouldn't go.

I felt dizzy, grabbed on to the door to stop myself falling off the balcony, used it to pull myself inside. It was cold, too cold, I could feel it all the way into my bones. Like cancer.

I took a breath. Another. Something flared inside me. Fear. Worse than fear.

I picked up my phone, dialling his number, waiting for his voice-mail greeting.

'Hey,' I said, staring at the postcards on the wall, not sure what I was doing. They made my chest ache, my stomach churn. So many places, none of them real. Just pictures. Just postcards. 'Lina's having a wedding crisis and she really wants to do our Tuesday dinner, so I said I would.'

I tasted bile. Guilt. The lie came so easily.

'We're meeting in Petersham so I'll just go home after and see you after work tomorrow.'

One word after another. I barely recognised my voice—steady, strong, normal. What was wrong with me? Something had to be wrong with me.

'I'll call you later though, okay?'

I blinked, felt a tear at the corner of my eye.

'Bye, Tom.'

Blinked again as I hung up. The tear fell and I wiped it away, shook my head, took a long breath.

'Come on, Cait,' I said softly, pacing the length of the room. 'Get it together.'

I kept pacing and pacing, not sure what to do, but knowing I had to do something.

It came to me suddenly, formed whole. I found my bag, the keys on the bench, and let myself out, forcing myself to keep breathing, keep going, until I was out on the street, heading into the city.

I had to be careful. I'd been careless, and somehow, I'd made it this far. I'd been lucky. But I had to be careful. Just in case.

◆

'I'm old,' Beryl said. 'I know I am. I can see all of you getting ready to tell me I'm not but I know I am.'

I'd been early. Ridiculously early. Even after walking until my feet ached, I'd had to sit on the bench outside for what felt like hours, waiting for Abraham to show up. I assumed it would be Abraham, although it had been a month, so it could have been anyone. I'd been the first one in the room, helped him set up the seats, picked one as far away from him as possible. He didn't ask how I was, where I'd been. He didn't seem to care.

Donna had smiled when she saw me. *Welcome back*, she'd said, sliding onto the seat next to mine. Her hair was freshly bleached, almost glowing, loose over her shoulders. It made me itch, touch my own, make sure it was safely tucked away at the back of my head. *We were wondering where you'd got to.*

I've been busy, I'd replied, shrugging. I'd been careless. I'd forgotten what happened last time and I'd been careless. *Work.*

I didn't know why I lied, but it seemed easier than explaining.

'I've lived a good long life,' Beryl went on. 'I have kids and grandkids and I outlived my first husband—who was a right bastard and it's not nice to say it but I was a little bit glad when I heard that he'd gone under that truck. It would have been nice if he'd suffered more, maybe, but I was just glad he was gone.'

Geoff had touched me on the shoulder and told me I looked good. I hadn't said anything. I didn't feel like I looked good. My throat hurt from all the cigarettes I'd smoked and the Thoughts were rattling me. So many, so suddenly, and I didn't understand why. It was just a picture. It didn't mean anything. He wasn't with her. He was with me, and he wanted to go travelling with me—he grinned, his eyes twinkled. He wanted to. It didn't change anything we'd talked about. If I asked him, he'd go to New York. 'I've been once,' he'd say, 'but we should go again.' It would be fine.

But still, I'd left, and now I was here.

I pushed my hands into my hoodie, trying to imagine being as old as Beryl, being married twice, once to a violent arsehole and then to the love of her life, who died of bowel cancer at fifty-five, having all those kids and grandkids and just marking off the days, wondering how many were left. I wondered if it got boring, being around that long, seeing the world spin around the sun that many times. I wondered if anything surprised her anymore.

'I get these headaches,' she went on. 'Real blinders. Last week I forgot my daughter's name. The doctor says that's not dementia on its own, but he's just trying to make me feel better, isn't he? That's how it starts. I've seen it. One minute they're calling their son by their husband's name and the next they've forgotten how to swallow food and the nurses just shake their heads sadly and wait for them to starve to death.'

She looked exhausted, like the years were catching up with her, weighing her down. It made my chest hurt.

'Oh, hon,' Fran said. 'It won't happen like that, I promise.' She didn't sound so sure.

'Absolutely not,' Donna added, equally hesitant. 'I was reading up about dementia. You're much too active. Plus, you do those crosswords. They say that's the key.'

Tom had called. Twice. I'd let it go to voicemail and hadn't listened to the messages. I didn't know if I could stand to.

'Thanks, girls,' Beryl said. She looked at them, and then at me, smiled. 'You're all so kind. That's why I come here.'

I gave her a small smile back, then looked down at the floor. Beige, but the same as it had ever been. Solid. Safe. I pressed my lips together. Everything was going to be okay. I'd been careless, that was all. Everything would be fine. I took a breath, inhaled the positive thoughts, like I'd read in some bad magazine. Exhaled the darker ones I'd been fighting all day. One by one, I pushed them out into the beige room, watched them float away.

Everything would be fine. It had to be. I just had to be careful.

21

WEDNESDAY, JULY

It was busy and Holly was off sick, so the floor was short-staffed and Nic couldn't help me, but it was exactly what I needed. I'd been careless. I'd been showing up and doing the work but I'd been distracted. Nic knew it and I knew it and he hadn't seemed to care but I knew he did. Now, whenever he glanced in my direction it was different, satisfied, impressed, and at some point I stopped seeing Tom and Sophie dancing on the Brooklyn Bridge.

By the time Tom arrived, I was exhausted. My legs ached and my shoulders were sore. I'd walked for hours after group, taken the long way home, and while I'd slept it hadn't been the same. The smell of cat piss and the noise of King Street had kept jolting me awake. I couldn't remember dreaming, but I woke up feeling like I had, a residual unease that it had taken me the entire lunch shift to shake.

'Hey,' he said, sliding into his usual seat.

I forced myself to look at him, to smile. God, he was beautiful, and he looked at me like nothing was wrong, like everything was fine, like *I* was fine. My smile turned real.

I reached for a glass automatically. 'Hi,' I said, leaning over and giving him a quick kiss. I'd missed his smell. Missed his warmth. It had only been a day and a half but it felt like so much longer. 'The usual?'

'Of course.'

I turned and got the Glenmorangie, poured some into his glass.

'I missed you last night.'

I bit my lip, eyeing the pour.

'Did you get my message?'

I nodded, putting the whisky back, making sure the label faced the right way. I glanced at him and smiled, then touched the bottle again, and the one next to it, made sure they were lined up perfectly, their labels exactly right. 'I'm sorry. I didn't hear my phone and by the time I noticed it was really late. I figured you were probably asleep.'

I poured some water into a glass, floated it on top of the whisky. Focusing. Careful. Absolutely perfect, I thought, straightening and pushing the glass towards him.

'You could have woken me.'

I looked up. He was smiling and it made me smile. I didn't want to admit it but I'd been nervous about seeing him, and now I could hardly remember why.

'I know,' I said, putting a hand out and touching his. 'But I feel like I'm always waking you.'

'I like it.' His fingers tucked around mine, and he squeezed. 'How was Lina? Everything okay?'

I nodded. 'Fine,' I said. I looked past him at the dining room. All under control. Quietening down. Back at my docket machine. Empty. I'd started a stock list, and I'd already cleaned the fridges. All okay. Everything was fine. I let go of his hand and began straightening up the napkins and the cutlery at the end of the bar, lining up the spare salt and pepper shakers, the pile of menus. 'She's just stressing about the wedding, I think.'

'Weddings do that.'

'I know. And she stresses about things at the best of times.' I frowned, spotting an oily fingerprint on the top menu. I grabbed a cloth and wiped at it until it disappeared. 'Something about the flowers and Matt's allergies, I think.'

He laughed.

'I don't know.' I shrugged. 'It's all fine though, I think.'

Again, I hated how easily the lies came. He was looking at me the same way he always did, his face open and warm and happy and I wanted to be the person he thought I was. So much. I pushed down a burst of guilt, of fear, let myself look at his eyes, lose myself in them.

'That's good,' he said, sipping his whisky. 'You sounded worried, in your message.'

'I was a bit. But everything's fine.'

Nic walked past with a fistful of empties, clearing his throat. I glanced at the docket machine—still empty.

'I think I might need to keep my Tuesday nights free for a while, though,' I said, looking down. The corner of the mat had rolled up, creating a trip hazard, and I kicked it flat, ran my shoe over the edge. I had to be careful. 'If that's all right.'

I didn't have to do anything drastic, nothing extreme; I just had to be a little bit more careful.

'Of course it is.' I could hear the light in his voice. 'I've probably been hogging you a bit this past month.'

I smiled, picking up the cloth again and wiping the bench. It was fine. Everything was fine. 'I've been letting you.'

'I know, but it's only fair I let other people have you for a bit.'

'What's that?' Nic asked, suddenly next to me, eyes wide with excitement. 'Does that mean she's coming drinking with us tonight?'

'No,' Tom and I said at the same time. I looked at him, suddenly overwhelmed, my heart ready to burst. 'Not tonight,' he went on, holding my gaze. 'I've missed her too much.'

'Gross,' Nic said. 'Caitlin, are you going to let yourself be controlled like that?'

I shrugged. 'He's missed me, what can I do?'

'Well, you could stock this bar, for a start.'

Tom laughed.

'I'm all over it,' I said, pushing off the bar and giving Tom one more look. 'I'll be back.'

'I'll be waiting.'

I grinned. Everything was fine. Everything was perfect.

He waited until I finished like he always did, and we walked down the hill to his apartment holding hands and talking about nothing and everything and when our eyes met it made my heart hurt, but in all the best ways, like it always did.

The picture was still there, but I could convince myself that it was just a picture, ancient history, barely real. Tom was real. He was real and he was with me, looked at me like I sparkled, said my name in that way that made me tremble, and it was all I needed.

◆

I woke up suddenly, gasping for air, not sure why, not sure where I was.

My chest hurt, like I'd just run a marathon. I couldn't remember dreaming but I must have been dreaming, and it was so dark I couldn't see.

'Hey.' Familiar. Safe. A hand touched my shoulder—cool, because I was hot. Soft. Perfect. Tom.

'Hey,' I whispered, finding my breath. I rolled into him, felt my heart hammering in the confined space, the only thing I could hear.

'You okay?' His voice was sleepy, far away.
'Yeah.' I exhaled. 'Just weird dreams.'
So bloody quiet.
'Good,' he mumbled. 'Go back to sleep.'
I closed my eyes.
It was already gone, if it had ever been there at all.
Okay, I thought, as I drifted off. Everything was okay. Better.
Everything was perfect. I just had to be careful.

22

Tuesday, July

I went back again. Forced myself to be careful, to keep going. Tom didn't seem to mind, told me to have fun and say hi to Lina. A part of me wondered if he was relieved.

Frannie was talking about her son's birthday. She'd planned something huge, with themed food and a jumping castle and a face painter, and her words tumbled out of her mouth, one on top of another, in waves, and in between they'd run out and she'd stop and look around and it was as though she'd forgotten where she was. The first time it happened I felt something dark brush up against my insides, the spark of a memory, but it took her finishing her story and staring blankly at the wall behind me to figure out what she'd reminded me of.

Lina's mum. Afterwards.

She would be fine, a little jumpy but fine, and then her eyebrows would move, just a fraction, just for a second, and it was as though she'd remembered something she'd been trying to forget. Lina caught it too, every time; her face would change, and she'd start talking, too fast, too much.

Hey, Mum, I have some holidays coming up and I was thinking we should go to Fiji again. Remember the breakfast buffet? I have been dreaming about those waffles for weeks. Let me look into flights. It's no big deal, but it would be fun, wouldn't it?

So I was going to surprise you for your birthday but I bought us tickets to Wicked. We'll have dinner in the city first. There's this great Italian place in the Strand Arcade. Meant to be amazing, isn't it, Cait?

Mum, Cath at work was asking about your orange cinnamon spice cake. I was telling her how you used to make it for Easter every year and it was the best thing ever. And that icing. Do you think you could write the recipe down for me?

Hey, Mum, do you remember when my first tooth got wobbly and I tried to pull it out on a doorknob because I saw it on TV? You were so mad.

Anything, just to bring her back.

I liked Jenny, I'd always liked Jenny, but afterwards it was hard to be near her. There was something in her eyes I didn't like seeing.

I felt cold, wrapped my hoodie tighter around myself, stifled a yawn I hadn't felt coming. When I looked at Frannie she looked normal again, her face still and calm and thoughtful.

'It's our anniversary next month, Tanya and I,' Carlos was saying. He was smiling, but it was sad, wistful. 'Ten years. Tanya's got some time off and wants us to drive up to Port Macquarie to see her family, then on to Coffs and Byron to see friends. People we haven't seen since the wedding.'

Geoff took a sharp breath, and he wasn't the only one. We'd all seen the footage—cars wrapped around trees or torn in half by semitrailers all the way up the north coast. Glass everywhere.

We'd driven up to the Gold Coast every January when I was a kid, the car packed full of bed linen and boogie boards and the back seat much too small for Jack and me. Mum and Dad would share the driving, and I would look out the window. It hadn't been a big deal then. Dad did the speed limit all the way, never went over, while Mum pushed harder, laughing when I told her to slow down, telling me I was seeing the needle on an angle.

I shivered. It was so cold. Abraham must have forgotten to turn the heating on.

'It's a beautiful part of the world,' Glenn said sadly. 'We used to go up there all the time. Camp right on the beach, even though you're not supposed to. My mates still do sometimes.'

Carlos nodded. 'She's even talked about hiring a campervan. At least her car has a five-star safety rating, but those things . . . who knows? Who knows how regularly they're serviced, or what the person who hired them before you did to them? It's ridiculous.'

'So what are you going to do?' Geoff asked.

Carlos shrugged, and I knew the answer.

'Stay home. I've told her I can't get away from work.' He said finally. 'I feel so guilty for lying, but I don't want her to lose me and then blame herself for suggesting the trip in the first place. She wouldn't be able to live with herself.'

I closed my eyes, a sharp ache pushing into my chest.

'I promised her we'd go to Fiji in March.'

'Cyclone season,' Glenn mused.

Carlos frowned. 'Maybe not then. Jesus.'

'You've got to be careful, mate.'

The way Glenn said it was strange, and it took me a second to figure out what he meant.

I thought about Lina, for some reason, planning her dream wedding long before she met Matt. I used to tease her about it. *What?*

she'd say. *Just because you don't let anyone hang around for more than a month.*

I'm just being careful.

Too careful.

And I'd laugh but it didn't feel funny. I had to be careful. To be safe. To not end up like Jenny.

I was still being careful, I thought, looking around. That was why I was here. That was why I kept coming.

Careful.

We were all just being careful.

August, Once

'I'm sorry again, love. I didn't even think when I was heading out of the house.'

I looked up at the rear-view mirror, smiled at the reflection of the driver's eyes. Gerry, the app told me his name was. Gerry had an Irish accent, which softened the bristle of him calling me *love*. 'It's fine,' I said. 'Really.'

I'd gone to sit behind him, where I always sat. *The Caitlin seat*, Lina would tease me. *Statistically safest.* I'd walked across the street and pulled the door open and there had been a bulky grey car seat blocking my way. Gerry had sworn and started apologising—first for the seat, and then for the swearing, then the seat again. He was still apologising by the time I got around to the other side, opened that door. I'd told him it was fine but he kept apologising.

'I'm pretty new to this gig, I have to confess.'

'It's okay.' I glanced at my phone. There was a message from Lina. *Text me when you get home.*

She must have sent it before she even went back into the pub. *Of course, Mum,* I replied.

'Busy night?'

'Nah, just started. Otherwise I would have noticed Luka's seat earlier.'

I looked out the window.

Ha ha. You sure you're ok?

'Is Luka your little one?'

'Sure is.'

'Boy or girl?'

'Boy. As it should be.' The car turned, and outside I saw a line of trees. I didn't come to Balmain often, wasn't sure where we were. 'Everyone thinks because of the song that Luka is a girl's name but she was singing about a boy.'

I smiled. 'Her neighbour, right?'

I'm ok. Just work driving me nuts. Sorry.

'Yeah.'

The car turned again, onto Victoria Road. My eyes followed the darkened storefronts, the tyre yards.

'He had a doctor's appointment today. Nothing serious, but Ailie, my wife, wasn't well, so I took him. I don't usually have a car seat in here.'

I nodded, not sure what else to say.

So long as it's just that. Coffee Monday for sure.

I bit my lip. It wasn't just that.

I had to tell her. I didn't know why I hadn't told her yet.

We turned again, curved around the end of the bay into the bottom of Annandale, under the bridge. I looked out the window. Terrace houses.

Or row houses. In New York they had stoops; they were different but they were the same. I'd seen them in movies.

The car turned. Gerry went to say something else and then everything went white.

23

Thursday, August

'Hey.'

I looked up from the fridges, felt my heart shift at the sight of Tom sliding onto his usual stool. Still. It had been weeks, but looking at him still made this happen, made me want to fall into him and never come out. He still made me feel so much. I was being careful, but whenever I saw him, when his eyes found mine and he looked at me, I forgot why I had to be.

'Hi,' I said. He seemed tight, tired. 'Long day?'

'Yeah.' He shook his head, smiled. 'Better now.'

I stood up, gave him a quick kiss over the bar. 'Good.'

'How was your night?'

I looked around. The bar was a mess. 'Busy. Rachel was in here earlier and we had some big corporate dinner. I hope you don't mind waiting.'

'It's okay.' He smiled again, looser this time. 'I like watching you work.'

I grinned playfully. 'You just like me making you drinks,' I said, turning to the whiskies.

He laughed. 'It does make you seem nurturing and trustworthy.'

I bit my lip as I found the right bottle. I didn't feel trustworthy.

'Ew,' Nic said, watching us. 'Holly, the straights are being gross again.'

Holly came around the bar and dropped a fistful of empties into the bin.

'Let them have this one thing,' she teased. 'Look at Caitlin, she's all giggly and stuff.'

I giggled, as though to prove her point.

Tom watched us, his face brightening. 'Sorry about them,' I said, raising my voice enough so they could hear. 'They're children.'

'It's fine.' He shook his head. 'I like you giggly and stuff too.'

Holly looked between us. 'Nic and I are going to the casino and he thinks you should come,' she said. 'Both of you.'

Tom caught my eye, raised an eyebrow in question.

'Come on,' Nic said, before I could answer. 'You haven't been out with us in weeks.'

I looked at Tom. 'What do you think? You look tired.'

'A little.' He sighed, downing his whisky in one go.

Something bit at me; a niggle, a chill. I brushed a strand of hair off my face and found his eyes. 'You okay?'

'Yeah. Just work stuff. I promise.' He gave Holly a smile. 'The casino? Really?'

'It's classier than it looks,' she said. 'I promise.'

He looked at me. God, he was beautiful. I smiled, despite myself. 'Fine,' he said. 'No shots, though.'

'Oh no,' she said, feigning innocence. 'Never. They don't sell them that late anyway. We drink cocktails, mostly.'

I studied him as she walked away, touched the bar. Still there. 'Are you sure? We can just go back to yours.'

'I'm sure, Cait. We can go back to mine afterwards.'

I looked around. 'If I ever get out of here, that is. Nic's made a mess back here.'

Tom grinned. 'I'm sure you can handle it.'

'Oh—' I laughed '—I can.'

I turned to the coffee machine and picked up two empty milk jugs, the last dregs of froth coating their insides, took them over to the sink to rinse them.

'Hey, Nones.'

I looked up. Dex was standing by the sink, arms crossed, leaning against the wall. I frowned, letting the jugs fill and then turning the tap off. 'What?'

'I need some wine.'

I rolled my eyes. 'Don't we all?'

'Ha ha,' he drawled. 'No, we're all out of merlot in the kitchen. For the rib eye.'

'And you've forgotten where it's kept out the back?'

He shifted. 'I can't find it.'

I pushed a brush into the first jug, ran it around the edges. Tepid milky water spilled out over my hands. 'Third shelf, under the pinot.'

'I looked there.'

'Look again,' I said, emptying the jug and starting on the second one. 'I'm busy.'

'You have to go down there to stock anyway, don't you?'

'Yeah. To stock the *bar.*'

He sighed. 'When did you get so unhelpful, Winona? I remember when you used to bring me a coffee at the start of every shift, and I didn't even have to ask.'

'We're all young and foolish once. Just look at Emma.'

He didn't answer, but he didn't move either. I emptied the second jug and held it up, giving in because I knew he wouldn't. 'Fine,' I said, 'I'll go down in a sec.'

'You're a gem.' He pushed off the wall. 'Truly.'

'Fuck off.'

'I mean it. Hey . . .' He put his hand out, pressed a thumb into my arm and rubbed. I stiffened at the unexpected contact. 'You've got some coffee grounds there.'

I pulled my arm away. 'Right. Thanks.'

'No, thank *you*, Nona.' He fixed his eyes on me, and then walked away. I looked back down at the sink, annoyed, tired, faintly confused.

'You right, Cait?' Nic asked from behind me.

I nodded. 'All good.'

I set both jugs by the sink, turned back to where Tom was sitting. He was watching me, holding his whisky up in front of his face, and when he caught my eye he gave me a smile, but it was small and unsure, and it took me a moment to return it.

◆

At the casino, we arranged ourselves into the same overstuffed gold and pink lounges we always occupied. I sat on Tom's lap, even though I probably didn't need to, even though it made Nic wrinkle his nose in disgust. I wanted to be closer to him, to savour the feeling of his hand on my waist, mine locked around his neck. Nic told him story after story, some of them silly and pointless and others ending with some nice thing I'd done or some way I'd saved his arse at work and I could tell he was trying to impress Tom, trying to make sure I impressed him. Tom would laugh and tease me and I watched him, my heart thundering at the look on his face, open, warm, bright. Happy, his earlier weariness fading away, replaced with the brightest light in the whole room, brighter than any thousand-bulb chandelier and all the pokie screens, and warmer than every single one of the fake fires that decorated the edges of the gaming floor. A word kept knocking around my stomach, a big word, almost too big.

When Tegan finished she came over and sat next to Holly and the two of them started talking softly and Tom pulled me closer and closer with every cocktail, his hands creeping under my shirt and his mouth seeking mine out more and more frequently. He was watching me even more intently than usual.

'What?' I asked at one point.

He shook his head. 'You're so beautiful,' he said.

My whole body fizzed. 'You too.'

He went on, as though I hadn't spoken. 'You know how I feel about you, don't you?'

I smiled. 'I think so.'

His hands tightened around my waist and he put his head on my shoulder.

'You sure everything's okay?' I asked.

He exhaled. I felt it on my skin. 'I hope so.'

I caught a frown flicker across his face. 'Tom?'

He paused. 'So before,' he started. 'At Sawyer's. Who was that?'

'What?'

'The chef you were talking to.'

'Oh.' I felt myself straighten. 'That's just Dex.'

Tom laughed. 'Wait? *The* Dex?' I hesitated, unsure what he meant. '*MasterChef* Dex?'

I breathed out. 'The one and only.'

He gave me a look. 'You two seemed—'

'No.' I knew I sounded strange. 'He's just like that. It's nothing.'

His jaw twitched. 'You sure?'

I was vaguely aware of Nic sitting next to me, staring into the middle distance and not saying a word. 'Of course,' I said, smiling, not sure I felt like smiling.

Nic moved, leaned forward to pick up his drink, still not saying anything, but I felt his eyes on me.

'Hey,' Tom said softly, changing the subject as I leaned in closer to him. 'It's my sister's birthday in a couple of weeks. Come for dinner?'

I blinked, momentarily disoriented. 'To meet your sister?'

He shrugged. 'Maybe my mum.'

My eyes widened. 'Really?'

'Really. If you want to.'

'Really?' I asked again, a warmth spreading through my chest.

He laughed. 'God, you're adorable. It's not that big a deal.'

'Meeting your family?' I shook my head. 'Of course it's a big deal. They make movies about how big a deal it is.'

He laughed again.

'Are they like you?'

'Like me what?' He frowned.

'You know.' I touched his chin. 'Polite. Nice. Doctorly.'

'I guess. Except Sarah. She's an architect.'

'How embarrassing for you.'

'Yeah, we don't talk like to talk about it.' He grinned. 'So? Mum's asking to meet you.'

I raised an eyebrow. 'You've told her about me?'

A flicker of uncertainty crossed his face. 'Of course I have.'

My heart thumped in my chest, reminding me it was there. 'Please?'

'Yes. Of course. What night? I'll need to get Nic to—'

'Tuesday. Not next week but the one after.'

My breath caught.

'I have plans,' I said, looking down at my lap. 'Lina, remember?'

'I know, but it's the only night Sarah can get a babysitter.' He sounded confused. 'And I'm not working and . . .'

I squeezed my fingers into a fist.

He noticed, frowned, his hand loosening on my hip. 'Lina will understand, won't she? Can you two have dinner on Monday? Or weekend brunch or something?'

A part of me wanted to say we could, wanted to skip group and meet his family, maybe never go back, never have to lie to him again. But something stopped me. The photo. Something else.

Careful.

'I don't know.' I paused. 'With the wedding and everything, she's kind of . . .'

I could feel his eyes on me, but I couldn't look at him. I'd never met anyone's mum before, except once unintentionally, after a big night. It seemed too soon to meet his. It seemed like a lot, a step. A part of me wanted it so much but it was too soon.

I hadn't even mentioned him to my family, I realised. Whenever Mum rang all she wanted to talk about was Lina and the wedding and it had never felt like the time. I bit my lip, feeling my chest tighten.

He sighed. 'Okay. Maybe next time.'

I reached for his hand, feeling guilty. 'I can ask,' I said slowly. 'If it's—'

'No, it's okay.' But it didn't feel it. 'Don't worry.'

'Are you sure?'

He took a moment to answer. 'Yeah.' His hands tightened around me again. 'We'll work something out. Another night.'

I relaxed, just a little. 'Thank you.'

'You're a good friend,' he said. 'I'm looking forward to meeting her.'

I tried to meet his eye. 'I know,' I said. 'Soon. We'll have lunch or something.'

'Maybe I can crash one of your Tuesday dinners.'

'Maybe.'

He looked at me again. 'Are you all right?'

I nodded. Everything hurt. 'Yeah.'

'It's fine, Cait.' He squeezed my waist, smiled. Genuine, like it really was. 'You can meet Mum another time.'

'I know.' It was fine. As long as I was careful, everything would be fine. 'I've just got a headache. The noise.'

He sat back, studied me. 'Should we go?'

I looked around. Nic had stopped watching me and was deep in conversation with Tegan and Holly, and I wasn't lying about the headache. The cocktail churned in my stomach and suddenly I felt completely exhausted.

'Yeah,' I said. 'Let's go.'

♦

We walked back to his apartment in silence, our feet never quite finding the same rhythm, so his hand kept pulling mine in the wrong direction, or I was pulling him. At one point he let go completely, knotting his fingers together and looking down at them as he walked.

'You know,' he said, studying his palms. His voice was slow, deliberate. 'If this is too much for you, or you need space or time or anything, you can just tell me.'

I stopped walking, or maybe he did. We both did. I looked at him. His eyes were down and he looked worried and I hated that I'd caused it. I wanted to tell him everything, but I also wanted to tell him it was fine, everything was fine.

I wanted everything to be fine.

'I know you haven't done all this before and it's all been really intense and if you . . .'

I could just nod, I thought. I could just say he was right. But I felt a rush of fear, of what that might mean. I didn't want it to slow down. I didn't want space. I wanted him. Still. So much it made my eyes water.

'No,' I said, my voice breaking. 'No, I'm sorry. It's okay.'

I wasn't sure it was, but it was going to be. I was going to make it okay.

He looked at me. His eyes holding mine so entirely my breath caught. 'Cait, I—'

'What?' I cut him off, too quickly. He frowned, surprised, opened his mouth as though he was about to go on, but didn't. My stomach hurt. My chest. Pulmonary embolism. I didn't even know what that was, except that it was fatal.

'Nothing. It's all good.' He paused for a second, then took my hand, and we started walking again. He didn't say anything else.

◆

Back at his apartment, he kissed me, and I kissed him back, maybe a little too hard, strangely urgent, and we had strange, urgent sex, never quite finding the same rhythm. I'd feel his eyes on me, but when I looked at him he'd look away and everything felt too intense, too big. Words rattled around my head; big, small, short sentences, long stories, so many words I wanted to say but I couldn't, and it took me a long, long time to fall asleep.

August, Once

I kept hearing the sound. So loud but so—not loud. Like a tin can, crumpling; a beer bottle falling onto concrete; plastic, snapping. I kept hearing it, over and over again. Loud, but not loud enough. It should have been louder. I'd always imagined it would be louder.

'You should get checked out,' the officer said. He wasn't looking at me and I wasn't looking at him. We were both looking at the ambulance, the gurney being wheeled into the back. Too slowly, the paramedic's lips pressed too tight, no sense of urgency.

I nodded. My neck hurt. 'I will.'

'I can take you up to RPA.'

I kept hearing the sound. The silence. The sound. The silence.

'Do I have to?'

He frowned. 'You can go tomorrow. But you should get checked out, just in case. I'll drive you home instead, if you prefer.'

'I'm not far,' I said. Lied. 'My boyfriend lives around the corner, I'm just going to go there.' So easy.

'We can call him, get him to come and get you.'

I shook my head. My hair sparkled at the edge of my vision. Pink, like fairy floss. Glittery. Where had the glitter come from? 'It's fine.'

He shrugged. 'I don't like it, but I can't force you.' He handed me a card. 'Give us a call on Monday. We'll need a statement when you're thinking a bit more clearly.'

'I'm fine.'

I looked at the car. Bright red, a great big gaping crater in the side. I could see the baby seat through the space where the window used to be. Even from across the road in the dark I could see it was broken, bent, thrown across the car when the spot it was in disintegrated. That was my spot. The Caitlin seat. That was where I was supposed to be sitting. Statistically safest. I hadn't even known that until Lina teased me about it. It probably wasn't even true.

It wasn't true now. It was a hole. An absence. A gap in the fabric, the metal, the plastic. My head was supposed to be where the missing window was, the twisted metal in line with my spine. I felt dizzy.

The van driver hadn't seen us, hadn't been looking. He was sitting in the gutter, head in his hands, another officer squatting over him with a notepad. Blond hair, cropped short. Work boots. Normal. You wouldn't notice him on the street.

'I've written another number on the back. Trauma team. In case you—'

I shook my head again. More glitter. Had there been glitter before? At—'I'm fine.' A party. A birthday. I couldn't remember whose. 'I'm okay.'

'I know. But you might be in shock.'

'I'm fine.'

'I know it might not feel it, but you were lucky.'

I nodded. Lucky.

'If I were you, I'd be buying a lottery ticket tomorrow, that's for sure.'

'I will,' I said, not meaning it. 'Thanks.'

♦

But I kept hearing the sound.

I just needed to get home. Across the park, up the hill, left at the second street, up the steps, inside. I'd get home and make a cup of tea and it would all be okay. I looked at my phone. The screen was cracked. It wasn't even midnight. Helen might still be awake. We could have tea together. She made good tea. I just had to get across the park. My shoulder hurt. My head hurt. I'd been drinking. Maybe that was why. Maybe it was shock. I wasn't in shock. I was just tired. Dead tired.

Dead.

No.

I wasn't dead.

Someone was dead. They hadn't said it but we all knew. Gerry. How did I know that? The app. When I'd booked. Gerry. And he'd told me. He was Irish. He had a—a car seat. A kid. A doctor's appointment. A sick wife.

I wasn't dead. I turned my head, side to side, to make sure I could. It hurt, but I could. And I saw glitter. Again.

Not glitter. Glass.

All the glass had shattered. The windscreen. The windows. Glass everywhere. All over the seats.

Not glitter. I touched my hair—fairy floss—and I felt it in my palms. Stinging.

Oh God.

Something broke. A bottle hit concrete. A tin can crushed in a fist. Another sound. Closer. A siren. Or a wail.

'Oh God.'

My throat burned. I looked at my hand and it didn't look like my hand and I could see where it stung, a sliver of red. I shook it, looked again, but it was still there. I could feel it. On my hand on my arms in my hair on my face, crawling, stinging.

Lina.

That was where I'd been.

Lina's birthday.

No.

Matt's birthday.

I was going to tell her.

I shook my head. More glitter. Glass. My chest hurt. My eyes hurt. Was there glass in my eyes? I blinked and it burned. There was glass in my eyes. Hot.

No.

I blinked again.

Just tears.

Hot. Burning.

'Noooo . . .'

I'd stopped walking. Somewhere, there were voices. Other people. Somewhere far away. One laughed. It felt too close, too mean.

My chest hurt. Glass there too. Burning.

So much glitter.

24

TUESDAY, AUGUST

'Have you guys ever heard of carbon monoxide poisoning?'

Geoff was sitting forward, elbows on his knees, looking at each of us intently, one by one, making sure we were listening.

When it was my turn I'd looked away, straightened my fingers in the pockets of my hoodie, tips straining the fabric. We'd done this before. Months ago.

Tom had the night off and I'd been so close to staying home with him. A part of me wished I had. I could have told him Lina was fine. Or that she was sick, that she had to work. Something. Anything. Just one time.

But I had to be careful.

Everything was strange. I had been trying to fix it but since the night at the casino everything was different. Harder. Tom was the same. He felt the same, looked the same, but sometimes when I looked at him I felt cold, like I had the flu, the bad kind.

I had to be careful. I was being careful.

'I was up late the other night and I found this amazing thread on Reddit, where this guy was convinced his landlord was plotting against him. Someone suggested he might have been hallucinating due to a carbon monoxide leak in his apartment. Ended up being right and saving his life. It got me thinking . . .'

'I read that!' Louise exclaimed, so loudly it made me jump in my seat. 'I know Reddit has a terrible reputation but that was amazing.'

'Hi,' a familiar voice said from the doorway, shaky and small. 'Sorry I'm late.'

I turned.

Frannie walked in, pale, her eyes like saucers as she found an empty seat and sat down. She put her hands in her lap and her jacket rode up, and I saw thick white bandages around her wrists.

My breath caught, shook.

The room started to spin around her and I could feel my ribs closing around my lungs, so tight it was terrifying.

My mum's sick.

Is she going to die?

Abraham shifted in his seat. He'd seen the bandages too.

My eyes found his and I begged him silently to fix it, to make it not real. He was the professional, I thought, as he frowned and looked away. It was his job to fix this. To fix us. That was why we were here.

'Sorry I'm late,' she said again.

'It's fine,' someone murmured.

'Welcome.'

'Hi, Fran.'

All the voices blended into one, and then stopped. Someone started talking, stopped. Someone else.

I felt myself falling. That smell. Hot and sour.

My mum's sick.

'I'm not crazy,' Frannie said suddenly.

I couldn't look at her. I could smell it, from across the room.

'I'm sick. I know I am. I can feel it. I look at myself in the mirror and I can see it. Why can't they find it?' Her voice was weird and low and desperate.

My mum's sick.

'They will,' Geoff said kindly. I looked at him. He was pale, but otherwise normal. Carlos was nodding. I felt my breath quicken, my stomach churn, something awful rise up in my throat.

'I know,' Frannie said. There was a strand of hair on my face and I brushed it behind my ear. Another, and another, tickling but not tickling. Scratching. I brushed them all back. Slivers of glass stinging my forehead. Glitter.

'It's just so hard. I can't start treatment until they find it. I'm rotting from the inside and they can't find it.'

Donna shifted next to me. Everyone else was nodding and smiling at her like it was normal. Like this was normal. Like nothing had happened.

I made a sound. Odd, low. Geoff looked at me, and I glared at him until he stopped.

'I'm so tired. I don't know what to do anymore. I'm sick and nobody will help me.'

My mum's sick.

Is she going to die?

A surge of anger charged up my spine. 'What if you're not?' I asked, before I could stop myself. I heard Donna say my name, hated the sound of her voice. Hated everyone, everything in this room. The calm, patient nodding like everything was going to be okay. Not fixing anything, not even trying. And I'd been trying so hard. 'What if you're not sick at all?'

My mum's sick.

I took a breath, but I wasn't there anymore.

I was fourteen, standing in a bathroom, pink and white, and stinking of vomit.

Lina was getting a textbook from her room and I needed to go to the bathroom and that's where she was, head bent around the toilet, feet blocking the door. It smelled like vomit, but worse. Hot and sour.

Like death.

I liked her. I'd always liked her. Sometimes when she spoke it was like I understood her better than anyone.

I blinked. Frannie was looking at me, surprised, her eyebrows knotting together in a confused frown.

'What if the reason they can't find this cancer is because there is no cancer?' I inhaled sharply. 'What if you're perfectly healthy and you're going to be perfectly healthy for another forty years? What then? What if you're not dying?' My voice was too fast, too loud, and when I stopped everyone was staring at me, cold, hard eyes telling me how stupid I was for not understanding. 'What if none of us are? This is horrible. This is absolutely fucking horrible.'

My mum's sick.

I hadn't understood when she'd said it, but I'd understood then. The second I'd seen her, I'd known. I felt like I'd always known.

I'd tried to stop Lina coming in, but I hadn't known how. I'd tried to stop her seeing, but I couldn't. And then she was wailing, begging for help, begging me to do something, and I'd tried to help her but I didn't know how. I didn't know what to do.

Acid. Vomit. Hot and sour, and she was bent at all the wrong angles.

Lina pulled her up and she was floppy, like she was dead. Lina kept saying her name, or not her name, but *Mum. Mummy.* Begging.

I thought she was dead. The smell was so strong, so impossible. It made my throat close up. And Lina just kept saying her name, kept begging her to wake up.

'Caitlin,' Abraham said sharply. I blinked, not sure where I was. There. Here.

'Why?' My voice was small and my throat hurt. 'Why would you—'

Frannie looked down at the floor, at her wrists. Acid. Blood. Vomit.

'This isn't normal. This is fucking horrible. Why are all of you acting like this is *okay*?'

Nobody said anything. Geoff's eyes flickered down to his hands, but for once he didn't say anything.

'Why aren't any of you *doing* anything?' I looked at Abraham. 'Why aren't you? You're supposed to be helping us.'

He didn't answer.

I could smell it again, suddenly. Hot and sour. I turned. Everyone was still silent.

'This is wrong,' I said, standing up and putting my bag on my shoulder. 'This is all wrong. You're not doing anything. You're not helping at all.'

Everything was wrong.

I heard someone say my name, ignored them. All wrong. I turned back to Frannie. She looked sick. She *was* sick. 'Sorry for swearing at you,' I said.

She nodded, her eyes huge and hollow, and I walked out of the room.

◆

I called an ambulance, in the end. I don't remember who called Lina's dad. He came and he was different from what I'd imagined. He didn't touch Lina once. Didn't hug her. He stood there talking to the paramedics with his arms crossed, frowning, shaking his head.

Mum came too—she'd been home the whole time, cleaning the floors. She'd come out when she'd heard the screaming. Lina.

Lina wouldn't stop crying. Couldn't. I sat with her and the grown-ups talked. Mum, the paramedic, Lina's dad, another lady in a suit who'd shown up with a briefcase. Her dad looked angry, annoyed. At one point he stopped to take a phone call. *What a pain in the arse*, I heard him say into the phone.

And Lina wouldn't stop crying. I held her hand and told her it would be okay. I promised her that I would make it okay.

♦

I stumbled down the stairs, feeling my eyes get hot.

Ever since then, I'd been so careful. I'd been careful for years, about everything, everyone.

And then I'd been careless. Once. Just once. I'd booked that ticket. February fifteenth. And then—

I was trying so hard to be careful again. That was why I had come here, when all I wanted to do was be careless and stay home with Tom and let myself go, over and over; fall, harder and harder.

I needed it to work. To keep me safe.

At the bottom of the stairs I pushed the door open and stepped onto the street, the cold slapping me in the face, catching the tears on my cheeks and turning them to ice. I stopped, reaching into my bag for my tobacco. My phone was flashing but I ignored it, desperate for nicotine, for something, anything.

The cigarette I rolled was crooked, fat in the middle and the filter dangled out the end, but it was something, and I tapped the end with my index finger and put it between my lips, searching my bag for a lighter, finding cold plastic with my fingertips.

'Cait.'

I jumped, the lighter slipping away. 'Shit,' I said, fumbling for it again, taking a second to understand what I'd heard.

'Hey.'

I looked up, still not knowing, not right away.

Tom was standing in front of me, hands in his pockets, frowning. And everything stopped.

I tried to take a breath but it caught.

'Hi,' I said, my voice shaking. I took the cigarette out of my mouth and watched it wobble between my fingers, wiped my cheeks, tried to wipe it all away. Frannie. Jenny. I felt a flicker of confusion. His face was so strange. Hard. 'What—'

This wasn't right. None of it was.

My mum's sick.

I felt my face rumple, a sob, forced it back.

'Hey.' His voice softened, tugged at me, frown disappearing. 'What's wrong?'

Something broke, somewhere just below the surface. I wanted to cry. I wanted to fall into him and have him hold me and tell me everything was going to be okay.

But it wasn't. It hasn't been for a long time. Days. Months. Years. *You're too much.*

I managed to shake my head. 'I'm fine,' I lied, begging him to believe me even as I knew he wouldn't.

'Cait.' His hands came up to my shoulders, my cheeks. Warm. Terrifying. 'What's happened?'

I pulled back, stepped away. 'Nothing.' I put the cigarette back between my lips and found my lighter, but my hands were trembling too much to get it to work.

'Here,' Tom said, taking it from me and sparking it, one hand up to shield the flame. It caught.

I took a drag. So hard I immediately felt sick. 'Thanks.'

He held the lighter out and I reached for it, letting his hand wrap around mine as I did. His fingers were warm from being in his pockets and mine shivered against them, so cold they burned.

'Cait . . .'

'Don't.' I didn't mean to say it, didn't mean to pull away.

His eyes widened, face frozen in confusion, hand hanging in mid-air. 'Sorry.'

I looked down. 'It's okay.'

But it wasn't. All I could see were Frannie's wide, hollow eyes and her wrists; all I could smell was vomit and death.

Something was wrong. Something else. Not just with Frannie—with everything. Something had happened right in front of me and I didn't understand it yet but I could feel it.

You're too much.

It's why my dad left.

Something was wrong with me. Something awful. Terrible. Incurable. Fatal.

My stomach tightened, my spine, my jaw. I tried to swallow—all of it, down. Careful. But there was no careful. There was just a beige room full of death and it wasn't helping and I didn't know what possibly could. Still, I forced it down, forced a smile onto my face, forced my eyes up.

Tom looked so different, his expression one I'd never seen. Wrong.

He looked away, past me, at the door I'd just come out. Stared at it for a long time. I almost expected it to open and someone to emerge. Geoff. Frannie. Abraham, in his standard-issue polo, holding his standard-issue clipboard. Something crept up my spine. Something that had been there since the moment I'd heard his voice but which I hadn't recognised. I went to say something but he spoke first.

'What's going on, Cait?'

Something awful. Terrible.

I put my cigarette in my mouth, my hand trembling so much I nearly missed, caught it with my lip, inhaled. The paper crackled as it burned.

Too much.

I'm sick.

'Caitlin,' he sighed. Sad. 'Please.'

I shook my head, pretending not to understand, begging him to stop.

He made a sound, a low rumble. It shook my bones. 'What are you doing? What is this place?' Looked at the door again.

A tiny earthquake. Somewhere close. Right underneath our feet. He hadn't even noticed, or maybe he had.

'I called you.'

The flashing phone. A tsunami. An earthquake, and then a tsunami. If one didn't kill us, the other would. 'You did?'

'Yeah.'

'How come?' Trying to pretend I didn't know.

He sighed; guilty, tired, something else. 'I wanted to know what you were doing in there.' He sounded apologetic. Nervous. The penny dropped, took my stomach with it.

'You followed me?' I didn't realise what I was asking until I asked it; didn't believe it. My ribs closed around my lungs, squeezed, and whatever it was rolling up and down my spine turned hot, shot through into my eyes and my fingers and my lips.

He didn't say anything.

'You followed me.'

It wasn't a question this time, and he didn't deny it.

'No,' I said, shaking my head, trying to deny it for him. 'No.'

'Caitlin.'

Heat prickled along my skin, lifting every hair on my scalp, burning my cheeks, my jaw. 'Why?' It was part wail, part whisper, part yell. 'Why would you do that?'

He hesitated. Took a breath. 'I'm sorry. I wanted to . . .'

I turned away. 'No.'

He moved in front of me, reached out to touch me, hold me. 'Cait.'

I pulled back, dropping my cigarette and watching it roll into the gutter. 'Fuck.' I kicked the concrete. 'Damn it.'

'What's going on, Caitlin?' he asked again. Louder this time. Or maybe it just felt louder. More desperate.

I stepped away, bringing my arms up around myself. My chest hurt so much I couldn't breathe.

'What happened? Why are you—'

'Nothing. I'm fine.'

'Please.' Urgent. I hated it, hated the fear in it.

'*Nothing.*' I kicked the ground again, as though I could stop what was happening.

'Cait.'

'Please. Stop.'

I was vaguely aware of the bodies on the other side of the street changing. Heads turning, feet shuffling. Hushed comments, not hushed enough before they were drowned out by a passing motorcycle.

I forced my arms down. Tom was still in front of me. Tom. My Tom. I couldn't see his face, but I could hear him breathing. I could see his hands on his hips, shoulders wide and stiff, his jaw twitching. Waiting. I'd never seen him like this. Hurt. Scared.

'Caitie.' So much fear. Sickly sweet and ice-cold. 'Please.'

I thought back to when I'd left his flat, kissing him at the front door and telling him I'd see him tomorrow. He was going to order pizza and watch a movie and have an early night. Everything had been normal. Perfect.

We were just going to get Lina's textbook and then go back to my house. There was leftover cake in the fridge and Lina had a new manicure kit but we had to study first. Fine.

And then it wasn't. And maybe it hadn't ever been.

My mum's sick.

Is she going to die?

How does it end?

Everybody dies.

Everything had been perfect and now it wasn't and nothing was ever going to fix it.

'I can't fucking believe you followed me,' I said, a rush of anger the only thing keeping my body from collapsing onto the footpath. 'How could you? This isn't about you.'

'So what is it about?'

The earth shifted again, just a fraction of a degree, but that was all it took. Another tsunami, water bubbling out through the drains, dissolving the ground beneath us. Liquefaction. 'I don't . . . I can't tell you.'

'Oh.' He straightened, shoulders tensed, jaw locked so tight. 'Okay then.'

'I want to.' I took a breath. 'I've wanted to since . . . But I can't.'

'Why not?'

You're too much.

She gets weird sometimes. It's why my dad left.

'I'm scared,' I said finally.

He stared at me like I was a stranger.

'You're scared?' he asked, after a long time. His voice had dropped to nearly nothing but it was so hard he may as well have shouted it. 'You?'

There was something awful in his expression, and I couldn't respond.

'Cait.' He shook his head. 'I have been all-in here. From the beginning. Before that. Anything you wanted. *Everything* you wanted. I wanted you to meet my family, be a part of my life. Because I—' Another shake. A sigh. Defeated. 'We've been together for, what? Two months? And you said I was never coming to your flat and I thought you were joking.' His voice changed. 'But I've never been to your flat, have I? You don't even let me drive you home.'

I bit my lip, looking down.

'I don't even know where you live.' He exhaled.

I couldn't answer. There was something wrong with me.

'You told me you've never done this before, but then . . .'

A brain tumour. I had a brain tumour. God, it had to be a brain tumour. That was why I was like this. That was why I had done this. 'I haven't.'

Why I was still doing it. Why I couldn't stop.

'Come on, Cait.' He pleaded. 'I wasn't just being paranoid, was I? About Dex?'

My breath caught. I just wanted it to stop. All of it.

'I see you at work,' he went on. 'After work, at my place. Or the pub. You don't talk about yourself. You joke. You tell me stories about being a kid, or who you used to be, but not . . .' He looked up at the sky, at the impending missile strike that was going to take us both out. 'As far as I know, you have exactly one friend, and when I've suggested meeting her, you make excuses.'

'It's not—' A freak lightning bolt from a storm we hadn't seen brewing.

'I've known you for *months*, Caitlin.' His voice came up again, just a fraction, another rush of anger. 'And I have let you all the way in. And I've been waiting for you to do the same but you *won't*. And *you're* scared?'

I looked at him, not sure what to say.

'You won't tell me anything. You—'

'You didn't tell me you'd been to New York.'

The words came out before I could stop them, and as soon as they had I wanted them back. I felt naked, completely exposed.

He frowned, confused. 'How . . .' He sighed. 'What does that—'

'Nothing.' I shook my head, felt my eyes get hot. I pressed the heels of my palms over them, trying to make it stop, all of it. 'Never mind.'

'Cait.' His voice softened, and I knew he'd moved closer. I could almost see him, the look on his face. I knew that look.

It's why my dad left.

I just wanted it all to stop.

'What happened, Cait? Tell me.' He was begging, desperate.

All of it. I wanted it to stop.

The thought pushed me back, and he had to hold on to my arms to stop me from falling over. 'Whatever it is, we can fix it. I can—'

'You can't fix it.' Owen hadn't fixed Frannie. Twelve years they'd been together. She'd told us that once. Twelve years, and still—

'We can try.' He exhaled. 'Caitlin, please.'

'Don't.' I pulled away, stepped back. Lina couldn't fix her mum. I couldn't fix anything. My hands shifted and I could see his face again. Different now. Lost. Scared. Scaring me.

'Please. Just tell me.'

It was so small it shattered something inside me. Glitter. Glass.

'You want to know?' I asked.

He didn't answer.

'Do you?' I asked again. 'Because if I tell you it's there and then . . .'

I looked at his face. Still. Scared. Desperate.

'Okay.' I gave in. *Too much.* 'Okay.'

I took a breath. Another one. He didn't move.

'This is a support group. People call us the Morbids.' My voice shook. I paused, tried to steady it. 'Do you remember when you asked me if I ever thought about dying?'

He nodded, just a fraction.

'Well, I do. I think about dying all the time. I think about how I'm going to die, how one night someone is just going to come up behind me on the street and put their hands around my throat and drag me away.'

I tasted bile.

'I think about that moment when it all disappears. All the ways it could happen. It's why I don't sleep. When I sleep I have nightmares about it. All the fucking time. All the time.' I looked away. 'Or I did. Until we—'

He winced, small, soft. I glanced up, at his face. Pale, even in the darkness. His jaw tight, eyes fixed on me.

'I was in an accident. A couple of years ago. It was Matt's birthday party and I got an Uber home, and this van just—'

I heard him exhale.

'We got hit. From the side. Hard.'

There was glitter. And blood. At first I thought it was my blood and when I saw it I went cold, so cold I was drowning in ice, but it wasn't mine. The windscreen had come apart and there was blood and the driver was impossibly still and it smelled like rusty nails. Hot and sour.

'The driver was unlucky. I—'

I was fine. I had glass in my hair and when I moved my head it looked like glitter. I couldn't lift my arm, but I didn't say so, because I just wanted to go home. I wanted people to stop talking to me.

But I was fine. Lucky.

The baby seat had come loose and slammed into my shoulder, but I didn't notice, didn't even feel it, not until the next day.

'I walked away.' I looked down at my boots. I'd been wearing heels that night. Stupid shoes for walking. Stupid shoes for doing anything.

'But ever since then . . .' I blinked, and everything blurred. Tears again. 'It's all I can think about.'

The next day I couldn't get out of bed. Everything hurt. The day after the bruise came up on my shoulder, down my arm, where the seatbelt had yanked me back. Helen, my flatmate, insisted I see a doctor. She drove me in her car and I sat in the passenger seat like a frightened rabbit, bracing for impact. The doctor said I was in shock and gave me some valium which I didn't take because I was fine, and some painkillers for my shoulder. I took those—two with water every eight hours, and I slept and slept and slept, for I don't know how long. All I could think about was dying, that I was supposed to be dead, I was supposed to be sitting where that baby seat was, I was supposed to have a tonne of metal and glass and moulded plastic impaled in my chest. All I could think about was that walk home. How quiet it had been, how easy it would have been for someone to snatch me, to pull me into their car. I looked at the painkillers and forgot how many I'd taken and wondered if they should have killed me too.

'Cait . . .' I saw his head shake, turn.

'My flat smells like cat piss.' I went on. 'It always has. The windows don't seal properly and the paint is peeling off the ceiling in sheets and it's so noisy. Sometimes the trucks come so close I think they're going to tear the walls off. And sometimes I want them to, because at least then I wouldn't be lying there hating myself for not being able to sleep.'

He made a sound, achingly sad.

'I moved there after the accident. It was only supposed to be temporary, because I was going to die, so it didn't matter.' I laughed softly. 'I can show it to you if you want. But we'll have to walk, because . . .'

I didn't want to finish the sentence, and I knew I didn't have to.

'You're right about Dex. It was a long time ago.' I frowned. 'It was stupid. I—' I shook my head. 'It wasn't important. It felt important at the time.' The time. The date. 'I was having a hard time and I just wanted to feel—'

Something. Anything.

'I didn't come here at first, not for a few months. My doctor gave me a pamphlet and I thought it was ridiculous. I thought it would go away. It did, a little bit. Enough.'

Enough that I could get a job, enough that Lina left me alone, stopped looking at me like she pitied me, like I was pathetic. And the days ticked by. Christmas. New Year. February.

'But then it got worse. So I started coming here. There are nurses and we talk about it and it—' I closed my eyes, saw Frannie's. 'I thought it was helping, keeping me safe. I thought as long as I kept coming here, I was okay.'

Frannie. Geoff. Carlos. All of them. Just sitting there. Waiting.

'I was careless. One time. I did one thing. One stupid, ridiculous, horrible, selfish thing, and someone died.'

'What did you do?'

I didn't answer. It didn't matter. 'I'd always been careful. I'd been so careful. My whole life. For years and years. I'd been so careful and then the one time I wasn't . . .'

'Cait.'

For a moment I'd almost forgotten Tom was there. His voice was soft and so, so sad. When I looked up his eyes were huge, defeat pushing down his shoulders. It hurt to look at him.

'So now you know.' I turned away.

Everything hurt. Everything had fallen over and broken as it hit the concrete. Shattered. Broken plates. Broken glass.

'I was being careful. Coming here. It was helping.' I shook my head. 'I can't believe you followed me.'

'I'm sorry.' He stepped forward.

'I wanted to tell you. I've never told anyone.' I gestured towards the door. 'Not even in there.'

I'd never told them about the accident, what happened after. About taking the pills, two at a time, and sleeping for days, finally getting up and dragging myself to the corner shop to buy cigarettes, cutting my hair over the bathroom sink, because it was still full of glitter and I couldn't get rid of it. About going back to bed and only getting up to chain-smoke in bursts, and Helen kindly suggesting that I do it further away from the windows and then kindly suggesting I look for another place to live—no hurry, just when I was ready, it wasn't personal and she was very sorry. About ignoring all the calls from work, from Lina, waking up to find her sitting on my bed and the awful look on her face, and how nothing had ever felt the same since.

I'd never told them about Jenny. About the vomit. About how Lina had wailed.

'From the first night, I wanted to tell you the story, the whole story. And I didn't know why. I still don't. But you made me feel safe and it made me want to just let it out.'

'I wish you had.'

I glanced at him, away. *Too much.*

'I just wanted you to like me.' I swallowed. 'I wanted to—'

It's why my dad left.

I wanted everything. I wanted him, all of him.

Too much.

'Caitlin.' He stepped forward again, and this time I was too tired to step back. I let him pull me in, let him wrap his arms around me and squeeze gently and let his lips touch my forehead and I felt the heat in my eyes turn into something else. Tears. Let them fall, silently.

'Somebody died, Tom. And it was all my fault.'

'It wasn't.'

'It was.'

'Why? How?'

I shook my head.

'It's okay,' he said, his arms tightening. 'It's okay.'

But it wasn't, no matter how many times he said it. Still, he held me. It felt strange, final, but I let him do it, needed him to do it, one last time.

'I should go,' I said, after a long silence.

His hands fell, almost against their will. 'What?' He frowned. 'Where?'

'Home. My place.'

'Come to mine.'

I looked at him. He seemed to mean it. Maybe he actually did.

'Cait, please.'

I wanted to. I wanted to take his hand and go with him and let him fix all of this—let him try—but I shook my head. 'I need a walk.'

'I'll come with you . . .'

I shook my head again.

'I'm sorry, Cait.' He looked at the ground. 'I'm sorry I followed you.'

'It's fine.'

'Are you sure? Are we . . .'

It was small and unsteady and I nodded, cutting it off before it gathered any air. 'Yeah. I just need a walk. I'll see you tomorrow? After work?'

He exhaled. 'Of course.'

'Okay.'

'Cait, you know I—'

'I know.' I cut him off. I had to keep him from saying something he might regret, something he didn't mean.

'Night, Caitlin.' He kissed me, but it felt wrong. Empty.

I tried to look at him, but I couldn't. 'Night,' I said to the ground.

He didn't move, so I did. I turned and walked away, not letting myself turn back, not even for a second.

Careful.

◆

I walked for a long time, felt Tom's arms around me and his breath on my forehead and saw that look on his face. Heard his voice telling me it was okay, telling me we could fix it. Wishing we could.

Jenny wasn't careful. She was young when she had Lina. The pregnancy was an accident but Jenny was madly in love and she thought they could make a go of it. So she married Lina's dad and they tried. She tried. She loved him so much. He was different then. Nicer. They were happy, for a while.

She told me that once, years later. Afterwards. Lina and I had fallen asleep watching TV and I'd woken up to go home and found Jenny sitting in the kitchen with a glass of wine, a pack of cigarettes next to her, not even bothering to hide them like she usually did. Maybe she was bad again then. I didn't know. I didn't know if Lina knew either. I'd sat with her for a while, not wanting to leave her alone. She never slept very much.

It's so quiet here, she'd said, staring out the window at the black sky, like she was waiting for something. *So bloody quiet. It drives me crazy.*

You and Mum, honestly.

I walked and walked. Fast. Until it hurt my chest and I had to gasp for breath and when I smoked cigarettes they stabbed and bit at my lungs. Walked until I was hot, sweaty, my face damp; until the cold sliced at my skin like broken glass, like glitter in fairy floss. Walked until I was lost and there were fewer people and the buildings weren't so tall, and there wasn't so far to fall.

She said it all the time.

You and Mum.

That we were switched at birth, that we were the same, Jenny and I.

So bloody quiet.

She didn't know how I could sleep with all the noise.

I didn't sleep. I listened. I waited.

New York, I imagined, was never quiet. On TV it was never quiet. Even in pictures, even on postcards, it roared and beeped and flashed and wailed and clanged. It shone, but mostly it roared.

Jenny was sick, and Lina hated being there, hated seeing her like that, so we decided to go somewhere else. Somewhere loud and shiny. I thought she wanted to. I thought I was helping her. I promised I would look after her, make it better. I wanted to take her away.

◆

I was so careful, afterwards. I was always so careful. I didn't want it to happen to me, didn't want to hurt like she hurt. I was safe. I did all the right things, all the safe things.

I looked after Lina. I was going to take her away, help her, like I hadn't been able to that day. It was all for Lina . . .

Until it wasn't. Until it was for me. Until I wanted it, so much it hurt. I wanted the noise, the lights, the roar. The wildness, the craziness. I wanted it so much I was willing to give up everything for it.

I was careless. Just once. Just for a second, and it ruined everything.

I had to be more careful. I tried to be careful but I wasn't careful enough. I needed to try harder.

I walked. And I walked. And I couldn't remember getting home.

25

WEDNESDAY, AUGUST

'You okay, Caitlin?'

I blinked. Nic was looking at me. 'Yeah.'

I wasn't, and I'd forgotten how to fake it. I hadn't slept. Not for a second. There was a shake in my words and my hands and that thing rolled up and down my spine constantly. Tom had called in the morning but I hadn't answered. *Hey,* his voicemail message said. *I just wanted to make sure you got home okay.*

Then a pause.

I missed you. I'm sorry about last night. I got scared and paranoid and I—

Another pause, pulling himself back.

I'm glad you told me. Can we talk tonight?

A sigh.

Anyway, call me. Or I'll see you at Sawyer's. I finish at ten. I miss you. I—

Then his breath, catching.

Have a good day, Cait.

Then a click, and the robotic voice on my phone asking me if I wanted to listen again. And I did, over and over, and every time his breath caught in that same moment mine did. I wanted to know what he was going to say and every time he didn't say it my heart hurt. I itched to talk to him, couldn't stop thinking about it. Aching for it and dreading it at the same time.

'Caitie?'

I made mistake after mistake. Little ones that nobody else noticed. The wrong wines, too much sugar syrup, skim instead of full cream.

It was quiet, even for a Wednesday, so I had no excuse. I'd already stocked the bar and started cleaning the coffee machine, but everything felt harder than it should. Nic had replaced the usual bluesy instrumentals with French electronica and it seemed to echo off the timber, off-beat. He didn't seem to care. I looked at him, polishing glasses.

'You okay?'

"Course.'

He studied me. 'Is Tom coming in tonight?'

I tried to answer but I couldn't. Tried to plaster on a smile and make a joke, but the cracks ran too deep and nothing seemed funny.

It was hot. Too hot.

He held a glass up in front of the light, squinted, then put it back into the tray with the others. It crashed into them, too loud, and the sound made me jump. So loud. All I could hear. Nic didn't seem to notice, to care.

Too hot, and then cold. A prickle of . . . something . . . up my spine. A tightening in my chest. My heart skipped a beat and took the next one twice as hard.

'You sure you're okay, Caitie?' He was looking at me again. 'You look terrible.'

I tried to answer but I couldn't. My eyes were wet, hot. There was something around my throat. Hands. Squeezing. Ice-cold. Sweat dripping along my hairline.

Dying.

Dying. This was what dying felt like. Multiple organ failure. Heart attack. Stroke. Pulmonary embolism.

Dying.

'Cait?'

He had his hand on my arm but I could barely feel it. Dread. Dead. Dread.

I tried to move. To breathe. To do anything.

I couldn't feel my face.

'Here, have some water.' Nic was holding a glass in front of me and I reached for it, felt the cool glass with my fingertips. 'Got it?'

I nodded, couldn't speak. He let go.

I didn't have it, and it crashed to the floor. Crashed. So loud. Not loud enough. 'Shit,' he said, somewhere far, far away. He was under water. Or I was. Drowning. 'Don't worry. I'll clean it up. You—'

'Can I have a cigarette?' I managed. I had to get out of there. Out from under the light fixtures, away from zappy power points and sharp knives. I had to. Before . . . 'Please?'

When our eyes met his were huge, eyebrows drawn together, full of questions. 'Of course.'

I looked away. Straightened. My spine hurt too. Meningitis. Straightened and walked past him, not hearing what he said next, not hearing anything except a roaring between my ears and, as I made it out of the dining room, the sound of the front door opening and closing.

◆

'Cait.'

I didn't know how long it had been. I was holding a cigarette, one of Nic's, but it had turned into a column of ash. When I shifted at the sound of Tom's voice, it fell onto my thigh and rolled, intact, onto the concrete. I had a postcard on my lap. New York. I didn't

know why I'd taken it out of my bag, or when. I pulled my hand
over it to hide the photograph.

'You okay?'

I nodded. 'Just tired.' I was. I was so tired.

I'm so tired.

I was going to send it to Lina.

Lina. The wedding. I couldn't go to the wedding. There was no
way. I couldn't do anything. Could barely move.

'I've never been out here,' he said, trying to keep his voice light.
Trying so hard. 'Is this where you all come to get away from us?'

I inhaled. My chest, ribs, stomach hurt, like I'd just run a
marathon.

'I waited for you to come back but Nic thought I should check
on you.' He came closer, bent down in front of me, one knee on
the filthy ground. 'It's like getting VIP access. I even got to see the
staffroom.'

Trying so hard. And I couldn't move, couldn't say anything.

He exhaled, went to reach for me, my hand, stopped himself.
'How are you feeling?'

It was genuine, but polite, careful. Doctorly. I nearly laughed,
only I couldn't. A wave of sadness washed over me. Defeat.

I'm sick and nobody will help me.

Nobody can help me. Nobody could help Jenny.

'You can't fix me, Tom,' I said, my voice straining. 'I know you
think you can but I don't have a broken leg or a fucking virus or
whatever. You can't fix me.'

'I know.' He sounded sad, tired. 'I'm sorry.'

'You can't fix me,' I went on, like he hadn't spoken. Frannie had a
husband. A family. And it hadn't fixed anything. I wondered who'd
found her. I wondered where she'd been. How close she'd come.

I wondered who'd find me.

'I'm sorry,' he said again.

'I'm going to die.' It sounded different, even to me, something I'd known for years but suddenly bigger. Scarier. 'I'm going to die, Tom.'

'Don't, Cait.'

I dropped my head, too tired to hold it up anymore.

You're too much.

I had to be careful. I thought I was being careful but I wasn't. Not careful enough.

'I can't do this,' I said, before I could stop myself.

I had to be more careful.

'What?' Small. Scared.

I squeezed my eyes closed so I wouldn't accidentally look at him. Focused. 'This. You. Me. Us. I can't.' I swallowed. 'It's not going to work.'

I heard him inhale sharply. 'Cait—'

I shook my head. 'You're a doctor. I'm a fucking waitress. And not . . . not even a good one.' I remembered that moment at the bar, not even being able to hold a glass. All the mistakes I'd been making. For weeks. Months.

'So? That doesn't matter to me.'

I opened my eyes and looked at him, trying to figure out if he meant it. If it mattered.

'I'm going to die, Tom,' I said finally. 'Maybe not here. Not . . . but soon.'

'You're not, Cait.'

'I am. I'm going to fall down some stairs or the air conditioner is going to fall off the wall and crush me or we're going to get held up at gunpoint.'

He stifled a wince.

'Or I'll have an aneurism, from the smoking. Maybe I already have lung cancer, who knows? Or I'll get knifed on the way home. Fall off your balcony. I'm going to die, so all of this is pointless, none of it matters, none of it.'

'Cait.' He was trying, so hard. 'Please don't.'

'Are you going to save me?' I looked at him. His face had changed, gone pale. 'Stop the bleeding? Give me CPR? Talk me through it and tell me to hold on and that it'll be okay?'

'Caitlin. Stop.' His voice rose, his hands up again, hovering in the air, shaking. I found his eyes. God. I wanted him. So much it hurt. So much.

Too much.

'You can't.' I looked away. 'I can't.'

'Caitlin.'

I felt a shock as his finger touched mine. 'What's this?' he asked, nudging my hand away gently to see what was underneath. I pulled back, suddenly ashamed, felt the postcard bend as I shoved it into my apron pocket.

'Nothing. Don't.'

He sighed, shifted onto his heels.

'I can't do this.' I said again. 'I'm sorry. I thought I could. I thought . . .'

I wanted to. I closed my eyes and I could still see him in front of me and something I'd never felt charged through my bones. Warm. Urgent. Terrifying.

'I have to be careful, Tom.' My voice shook, and I begged myself to stop talking. 'I'm different to you. I have to be careful. I have to be careful or everything will break. I'm not like you.'

'Caitie.' Still trying.

'This is easy for you. You said so yourself.'

Tom hesitated. 'I didn't say it was easy.'

'You did. You said it about Sophie.'

'Cait.' His voice caught. 'I said it was *too* easy.'

I opened my eyes. He was looking at me, incredulous, almost angry.

'You honestly think this is easy for me?' He leaned forward and put his hands on my arms gently.

'Do you?' he asked again.

'I don't know.'

'It's not. Seeing you like this is—'

It's why my dad left.

'So, don't.'

'That's not what I meant.'

'I'm sorry.'

He shook his head. 'I don't want you to be sorry. I want you to let me in. I want you to trust me. I want you.'

I made a sound. A whimper.

'Caitlin . . .' His voice dropped, hands sliding off my elbows, down my arms, until they were holding mine. Holding on. 'My life might be easier without you in it. But that's not the life I want. Easy doesn't mean good. It doesn't mean happy. I think you know that.' He took a breath. 'I think that's why you're here.'

I frowned, not sure what he was saying. His eyes were nearly black and he was so damn perfect. Like a postcard. I felt the warmth again. The fear.

I looked away. At the wall. Old bricks piled on top of each other, the mortar crumbling under their weight, barely holding them together.

It wouldn't take much. Some building work nearby. One of those tiny earthquakes nobody even felt. A water leak in the bathroom upstairs. One would go, and then they'd all tumble down after it.

'I can't,' I said, pulling my hands away.

Silence. When I looked at him, he was looking at the ground, hands in front of him, fighting with each other. His jaw was tight, twitching and he was frowning. But he wasn't arguing. He wasn't saying anything, because he knew too.

'You should go.'

When he spoke his voice was raw and low. 'I don't want to.'

'Please.'

'Caitlin, I—'

'Don't, Tom. Please don't.'

His mouth opened, and then closed.

And slowly—achingly slowly—his chin tipped, just a fraction. Enough.

I'd been waiting for it, but it still stung, burned like a slap, so much that my hand flew up to my face to make sure he hadn't made contact.

'Okay.' He paused. 'If that's what you want, Cait.'

I nodded. 'It is.' It wasn't. And I wanted him to know it, to argue, to fight, to tell me I was wrong. To finish his damn sentence, make this all a hundred times worse but maybe better, somehow. But instead he nodded too, stood up.

'Okay.'

I let my head drop, closed my eyes and felt the tears form, the familiar tightness in my chest. 'I'm sorry.'

He didn't answer.

Finally, I felt his fingers graze the top of my head, stop for a second. 'Bye, Cait,' he said. 'I'll see you round.'

I nodded again, squeezed my eyes shut tighter and didn't say anything, and then his fingers were gone, and I heard the door open and close and he was gone too.

26

*T*HURSDAY, *A*UGUST

My phone was ringing.

And ringing and ringing and ringing. The sun streamed through my window, so bright that for a moment I couldn't see anything at all. I rolled away from the noise and the light and a scattering of postcards fell to the floor.

The ringing stopped, and it took me a minute to remember what had happened.

♦

I remembered tequila. The casino.

Before that, Holly.

Holly's arm on mine. Holly walking me out of Sawyer's. And then the casino and tequila, so shiny and so bright and so loud. So loud I couldn't hear my own voice. And the bathrooms. Shiny. Such shiny bathrooms, full of glitter, and so loud, so hot.

Acid, burning at my throat. Vomit. Hot and sour. Holly's hand on my back. Holly's voice, telling me I would be okay. Lying.

I remembered walking. Tripping. Walking. Someone asking where I was going and me laughing. Tinny. Empty, my throat torn open, raw. Tasting blood.

Nowhere.

Walking.

I had to send Lina a postcard. I'd been meaning to send her a postcard. For months.

We'll still do the postcards, won't we?

I just didn't know what to say.

Not going anywhere. Never going anywhere.

I remembered the postcards. At some point I'd made it home and there had been so many postcards. Reading all of them, all those fantasies, those lies. All those facts and none of them the important ones, the ones that mattered. Did she know twelve people died every year visiting the Grand Canyon? That eighteen people a year drowned in the canals in Amsterdam? Did she know at least twenty people died building the Brooklyn Bridge? That two hundred and twenty-eight thousand people died in the Boxing Day tsunami? And four hundred thousand died building the Great Wall of China? Their bones were buried in the wall itself and I wondered if Lina knew about them, because I did and I couldn't stop thinking about them, couldn't stop thinking about dying, all the ways I could die, the ways I *would* die. I couldn't sleep, I couldn't move. There were so many ways to die. No way to avoid it. None at all.

◆

The ringing stopped, then started again. I picked it up.

'Caitlin. Thank fuck.'

It was Nic. He sounded weird. 'Hey.' My voice broke. My throat felt like I'd swallowed a hundred acid-coated razor blades.

'Where are you?'

I blinked. It was so bright. My hands were shaking.

'I'm sleeping.' I rolled onto my back. My whole body hurt. 'What time is it?'

'Twelve thirty.' He exhaled. 'You were supposed to be here an hour ago.'

When I sat up, my head spun. I fought the urge to vomit. 'Shit.'

'It's fine.' There was something in his voice. Something awful. 'Just get here as soon as you can. We're fully booked.'

'Okay.'

'Okay.' He sighed. Awful. 'See you soon, Caitie.'

◆

It was a mistake. I should have just stayed home, told Nic I was sick and paid the price, let him fire me, as though that would make a difference when I drowned in my bathtub. And I *was* sick. More than sick. Dying.

I was sluggish, slow, my rhythm off. I left the vodka out of a martini; put three shots in another; sent the wrong hundred-dollar bottle of wine to a table, uncorked, wasted; opened all my beers too fast so they erupted onto my hands and my shirt and the floor; smashed a glass just trying to put it on the bar, the sound ripping through my spine. So many mistakes. I'd never made so many mistakes, and whenever I looked up Nic was watching me with his lips pressed together, an expression on his face I didn't understand. My hands were shaking so hard, my head pounding. I couldn't speak, and when I tried my throat throbbed and protested.

I'm sick. I know I am. Why can't they find it?

'You all right, Cait?' Holly asked in the staffroom after lunch. I was trying to roll a cigarette but I couldn't steady my hands. 'Where did you run off to last night?'

I blinked, not knowing how to answer.

'Hey,' she said, reaching out and putting her hand on my forearm. So cold it burned, dry ice, and I flinched, tobacco spilling everywhere. 'Are you okay?'

I shook my head, eyes hot. Everything hot.

'Here.' She reached into Nic's locker, handed me one of his cigarettes. I took it, tapped the end with my index finger. Over and over. 'I've never seen Nic like that.'

Over and over.

'He was freaking out. Thank God you answered the phone when you did or he would have sent an ambulance to your flat.'

'I just fell asleep.'

I'm so tired.

She looked at me. That same look. I couldn't stand it. Touched my arm again, rubbed. Cold. Bruising.

My mum's sick.

Is she going to die?

I'd swear we were switched at birth. You and Mum, honestly.

'You'll be okay, Caitie. You will.'

I didn't believe her, didn't see how she could possibly be right, but I nodded anyway, turned away from her, out of the room. 'Thanks.'

◆

'Nona.'

I hated his voice. Raspy. Grating. I just wanted to smoke my cigarette and now this. I hated it all so much. I closed my eyes. 'Jesus, please—not now, Dex.'

'What happened?'

'Nothing,' I said, staring at the ground. Concrete. Hard. Lethal. 'I can't do this anymore.'

I heard him take a drag, heard the paper crackle. It was so quiet. I didn't know when it had got so quiet. 'So quit.'

'No, not . . .' Not *this*. Everything.

'You'll get over it.'

I laughed. Nearly laughed. A flash of anger burning in my gut. 'And how would you know that?'

When I looked up at him he shrugged, did this thing with his face that was almost a grin, and the utter disregard of it—the utter *carelessness*—made me furious.

'How the fuck would you know?' I asked again, spat.

'Settle down, Nones,' he said. 'I just came out here to check on you. Everyone's worried.'

'Are they?' I could barely see. Barely hear. 'Are you?' I looked right at him, the perfectly pitched eyebrows, the disgusting smirk on his face, fading slowly.

'Nona.' His voice changed.

'I have a name, Dex.' I glared at him. 'I have a fucking name.'

I was yelling. Maybe. I could barely hear, my voice small and far away, but I had this feeling like I was probably yelling, because it was hurting my throat, because he was recoiling, because he'd stopped smirking. That was the only good thing—he'd finally stopped smirking.

'We all have fucking *names*.'

I looked at him, and I hated him so much. I hated myself for letting him in. I hadn't even wanted to. I'd just wanted to feel something. Anything. It was stupid, I'd been careless, too much. Too much everything, too much me. Wrong. Something wrong with me.

Too much.

It was all too much and I just wanted it to stop.

All of it.

I felt a tug in my stomach, a sickness, a blackness. My vision blurred, and my head dropped onto my knees as I felt a sob tear out of my throat.

My mum's sick.

I'm sick and nobody will help me.

Somewhere, a door slammed, and when I finally managed to look up Dex was gone. I was alone—the way I had to be. I didn't need anybody. I took a breath, another one. My heart was thundering against my ribs and I tried to slow it down before I had a heart attack.

Careful. I had to be careful.

More careful.

◆

When I got back onto the floor Rachel was behind the bar, Holly standing on the other side. They turned to look at me. Everyone was looking at me. I felt naked, exposed.

'Caitlin,' Nic said, from somewhere close by. 'Office. Now.'

I couldn't look at him. 'Just let me—'

'Holly will do it.' He paused. 'Now.'

◆

In the office, Nic lit a cigarette and handed it to me, then lit another for himself.

'Thanks,' I said.

He didn't answer.

He didn't say anything for a long time, just watched me, smoking his too-weak cigarette.

When he finished, he stubbed it out in an ashtray and immediately reached for the pack again.

'I'm sorry, Nic,' I said finally.

He nodded, tapping another cigarette onto the table before putting it in his mouth.

'I fucked up. I'm sorry.' I put my own cigarette out, brought my hands into my lap, knitted them around each other as though to stop myself doing something stupid.

The office was small and warm. Technically I wasn't allowed in here, but I'd spent hours sitting with Nic while he cashed up, watched him count coins, flick them off the table into his palm while muttering numbers under his breath. Sometimes I even helped him, though I wasn't supposed to.

I trust you, he'd said once, and I'd liked it more than I wanted to admit. Too much.

'What happened, Cait?'

I hesitated, not sure where he wanted me to start.

'Not today, not last night—I know all that.' He lit his cigarette, took a drag. 'I don't understand why exactly, but I know what happened.'

I unclenched my fingers, reached for another cigarette but didn't light it, just brought it back into my lap, looked at it. Perfectly cylindrical, as it should be.

'What's going on, Caitie?'

I bit my lip, shrugged. I didn't know what to say.

I put the cigarette in my mouth, lit it. Took a drag, exhaled.

'I broke up with him.'

He sighed, disappointed.

'It was my decision, so you don't need to feel sorry for me. You don't need to worry about me. I'm fine.' I inhaled again, felt a rush of nausea. 'It was the right thing to do. I'm sorry you've lost a customer but I'll be fine.'

'This isn't about Tom, Caitie.'

The sound of his name pierced something in me, sharp, awful.

I shook my head. 'Yes it is.'

He looked at me.

'It is,' I said. 'You're just mad because he won't be coming in anymore.'

'I'm not mad, Caitlin.' His voice was flat. Calm. Steady.

I took a drag, didn't answer.

'This isn't about Tom,' he said again.

I wanted him to stop saying his name. Every time he said it I wanted to scream.

'This has been going on for much longer than Tom. And it's not about Dex either, as much as I enjoyed hearing you yell at him. This is something else.'

I tried to ignore him, block him out.

'You need help, honey.'

I took a drag. 'No,' I said, exhaling. 'I just need . . .'

To be careful. More careful. I would be okay so long as I was careful. I took another drag, let my head spin, looked up past Nic's head at a stack of boxes in the corner. Precarious, ready to topple.

'You do.' His head turned, eyes looked past me. 'It's not about Tom.'

I looked at his hands in his lap, thumb tapping on his thigh, perfectly in time. Tap tap tap. Tap tap tap.

'I don't know what it is. I have an idea. But I don't know what specifically. Just that you weren't much better than this when you started. You just held it together better then.'

I wanted to argue, didn't know how. Everything was so quiet, so still, for just a moment. Sawyer's had never been this quiet. Tap tap tap. 'So why have you always—'

'Because you're good at your job. Damn good. Even today. You've got the sweats and you're clearly on the verge of something and you're still *good*. Most of the time, ninety-five per cent of the time, you're the best person I've got. And somewhere in there, you fucking know it.' He sighed. 'Ever since your first night. I gave you one shift and you took it like it was a lifeline.'

I nearly laughed. I hated how obvious it was. How obvious it had always been.

He'd been so sceptical, seen right through my lie about waitressing during uni. He'd complained to me about how Lenny kept hiring pretty young things with big boobs and how none of them ever knew what they were doing and I'd wanted to walk out but instead I'd pointedly looked down at my chest, barely there, and for some reason that had made him smile, and he'd given me a chance. *One night*, he'd said.

'You just worked so fucking hard.' He took a drag. 'I thought, *This one's got something.*'

It wasn't long after the accident. I'd only planned to stay for four months—if that, if I lived that long. I had a ticket to New York but my savings were running low and I needed the money, but more than that I needed something to do, a reason to get out of bed. A distraction.

I walked home that night, for the first time. I walked home and I felt it there, the fear, all the way, but it felt . . . right. It helped. I felt tired, exhausted. I even slept, for the longest time since the accident. Not the whole night through, but long enough. It helped.

'You didn't care about the tips, or the prestige, or anything. I don't know. Maybe it wasn't . . .' He sat forward, elbow on his knee, chin on his hand, staring off at something I couldn't see.

I finished my cigarette and put it out. The office was small and warm, full of filing cabinets and crates of glasses that didn't fit anywhere else—so that the room was padded, almost—and I felt safe. I'd always felt safe here.

'Maybe it wasn't healthy, but I thought . . .'

I straightened, and it seemed to bring him back.

'Go home, Caitie.'

My chest tightened. 'Nic, please—don't.'

'I'm not firing you.' He reached forward and took my hand. 'Take the rest of the week. Go . . . hang out with your friends. Do something fun.'

I shook my head, my eyes widening in fear. 'Nic, no. I can't.'

'I know.' He sighed. So tired. He sounded so tired. 'I know, Caitie. But being here, right now, isn't good for you.'

'I don't . . .' I inhaled. When I exhaled my breath shook and my eyes watered. 'What will I do?' My voice was so small. I was so scared. I wanted to beg him to let me stay, to let me work.

'I don't know.' He squeezed my hand. I didn't want him to let go, but he did, sat up and looked away. 'Maybe just get some sleep. Maybe that'll help.'

♦

I emptied my locker. I didn't have to—Nic said I didn't have to, specifically told me not to—but there was something in me that was telling me I wouldn't be back. I threw out the faded sock printed with a green cartoon foot, the crosswords I hadn't done, the empty cans of deodorant, and the full ones too, with their promises of teenage love and spontaneous ocean swims and afternoons spent rolling in fields of daisies; they all smelled like piss anyway. I shoved the dirty shirts in my bag, the aprons in the laundry bag.

As I pushed them down I felt something in one of the pockets, hard, but broken. I wanted to ignore it, leave it there to disintegrate in the wash, but I couldn't.

New York. It was worn away now, the picture crumbling off where the cardboard had bent. Soon it would be all gone. Soon it would be over.

I turned it over. Blank. There was a stamp in the corner and I couldn't remember when I'd put it there—months ago, when I'd thought I was going to send it.

A thought pushed into my belly. Sick.

My mum's sick.

I'm sick and nobody will help me.

I put the postcard in my bag, hitched it onto my shoulders, and walked out of the staffroom for the last time. As I walked past the kitchen I saw Dex working the pans, arms moving back and forth, head bobbing, like he was dancing, not a care in the world.

I had to be careful.

I just had to be careful. More careful.

Holly caught my eye as I walked through the dining room. 'See you soon, Cait,' she said softly. I couldn't say anything back, just nodded. Nic was behind the bar, head down, making coffee. I wanted to say something to him but I didn't know what, so I just turned and walked out the door.

◆

It was still light outside, and it hurt my eyes. I was still hungover, still aching from the night before, the week before, the year. My whole life. So tired.

Careful.

I could feel it. All of it. Everything. It hurt to walk, but I did. The wrong way.

Careful. I didn't even look up as I passed his building.

Down to the water. It seemed to take forever, take no time at all. He kissed me here, I thought, as I sat on a bench, my bag on my lap—full of shirts and tampons and pens that probably didn't work. Not here, but a few metres away. I could see the exact spot. He kissed me and I'd been careful then. I'd stopped it.

Not careful enough.

I pulled the postcard out of my bag. New York, fading away, like it had never existed in the first place.

A pen. Started writing. I didn't know what I was writing until I was done.

Dear Lina,

I can't come to your wedding. I thought I could but I can't. I'm so sorry. I hope you can find someone else to be your maid of honour and I'll pay you back for the ticket.

I love you. I hope it's wonderful. I'm sorry.

Caitlin

It was easier than I thought it would be.

Too easy.

Easy to stand up, to pull my bag onto my shoulder. I felt lighter, smaller, than I had in months, years. I felt like I was floating. Flying. When I exhaled it was like I was exhaling lead, clearing my lungs, my head. I could walk. I could feel the last of the sun on my back, the air on my face, the lightness of my body. I didn't hurt at all. I couldn't feel anything and it was such a relief I wanted to weep.

I was just being careful.

I'm always careful.

It was easier than I thought it would be to find a postbox, to slip the faded, broken piece of cardboard through the slot. Easier to let it go, like letting go of a weight. Letting go of everything.

And then I heard the hollow thunk of it hitting the bottom of the box.

Gone.

I heard it and I felt it all again, everything. A flood, a torrent. And I did weep, but it wasn't with relief, it was with fear.

'Oh God,' I said, to nobody.

What had I done?

What was I doing?

What would I do next?

My chest tightened and I felt the cold again, the blackness.

I started walking.

I walked home, straight home, for the first time I could remember. Almost ran. It was still light and there were so many cars and I could hear them, revving, braking, the squeal of tyres on bitumen. It was still light but there was something dark just behind me, chasing me, a gloved hand ready to seize my throat, an arm reaching across my chest. Tears ran down my face and they stung and there were so many people and they all looked at me and I had to run, to get away from them, to get away from the dark thing, whatever it was.

Be more careful.

My mum's sick.

I was sick. I was sick. I was sick. All the way across the park, all the way down King Street, past all the restaurants and convenience stores and weird kitschy lifestyle boutiques, all too busy, too full of people who had no idea how they were going to die, or when—how close it might be.

The lock gave first go, and the door opened so suddenly I nearly fell. When I shut it behind me, the darkness was still there. It had followed me in. I could hear it, feel it, smell it. Hot and sour. Blood and vomit. Death.

Marnie was in the kitchen, stirring something on the stove. It smelled like death. Like rotting flesh. Blood and vomit. 'Hey,' she said, surprised to see me. Maybe surprised. I could barely tell, barely hear her. She looked up and her face changed. A freak show mirror. Tilted. Disappeared. 'Are you okay?'

'Tired,' I said. I could smell burning. I could smell gas. I could smell death. Blood and vomit. Hot and sour. 'Need to sleep.'

Need it all to stop.

Careful. Careful.

And then nothing.

August, Once

The car pulled up and I looked at it. At Lina.

I've got to tell you something.

I cancelled the Uber. The car drove away.

I'm going to New York. I bought a ticket anyway.

I watched as he turned left, towards the city.

I turned back to Lina. She looked stunned. *You're going without me?*

I'm so sorry. I just have to. It's all I've wanted to do for years.

Have you given any more thought to what we talked about last week?

I closed the browser window and the flashing lights went away. *I'll do it.*

I didn't tell her. I pulled the door open, slid into my usual seat. The Caitlin seat. Statistically safest. Looked at the driver. He asked me how my night was. I started to say something, something meaningless, something unimportant. Then a sound. Loud, but not loud enough. My ribs. My spine.

◆

'Oh God.'

I kept hearing the sound.

When I moved there was glitter and Gerry the Irish Uber driver was dead. Luka's dad. Boy Luka.

I was in a park, not far from home. I just had to get home. I just had to get home but everything hurt and it was too hard to walk and I kept hearing the sound.

Oh God.

My stomach twisted, lurched, my knees buckled. Cold as they hit grass. Hot as the vomit poured out of my throat. Green.

Oh God oh God oh God.

Dead.

Someone was dead. Gerry. Luka's dad. Someone was dead and I wasn't dead. But—

Something broke. Broke all the way, the wailing so loud it was all I could hear.

It was my fault. Someone else was dead and it was all my fault. I could have stayed. I should have. Should have told her. I shouldn't have been going at all. It wasn't mine, but I'd stolen it.

More vomit. Bile now. Bright yellow, shining under the moonlight. Hot. All the heat pouring out of me and everything that was left was so cold. Ice. My fault. Someone was dead and it was my fault, because I'd stolen something that wasn't mine.

Because I'd been careless.

So cold.

It should have been me.

It hit me so hard that all the air went out of my chest, all the blood ran from my head. It hit me over and over and over again, smacked into me and broke my teeth and crushed my pelvis, snapped all my bones. Over and over again.

Over and over.

27

August, Now

Hours.

Days.

Sometimes, when I opened my eyes, it was light. Sometimes it wasn't. Sometimes it was in between, hazy and grey. Sometimes the orange streetlight stabbed me in the eye.

I died, over and over.

I didn't die, wished I could.

I was hot, my skin drenched in sweat, sticky and pink. Cold. Icy. Fingers white. I dragged myself to the toilet, my throat opened, lining ripped off, yellow bile, red blood.

I died. I didn't die. Hands grabbed at me and voices said things to me and the soft ones were the worst, vicious whispers. It was so hot. So hot the air bent and when I screamed my voice melted and disappeared before it made contact. I woke up pinned to the bed, hands on my shoulders, a mouth on mine. I woke up blue and cold.

I didn't wake up at all.

Sometimes I heard Marnie's voice. Other voices. Far away. Sometimes sirens. Coming for me. I hoped coming for me. My stomach hurt. My heart didn't beat properly. My throat closed. I couldn't breathe. Drowning.

Acid and hot. Shaking. Freezing cold.

I died. Nobody noticed.

◆

'Caitlin.'

A sigh. So tired. A hand on my forehead. Another, rolling me over.

'Oh God, Caitie.' I recognised it. It reminded me of something. A long time ago.

'Come on.'

Pulling. Pulling me up.

'Cait.' Soft. Tired. 'Sit up. Please, you need to sit up.'

Smelled like flowers. Wild. Clean, like a beach. I felt myself laugh.

'Okay.' Another sigh. 'Okay, okay. That's good. It's not funny, but you're okay. Okay.'

Practised. Tired, so tired of this.

Something cold, hard against my lips. A hand on my cheek. 'Drink. Come on, Cait.'

I felt the water run into my mouth, swallowed. Swallowed more. So thirsty. God. So thirsty. Reached. It moved away.

'Not too much. Slow.'

I whimpered, fell forward. Soft. Warm. Coming around me, a hand in my hair, stroking. My fingers reaching and finding other fingers. Squeezing. They squeezed back. Holding on, so tight.

'Okay.' A crack, a cry. 'God, Caitie. You're okay. Okay. Jesus.'

◆

Hours.

Days.

Voices, closer and then further away and then closer.

More nightmares. Brutal, violent, mean. In the dreams there was blood and vomit and broken glass everywhere, and it looked like glitter but it smelled like death and I was trapped in a broken car, dying, over and over again. Dying. Crushed. Buried. Bleeding.

I screamed, and the hands came back.

'It's all right, Cait. It's okay. It's just a dream.'

I reached, tried to hold on to anything I could but it was just blackness, just nothing.

Light. Dark. Nothing.

Slept.

♦

The hands were gone when I woke up, replaced with a pillow, clean, dry, and a blanket. It was light, but not bright. Early.

Everything was still. Quiet.

I blinked, surprised my eyes still worked. Surprised I was still alive. My head felt like it had been pressed between concrete, my throat raw and swollen, but I was alive.

Lina was sitting on the floor, knees bent to her chest, wearing old, faded jeans and a stretched-out jumper, her hands tucked into the sleeves, hair twisted at the top of her head, falling out around her face, starting to curl. She was surrounded by postcards, carefully sorted into piles, holding a creased piece of paper, reading it. From the way her eyes moved it looked like she'd been reading it for hours, trying to make sense of it. I couldn't see what it was, but I could guess.

Everything about her was wrong, hard. When she moved, it was stiff and harsh. The last time I'd seen her she'd been wearing a wedding dress, red lipstick. She'd looked like a princess, like a bride.

Now, she looked tired, exhausted and pale. I wondered if she was okay.

'Hey,' I said. My throat hurt. She jumped, surprised, looked at me for a long time like she wasn't sure I was really there; looked away, vaguely disgusted. Hurt.

'Hey,' she said, to the floor. She put down the piece of paper and wiped her eyes with the back of her hand. Familiar shapes. A logo—it should have been red and white but it had printed black. A booking confirmation. I'd printed it out right after I'd done it, stuck it to my wall at home.

After the accident, I'd put it in the box, under the postcards, next to the envelope that held my passport. That was sitting on the floor too.

'You never told me.'

'I wanted to.' It hurt to talk. 'I was worried you'd be upset.'

She looked at me. 'No, you weren't.'

I tried to respond, but I couldn't.

'How are you feeling?'

I didn't like her voice.

'I don't know.' I curled inwards, flexed my toes. Everything hurt, stiff and sore, but nothing felt broken, not all the way. 'Okay. I think.'

She nodded, as though confirming something.

I wrapped the blanket tighter around myself, trying to get warm. It was thick and dry but I realised the sheet under me was damp, icy cold. I shifted.

'Sorry,' Lina said. 'It's hard to change the sheets when someone's unconscious on them.'

'It's okay.'

'No.' She shook her head. 'It's really not.'

I sat up. My brain rattled against my skull in protest, but only for a second. Even my stomach seemed to cope, although I felt a dull ache through my middle as I tried to stay upright.

'How is any part of this in any way okay?'

She wasn't asking me. Her voice was small, worn down to a dull sadness. I slid off the mattress onto the floor. Mirroring her.

'Leen—'

'Damn it, Caitlin,' she whispered. 'Goddamn it.'

I opened my mouth. Nothing came out.

She caught her breath, trying to keep herself from crying.

'I came home and I got the mail and I was *happy*. I saw Central Park and I thought . . .' Her voice broke. 'I was so happy.'

'I'm sorry.'

'Why, Cait?'

I closed my eyes, dropped my head onto my knees. I wanted to tell her I hadn't meant it, or that I'd been drunk or it was a joke or any number of things, but none of them were true.

'Do you hate me that much?' I heard her shift. 'Still? After everything? After all that's happened?'

I frowned, confused.

'I'm sorry, Cait.' It was so tired, like she'd said it a thousand times and it had lost all meaning. 'I'm sorry my mum was sick and my dad was an arsehole and you had to look after me. But do you really hate me that much?'

I turned so I could see her, elbows on her knees, head tipped back, staring at the ceiling.

'I don't hate you.' My voice was so small.

She ignored me. 'I never asked you to, you know?' She closed her eyes, remembering, steadying herself. 'Or maybe I did. I don't know. I'm sorry.'

'No, Leen.' I had wanted to help her, look after her. Take care of her.

She hissed inwards, like she was in pain. It pierced my ribs and I had to turn away. 'How could you do that? On a postcard of New York, of all places?'

'Leen.' I'd never seen her like this. Never heard her. 'I don't—'

'You are supposed to be my best friend, Caitlin.' Her voice came up. 'Why couldn't you just tell me? Why couldn't you just talk to me instead of all . . . *this*? Fucking hell, Cait. Fuck.'

Footsteps. Shoes scraping timber.

'You promised me. You promised!'

She was in front of me, I could tell. I stared at the floor, tried to pretend she wasn't there.

'After last time. You promised, Caitlin.'

Breathing hard. I could smell her. Toothpaste. Clean.

'Caitlin. Look at me, Cait.' Trembling. 'Look at me right now or I'll leave and you will be all on your own.'

I shook my head, a rush of fear exploding behind my eyes.

'Caitlin.'

'Stop.' I lifted my head, set my jaw. 'Please. I'm fine. I'm okay.'

Her face was all I could see. Hard. Angry. Red. New tears on top of old, dried trails of salt. Spittle at the corners of her lips. Nose pink and swollen.

'You're okay?' She laughed, bitter, cold. 'Right. Good. I can go then. Because you need to know, Cait, I nearly didn't come. I am so, so, *so* angry right now.'

'Lina . . .' I reached for her arm, and she jerked it away.

'I wasn't going to come. You should know that. But then I got scared.' She deflated. 'I got scared that you were . . .'

My chest broke.

'I thought you'd . . .' She looked past me. Her voice shrank. 'That smell. God. It stinks here. It stinks like it did that day. That fucking smell and I thought this time . . .'

'I would never—' But I couldn't say it.

'Maybe not on purpose.' She shook her head. 'You promised you wouldn't do this again.' Her eyes came back to me, open so wide I could see the whites all the way around. Pupils like pinpricks.

Furious. Exhausted. She was whispering but it was razor-sharp and awful. 'You promised you would get help.'

'I didn't need help. It was just shock, after the accident. I was fine.'

'You hardly got out of bed for weeks. You—'

'Someone died, Lina.' I shouted it, too big for the room. 'Someone fucking died and he had a kid and a wife and now he's dead and it is all my fault.'

I looked at her, right at her. She was still, stunned.

'I did this,' I said, looking at the piece of paper still in her hand. 'I knew it was ours but I took it and I booked it anyway. And I wanted to tell you that night, I swore to myself I would, but I couldn't, so I went home instead, and someone fucking *died*.'

'Cait.' She shook her head. 'It was an accident.'

'No, it wasn't.'

'It was.'

She looked at the piece of paper again. 'Is that why you didn't go?'

'No. I just . . .' I couldn't remember why I didn't go. I got scared. The weeks went on and I got more and more scared.

'You should have fucking gone,' she said, looking away, her voice gently angry. 'I would have been jealous, because you were actually doing this amazingly fun thing and I was buying homewares. And I did want to go. One day. For a couple of weeks. A holiday. Just to see.' She frowned, as though in disbelief. 'I wanted you to go. You always wanted to go. More than I did.'

'No, it was—' But I couldn't even say it anymore.

She read the booking confirmation one more time, then folded it up and put it on the floor. 'I wish you'd just gone. I want to say I would have missed you but it's not like you've been here anyway. Not really.'

'I'm sorry.'

'You promised, Cait.' She hardened. 'You promised you would get help.'

'Leen—'

'You were not fine. You lost your job. You got kicked out of your house. Maybe you don't remember, but I do. I was there. I remember every single thing.'

I didn't remember all of it. I took two pills every eight hours, and I slept. I was just tired. I was just cold and I was supposed to be dead. And then one day I woke up and she was there. On a chair, that time. Her hair had been different. Or maybe mine had been.

When did you cut your hair?

That was the first thing she said to me after the accident.

It looks terrible.

'I got better.'

She laughed. Bitter. Sad. 'No, you didn't. Not really. You pretended to. You got a new job and a new flat and pretended it didn't matter. And then Dex, and you—'

'I got help, Leen, after that.' I reached for her hand but she wouldn't let me touch her. I wanted to tell her about group, about Donna and Geoff and Frannie . . . but maybe not Frannie. 'I did.'

'Not enough, obviously.'

'I tried.' So many times. Over and over. Every week. I was careful. 'I got better.'

'You pushed everyone away. When was the last time you saw anybody from before the accident? Your old work friends? People from uni? School? You know someone asked about you the other day, why you never come to anything anymore, and I didn't know what to say. Your family. God. Your mum asks me all the fucking time . . .' She hesitated. 'Tom.'

I winced at the sound of his name.

'Is that what happened?'

'No,' I said, firmly. 'He would have left anyway.'

'You don't know that.'

'I do.' I didn't want to talk about this, but she was wrong. He would have. He had. 'Like Dex.'

'You said yourself that he wasn't like Dex.'

'Still.' *Too much.* 'He would have.'

She shrugged. 'Maybe. Who the fuck knows? You never let me meet him. All I know is that you liked him so much that you invited him to my wedding and you have never, *ever*—' She blinked, stunned, like she'd just figured something out. 'God,' she said, looking away. 'You don't even know.'

I frowned. 'What?'

She pressed her lips together. 'Nothing.' Shook her head. 'It doesn't matter. You pushed him away, same as always.'

Something unfurled inside me, pushing into my throat. I forced it down.

'You pushed *me* away. I've kept calling you, kept trying, but how many times have you called me in the past two years?'

'It hasn't been . . .' I trailed off, suddenly confused. August. Matt was a Virgo. Two years, and I'd barely noticed. 'I'm sorry, Leen.'

She clenched her jaw, looked away. 'God. You're my best friend, Cait.' The way she said it made it sound like a weight, a burden she wished she could get rid of.

I swallowed.

'You always will be. I know we don't always agree and you think I'm basic.' She rolled her eyes. 'I probably am. But you were there for me when everything was so shit I thought I would never get over it. We're family, and I love you.' She took a breath, and her voice changed. 'But I don't know how to do this anymore.'

I felt my heart bend, break, crumble. Felt it all come up, spill over, all the pretending, all gone. And then just fear. 'Leen . . .'

She sighed. 'You need help, Caitlin. I want to help you, but I can't, not if you won't—'

I wanted to argue, to fight; to tell her she was wrong, to leave, that I was fine on my own and I'd go back to group and everything would be okay.

But I'd tried that. I'd tried being careful and it hadn't worked.

'Please, Cait,' she said. 'Please.'

I looked at her. She'd closed her eyes, and she seemed so young, suddenly, and much too tired. She looked completely lost. She couldn't do it anymore and neither could I. I couldn't lie anymore. The blackness that had chased me home nudged up against my spine, reminding me that it was still there, that it could still take me, if I let it. 'I'm so scared, Leen,' I said, my words tiny.

She nodded. 'I know.' She took my hand and pulled me closer, tightened her arms around me. My head fell against her shoulder. So heavy. So safe. 'I know, Caitie.'

'What's wrong with me?' I felt the heat behind my eyes. 'Why am I like this?'

She didn't answer.

'I need help, Lina.' And I started to cry. Hard, heavy, thick sobs. 'I have tried so hard and I can't do this anymore. Please help me.' Cried and cried and cried and cried, finally, and through heaving sobs I said it over and over again. 'I need help.'

◆

Lina picked me up, undressed me, put me in the shower. She was gentle when she touched me, like I frightened her, and I should have hated it, but I didn't. I was too tired. When the hot water ran out she wrapped me in a towel and helped me get dressed. I was so weak, I realised. I'd cried forever but there had been hardly any tears. My body had nothing left.

I felt numb, exhausted, and something else. A strange sort of calm. I felt a thousand years old, like a decade had passed in just a few minutes and I couldn't remember anything that had happened.

I felt lost, completely.

'What day is it?' I asked, as she helped me into my hoodie.

'Tuesday.' Like it was the most normal question in the world.

I bit my lip. I'd left Sawyer's on Thursday. A hundred years ago. 'How long have you—'

She shook her head. 'Don't ask.'

'I'm sorry.'

Another shake. Stop. 'Are you hungry?'

I shrugged. My stomach made a sound, wanting tangled with terror. 'Thirsty. Yes. Maybe.'

She made me toast, brought me a glass of water, settled me on the floor with a pillow while she stripped my bed, rolled everything up in a sheet and cast it aside, like she'd done it a dozen times. Like she'd done all this a dozen times. I watched her face, set, bottom lip pulled under, perfectly still. Decades of practice.

'How's your mum?' I asked while I chewed. The first mouthful went down hard, nearly came back up, but the second was easier. I couldn't remember the last time I'd eaten and my stomach hurt.

'Huh?' She touched the mattress and wrinkled her nose. 'This needs airing.'

I chewed, waiting.

'She's okay,' she said softly.

I hesitated. We never talked about this. 'Did she ever try again? After . . .'

I expected her to flinch, or react, tell me to stop, but she didn't. She just shook her head, as though I'd asked her if she liked olives. 'I don't think so. Meeting Colin helped. Mum never was much good at being on her own. And medication helped too. Bucketloads of medication.'

'Does she still take it?'

'As far as I know.' She shrugged, thoughtful. 'She always will, I think.'

She picked up a pillow, held it still, eyebrows pinched together like she was studying it.

'She doesn't talk about it much. Colin tells me. She'll be good for months—years, sometimes—and then she'll be less good for a while. But she's better.'

She paused for a long time. 'She tried a few different things before one stuck, you know?'

I didn't, but I nodded.

Lina pulled an empty backpack from next to my bedside table, shook off the dust.

'But it did help. Therapy too. I don't know.' She opened it up on the dry end of the bed. 'Lots of things. I think that's the trick. No one single thing.'

I liked the sound of her voice. Calm. Wise. She picked up a basket of clothes I didn't remember washing, held up a pair of jeans and folded them.

'What are you doing?'

'Packing.' Put the jeans in the backpack, reached for a t-shirt. 'I talk about it with my psych a lot. What the trick is. Whether there is one. I don't think there is.'

'Wait. Where am I going? And when do you see a psych?'

'Caitlin.' Lina stopped, a jumper rolled around her forearms. 'My dad's a fuckwit, and my mum tried to kill herself, and my best friend and I found her. And now my best friend keeps having breakdowns, and it feels like it's my fault and I don't know what to do.'

'It's not your fault.'

'I know.' Her mouth twisted, tightened for a moment. 'But it makes me so angry that sometimes I just—' She finished folding the jumper, put it in the bag a little too forcefully. 'Of course I see a psych.' She sighed. 'I'm okay,' she added, too fast, before stopping, shaking her head. 'Or, no. I'm not.' She studied her hands, stretched out her fingers. 'I'm not okay with it at all. It sucks. It's not fair. But it's not like I can tell you how horrible it is to watch you come apart like this. It's not like I can just say, *Hey, Mum, remember that time you decided you'd rather be dead than keep being my mum? Well, it sucked, and I hated you for it for a long time.* I can tell my dad I hate him but it's not like he even cares, so there's no point. And the two of you . . .'

I bit my lip. It tasted like guilt, like sadness. Stale and old. 'I'm sorry, Leen.'

She sighed, went back to the washing basket, grabbed a fistful of underpants and packed them. 'At least Matt's normal,' she said, filling in the silence. Always filling in the silence. 'He's the most mentally well person I've ever met. I asked him once if he ever stayed up late worrying about things and he looked confused by the question. I think maybe that's why I'm marrying him.' Pulled out another pair of jeans, folded them. 'Oh, and you're coming to my place.'

She gave me a hard look, then went back to the clothes.

'It smells here, Caitlin. I've told you that before. It smells like cat piss, and—' She swallowed. Hard. 'Also, your mattress is a mess and you can't sleep on it until it dries. Have you never heard of a mattress protector?' She shook her head. 'Kids these days.'

I couldn't help but laugh. 'I'm older than you.'

'I'm wiser.'

'I know.'

I did. Maybe she always had been.

I remembered what she'd said. My stomach tightened, the toast threatening to come back up. 'Lina?'

'What?' She was folding t-shirts. I couldn't remember ever having folded a t-shirt in my life.

'I don't know if I can come to your place.'

She frowned, not looking up. 'It's fine. We have two spare rooms. Matt doesn't mind. He's working all the time anyway.' She drew in a long breath, exhaled. Shaky. 'He got a promotion just before Christmas. A big one. I would have told you, if you'd ever let me. He's working all the time now, but the money is good. It's how we can afford the wedding.'

'Oh.' I felt a flood of guilt for thinking all the things I didn't want to admit I'd been thinking.

She hesitated. 'I didn't lie, back then. We needed all our money for the deposit. Every cent. You know, our fridge died during the move and we had to borrow money from Mum to buy another one.'

I went to say something, but she cut me off.

'But it's not like I was forced into it. I could have gone with you. I could have said no to the house. We could have bought something smaller or older. I made a choice, and it was the right one for me. I hoped it would be the right one for you too. I'm sorry.'

'Leen—'

'Come to my place.' She smiled. 'It's only a townhouse, but it's nice.'

'No, it's not . . .' I shook my head. 'I don't know if I can get there.' I felt ridiculous and pathetic—and even more ridiculous and pathetic for ever thinking this was normal. 'In a car, or . . . since the accident. I can't.'

Lina stopped, the pieces falling into place. She put down a pair of socks and came around the bed. 'Cait.' She kneeled in front of me. 'It'll be okay.'

I looked at her. 'I'm scared.'

'I know.' She took my hand, squeezed it. Holding on.

'Why are you doing this?' My voice shook. 'If I'm so . . . why?'

She looked down at our hands. 'You're my best friend. What else can I do?'

A wave of sadness rumbled over me. Another one. I wanted to close my eyes and wish it away but I had been doing that for so long and I didn't have the strength anymore. I let it come. 'I'm sorry, Lina. I'm so sorry.'

She sighed. 'It's . . .' But it wasn't, and she couldn't say it was. Instead, she said, 'I'll drive carefully, okay?'

♦

It wasn't that simple. None of it was. But she put me in the front seat and did up my seatbelt and put a pale blue elephant in my lap. 'In case you get scared.'

I pressed its belly. 'It's a boy!' a tinny animated voice squawked. My eyes got hot and if I could have cried, I would have.

'Oh God,' Lina said, getting into the driver's seat and doing up her own seatbelt. 'You better not do that all the way. Go for the head.'

I went to laugh, but it came out a whimper.

♦

I'd never seen Lina so in control. She navigated traffic without a single wrong move, while I gripped the elephant so tight its trunk came loose, counted to five, ten, fifty, six hundred. It was awful and my chest hurt the whole time but she kept going and I didn't leap out and run away, no matter how many times I wanted to.

I felt wrung out. The past—week? I couldn't quite believe it had been a week since I saw those bandages on Frannie's wrist, since everything went sideways. It felt like it had been a year, a minute, but it had hollowed me out, hollowed out the good and the bad, leaving just skin and bones.

Lina's townhouse looked like every other townhouse. Pale grey render with dark tiles and a square of green lawn next to the driveway that looked like nobody had ever walked on it. But she was right: inside it was nice. I liked it—even the island bench and the giant oven and the butler's pantry. It felt like a home, warm and safe.

She got me to have another shower. The steam rose up around me and made me nauseous. I felt hungover, even though I hadn't had a drink in days. My mouth was dry and I let it fill up with hot water, desperately thirsty. When I came out she was on the phone, telling my mum everything was all right and she would keep her posted, and I wanted to cry, for the tenth time, for the thousandth time. This time with gratitude, with relief. And when I did, she held on to me, and then she made me dinner and set up a TV in the spare room and put my phone on a charger. All the things I should have been able to do for myself but seemed to have forgotten how.

She flicked through TV shows while I checked my phone. There were calls. Messages. Nic. Holly. Mum. Even Dad. And Lina. Over and over. Voicemails I didn't even want to imagine. Finally, she settled on *The OC*.

'Dumb melodrama,' she said, climbing onto the bed. 'Perfect.'

She curled up next to me, put her head on my shoulder and I let her, surprised by how easy it was, after so long. She smelled like the beach, clean and safe. I couldn't remember the last time we'd been so close. I missed it so much.

'Where's Matt?' I asked after a while.

'Work. Late conference call with Tokyo.'

I took a breath. 'Are you sure he's okay with me being here?'

'Uh-huh. He doesn't have a choice, but he is.'

I exhaled, more relieved than I wanted to say.

She sat up slowly and paused the television, folding her knees to her chest and wrapping her arms around her calves.

'What happened, Caitie?' she asked, without looking at me. Her voice was kind, but it made my breath catch. I knew she'd ask eventually.

'I don't know.' It was true, and it wasn't. 'I got scared. You were right. I wasn't being careful, and I got scared.'

She frowned. 'Caitie, I—'

'I know.' I shook my head. 'I know that's not what you meant. I tried. I tried to tell myself it was okay and it was and then it wasn't.' I couldn't tell her about Frannie. Not yet. One day I would. Even thinking about her made my throat tighten.

She hesitated. There was something else.

'I don't remember everything,' I said, after a long time. 'But I didn't do anything Leen. I didn't take anything or try to . . . I didn't want to die. I just wanted to sleep. I was just so tired.'

She nodded as though confirming a hunch, still avoiding my eyes, and I wasn't sure she believed me. I wasn't sure it mattered.

'So,' she started, her voice trembling. 'Your mum got you in to see your doctor tomorrow.' Her hands tightened on her calves. 'I'll take you. If you want.'

That familiar urge to argue rose up, stiffened my spine.

'You have to,' she said. 'I'm sorry for what I said before, when I said I'd leave. I didn't mean it. I would never just abandon you.' She sighed. 'But I can't do this, not by myself.'

I nodded, understanding. Hating that she had to do this. Hating everything about this, but not hating that I was here.

'I feel like this is too much. What you're doing.'

She frowned. 'Do you want to leave?'

'No.' I shook my head. 'No, I don't. But I'm scared I'm not going to be able to—'

She exhaled. 'I just want you to try. Please, Cait?'

'I don't want to mess up your life.'

'My life is fine, Caitlin.'

There was more I wanted to say, but she grabbed the remote, made the faces on the screen move again. 'Besides, I'm being selfish here too.'

I bit my lip. 'How?'

She settled herself, head on my shoulder again. I let mine fall onto hers.

'I want my best friend at my wedding.'

28

WEDNESDAY, AUGUST

I cried a lot. Cried when I woke up and realised where I was, when I realised that I'd slept the whole night through, that I hadn't had a single nightmare. Cried when I remembered I was supposed to go to work and Lina said she'd called Nic and told him I needed a couple of weeks off.

'He said hi,' she said to me. 'He said to get better. Something about coming back to clean the fridge seals.'

I laughed then—between tears.

Cried over the pancakes Lina made me—my favourite, with lemon and brown sugar; cried on the drive to the doctor's, holding on to my blue elephant and bracing myself at every intersection; cried in the waiting room, and when Lina offered to come in with me.

I cried right through the test the doctor gave me. When he asked if I'd been crying more than usual recently, I cried harder.

I cried when he told me I was severely depressed. 'And probably quite anxious too,' he added, his face as full of pity as it had been when I was ten and had to miss the school swimming carnival because I had chickenpox.

Afterwards, I sat in Lina's car and cried for a long time, because then it was real, and I couldn't pretend anymore, and all I wanted to do was keep pretending.

◆

'Where to?' Lina asked, when I'd finished. She started the car and the vibration of the engine made my spine tingle. I hugged the elephant tighter.

'It's a boy!'

'I don't know.'

She chewed on her lip, looking through the windscreen, thinking.

'Remember when you used to make me go on those stupid train trips with you?'

I frowned. 'Yeah?'

'I used to hate it, sometimes. I just wanted to stay home and watch TV and throw things at the walls to annoy Mum, but you'd insist.'

I blinked, wanting to correct her, remind her that she hated being at home, but I didn't.

'It took me ages to figure out what you were doing.' She sighed. 'I don't know if I ever thanked you.'

I looked at my hands.

'You were there for me when everything was shitty, Cait. You gave me hope when I thought everything would be terrible forever.'

The elephant. My fingernails, jagged and bare. My eyes filled with tears. Again.

'I have an idea,' she said, after a long time.

'What?' My voice cracked, thick with phlegm.

'It's—' she glanced at the display on her car stereo '—it's August thirtieth.'

I nodded.

'That means we fly out to Bali in two and a half months.'

I hadn't realised it was so soon.

'Matt will drive us to the airport. Then we're getting on a plane. It's a seven-hour flight, give or take.'

'It's a boy!'

She jerked at the sound, but went on talking. 'And then there's the transfer. Which will probably be a minivan. The road is—' she wriggled her shoulders '—not the best. Busy. Lots of buses. Insane drivers.'

'It's a boy! It's a boy! It's a boy!'

She inhaled sharply. 'Cait.'

'Sorry.' I released my grip. 'It wasn't me.'

'I want you to do this,' she said, annoyed, frustrated.

I hesitated. I'd been trying not to listen to her but I'd heard every word. 'I know.'

'I want *us* to do this.'

'I know.'

'So.' She sat back in her seat, looking straight ahead. 'I think we need to practise. And I think we need to start right now.'

My breath caught.

It was always catching. Always tight, always hard. It had been so long since I could breathe and I was sick of it, the constant ache in my chest.

She turned to me, and I could see the pleading in her eyes. 'Trust me, Caitie?'

I took a deep breath, and nodded.

◆

She didn't drive far, just north until the houses started to separate out. I squeezed the blue elephant's trunk and its legs and once its belly, and she told me she was going to throw him out the window, asked me where I'd got him from anyway, and I'd cried then, just for a little bit. I was sick of crying.

It was hard, but it wasn't as hard as I'd thought it was going to be, wasn't as momentous as I'd made it in my head. Fear rumbled through me but it didn't burn, and we crossed intersection after intersection and nothing happened. We kept going.

I felt myself relax, sink into the seat, watch the houses instead of frantically checking for other cars. At one point I closed my eyes. When I opened them Lina was smiling, satisfied, and it felt like we might be okay after all.

29

Thursday, September

Georgia wasn't much older than me. She wore funky colourful shoes with thick heels and had a peacock feather tattooed up one side of her calf. I don't know what I'd expected, but it wasn't that. Her office was plain but warm, a series of insipid pastel watercolours on the walls. She caught me studying them and apologised. 'I share the room with someone,' she explained.

I didn't say a lot. Not at first. Eventually, I told her about the accident. Sketched it out, rough and meaningless, the way I'd been sketching it out for myself since it happened, pretending it wasn't a big deal, that it didn't matter. That everything that happened after was normal—shock—and everything before was fine, just life.

Lina had taken the day off, and afterwards she drove me to the mountains.

She'd gone back to work at the start of the week, and I'd been home alone for days, mostly sleeping, catching up. My head still hurt nearly all the time and sometimes when I moved my joints creaked and groaned, but it wasn't like it had been, it wasn't as raw. I didn't dream, not that I remembered, but sometimes when I woke up my chest felt tight and there was a sick dread in my stomach and then I cried again. The silence took turns being deafening and comforting. In between, or when the dread got too much, I watched shitty TV. I finished *The OC* in a matter of days, moved on to *Veronica Mars*. It made me cry. Lina called at lunch, on her afternoon break, checking in. Did we need milk? Was there enough lettuce? Code for *Are you still there? Still alive?* I told her she didn't have to but, truthfully, sometimes I waited for her calls with bated breath.

But I didn't say all that to Georgia, not the first time. I didn't know how.

The mountains were terrifying. The roads curved around cliffs and they made my heart race and at first I felt my heart jump with every curve, every bump, but then it steadied, found its rhythm. I clutched the blue elephant, grateful its batteries had run out so Lina didn't have to throw it out the window. We had lunch in a bakery that opened out onto a little garden, so green it looked like a postcard I'd once found of somewhere in England. 'Thank you, Caitie,' she said, as we got in the car to drive back.

'What for?'

'For trying.'

I cried then, again.

♦

The next appointment, I inked in some of the lines, added the merest hints of colour, of truth. Sawyer's. Dex. Tom. After. Georgia asked me questions but she didn't push. Sometimes, she asked me how I'd felt—after the accident, after leaving Sawyer's, all the times in between—and I tried to tell her, tried to remember, but I didn't like going back there, didn't like thinking about it. The blackness, the certainty that this was all wrong and I wasn't supposed to be here, the way it had chased me home that afternoon, demanding I give in to it.

'Why didn't you?' she asked.

And I didn't know. I didn't know why in that moment, standing in the kitchen of the cat-piss house, I'd decided to go to bed and not do something worse. Something in me had fought it, and won. Somehow.

It scared me to think about it, to talk about it, in case I brought it back, but I knew I had to. For Lina.

For me.

◆

Lina drove us to the beach. She'd taken Thursdays off until the wedding—not because of me, she said, when I asked. To plan. There was so much to plan, she said, but all she seemed to do was take me for drives and read trashy romance novels.

It was too cold to swim, but we ate hot chips and she told me it would be warmer in Bali and described all the cocktails she'd selected for the reception and it was hard to hear, and hard to respond. We didn't talk about the postcard I'd sent, but sometimes I felt it there, too aware of how close I'd come to ruining everything. It was all hard, but the breeze skimmed my arms and when I went to take a breath it only hurt a little.

Sometimes I caught one—a stray Thought. A cluster of them, one after another. I became aware of the pointiness of the shower taps or the slipperiness of the laundry tiles or that there was a single step into the garage, and they'd tumble out, one by one, demanding my attention. I told Georgia and she suggested strategies, so simple I didn't think they'd work. Breathing. Refocusing. Writing the Thoughts down, accepting them instead of fighting them, acknowledging them, letting them go. Different strategies. A toolkit, she called it. I didn't think they'd work but they did, usually, eventually.

Lina called less, only once a day. I ran out of television, found a book to read, something pink with a woman dancing on the cover that I probably should have hated, but I didn't. When I finished the book, telling myself I despised the cutesy happy ending but secretly liking it, I went for a walk, just around the block, getting used to the feeling of moving, getting used to the air, to breathing.

To being alive. Somehow. Still.

30

SUNDAY, SEPTEMBER

Lina invited Mum and Dad for dinner. Jack too, but he had a birthday party, she told me.

I knew Lina had been talking to Mum, and not just about the wedding. Sometimes Lina encouraged me to ring her but I never felt ready. I hadn't seen them in months, I realised, not since we'd had brunch in Newtown and I'd had to leave before I started crying in front of them. We weren't close at the best of times, but it was harder now. So much had happened, and I didn't know what to say.

So I didn't say much. Not at first. They seemed nervous too, especially Dad. He gave me a quick hug and said I was looking well and then made a beeline for Matt, asked him about the football.

I hadn't seen much of Matt. He worked a lot and by the time he came home I was usually half asleep. I knew he and Lina stayed up. Some nights I could hear them talking late into the night, tiny bursts of laughter. I'd never given him much of a chance before, but I'd come to like him. He made Lina happy.

Over dinner, Mum grilled Lina about the wedding, wanted to know all the details, cooed and smiled at everything. I should have hated it, but I didn't. I didn't hate much these days, didn't have the energy, the anger. 'Have you got your dress yet, Cait?' she asked me.

I shook my head. 'Not yet.'

'You need to do that soon.' She looked at Lina. 'I can help you if you want. What colour do you want her to wear, Leen?'

Lina picked up her wine. She'd poured me a glass too but just the smell made my jaw hurt. 'I don't care. Whatever she wants.'

Mum sighed. 'Long? Short? Strapless? They're doing some lovely jumpsuits these days.'

'Not a jumpsuit,' I said quickly. Lina had made spaghetti and it was amazing and I was having a hard time not shovelling it all in at once.

'Well. There's a start. A dress. You'd look lovely in something pink, Cait, with your colouring.'

'Not pink.'

Lina laughed, and Mum made a face. 'Fine, not pink,' she said. 'Satin? Lace? Organza? Chiffon? Tulle? I could make something if you find a pattern.'

'Mum . . .' I took a breath. 'It's okay. Leen and I have talked about it, and I'm going to find something off the rack.'

'Honestly, Sue,' Lina said, 'my dress is enough of a meringue. Caitlin's can be super simple. And we're just having white flowers so the colour doesn't matter.' She looked at me. 'Just not pink.'

Mum didn't seem convinced, but she gave in. 'Okay then. I just think it's better to be prepared with these things.'

Lina smiled reassuringly. 'Literally everything else is organised, isn't it, Matty?'

'Absolutely. Amanda has been amazing. Seriously, Cait—' he looked at me '—when you get married, do it in Bali. Someone else does everything.'

Lina's face froze in shock, but the thought seemed so alien to me right then that I just laughed, hard. *Matt doesn't think too much,*

Lina said once, years ago. Back then I'd thought it was a complaint but now I realised it wasn't.

'Thanks,' I said, 'I'll keep that in mind.'

◆

After dinner, Lina took Mum into the lounge room to show her some pictures of the resort, and Matt disappeared into the study. I carried a stack of dishes into the kitchen, started rinsing them in the sink.

'Hi, Cait.'

'Oh.' I turned around in surprise. 'Hey, Dad. I thought you were . . .'

I didn't know what I'd thought he was doing. He was quiet through dinner, letting Mum talk, like he always did.

'It's all right.' He leaned back against the bench, crossing his arms. He looked older, his hair greyer and mulleting like it did whenever he was overdue for a haircut.

'Did you enjoy dinner?' I pulled the dishwasher open.

'It was great.'

'I swear,' I started awkwardly—I couldn't remember the last time we'd been alone in a room together. Mum was always there, taking up all the air. 'At Sawyer's we had chefs making us dinner every night but Lina's cooking is so much better. It's like she cares more, I think.'

Dad paused. 'Are you going to go back there?' he asked. 'You've been off for a while.'

I shrugged, turned back to the sink. I'd been thinking about it a lot, talking to Georgia about it. 'I think so.'

'You liked that place, didn't you?'

I thought for a minute, staring at the water running into the sink. 'Yeah,' I said finally. 'Yeah, I did.'

I missed the bar, I missed the way my body knew exactly what to do, my brain quiet, and the strange satisfaction I felt at the end of a crazy busy night, being part of something that just worked, that made people happy, even if it was only for a few hours. I even missed the parts of it I hated—I missed caring enough to hate them.

Nic messaged every week or so. *No pressure, I just want to make sure you're okay.* I always replied and told him as much of the truth as I could. That I was getting there, that I was trying. *Soon,* I said. He always said it was fine, and for some reason I believed him.

Holly had messaged too, a couple of times. I'd only replied once. I missed her as well, but I wasn't ready yet.

'How are you, Cait?'

The question startled me. I was expecting more small talk.

Dad pushed off the bench, came around and took the dish I'd been holding, packed it into the dishwasher. 'Don't worry.' He made a face. 'Your mum's been teaching me how to load one of these the right way for twenty years.'

I laughed, knowing exactly what he meant. I picked up another plate, ran it under the tap.

'You know,' he said carefully, 'I used to drive her mad when you were a kid.'

'How so?' I handed it to him.

'After you were born, I was convinced we were going to stuff you up.'

I bit my lip. 'This isn't your fault, Dad.'

He gestured at the stack of plates. I picked up another one. 'I worried about everything. I read all the books—you know, they all contradict each other. Some said to let you sleep whenever. Some to wake you up every hour. Some to, you know—' he hesitated, not sure he could say the word '—breastfeed.'

I smiled.

'I just worried a lot. I worried we were going to overdress you, and you'd get sick. I worried that if you didn't have a feed, there was something wrong. I worried that your mum would get distracted walking you and the pram would roll off . . .' He shook his head as he studied the dishwasher. 'She used to joke that I wanted to wrap you in bubble wrap.'

Another plate. A part of me wanted to laugh, but it wasn't really funny.

'Why not? I'd ask. It'd keep you safe. A bit of a suffocation hazard, though.'

I did laugh then, softly. He didn't seem to mind.

'Sometimes it got a bit worse than worrying, you know? I'd have these nightmares about something happening to you. Your mum hated it. She thought it was because I didn't trust her.'

A familiar tightness spread through my chest. I handed him the last plate, turned off the tap.

'I did. Trust her, I mean. It was just . . . I worried a lot. I don't know. They didn't call it anxiety then. And every time we took you for a check-up they asked your mum how she was feeling, but you know her, she can handle anything. She was fine. The best mum. It was me who . . .'

I looked at him. 'I'm sorry, Dad.'

He finished packing the dishwasher, and went back to his spot against the bench. 'As you got bigger, it got easier. You'd bounce. You fell over, but you bounced. You scraped your knee, it got better. I got used to you bouncing.' He paused, thinking. 'And Jack—he was different, or maybe I'd just got the hang of it by then.'

I laughed, remembering the number of times I'd whined at them as a teenager. *How come he's allowed? You never used to let me.*

'But you got older, and I noticed it sometimes.' He frowned. 'You were always careful.'

Careful.

'Always trying. You worked hard at school and uni and everything, but you never seemed . . .'

I blinked, felt that too-familiar heat behind my eyes.

'Happy. Not really.' He shook his head. 'You weren't unhappy, I don't think. But it felt like you were always working, you know? Always holding back.'

The words stung. I locked my fingers together, looking at them through tears.

'And with Lina, after Jenny, the way you tried to look after her, the way you worried about her. But at the same time you . . . I don't know. I tried to tell myself I was imagining it. Putting my neuroses on to you, your mum said one time. Easier to think you're crazy than your daughter—'

'Dad.' I put out a hand. We weren't huggers, but he took it, and pulled me in until my head found his shoulder. I felt like a little kid. 'It's not your fault.'

'Lina told us about the accident,' he said. 'You could have told us yourself, you know? But I get why you didn't. I probably wouldn't have let you get in a car ever again.'

I laughed, but it was wet, through tears.

'Your mum would have told you you were fine, and to get on with it. She's different. I think that's a good thing,' he added. It reminded me of someone else.

'Yeah.'

'She didn't really want to talk about it. I think she still doesn't. She doesn't get it, not really.'

'I know.' I pulled away.

'But she loves you. She does. She always has.'

I nodded. I knew that too.

'You okay, sweet?'

'Yeah,' I said. I felt tears spill down my face, but I was smiling. 'Yeah, Dad. Thank you.'

31

Thursday, September

'I found her.'

Georgia straightened in her seat, looked at me in surprise.

'Who?' she asked. 'Jenny?'

I nodded. Georgia's shoes were purple, patent leather with three silver buckles up the side.

We hadn't been talking about Jenny. We'd been talking about fear, about how it was our brain's way of protecting us from threats, and it had sparked something in me.

'I thought she was dead.' I closed my eyes, remembering. I hated thinking about that day, about how I'd felt when I saw her. Scared—more than scared. My blood had gone cold and a shock of terror had bolted up my spine.

My mum's sick.

Is she going to die?

'That would have been awful for you.'

I shrugged. A familiar shrug, brushing off her words. Brushing off the memory. I didn't know why I'd brought it up now. 'It was worse for Lina. It was her mum. She was so upset. She was screaming and crying and begging me to help her.'

'And you did.'

'I tried to.'

Georgia paused. Studying me. 'What about you? Were you upset?'

'Of course. It was horrible.' I felt cold. 'But it was worse for her.'

'Caitlin.'

'What?' But I knew, and she knew I knew, because she didn't say anything, just tapped her notepad with her pen. She did that while she was waiting for me to get to the point. It was one of her tells.

I shook my head, my eyes filling with tears. 'I don't want to talk about this.'

'You brought it up.' It wasn't an accusation or a challenge, just a reminder. I had.

'Did you talk to anyone afterwards?'

'Lina did,' I said. 'Jenny—when she got better, I guess, I can't remember—wanted her to see a shrink. She did. Only a couple of times.'

'And you?'

'No.' I frowned. 'I was okay. I was just worried about Lina.'

Everyone was so worried about Lina. Mum kept asking me how she was. *The poor girl.*

'Lina had told me her mum was sick, but I didn't understand what she meant. I didn't wanted to. And then when I found her, I understood, and I felt like I'd let Lina down, I hadn't listened to her.'

I looked away at the pastel watercolours on the wall. They were supposed to be soothing yet they were anything but.

'Lina had no-one, after that. Jenny was still there but Lina didn't want to be around her. She was so angry. And she had no-one.'

'Except you.'

I nodded. 'I looked after her. I tried to help her.'

'And you? Who helped you?'

I shook my head, trying to figure out what she was getting at. Wishing—as I'd wished many times—that she'd just spit it out.

'You went through this awful, horrible thing,' Georgia continued. 'Who helped you through it? Who did you talk to?'

'No-one.' My voice sounded funny. 'I was okay. I didn't need anyone. I coped.'

'How?' she asked. 'How did you cope?'

I shrugged. 'It didn't affect me that much.' But my tongue seemed to stumble over the words.

She sat forward. 'Caitlin.' Her voice was so soft and suddenly I wanted her to give me a hug. I wanted someone to give me a hug. I was fourteen again and I was sitting outside holding Lina as she cried and I just wanted someone to give *me* a hug. I was so scared. I'd been so scared. Scared that Jenny was going to die, scared of what would happen to Lina, to me. 'I want you to think about this more. Not now, maybe. But let's come back to it again soon. I want you to think about whether it's true that it didn't affect you. Can you do that?'

I looked at her. She was waiting, not tapping her notepad, not doing anything, just watching me, her face so kind, so patient. I wondered what she'd say if I did ask her for a hug, if she'd give me one. Instead, after a long, long time, I nodded. 'Okay.'

◆

When we finished, I cried in Lina's car for a long, long time. My body doubled over and I fell into her lap and she rubbed my back, holding me, the way I'd once held her.

I'd promised her that I'd look after her. That I'd always be there for her. I'd promised myself.

She'd tried to tell me about her mum, that she wasn't all right, that she needed help, and I'd ignored her, brushed her off. I hadn't paid enough attention to what she was saying. I'd been careless, thoughtless.

I promised myself. I'd pay more attention; I'd be more aware.

I promised I'd be more careful. About everything.

'I'm sorry,' I said, between tears. 'I'm so sorry.'

Lina rubbed my back and said it was okay, over and over, but I wasn't apologising to her. It wasn't her forgiveness I needed, and the realisation just made me cry harder.

32

THURSDAY, OCTOBER

I slept.

I didn't sleep.

Some nights I had nightmares—I could never remember them, but I could feel that familiar sickness in my stomach—and I'd lie there awake and it was so quiet I didn't know how much time had passed and it was terrifying, still, but then I'd sleep and when I woke up I couldn't remember why.

I didn't walk; not at night. During the day I walked around the block or to the service station on the main road, but at night I had nowhere to go.

Some nights I went out and stood in the middle of the street, looking around at all the quiet houses, smoking cigarettes—it was the only time I did anymore—sure if anyone saw me they'd think I was crazy but sure no-one would see me, and they'd be right anyway. Stood there, with nowhere to go, waiting, not sure if I was hopeful or petrified of what would happen next.

I saw Georgia again and again. I told her about Careful Caitie.

About how at first she just worried about Lina, wanted to help her, to make sure nothing bad ever happened to her again.

And then she started worrying about other things. About herself. She kept thinking about Jenny, what had made her the way she was, driven her to do what she did, worried about the same thing happening to her. She worried about caring too much, feeling too much, loving too much, like Jenny had, and so she created a world in which she wouldn't, in which she was safe.

And, still, she worried about Lina. Even when it became clear that Lina was okay, she worried about her more than anything. She planned a whole trip just to make Lina happy, ignoring the fact that Lina was already happy, because she worried about what it would mean if Lina was happy, if Lina didn't need her anymore.

She was so careful. So safe.

And then one time she wasn't, and everything fell apart.

It took weeks. Sometimes I'd talk for an entire hour; sometimes I'd only talk for ten seconds and then there would be these long, awful silences as I tried to untangle it all in my head, tried to figure it out. 'I know it doesn't make a lot of sense,' I said once, and Georgia had frowned, told me it did make sense, but that maybe it didn't need to.

◆

I told her about the trip. I hated talking about it, but I wanted to. I didn't realise how much until I started. I told her how I'd planned it for Lina but I'd wanted it for myself. How the more safe and careful I was, the more a part of me wanted to do something that wasn't. Go somewhere I didn't know, somewhere noisy and wild and alive.

I told her how it was easier to tell myself it was for Lina than to admit it was for me, because then it felt safe, it didn't feel like such a risk.

'Why didn't you go?' she asked.

'Because of the accident.'

She waited, tapping her pen on her notepad. I wanted to tell her I knew what she was doing when she did that, but instead I told her the truth.

'Because I had to be careful. I wasn't careful and somebody died.'

'It wasn't your fault, Caitlin.'

I shook my head, not sure I believed her. Not sure I wanted to.

'It was silly. It was a fantasy,' I said. The words came hard and even I didn't believe them. 'And risky. Dangerous.' I thought about all the things.

The planes. The guns. The subways.

'I was scared. I got scared.'

'Of what?'

After the accident, all those worries turned into cold, raw fear, and I was just scared of everything. Dying. After the accident, it was all I could think about. Dying became inevitable, and it scared me so much.

'Everything.'

She shifted, tucking her purple shoes and their silver buckles behind the leg of her chair, studied me.

'What do you want, Caitlin?' she asked finally. 'I know what you wanted before the accident, but what do you want now?'

I looked at my hands. One thing.

'I don't know.'

But that wasn't true either, and maybe from the way she looked at me and nodded, she knew that too.

◆

Afterwards, Lina drove us to the Northern Beaches. The blue elephant lived in her car and the sunlight had bleached its fur, turned it nearly white, but still I clutched it as she drove, held on.

'Tell me about him,' she said, catching me looking at its broken trunk.

'Who?'

She glanced at me, shrugged and looked back at the road. I squeezed the elephant, so worn out I could feel the plastic battery box in its belly.

'He was just nice, Leen.' I could feel my eyes getting hot. 'I felt like I could talk to him, you know? About anything.' I shook my head. 'I didn't, but I could have. I wanted to.'

I looked up at the road. There was a ute in front of us driving slowly, like he was lost. It was almost comforting.

'He listened to me. Properly. Like what I said mattered.' It hurt to talk about him. Even with Georgia, I struggled. 'I don't know. It's hard to explain. He just made me feel . . .' Everything.

Still.

It had been ages, but when I thought about him it felt like yesterday. It stung.

'On paper, he was like all those guys I used to date, you know? The ones you used to tease me about? But he wasn't. He never tried to impress me or outsmart me or make me feel like I should admire him for being accidentally born into the right family or being a doctor or living in a fancy apartment.' I paused. 'I just liked him. A lot.'

I heard her make a sound, but when I looked over at her she was staring straight ahead, her expression unreadable.

I remembered something suddenly, something she'd said the last time we'd talked about Tom. Weeks ago.

'Leen?'

'Yeah?'

'What don't I know?'

She frowned, but her eyes didn't move, burning into the ute in front of us, as though willing it to move.

'You haven't figured it out yet?' she asked, eventually.

I blinked. 'I don't think so.'

'Oh.' She sounded surprised. 'You will.'

'Leen . . .'

She pressed her lips closed, changed gears, checked her mirrors. 'It's a good thing, don't worry.'

I watched her, waiting, but she seemed determined not to say anything else. Finally, she turned on the radio. I didn't recognise the song that came on but she started singing softly. Her eyes shifted in my direction and when she caught me watching her she looked at the road again.

'You changed, Cait,' she said, almost absently. 'After the accident.'

'I fell apart.'

She hitched one shoulder up a fraction, like that didn't matter.

I sighed. 'I thought you said it was a good thing.'

'No, not—' She shook her head. 'You'll figure it out.'

She kept staring at the windscreen, the faintest hint of a smile on her lips. I was confused, trying to solve a riddle I didn't understand. There were so many riddles and I was so tired.

'Why can't you just tell me?' I asked, hoping I didn't sound as petulant as I felt.

'Because it doesn't work that way.'

I looked out the window, annoyed.

But I *had* changed. After the accident I felt so much more. More of everything. More scared. More alone. More needy.

Too much, and I didn't get how that could possibly be a good thing.

I felt a surge of frustration—at Lina, at Georgia, at everyone; wondered why everybody kept expecting me to figure it all out, why nobody would just tell me what to think or how to feel or what to do. Why I had to do it by myself, when they knew the answers. Suddenly it felt incredibly unfair.

I pulled my tobacco out of my bag, finding a filter and touching it to my lip. I wasn't allowed to smoke in Lina's car, but she let me roll cigarettes, just for something to do.

I touched again, put the filter back in the packet, not in the mood.

'Cait . . .' Lina sighed. She turned the steering wheel, taking us around a bend. 'You're going to be okay,' she said, still looking at the road. 'I know it.'

She was smiling, and I didn't know why but there was something about her expression that broke the tension, and I smiled too. She turned the music up, and my shoulders softened as I sank into the seat, clutching the blue elephant and staring out the window. In that moment, I believed her.

◆

Lina and Matt stayed up watching television but I went to bed early, exhausted—by Georgia, by the drive, by my own thoughts, which seemed louder than they had been in a while. Different thoughts; not about death, but about everything else. Trying to solve riddles I didn't understand. Answer questions I'd been ignoring for years . . . for my whole life.

What did I want?

Hey. I'm sorry. I'm so sorry for everything. I'm trying to fix the ending. I hope one day I can. Caitlin

It took a long time to tap out, longer to send. And after I did I stared at my phone for a long time, wondering if he'd get it, if he'd respond, if it even mattered. Then I turned the phone off and put it down, tried to sleep.

It didn't feel like progress, but maybe it was.

◆

I walked more and more during the day, my body feeling more and more solid. I read books and flicked through the newspapers Matt brought home.

Mum came round and took me out for lunch on her days off. I'd never been much for housework but I found myself tidying up, just for something to do, folding laundry and cleaning the bathroom and vacuuming the carpets. Lina said I didn't have to; she thought I was doing it out of guilt, obligation, but I wasn't. It was just something to do with my hands, with my body.

I was halfway through rearranging her butler's pantry when I realised I was bored. There was a little over a month until the wedding, and suddenly that seemed like an impossibly long time to spend cleaning Lina's already much-too-clean house, as nice and safe as it was. I needed something else.

I wanted something else.

I called Lina, told her first.

'Are you sure, Caitie?' She sounded worried.

'I am, Leen.'

'Now?' she asked. 'Can you wait until—'

'I can't.' I couldn't. I didn't know why. I'd made the decision and I had to do it before I changed my mind. 'I have to try, at least.'

And then I called Nic.

33

Tuesday, October

It was a package deal.

I couldn't drive, so if I was going back to Sawyer's, even part-time, I had to go back to the cat-piss house, which still wasn't a house but I knew would still smell of cat piss—so much more strongly now because I was used to the smell of Lina's deodorant and Matt's shower gel and the fresh-cut flowers Lina brought home from the markets every Saturday.

Lina offered to take me and help me get settled in, but I worried that if she did I'd change my mind and come straight back with her, so in the end I asked if Matt would drive me. He even took a few hours off work so he could. 'Not that he wants you to leave,' she said. 'It's just easier during the day.'

'I know.'

'You don't have to go.' She picked up a hoodie I hadn't packed yet, sat down on the bed holding it. 'You could find a job closer or a day job. Matt likes having you around. I don't think he'd care if you stayed.'

I nodded. I knew all of that. It wasn't the first time she'd said it and it wasn't the first time I'd thought about it. I'd thought about it a lot. I'd talked to Georgia about it, how tempting it was to start over, the way I had after the accident; to walk away and pretend nothing had happened.

But, I'd said, my eyes watering, *I can't just keep starting over. At some point, I have to deal with things, don't I?*

But it wasn't just that.

I missed Sawyer's. The warmth of the timber and the orange glow of the lights in their industrial cages. The bluesy instrumentals and the smell of pork shoulder dissolving slowly in a barely warm oven. Nic. Holly. Rachel, even though I'd never admit it to anyone else.

'What about Dex?'

Not him.

I took a breath, looking out the window into Lina's backyard and the backyards beyond. I couldn't decide if they were too empty or just right. I hadn't thought about Dex. It was as though he'd never existed.

I bit my lip. 'I don't know, Leen.'

I felt cold, suddenly. More tired than I'd felt in a while.

I have to try, I'd said to Georgia. And I did—even if it was hard. Especially when it was hard. I said it again to Lina and she nodded.

'I'm not better. Not all the way,' I added, watching a bird fly into a tree and then land, rest. Thought about what would happen if the branch broke. Counted down from ten and let it pass. 'But I don't know if I ever will be, if I don't do this.'

Too quiet. Too still. Too much time to think.

'Can you call me?' She put down the hoodie. 'Every few days at least?'

I laughed. 'I'll call you every day,' I said. 'And I've got Thursdays off, so we can still practise after Georgia's.'

Thursdays and Tuesdays off. Every second Sunday. I hadn't asked for Tuesdays, but Nic had assumed.

◆

I was scared. The second Matt drove away I wished I'd gone with him, even though he drove like a demon and I'd spent the entire trip over gripping the dash. I'd been alone in Lina's house for whole days but being alone in the cat-piss house for even one minute made me breathe harder. It did smell. It smelled really bad, and it was noisy and the windows shook every time a bus rolled past, but at least my mattress was dry and Lina had bought me a mattress protector as a welcome home present. I put it on, and a sheet, unpacked all my clothes, walked to the supermarket and bought bread and milk and butter and cheese and tobacco. My chest thrummed as I walked down King Street, the familiar stirrings at the corners of my mind, chill in my bones. I was starting back at Sawyer's the next day and the sun was setting and I didn't know what to do, where to go. How.

Until I did.

◆

'Hi.' I looked around at the faces, all a little bit beige. 'I'm Caitlin. I'm twenty-eight and I'm a waitress.' I hesitated. 'I think.'

'Welcome, Caitlin,' a nurse called Evelyn said.

She was new, but at first it felt like nothing else had changed. Beige chairs arranged in a circle, on beige lino. Maybe the circle was neater than I remembered—Evelyn still cared—but the coffee was still the same beige mud served in beige cups, and the crack in the wall was exactly the same size as it always had been.

I didn't know what I was doing there, what I was looking for.

'Hello, everyone, I'm Carlos. It's been two weeks since my last confession. I had a cold last week.'

It was so familiar it hurt, right in my heart.

◆

'The other day I was in a shopping centre and they were doing that thing, you know, where the lady walks around with the little cups of chicken? So many people took them. It's crazy. You don't know when it was cooked or how it was stored or anything. I mean, maybe salmonella isn't a big deal for most people, but if you're immuno-compromised it could kill you. E. coli. All that stuff. And I mean, chicken? They pump those birds so full of hormones it's making girls go into puberty early, you know? Breast cancer rates are nuts.'

Frannie flinched at that. Her bandages were long gone but she wore long sleeves and, despite the heat, she kept pulling at them with her hands. When she first saw me she'd frowned, looked worried, and I'd given her a smile to let her know it was okay. We could talk, I thought. Later, maybe.

Somewhere else.

Flynn was eighteen, with big, frizzy hair and ice-blue eyes and a beakish nose he'd be lucky to grow into one day. He talked for a long time, seemingly plucking new theories out of the air, his sentences running on, from hormone-filled chickens to chemtrails to vaccines to a secret government weapons facility a hundred kilometres west of Alice Springs. I could see Geoff making fists in his lap, Carlos's foot twitching against the leg of his chair.

He didn't bother me. What he was saying may have sounded ridiculous but I could see the way his eyes flicked around the room. He just wanted someone to talk to, someone who believed him, made him feel normal.

As he spoke, I took my own personal rollcall. Louise, Frannie, Geoff, Carlos. Glenn, Donna. Flynn. Amara, who'd come for a while when I first started—murder, most likely by serial killer—and Chris, who I didn't know but was worried about terrorist attacks.

All the same, telling all the same stories.

Beryl was gone.

Not dead; just stopped coming. Carlos helped her with her shopping every Friday, he told me during a break—Evelyn liked breaks; she believed in 'resetting the room'—and she was doing fine, better than fine. He told me she'd met someone—Neville, who'd been a biker in the seventies and had tattoos on his fingers. Neville had come along on her last night, admitted that he'd made some mistakes in his day but he'd served his time and now he was focused on making Beryl happy. She thought she was going to live to a hundred, at least.

I had a feeling she was right.

And something else had changed. It took me a while to figure out, but when I did it was like it was the clearest thing in the world, like I'd known it all along, from the second I'd decided to come back.

♦

'A couple of years ago,' I said into a short silence, my voice shaking; it was late, and I was tired, but I'd been waiting and it was time, 'I was in an accident.'

I told it again. All of it this time. The accident. The aftermath.

'After that, I couldn't get in a car. Or on a bus or a train.' I didn't look at Carlos or Donna, but I heard them shift in their seats. 'I didn't go anywhere, for two years. I told my parents that I had to work on Christmas Day, so I wouldn't have to go home.'

I felt a flush of shame as I remembered. Mum had been so hurt—Dad too, probably, but he would never have admitted it. I'd pushed them away, like I'd pushed away Lina, so I wouldn't have to deal with all the guilt I felt every time I was near them.

'I walk everywhere,' I said. Louise's eyebrows shot up, and I tried to ignore them. 'And sometimes it's terrifying. Sometimes it's so quiet and I'm so sure that someone is going to just—' I shook my head. 'But it's less terrifying than everything else. I thought I was being brave and in control but I was just being scared. I just didn't want to deal with it.'

Like all of them, I thought, looking around. Like Geoff, who'd moved again, this time because of a loose floorboard in his dining room. Or Glenn, whose eyes were the same colour as the ocean, but who might never see it again. Louise, who'd given up macramé and baking and capoeira and knitting and pottery.

Like Carlos, who'd put his trip to Fiji on indefinite hold after reading a brochure for travel insurance. *Have you ever read one of those policies?* he'd asked earlier. *They're a shopping list of tragedies, and all the big ones are excluded.* And I'd nearly laughed, and then nearly cried, because I'd had the same conversation with Lina just a few days before.

Frannie.

I could barely look at Frannie.

'I'm still scared,' I went on. 'But it's different now. I think maybe I'm different now.'

Mum had called the day before and I'd told her I was going back to Sawyer's. She'd seemed surprised, happy. *That's good*, she said. *You'll be back to your old self in no time.* And I hadn't known how to respond.

'Thanks, Cait,' Geoff said, when I stopped. I looked at him. Our unofficial leader, who cared so much about all of this. 'It's good you're finally talking about it.'

I looked away, at the floor, beige lino, faded and starting to bubble. Someday someone would tear all this up and replace it with plush carpet and an office full of web developers. Or knock down the whole building and put up apartments. It might be for the best.

One day, we'd all be dead, I thought. Cancer, car accident, electrocuted by a dodgy kettle. Maybe none of the above. One day, it would all be over, and maybe we'd be ready or maybe we'd be looking the other way—it wouldn't matter; not really.

All this time we'd spent talking about it would be for nothing.

'It's not enough,' I said softly. 'I don't think it's enough, to just keep talking about it.'

Your old self.

A different person.

You changed.

'I think I have to do more than that. I have to keep trying. Keep fighting.'

When I forced my eyes back to Frannie, she was staring at her fingernails, baby blue, like the elephant I'd left in Lina's car.

'I think we all do,' I added softly. She smiled, small and uncertain, but I saw it.

I saw hope.

◆

When we were done, I walked down the stairs alone, hands in my pockets. I felt strange, but I couldn't pick why, not right away. I felt strange all the time now, different, and I was still trying to figure out how all the pieces of myself fit together, how they worked and how to keep them working.

'You okay?' Donna asked, coming up beside me as I stood on Crown Street and pulled out my tobacco.

I nodded.

'Want a tailor?'

I nearly laughed. 'Thanks,' I said, putting a filter on my lip and shaking my head. 'I don't really like the taste.'

And she did laugh.

I rolled my cigarette, lit it and took a slow, gentle drag. I didn't like the taste of that either, truth be told, but it was something to do.

'How are you?' I asked. 'Is it helping?'

Donna shrugged. 'I think so. Sometimes.'

'How's Frannie?'

'She's okay,' she said. 'She's getting a lot of help, which is good.'

Help.

'Not just here,' Donna added quickly. 'She's seeing a psychiatrist and she's on medication. It's good.'

'Do you think she'll be all right?'

I didn't know what I was asking, or maybe I did. It was about Frannie, but it wasn't.

She thought for a long time. 'I think so.'

'I hope so.'

'Me too.'

I took another drag of my cigarette, exhaled, stared at the Vietnamese takeaway across the road. 'Tell her . . . Tell her I'm sorry.'

Donna nodded. 'I will.' She paused. 'Are you coming back?'

I blinked. Took another drag. 'No.'

'Good.'

I didn't know if it was good. I didn't even know if it was true. But it felt right. It felt like it was time.

I'd thought I was being careful, and maybe I was, but maybe I didn't need to be so careful anymore. Maybe I could try something else.

She tried a few different things before one stuck.

'Take care of each other, okay?'

Donna hesitated, then she nodded again. 'Of course,' she said. 'Want a lift?'

March, Once

The pamphlet didn't tell me how weird it would feel, sitting in a circle with a bunch of strangers. The seats were the same ones I remembered from school, plastic, beige, like everything else. There were only eight people. I don't know why but I'd expected more. I'd wanted more, to be able to sneak in the back and listen and convince myself that I was in the wrong place, because I *was* in the wrong place.

It was getting better. I had a job. I had a new place to live. Lina had stopped calling every day and clicking her tongue at me and telling me it would be okay.

But I still couldn't shake it. I should have died. I'd been lucky but my luck was bound to run out eventually. It was what luck did. Every time I stepped out of my flat I thought about the hundred, thousand, different ways it could happen. My arm still hurt and it was probably cancer. The awnings along King Street were all rotting and ancient. Scaffolding could collapse at any minute. A driver could have a seizure and take me out as I walked down the street. It was inevitable. You didn't dodge death twice. It always got you in the end.

I hadn't gone to New York. In my bones, I knew I never would. I didn't remember when I'd decided not to, but maybe I'd never intended to go, even before—maybe it had all been a fantasy.

You're in a hell of a mood tonight, Nones.

I just hate Valentine's Day.

It's not Valentine's Day anymore.

Still, look at this—we were passing a florist and I stopped, gesturing wildly at the red roses and teddy bears and love hearts in the window. I was slurring. Drunk. *It's fucking gross. It makes people stupid. Makes them spend stupid amounts of money on something that's just going to fucking die anyway.*

And then I'd been as stupid as any of them. More stupid.

I shook my head, not wanting to think about Dex. I'd been thinking about him too much. I'd never even liked him. I didn't need him. Didn't need anybody. I never had.

Paulie looked like a sitcom dad. He had a bigger belly than he should have and a big welcoming face.

Geoff had curly brown hair, didn't stop fidgeting once. Whenever anyone else spoke he stared at them, squinting, listening, waiting.

Carlos looked like he'd come straight from work, his cuffs and collar unbuttoned, a shadow of a beard across his face.

Beryl reminded me of my nan. But all old people reminded me of my nan.

Frances—Frannie, maybe, I wasn't sure—had that worn-out mum face that I saw in the park sometimes on my lunchbreak. Like she hadn't slept in a week and would tell you about her kid's feeding habits if you looked at her for more than five seconds.

Callum was young, surprisingly young, and looked like he'd come straight from the surf.

Bernie was a nurse. She wore a badge and held a clipboard and she spoke in soft, careful tones that reminded me of the paramedics that had come to Lina's house that day.

They all looked normal. Bernie *was* normal, I supposed, but the rest of them too. Like my parents' friends and people I went to school with—and my nan.

'My name's Caitlin,' I said, when it was my turn to introduce myself. 'I'm a waitress.'

It was the first time I'd said it like that, and I fought the urge to qualify it, to add that it was temporary and that I used to be a campaign coordinator and I'd been offered acting head of campaign strategy—that I wasn't *just* a waitress.

Everyone mumbled hello, and I eyed them with a tight smile, settled in to listen, to find out I was definitely in the wrong place. I was fine. I hadn't been fine; I'd been careless—the trip, the accident, Dex—but I was being careful now. So long as I was careful, everything would be fine.

I looked at their faces, at Bernie, her badge and her clipboard. This would help, I thought. It had to.

◆

It was Paulie who got me to speak, finally.

Carlos was talking about airbag fatalities, and it was making me edgy. I kept remembering the sound, the rush, the glitter. Carlos didn't have his licence. His wife did, but she didn't drive much either. He didn't like her to. They lived on the train line, so he could get to most places he needed to go, or if not he got a cab. *They're professional drivers*, he'd said earlier, *safer*. I hadn't known how to answer. He'd been explaining it for my benefit and everyone else had been nodding along, like it all made perfect sense, like the best way to deal with this was to just . . . not.

It seemed so easy, but it made my stomach hurt.

Trains weren't safe either, I thought. They seemed it, but there had been so many disasters—Granville, Glenbrook, Waterfall—and that was just in Sydney. I wondered how many people died in the subways of New York. Probably a lot. I'd been right not to go.

'You okay?' Paulie asked.

Carlos stopped at the sound of Paulie's voice, looked at me. They all looked at me, faces full of concern and barely hidden curiosity.

I nodded, not sure what else to do.

'Been dying long?' He was so flippant, like it was nothing.

I looked around. Paulie waited. They all waited. 'Not long. I think it'll pass but my doctor thought it might be good to come here.' I glanced at Bernie. She was making notes on her clipboard. 'To do something.'

To be careful. I was having trouble being careful. I'd been careless with Dex, and thankfully he'd ended it before anything bad could happen, but it hurt so much. I had to be more careful.

'That's why we're here.' Bernie smiled, eyes darting around the room but not meeting anybody else's, slightly nervous. 'We do recommend that this is just a part of a—'

Geoff scoffed, and she hesitated.

'We'll get to that,' she said hurriedly. 'For now, this is a great first step. Welcome.'

I nodded, looked around. All so normal. All fine, just careful. This would help.

'Thanks.'

34

WEDNESDAY, OCTOBER

I came in early; so early Nic wasn't there yet. Everything was so familiar—the timber, the lights; the smell of fresh coffee not quite overriding that of stale milk, bacon and slow-roasted garlic wafting up from the kitchen; the sound of knives on boards, of carrots splintering into sticks, onions being peeled, generic, low-tempo dance music and the mumbled chatter of the prep cooks. I got changed slowly in front of an empty locker, put my things inside it, rolled a cigarette and went out into the back alley to smoke it.

It was bin day. I could smell it.

'Welcome back.'

I turned around. I hadn't heard anybody come out.

Everything was the same, and when Nic hugged me, so tight I could barely breathe and I worried I was going to set him on fire, that felt the same too. My eyes filled up and I held on to him regardless.

'You look good,' he said, when I pulled away. 'I like your hair.'

I wiped my eyes with my hand, put my cigarette back in my mouth. 'Thanks.'

Lina had taken me to get it cut. *Nicely*, she'd said when she'd suggested it, watching me twist it into a bun for the hundredth time, brush the loose strands from my face. *Before you take to it with a pair of scissors again.*

It had been oddly scary. The hairdresser had washed it and I'd spent the whole time thinking about Tom and how he used to touch it, how he was the only person who had since the accident.

'Are you okay?'

'Of course.' I went to nod, then switched to a shake. 'No. I'm fucking terrified.'

He frowned. 'Of what?'

That question again. I sighed. 'Everything. What if I've forgotten how to do it? What if I was only good because I was a mess, and now I'm too slow?'

Nic hesitated. 'You'll be fine.'

I ignored him. 'What if I can't stay up until eleven? I've been going to bed at nine like some old lady. What if my feet hurt too much? What if you've changed all the wines and I don't know which ones are good anymore?'

'Cait . . .' He took me by the arms. 'You'll be fine. Just recommend the expensive ones.'

I laughed.

'There,' he said, pulling a cigarette out of his apron and lighting it. 'Now go, start.'

I nodded, taking one last drag.

'Oh,' he said, as I bent down to drop my butt into the sand bucket. 'So you know . . . Rachel's given notice. We're going to need another supervisor, someone who's good with the newbs, and knows how things need to be done. Part-time, at least at first, but better money.'

My heart jumped, I couldn't tell with what. 'I'll think about it.'

'Good,' he said. 'Now go. It's eleven-oh-one. You're late.'

I rolled my eyes, and went inside.

◆

I *was* slow, at first. Nervous. Someone had rearranged the fridge and I kept reaching for things where they used to be, the muscles in my shoulders and elbows and hands not willing to learn new tricks. But it got busier and busier, and eventually everything clicked into place. When I touched the bar it felt solid, like it would take my weight if I fell, but I didn't feel like I was going to. My brain switched off and let me work. Mindfulness. Distraction.

Just another thing. Not an answer. Not a solution, but part of it.

Holly came in, hugged me hard. Dex. He didn't say anything to me and as I watched him shuffle into the kitchen, looking strangely small, I realised I felt nothing. I never had. I'd been hurting and he'd been there, but that was all it had ever been.

Emma had quit, but there was another newb on the floor. I asked her name, made a point of remembering, but still needed a reminder halfway through dinner service.

'You're hopeless,' Nic said, with a laugh.

'And you trained me,' I found myself saying, feeling completely at home, completely at ease. 'So whose fault is that?'

◆

I went back again and again.

Back to Sawyer's. I told Nic I needed a week off for the wedding and he called me a brat. 'Fine,' he said. 'But when you get home, you're applying for Rachel's job.' It seemed like a small price to pay, and it terrified me, but I felt something else, too; something almost good.

Back to Georgia. Talked until I was wrung out. Or didn't talk at all. Cried. With sadness or anger or frustration. With gratitude. That I was still there, that Lina was still sitting in the car outside, reading a book or mapping out the latest place she was taking me.

It was hard. Sometimes everything was hard. Some nights I didn't sleep, and I wondered if it was working at all, and I asked Georgia to fix it all for me, and she shook her head and said it didn't work that way, and I knew she was right.

'If it makes any difference,' she said, 'you're doing that really well yourself so far.'

And I smiled and then I cried, because it was hard and maybe it would be forever. But I had to keep doing it.

Back to Lina's car, the seat changing shape to suit my bones.

'You're not just doing this because of the wedding, are you?' Lina asked me, speeding up the freeway towards Newcastle as I clutched my blue elephant, Thoughts about the road toll flickering through my mind, forcing me to breathe a little harder. But manageable, as Georgia would say. Nearly normal.

'No,' I said, too fast, because it was a fear I'd had too. We flew out in a few weeks and I was still tensing every time she changed lanes. I was dreading it, but more than that I was dreading it being over.

'What are you going to do after?'

'I don't know.' I stared out the window, at the trees and the sky and the vast, huge expanse of space that I'd never explored, feeling terrified. And something else. Something almost good.

35

MONDAY, NOVEMBER

Matt drove us to the airport, so early the sky was still a bruised grey and the roads weren't completely clogged. Lina sat in the back with me and held my hand, squeezed it tight. My stomach hurt. My head hurt. My chest hurt. When I'd seen Georgia the Thursday before she'd told me I'd be fine, but I didn't feel fine. I wasn't ready, but then I looked at Lina beside me and her face was so much—excitement, happiness, fear—and I knew what I had to do. What I wanted to do.

At passport control, Matt and Lina stood entwined for what felt like hours, whispering things to each other and touching each other's hair and faces and laughing softly. I looked down at my hands, and in between studying my fingertips and wondering if I had time for a cigarette, I felt something spark to life in the pit of my stomach. A feeling that wasn't new but I hadn't let myself acknowledge before. A memory of something that had never happened.

'You okay?' Lina asked, as Matt walked off.

'I think so.'

'Good.' She pulled a bottle of water out of her bag, had a sip and handed it to me. 'We can't take it through.'

I took it, sipped slowly, my eyes flickering over all the people, going to all the places. Most of them in suits and ties but some in sundresses like Lina and me. Some in cargo pants and Birkenstocks with giant backpacks and matted hair, so at ease that I wondered if they ever went home.

'You know, you're safer up there than almost anywhere.'

'I know.'

'It's loud. Nobody ever tells you it's loud but it is. And sometimes it feels like there's not enough air for all the people, but there is.'

I laughed. 'I've been on a plane before, Leen.'

'Of course you have,' she said. 'But in case you'd forgotten.'

◆

It was loud. I had forgotten how loud.

It was loud and it was busy and chaotic and small, but mostly loud. I couldn't hear myself think, and maybe that was a good thing. When Lina gripped my hand during take-off it was harder than it needed to be, but when I looked over at her she was frowning and had her eyes closed and her chest was rising and falling and I realised that maybe she was terrified too.

Maybe we all were, and for some reason that thought made it easier to breathe, and when I squeezed her hand back it was as much for her as it was for me, and then we were up there, floating in the sky, and I kept thinking about all the ways it could go wrong, all the times it had, but when Lina grinned at me, her face full of excitement and joy, the risk seemed worth it.

We landed funny, or maybe it just felt that way. The wheels of the plane bounced a little too hard on the tarmac and as they did my heart jumped into my throat. I glanced at Lina and she looked so happy, and I wanted to be happy for her—for me—but my breath stuck in my chest. Something felt wrong.

'We're here, Caitie,' she said, nudging me to stand up. 'We made it.'

I pulled myself up on the seat in front of me, gripped it, unsure my legs would hold. My stomach hurt, into my spine. Maybe it was just the sitting, I told myself. Maybe I was just stiff, but it didn't feel like that.

It felt like—

'Cait.' Lina nudged me again. I moved. I didn't know how I moved. It was cold. It wasn't supposed to be cold but it was so cold. 'Bags.'

'Oh,' I managed. Choked. 'Yeah.'

My arms went up. Back down. Up. Back down. Everything still worked but it hurt. I tried to take a breath but my throat was still blocked and my heart was pounding so hard.

I kept feeling that thud, wheels hitting the tarmac, the whole plane bouncing.

Death. It felt like death.

Maybe I'd be better once we were off the plane, I thought, dragging myself into the aisle, Lina following; maybe I'd be okay once we were outside. Maybe, but I felt it all around me, a horrible dread, a terrible fear. This had been a mistake; I was finally going to die and I was going to take Lina with me and that was the worst thing. I looked back at her—not ready, not thinking about it at all. She looked so far away. Impossibly far away.

'Leen.'

'Yeah?' Not paying attention. Not ready.

'*Leen.*'

I felt like I yelled it, but nobody stopped, nobody looked around. We all just kept moving forward, forward towards—

I heard a sob, from somewhere too close. A wail.

'Hey.' A hand on mine. Cold. I felt so cold. 'Cait. Are you okay?'

I tried to answer. Couldn't.

It was so cold. Like ice, like death. Charged with guilt and anger. Not now, I wanted to scream at myself. Not fucking now. What

the fuck is wrong with you? You're fucking everything up. Again.
I took a breath and my head spun.

'We're *here*, Cait. We made it.'

'No.' I tried to walk faster but there were so many people in the
aisle, barely moving. Inching forward.

Not yet.

'No, we're . . .' Something was going to happen and I wasn't going
to be able to stop it and I was suddenly so *sure* and everything was
getting dark around the edges and my chest hurt and my stomach
hurt and there was a heat, a cold, rushing up my spine, around my
neck, my face. Earthquake. Tsunami. Terrorist attack. Bus crash.
Kidnapping. We moved forward, but too slowly. No time left, and
I wasn't ready.

'Caitie . . .' A hand on my wrist, pulling me out of the way.

Stumbling. Falling. Sinking. Back into those tiny seats.

'Hey.' Two hands now. One holding each of mine. Mine were all
tense and when I looked at them my fingers were twisted around
each other, bent, tight. I tried to straighten them but I couldn't. 'Hey.'

Two hands, holding mine, pressing gently into my palms. I took
a breath, another, another, gulped them down, desperately thirsty
for air. Gasping. My chest was so tight and there was a sound in
my throat, a hammering wailing.

'Slower, Caitie.'

But I didn't want to breathe slower. There wasn't enough air;
I needed more. There wasn't enough air and I was going to die.
Suffocate.

Thumbs pressing into my palms, firm but gentle. 'Caitie. Hey.'
Pressing. 'Slow.'

'I'm dying.'

'No.' Pressing, rolling. 'No, you're not.'

'I'm sorry, Leen, I'm sorry. I'm—'

'It's okay. You're fine, Caitie. I promise.' My hands dropped free. 'Thanks. Thanks, she's okay. We just need a minute, sorry.' Far away.

'Leen?' I reached out. My heart thundered. Thudded. Thrashed. Cold. Awful.

'I'm here.' A plastic cup. Cold on my lips. 'Drink, Cait.'

I tried. I felt some spill down my chin but some rolled over my tongue. Cold. Strange. I swallowed. It hurt. More. Swallowed again. Something cold at the back of my neck, another hand, pressing.

'Good.' She sighed, picked up my hands again. 'Good. Now breathe. Slowly.'

I tried, but everything was still racing.

'Count to five.'

I did. Back to zero. No time left. Not ready. I let out a sound, tried to tell her.

'Again.'

And again. Slowly.

And again. And again.

I focused on the feeling of her thumbs rolling around on my palms. Circles. Small at first. Then bigger. Smaller. Slow, then fast, then slow.

I blinked. The fog cleared, just a little.

I was in an exit row, and Lina was kneeling in front of me, head down. I traced the part in her hair with my eyes. I could see her eyelashes flickering, see her breathing, her lips moving as she whispered things I couldn't hear. Her hands holding mine.

'Leen,' I said finally, as it lifted, whatever it was. Much too slowly. My voice was raw, like I'd been crying.

She looked up. Her eyes were red, glassy, wide, her lips pale, mouth tight. Impossibly sad. Impossibly scared.

'Are you okay?' she asked, impossibly small.

I nodded. My heart was still racing and I felt dizzy but the dread had passed. I just felt tired. Tired and awful.

'I'm sorry,' I said, looking around. Two flight attendants stood in the aisle, holding towels and cups of water. Otherwise, the plane was empty. I felt a surge of embarrassment. 'I'm so sorry, Lina.'

'It's okay.'

'What is wrong with me?' I asked. My throat hurt.

She took a breath.

'What the hell is wrong with me? Why am I like this? Why am I still like this? After all this time.' My eyes flooded. 'I thought I was different now. I thought I could do this.'

'Cait.' Lina frowned, squeezed my hand. 'You are doing it. We're here.'

'I know, but I'm still so . . .' I felt the tears prick at my eyes. 'I'm still not okay, am I?'

She shrugged. It should have felt callous but it felt exactly right. 'You're getting there, Cait.' She dropped my hands, sat up in the seat next to me. 'Progress,' she said, less to me than to herself. 'It's all progress.'

'I hate that you keep having to fix me.' I bit my lip. 'You shouldn't have to keep doing this.'

She shook her head. 'You're my best friend.'

'Still . . . It's not fair.'

'I know.' She sighed.

'I'm sorry.'

'It's not your fault, Cait.' Lina sounded tired. 'It's not. It's shitty. But it's not your fault.'

I blinked, not sure what to say.

She sat forward, eyeing the flight attendants. 'We should get off this plane before they call the police. Are you ready?'

I nodded.

I wasn't entirely sure I was, but I had to try.

◆

The last of the dread stayed with me on the bus trip to the resort and through dinner, a weight pressing against my spine, making it hard to move. Lina tried to be upbeat and positive but I felt guilty and more tired than I had in weeks, so in the end I went to bed early. She said it was fine, but she hugged me for a long time and it didn't feel fine.

Still, I was so tired I slept solidly, right through the night, didn't wake up until morning, the sun streaming through my window making everything glow. I looked outside and took a sharp, hard breath, because I was in paradise, and it looked like a postcard, but so much more. I saw a semi-circle of villas clustered around a beautiful, still swimming pool, surrounded by palm trees and garden beds full of flowers and lush glossy foliage. Everything was bright, bold and colourful—the greens, the blues, the yellows, the reds, all too vivid to be real. Except they were. It was all real.

I dressed and went out onto the verandah. Lina was sitting on a lounge outside my door, reading a book and glowing like an angel, and my heart jumped, not with terror, but with happiness.

Maybe I wasn't normal. But maybe normal wasn't the point, had never been the point. Maybe this was. Maybe I wasn't supposed to be here but I was, and I wanted to be, and that was so much more important. She grinned at me, and I grinned back and my chest nearly exploded. 'We're here, Leen,' I said. 'We're fucking here.'

36

WEDNESDAY, NOVEMBER

'So,' I said, cigarette in one hand, oversized cocktail with a fruit salad impaled on the rim in the other. 'You're getting married.'

Lina laughed, lifting her own insane creation.

We'd spent the past two days lying by the pool talking about swimming, and lying on the beach talking about swimming, and talking about going for walks and getting massages and taking day trips, but mostly talking. Or not talking, just being. Doing absolutely nothing. My bones had defrosted, my skin had softened, the muscles that had been holding me so tight for what seemed like forever had relaxed, letting me go floppy. I never wanted to go home.

Matt was arriving the next day, and they would be running through all the final details with Amanda and the celebrant and the caterer. The day after, everyone else arrived—Jenny and Colin and Mum and Dad and Jack and Shay, Matt's family and thirty of their closest friends—and then the day after that they got married. It was nearly over, and I didn't know what would happen next.

'I am,' Lina said.

'Are you happy?' I took a drag, coughed. Away from work, I rarely smoked and I felt it in my lungs.

She laughed again. 'Of course.'

'Really?'

'Yes, really.' She sucked on her straw. 'Really really really. I wouldn't be doing it if I wasn't.'

'And Matt's the one?'

'He is.'

I could tell he was, see the certainty all over her face. 'How do you know?'

She hesitated. 'I just do. I feel it in my gut, right deep in there. He's a part of me, and he always will be.'

I sipped my drink. It was strong, probably stronger than I'd had in months.

'Like you. Like Mum. He's a piece of my soul. I don't know. But different, because I also want to touch him all the time. And I always know where he is, if he's in the room. Like—I can feel him.'

My breath caught.

'I just know.' She smiled. 'And I know you two haven't ever got along, not really, but he does adore you. Especially after this year. He was kind of bummed when you moved out.'

I took another drag of my cigarette. Hot. Toxic. I stubbed it out, half finished, as I exhaled.

'He was!' Lina insisted. 'He wanted you to move in properly. At least until we need the room for something else.'

Something fluttered in my chest. 'Something else?'

She grinned. 'You know . . .'

'But you're not—'

'God!' She picked up her cocktail, sucked on the straw until her cheeks caved in, as if to prove a point. 'God, no. Not any time soon, either. But we've talked about it. That's what you do. Meet

333

someone. Get engaged. Talk about babies. Get married. Talk some more. Then . . .'

'You stop talking?'

'Exactly.'

The strange thing I'd felt at the airport in Sydney sparked in my stomach again. I looked at the ashtray, wished I hadn't put my cigarette out.

Want.

'Are you all right, Cait?'

I nodded, but obviously my face wasn't so convincing.

'Have you . . . you've felt okay, haven't you? Since the plane?'

I looked at her, figured out what she was asking. 'I have,' I said slowly. 'It was . . . a panic attack, I think?' I was getting better at describing how I felt, but sometimes I still wished I didn't have to. 'It just hit me, you know? All of this. I didn't think I'd be here.' I caught the look on her face, winced. 'So many times over the past few months, I thought I wouldn't make it. I thought I'd die, or I'd fuck it up, or a million other things.'

'I'm glad you were wrong.'

'Me too.' I paused. 'But now . . . I kept telling myself that all this work wasn't just about the wedding, about this trip, but I'm scared. I don't know what's next.'

She looked at her drink, thoughtful.

'This feels like the end and I'm not ready.'

How does it end?

Everybody dies.

Lina's mouth came open, like she was going to say something else, then closed, and she looked away towards the bar, suddenly nervous.

'Did I do the right thing?' she asked, after a long time.

I frowned, not sure what she meant.

'When I got your postcard, when I read it, I was so upset, and angry, and scared. Mostly I was scared. I thought you'd . . .' Her voice trailed off.

'I know. I'm sorry.' I reached out, touched her arm, needed to make sure she was there, that she knew I was there.

'It's okay. But then you were so sick. I don't know if you remember.'

I shook my head.

'It was awful. And I didn't know if you'd taken something or if you were actually going to die or . . .' She took a breath. 'Your mum wanted to put you in hospital.'

I sat back, not sure what to say.

'She'd called the bank and pulled out a chunk of their super and was ringing places.' She took a sip of her drink. 'My mum hated the hospital. She went once when I was a kid, before the divorce. Dad kind of insisted, and it helped, I think, for a while, but she hated it and she was mad at him for months afterwards. And I got scared that if we did that, that if *I* did that, you'd hate me too.'

I wanted to tell her I wouldn't, but I realised I didn't know.

'Maybe not forever. You'd get over it—but not in time.' She looked away. 'I just wanted you at my damn wedding. Maybe it was selfish, but I knew if we put you in hospital, you wouldn't come, so I told her I'd take care of you. And I promised it would be okay, and that if it wasn't, we'd do it. No arguments. But I wanted to try first.'

Lina looked small, and tired, but something else, too. Something I'd never really thought about. Determined. I felt a surge of awe.

'I wanted you here. And now you are. But what if—'

'Leen, you did the right thing. Thank you.'

She shook her head. 'You're the one who did it, Cait. Not me.'

'Only because you helped me.' I picked up my forgotten cocktail. The glass was wet and I nearly dropped it. 'I'm so stupidly lucky.'

She raised an eyebrow.

'I am.' I took a sip. Too strong. 'I'm lucky I have you. And I'm lucky it worked. I still think about it sometimes—I still have Thoughts, and I'm still scared—but it's different.'

'That's good.'

'I'm lucky to be here, I think. After the accident. After everything.' I took a breath, felt it for the first time. Lucky. Grateful. Insanely grateful. 'Thank you.'

'For what?'

'Everything. Being my friend. Saving me.'

She picked up her cocktail and finished it off. 'You saved me first.'

'So we're even.' I laughed.

'Yeah.'

I finished my own cocktail, wondered whether I should have another one, not really wanting to, but not ready to go to bed, for this part to end. We had to come again, I thought. Just us. Soon.

I put my glass down and looked around. There was a scattering of people in the bar, strangers, mostly couples. They'd all go home in the next two days, replaced by family, friends, more strangers. That thing sparked in my stomach again, bigger.

I stared at my empty glass. Thinking. About everything. 'I miss him,' I said slowly, a dull ache of need in my chest.

She looked at me. I couldn't read her expression. 'Do you?'

'So much.'

She nodded, confirming a hunch.

'I fucked up, Leen.'

She shrugged. 'So fix it.'

'How?'

I still couldn't read her expression. 'Do you want him?'

I closed my eyes. That same dull ache, but it wasn't need. It was bigger. Better. Scarier.

Want.

'Yes.'

'So . . . maybe that's what you're doing once you get home.'

I felt a rush of fear, but I smiled anyway. 'Maybe.'

◆

I had another cocktail. We talked about the wedding, and babies, and then work, and when we finished I was drunk, for the first time in months. I wasn't sure I liked it. When I fell into bed, my head spun, and when I dreamed it was too realistic, too big.

I dreamed of flying, of walking, down streets I didn't know, that I'd only seen on postcards. I dreamed of beaches and the wind on my skin and my heart beating. Of being warm, held tight. I dreamed. I heard laughter. Voices. One so familiar and so close that I dreamed I woke up, confused, more confused when I could still hear it. I dreamed I got out of bed and opened the door of my villa and I couldn't see anything but I could still hear it, whatever it was, over the faint sound of love songs drifting across the pool from the bar.

I dreamed. I wanted.

37

THURSDAY, NOVEMBER

I woke up to birds singing and another blue sky, and a postcard, slipped under my door. The Empire State Building, lit up in red, white and blue. It looked at once new and old, like it had been treasured for a long time.

> Cait,
> I'm so glad you did this with me. I'm so glad you're going to be my maid of honour. Thank you. Thank you so much—for trying, for doing it.
> Have a beautiful day. I'll see you tonight.
> L xxx
>
> PS Did you know the Empire State Building was built in 410 days? Well, now you do. Love you. Thank you.

When the tears came this time, I let them. I wasn't sad, I realised, with a shock. I was just feeling everything, all the things I'd tried not to feel for so long. And it was too much, but it was also just the right amount.

◆

Lina had gone to the airport to meet Matt, and it was the first time I'd been on my own in days. I went out to get breakfast, sat at a table by the beach and watched the waves roll in, the sand so pale it shimmered. My head hurt and I realised I was hungover. It was an unfamiliar state and I'd forgotten how to do it, didn't like it.

And there was something else. I was aware of something. Too aware—snatches of voices, a short burst of laughter that made me spin around and search the resort, abandon my pancakes and run down to the shoreline, looking for something, scanning every face, but all of them were strangers. My mind was racing.

'Just a hangover,' I said to myself, as I changed into my swimmers back in my villa. 'You're fine.'

And I was. My head hurt and that feeling in my stomach wouldn't go away, but I was fine. I was just awake, in a way I didn't remember being for a long time, and I couldn't figure out why. Maybe it was just that I wasn't used to being alone, or maybe the conversation I'd had with Lina had shifted something.

Or maybe it was just a hangover, and I'd forgotten what they felt like.

The pool was empty when I got there, and I dived in without testing the water first. It was bracing, colder than I'd expected, and when I came up I gasped for air before diving back down again, deeper this time, opening my eyes and feeling the sting of salt and letting myself float back to the surface. I swam a lap, two. A third. Got bored with laps and dived down again, this time all the way to the bottom, skimming the pool floor with my fingertips and letting my breath out in small bubbles as slowly as I could, until my lungs felt empty. My body felt soft, barely real. I couldn't feel where I ended and the water began.

I kept my eyes open as I floated up, letting the salt and the sunlight blind me for a second. I saw a shape off to one side, strangely

339

familiar. My face broke the surface and my eyes blinked involuntarily against the air and the light and I took a breath, huge and deep, and the shape was still there and from somewhere, I heard my name, what sounded like my name, couldn't be my name.

I dived down to the bottom again, touching it, solid. Fingertips on concrete. Real. Definitely real. My body drifted upwards but I fought it. This wasn't real. This was a dream. Or it wasn't, and I was finally going crazy. All the way insane. I exhaled as slowly as I could, so slowly my chest hurt, wondered if I could just stay under water. If maybe this was it—that I wasn't supposed to be killed in a car accident or be raped and murdered by a stranger or die in a plane crash; I was supposed to go insane in a swimming pool in Bali and drown myself through sheer will.

Only I didn't have that will. I didn't want it to end. Not now. My body pushed towards the surface. The shape was still there. Maybe closer this time. My name. Again. Louder. So familiar my whole stomach came alight. Not real. Couldn't be real.

'Cait.'

I blinked. My eyes stung. Sunlight and salt and tears. Tried not to react. I was just hearing things, imagining things. It was just the hangover, doing strange things to my head.

'Caitlin.'

Everything felt so real. When I got out of the pool the concrete was warm under my feet, the smell of the ocean and the flowers, the sound of birds, animals, low voices of strangers talking, all real. Couldn't be real.

I walked to the spot where I'd left my towel and wrapped it around myself. The sun lounger was cold and hard under my thighs, my hair wet on my shoulders. Real.

Footsteps. A body. Next to me. Sitting. Not too close. Dark jeans, ancient trainers, bare arms.

'You're overdressed,' I said, staring at the trainers. 'It's going to get really hot today.'

I was talking to someone who wasn't there. Lina was wrong. Georgia was wrong. Everyone was wrong. I wasn't getting better at all. I was going completely and utterly insane.

A sigh. 'I know. I miscalculated.'

His voice was like honey. Like sugar. Like arsenic.

He laughed. It made me ache. 'I packed shorts. Don't worry.'

'How did you know where I was?'

'I found the invitation a couple of months ago. It had fallen down behind your—my bedside table.'

I made a sound. I hadn't even realised I'd lost it.

'How did you know I'd come? I nearly didn't.'

A shrug. 'I had faith in you.'

My breath caught, hard.

'And I RSVPed,' he said. 'Sort of.'

Harder.

'I'm sorry,' he added, before I could say anything. 'I probably shouldn't have. I just wanted to know you were okay but I didn't want to upset you or intrude or . . . and Lina's email address was on the invitation. And then I got your message.' I blinked. I'd nearly forgotten about that message. Sometimes I managed to convince myself I hadn't sent it at all. 'I'm sorry I didn't reply. I didn't know how.'

'It's okay,' I said, when I found my voice.

He shifted. 'Lina's nice.'

'You've met her?'

'Not in person, but we've emailed. She adores you.'

'I know.'

We sat in silence, listening to the birds and staring at my feet. I felt as awake as I had in weeks but he was still there, elbows on his knees, those same trainers. I could hear him breathing. I could smell him, feel the heat coming off him. Not real. Not real. Not real.

'This is ridiculous,' I said finally, still looking at my toes, my feet.

'What?'

'You're not here. This is a dream.'

'Cait.'

'A silly, stupid dream and if I look at you I'm going to wake up.' My voice cracked. I'd had this dream so many times, but it had never felt like this. I'd never been so aware of it.

'Try it.'

I shook my head, terrified. 'No.'

'Come on.'

'I don't want to.' My voice was tiny. I did. So much.

'Please. Look at me, Cait.'

I turned my head. His face was tilted towards me and our eyes locked and he was so real I couldn't breathe.

'What are you doing here, Tom?' I asked softly. Everything was shaking.

He sighed, didn't answer for a while. Then: 'I said I'd come.' A long pause. 'I wanted to come.'

Wanted.

He moved, and for a second I thought he was going to hug me and I was going to push him away, but he didn't. He cleared his throat, straightened his legs, put his hands down in his lap, knotting his fingers together. Reset.

'This is nice,' he said tentatively. 'This place.'

I looked around. Palm trees. Flowers. Paradise. 'Yeah.'

'Are you doing anything today?'

I bit my lip.

'We should do something. If you're free.' His voice was light but there was an edge to it. A tremble. 'And if you want to. It's okay, if you don't. There's a tour to the monkey retreat I can . . .'

'No.' A part of me wanted to run away, to hide, but the rest of me was alight. The thing in my stomach had caught, and I could feel it everywhere. 'No organised tours,' I said. 'I know how much you hate them.'

His whole body seemed to relax.

'I just—I need to shower and get dressed.'

'Okay.'

'And you need to put on shorts.'

He laughed. 'Deal.'

♦

I spent longer than I needed to in the shower, giving him time to change his mind and leave. To disappear, because he'd never been here at all. I washed my hair twice, brushed my teeth for an age. The water cooled and I barely noticed because I was so warm. I put on a sundress, one that I'd bought with Lina the week before, stared at myself in the mirror for what felt like a year, not really knowing what I was looking for. Or at. I looked the same as I always did. Still not ready. But maybe—

When I came out of my villa, Tom was sitting on my verandah in shorts and thongs, and it was so unexpected it made me laugh, and when I did he looked at me, and I forced myself to look back at him, to smile. He made me weak, still.

'Sorry I took so long,' I said.

'It's okay.'

'Okay,' I repeated, needing to look away.

My heart was beating too fast. I'd thought I was getting better. Everyone—Georgia, Lina, Dad, even Mum—thought I was getting better, but my heart was racing and I was terrified of what was going to happen next.

'Fuck.' It was a croak. I felt a wall at my back, let myself drop against it, closed my eyes. 'What am I doing?'

Sometimes, late at night, I thought about this. I brought his number up on my phone and I thought about calling him, suggesting that maybe we could have a coffee somewhere and talk, and maybe it would be nice and we could be friends. But I wasn't ready, wasn't ever ready.

'Cait.'

I knew Tom was standing in front of me. I knew the expression on his face. All of this was a repeat.

It was all exactly the same, and I knew how it ended.

Except it wasn't the same. Something was different.

I was different.

I opened my eyes. 'Come with me,' I said, to his chest. I pushed off the wall and turned back to the door.

'What?'

'Just . . .' I said, pushing it open and going inside. 'Just come.'

I didn't know if he was behind me. I assumed he was but I was shaking and I couldn't look. I sat down on the bed and picked up the postcard Lina had left me.

Have a beautiful day.

I stared at it, stunned all over again, wanted to go and find her and either yell at her or hug her. I wasn't sure which.

'So,' I said, turning the card over, tracing the Empire State Building with my eyes. 'This is so stupid.'

I looked up. He was in the doorway, hands in his pockets. The thongs and shorts still made me laugh, only now it was through tears, and I wanted to tell him everything. Always.

'I have a whole shoebox of these. I used to collect them. Lina and I would send them to each other. We talked about going to all these places, but especially this one. It was my one place. We made plans. I wanted to. So much. I tried not to, but I did.' I touched the picture, wishing it real. 'It's a long story.'

I found his eyes. They were so warm.

'I'll tell you one day,' I said. I would. 'They sell these at op shops. They come in with the deceased estates. It's pathetic, isn't it? Buying postcards from cities you've never visited to send to your best friend from the postbox at the end of your street, pretending that maybe one day . . .' I laughed, but it wasn't funny. It made my heart hurt.

'It's not pathetic,' Tom said softly.

'I wanted it. So much. We had a plan. At first it was for Lina, or I told myself it was. But I wanted it too. More. People keep asking me what I want, and I say I don't know but I do.' I blinked, not sure if I was still talking about New York at all. 'I bought a ticket. I was so close, and then—'

'Caitlin . . .' Soft.

'After the accident, I stopped sending them, put them away. I didn't go. I couldn't get in a car, never mind on a plane. But I still want it so much.'

I put the postcard down on the bed. I hadn't realised it until I'd said it, but it was true. 'I don't even know why I'm telling you this. I know you've already been, and it's probably not a big deal to you.'

'Caitlin,' he said again. 'It is a big deal. It's okay.'

I wiped my eyes with the back of my hand. I wasn't ready for any of this. Maybe I was still dreaming. Maybe it didn't matter. I stood up, looking around, looking everywhere but at him. 'Should we go?' I asked.

'Cait.'

I ignored the tone of his voice, grabbing my phone from the bedside table and putting it in my pocket.

'Caitlin.'

He kept saying my name, and he was still standing in the doorway, so eventually I had to acknowledge him. That or climb out the window. 'What?'

'It is a big deal.' He stepped closer. 'And I'm glad you told me.'

I bit my lip.

'You have no idea,' he said. But for once, maybe I did. 'I'm really glad.'

I nodded, felt tears.

'Cait, I—'

'Come on,' I said, wiping my eyes and moving around him out of the room, before I did something stupid. 'Let's go for a walk.'

◆

We walked up the beach, along a dirt road that took us inland, past a small village and then another, then along a trail into some rainforest, more green and lush than anything I'd ever seen. We wound our way up a hill, feeling the heat, the thickness of the air. The clouds had come over and the palm trees above formed an endless canopy but still I felt myself turning pink.

He was quiet. We both were. He seemed to be waiting for something, and I was just trying to remember how to breathe.

'So how are you going?' he asked, after a long time. 'With the ending?'

I thought about it for a minute, trying to figure out how to answer. 'I'm getting there,' I said slowly.

He nodded, didn't say anything.

'I had a breakdown, I guess.' I kept my eyes on my feet, trying not to trip. 'Another one. More of the same one.' I frowned. 'I had a breakdown after the accident, and I don't think I ever fully recovered. I just buried it, you know? I thought I was fixing it but I was just burying it.'

'I know.'

'So it grew. And then I couldn't control it anymore.' I swallowed. 'But it was there before. It wasn't the accident. I think that's been the hardest thing to face. I kept thinking it was the accident, but it's been there all along.'

Since Jenny. Since before. I took a breath.

'I have anxiety. Severe, sometimes. Sometimes less. A bunch of other things, maybe, but that's the main one.'

It stunned me to say it. Somehow I hadn't said it like that to anyone. It was awkward and frightening, but I knew I could tell him, and that was frightening too.

'I'm getting better, but it's still there.' I glanced over at him, watched his face. 'It might always be there.'

He nodded, listening—thoughtful, the way he always listened.

'It might get worse again,' I went on. 'I don't know.'

'I know,' he said. 'It's okay.'

'It's not. It's fucking scary. But it's there and I have to deal with it, or I'll—' I stopped walking. 'And it's not an excuse.'

He stopped too, and I turned to him. 'I'm sorry, Tom. I'm so, so fucking sorry. About all of it.'

'It's all right, Cait,' he said gently.

I shook my head. 'I wish I could go back and tell you everything, the truth, from the beginning. I wanted to. I can give you all the reasons I didn't, but they don't change anything. I fucked up. And I'm sorry.'

Our eyes met.

'I know.' He held my gaze for a minute and then looked away. 'Come on,' he said, turning to walk. 'We'll never get there at this rate.'

'Where are we going?' I asked, following.

'You'll see.'

'Have you been here before?'

He shrugged. 'I just saw it on a postcard.'

I hesitated. 'And when we get there? Then what?'

'Cait . . .'

The way he said my name was so warm, so kind, it broke something inside me. I couldn't speak. We kept walking, kept going—I wasn't sure where.

'My dad would have liked you,' he said, as we rounded a bend.

I frowned.

'I've been thinking about that a lot.' He sighed. 'It was the anniversary a few weeks ago, and so I was thinking about him a lot and for some reason I kept thinking about you.'

'Oh.'

'Not in a morbid way.' The word made my heart speed up. 'Not because of what happened to you or anything.'

'Okay,' I said, still not sure what he was saying.

'It was just—taking stock. Again.'

I wished I'd brought my cigarettes. Food. Something other than a phone that didn't have any reception. The silence stretched out, long and uncomfortable.

'And what did you decide?' I asked eventually.

He glanced at me, a flicker of confusion, like I should already know the answer.

'I decided to come to Bali.'

◆

We kept walking. Higher, deeper into the rainforest, closer to wherever we were going. It got hotter, but we kept walking.

'I'm scared, Tom,' I said suddenly.

'Of what?'

That question. 'Of everything. I'm scared of plane crashes and car accidents and tsunamis and falling off cliffs and scaffolding collapsing and—' I stopped. It seemed like the easiest, most obvious question, with the easiest, most obvious answer. 'I'm scared of the ending. Of dying.'

But it wasn't right.

I tried again. 'I'm scared of this. I'm scared of being happy. I'm scared of wanting things and not getting them.' I hesitated. 'Or getting them and then losing them. Or getting them, and having them, and it not being enough. I'm scared of what happens after the happy ending.'

I looked up at the sun, closed my eyes, the insides of my eyelids turning bright blood red.

'I'm not scared of dying,' I said. 'I'm scared of living.'

And that was it.

I exhaled, exhausted. Wrung out.

'Everybody dies,' I said slowly, finding a piece of the puzzle that wasn't a puzzle.

Tom shifted.

'That's the end of the story. The bit after the happy ending. That's the way it always ends. The only way it *can* end.' I took a breath, testing out the truth of it. 'But maybe that doesn't matter.'

We'd stopped walking at some point, I couldn't remember when.

'I kept thinking that the ending was the important part, but maybe the ending is just the ending, and it's everything before the ending that matters. We're all going to die. So why . . .' I laughed softly. 'Why be scared of anything? Maybe we should be doing all the scariest, hardest, most terrible things? Jumping out of planes and swimming in huge waves and taking all the drugs we can find and driving the fastest, scariest cars and falling in love so hard it—'

Everything stopped, went still, silent. Even the birds.

And I knew. Finally.

'Cait?'

I shook my head, swore under my breath at how obvious it all was.

'I love you, Tom,' I said. It was a whisper, maybe not even that.

He made a sound. A fraction of a question. I looked up. His lips were twitching, like his whole face was about to break open, but he was trying to stop it, just in case.

My heart felt like it was going to explode in my chest and I was sure I was shaking. 'Before the accident, I—' My words trembled. I had to pause just to steady them. 'I never let myself get close to anyone. Anything. I never let myself want anything. Anyone.

Love anyone.' My face felt hot. My bones felt hot. I felt raw, naked, exposed, completely real. Whole.

'I pretended to,' I went on. 'I dated all these impossible arseholes but I would never get attached, so I would never get hurt. I told myself I was just being careful. Sensible. I told myself I didn't need anyone. But I was just scared. I'm still scared.' Somewhere, far away, I could hear a wave breaking onto a beach, the wind through a tree. 'I don't want to be careful anymore. I don't want to be scared. I don't want to be that person anymore. And . . . and I'm not.'

You changed.

'And I am.' I exhaled, not sure what I was saying. 'I'm different now, but this is still me. I'm still scared. Maybe I always will be. This is me. But I just want . . .'

Life. Everything.

The birds started, again.

'Cait?'

I felt something graze my fingers, and when I looked down his hand was there, touching mine, asking me something.

'Tom.' I wrapped my fingers around his. Answering.

I looked up. He still wasn't smiling but he was so close. So beautiful. I knew everything, finally.

And nothing.

'Tom,' I said again. 'If—when, *when* I get to New York, can I send you a postcard?'

He blinked, surprised. His eyes fixed on me and there was something behind them I couldn't read, and I couldn't breathe, and then he shook his head.

I frowned, ready to argue.

'Not if I go with you.'

'Do you want to?' My heart was thundering in my chest and I was surprised I could speak at all.

His face broke open and he smiled, all the way, dimple and everything. He tugged on my hand, pulling me closer. 'I do.'

'Are you sure?' My voice cracked. 'This might be a really terrible idea.' Shaking.

'It might.'

'And you want to do it anyway?'

He hesitated, gave the slightest nod. 'Do you?'

I found his eyes. Real. So real. Achingly real. Worth it. 'Yeah. Yes.' Made a choice. 'I want to do everything.'

'Caitlin,' he exhaled. 'I—'

'What?' I asked, too fast. My chest was so tight. Terrified. Something else.

He laughed. 'Will you just let me say it this time? Please?'

Something good. I nodded, waited.

He took a breath. 'I love you.'

'I love you too,' I said.

And I leaned in until my lips touched his, barely touched. Then touched again. He took another breath and I could feel it and I kissed him again, and then again and again. My heart was pounding and the blood was rushing through my veins but I wasn't scared. I wasn't scared and I wasn't safe. I was completely and undeniably and impossibly alive.

Epilogue

Dear Lina,

I thought the point of a destination wedding was that you didn't need to go on a honeymoon. I miss you.

I got Rachel's job, as if there was any doubt. I start Wednesday. You two will have to come in for dinner and see me be in charge. I'll smuggle you a free cocktail.

Also, because I know you want to know. Yes, we are. Yes, I talked to Georgia about it and she thinks it's okay. No, I don't have any idea what I'm doing. And yes, it's all your fault.

I just know, L. Like you said. I'm terrified but I know.

I hope you're having an amazing time and doing lots of not talking.

Love you,

C xxx

PS Thank you. I don't know how to say it enough. I never will. Thank you. I owe you.

◆

Dear Lina,

I'm so sorry. I'm sorry you're going through this. I'm sorry I can't be there. I'm just sorry in general. Life is a bitch. You don't deserve this. Nobody does, but after everything, it is so fucking unfair. You, of all people, don't deserve this. And I know you know this, I hope you do, but what you said on the phone this morning—you're wrong. Matt loves you. He always will. He doesn't blame you. He loves you so much. I can see it every time I look at you two. I can't imagine how this feels but that is one thing I know.

And please don't worry about me. Everything is so weird. I miss Sawyer's. Tom's at work all the time and I'm so scared he's going to get sick and this apartment is so quiet. Everything is so quiet, but I'm okay. I promise.

I love you. Call me if you need me. Call me anyway.

Love you.

C xxx

◆

LINA!

I was about to start my shift when I got your message and I just started jumping up and down on the spot until Nic threatened to fire me. I'm so happy for you. So happy. Thank God. I'm so excited. I know it's only a blur on a screen but it's so beautiful. You're going to make the best mum.

Also, I know you've got months and months to decide but I think Caitlin is a great name if it's a girl. I'll tell you more when I come round on Sunday.

It's so strange being back here, still. It's the same, but different. There are fewer tables so it's quieter than it used to be,

but maybe that's okay. Everyone's talking about things going
back to normal but I don't know what normal is anymore.

Love you,

C xxx

PS Hug Matt too. I'm so happy I'm crying among the garbage
bins. Just like old times. God. XXXXX

◆

Dear Tom,

I'm at the top of the Empire State Building. It's windy, and cold,
and my legs hurt from all the walking I've done, but I'm so
stupidly happy I can't stop smiling. I look like such a tourist.
This whole city is everything I wanted it to be. After all these
years of building it up in my head and then worrying that
it was gone forever—maybe it's not the place I'd imagined,
but it's still so amazing, everything I've ever wanted. Nearly
everything.

I miss you. I wish you were here. I know it was my
decision, but God I wish you were here.

I know maybe you didn't get why I had to do this on my
own. I know it's probably stupid, and I know I'm being selfish.
I just had to know that I could, after everything. It was the first
thing I wanted so much it hurt. You're the second. I love you.

I love you so much.

Caitlin

PS By my maths, you're getting on a plane right about now.
Travel safe. I'll be waiting for you at JFK and I don't think I'll
be able to breathe until I see you so hurry up and get here. We
have so much to do.

ACKNOWLEDGEMENTS

It's taken five years and so many people to get Caitlin, Tom, Lina and *The Morbids* out of my head and into the world—a very different world from the one they were imagined in. First and foremost, I'd like to thank my amazing agent Grace Heifetz from Left Bank Literary for finding *The Morbids* in the slush pile and taking a chance on me when I was sure nobody ever would. You have made this dream come true, and done it while keeping me grounded and sane and well fed. I will be indebted to you forever. Secondly, a huge, endless thanks to my publisher Kelly Fagan, who has been a force of positivity and light since the first time our paths crossed. The love and care you have shown this story, even in difficult times, has been overwhelming. I'm so grateful to have you both in my corner, and to be able to call you my friends.

To my editors, Ali Lavau and Tom Bailey-Smith, thank you for your wisdom and insight and putting up with all my writerly tics, and saying so many lovely things about my work. I've been so lucky to have you for this process. And to the whole team at Allen & Unwin, my dream publisher from the very beginning, the unwavering enthusiasm from every single one of you has often brought tears to my eyes. I'm so fucking lucky.

Thanks also to Laura Thomas for the most beautiful, most perfect cover. If someone had told me a year ago my book would have a pink glittery cover, I would never have believed them, but now I can't imagine it being anything else.

For reasons I can't explain, this book wouldn't exist without the National Young Writers Festival, and in particular I owe an immeasurable debt to Alex Neill, for getting me writing fiction again after decades of being too scared to try, and then for convincing me that *The Morbids* was too important to give up on, when I was on the verge of doing just that. And for the postcards—always for the postcards. You're an absolute angel.

It wouldn't exist without Sheree Kable and Stephanie Holm, who read the opening scene when it was just a snippet of nothing and insisted I turn it into something—and then got stuck having to read the whole thing, multiple times. It wouldn't exist without the feedback and encouragement of my insightful and honest early readers: Beck Perrin, Laura Townson, Phoebe Fayolle, Adeline Teoh, Anamarija Regler and Belinda Cashel. It wouldn't be called *The Morbids* without Lex Hirst, who insisted that it was the only possible title. Thank you. Thank you.

Writing is hard and isolating and forces you to spend too much time in your own head, but I'm lucky to have met so many fellow writers throughout this process, whose insight and encouragement have made me feel like less of a fraud. Thank you to all of you, and to NYWF, A&U, Left Bank Literary and the Newcastle Writers Festival for welcoming me into your world.

Thank you to everyone who has ever had to listen to me rant and whinge and wail about this book—you've helped me to keep going. Thank you to everyone who has babysat my kids or driven them to school so I can go to yet another meeting or finish a round of edits.

Thank you to my bosses, Rosemarie Milsom and Jade McIntosh, for not firing me despite all the time I've taken off. Thank you to Andrew Webb and Nicola Stanistreet for supporting WIRES by bidding on this book in the Authors For Fireys campaign—your generosity brought me to tears.

Most of all, thank you to my dear husband, James Ramsey, for the endless patience, support and love, and for giving me the space to give my life over to this book for the past five years, and to Jacob and Finely, for being my biggest cheerleaders—and keeping me grounded, always. This book is for the three of you, above all else. I love you more than I can say in words.

Brains are strange, difficult things and mental illness is complicated—there is no one experience, or one answer. For me, like for Caitlin, putting voice to the thing that had been niggling at me for years and years was the most terrifying but empowering thing I have ever done—but I also know I've been incredibly fortunate in that. If any part of Caitlin's story resonates, the only thing I can tell you is that you are not alone, and things will get better. Keep going. It's always worth it, I promise.